LYDIA
A Story of Philippi

TRUDY J. MORGAN-COLE

D1468411

Autumn
House® Publishing
www.autumnhousepublishing.com
A Division of REVIEW AND HERALD® PUBLISHING
Since 1861

Published by Autumn House® Publishing, a division of Review and Herald® Publishing, Hagerstown, MD 21741-1119

Autumn House® titles may be purchased in bulk for educational, business, fund-raising, or sales promotional use. For information, please e-mail SpecialMarkets@reviewandherald.com.

Autumn House® Publishing publishes biblically based materials for spiritual, physical, and mental growth and Christian discipleship.

Some of the details and dialogue in this book expand on the biblical story but are based on what is currently known about the times and the culture of the biblical world.

This book was
Edited by Gerald Wheeler
Cover design by Ron J. Pride
Cover photo/illustration by Jupiter Images/Square One Studio
Typeset:11/13 Bembo

PRINTED IN U.S.A.
14 13 12 11 10   5 4 3 2 1

Library of Congress Cataloging-in-Publication Data
Morgan-Cole, Trudy, 1965-
  Lydia : a story of Philippi / Trudy Morgan-Cole.
    p. cm.

  1. Lydia (Biblical figure)—Fiction. 2. Women in the Bible—Fiction. 3. Bible. N.T. Philippians—History of Biblical events—Fiction. 4. Church history—Primitive and early church, ca. 30–600—Fiction. 5. Philippi (Extinct city)—Fiction. I. Title.
  PS3613.O7487L93 2009
  813'.6—dc22
                        2009037314

ISBN 978-0-8127-0485-3

Other books by Trudy J. Morgan-Cole:

Connecting   *Deborah and Barak*
Courage to Stand   *Esther: A Story of Courage*
Daughters of Grace

Visit us at **www.AutumnHousePublishing.com**
for information on other Autumn House® products.

To my home church:

The collection of flawed, fractious, faithful people
who have been there all my life,
and who have showed me what it means to live for Him.

Acknowledgements

As always, a book is never the work of a single person. I owe a debt to the many writers (too many to list here) whose work on the early church and the city of Philippi I read in preparation for this story. I am, as always, grateful to the excellent team at Review and Herald Publishing for their support of this project, particularly to Gerald Wheeler for his careful editing, and to Jeannette Johnson for her unwavering encouragement. Any errors that remain in the book are my fault and not those of the editors and publishers.

Thanks to my friend Tina for the brilliant suggestion of using search and replace to avoid typing "Epaphroditus" over and over, which would have worked really well if I'd been paying more attention.

Finally, many thanks to my family—my parents; my husband, Jason; and my children, Chris and Emma—for being such a supportive team.

LIST OF CHARACTERS

[Names in **boldface** are those mentioned in the biblical accounts of the church at Philippi, though in some cases only a name or brief designation is given, and no other details are known about the person.]

Agricola: a wealthy man in Philippi who owns several tenement buildings

Alexander: a friend of Epaphroditus

Alexius: Lydia's brother, who lives in the city of Thyatira

Andreas: a young Christian cabinetmaker who marries Clement's daughter Julia

Ariane: a slave in Lydia's household

Ariston: a Christian doctor in Philippi

Arius: a Christian in Philippi

Arsenios: one of Euodia's owners

Aulus Gabinus Sidonius: a magistrate in Philippi, the husband of Flavia

Benjamin: a leather worker; a Jewish convert to Christianity

Barnabas: a Christian missionary

Caius Livis: a city official in charge of the jail

Caius Memmius: a weaver, neighbor of Lydia

Calvus: a slave in the house of Demos

Chara: a slave in the house of Clement

Clement: a retired soldier who guards the Philippian jail

Demos: One of Euodia's owners, later a church leader in Philippi

Doris: a deaconess in one of Philippi's churches

Durio: Clement's late brother

Epaphroditus: son of Lydia

Euodia: a slave girl possessed by a spirit that enables her to tell fortunes

Flavia: a wealthy woman of Philippi, wife of the magistrate Aulus Gabinius

Gaius Fabius: a wealthy young man, a friend of Epaphroditus

Helena: Lydia's mother-in-law

Hermia: wife of Demos

John Mark: a Christian missionary

Joshua: a Jewish convert to Christianity in Philippi

Judah: a grain merchant and Jewish convert to Christianity

Julia: daughter of Clement and Syntyche

Lucia: wife of John Mark

Lucius: son of Clement and Synyche

Luke: missionary, doctor, and travelling companion of Paul

Lydia: a merchant of Philippi

Lysander: a Christian in Philippi

Mary: a Christian missionary, wife of Barnabas

Nerissa: a poor Christian widow

Nikolai: a leader of one of the Christian churches in Philippi

Paul: missionary preacher who brings the news of Jesus to Philippi

Paula: a friend of Julia's whose family disapproves of Christianity

Philip: Lydia's late husband

Rachel: a Jewish freedwoman who works for Lydia and is Simeon's wife

Rufus: slave in the household of Flavia, later a church leader

Sergius: a Christian freedman in Philippi, suggested as a possible husband for Euodia

Silas: Paul's traveling companion and fellow missionary
Sara: a Jewish woman of Philippi and daughter of Solomon
Simeon: Rachel's husband and a Jewish freeman who works for Lydia
Solomon: a tanner, one of the few Jewish men in Philippi

Syntyche: wife of Clement

Timothy: a young preacher who travels with Paul
Titus Cassius Placidus: a centurion of the Philippian garrison
Tacitus: a slave in Lydia's household
Tulla: a Christian woman
Urbanus: a Christian from Rome
Varro: a guard at the Philippian jail

CHAPTER 1
LYDIA

"It's a striking color," Rufus said, edging closer to the window to hold up the fabric samples to the slanting late afternoon light.

"More than striking," Lydia agreed, taking one of the two squares from him to display it to better advantage. "It's the true Tyrian purple, and you can see how it looks slightly different on the silk and on the linen. And of course, as always, the color will only grow richer with time. Is your mistress's gown made of silk?"

Rufus smiled. "Of course. Here, I brought a piece to show you." He drew forth a fabric sample of his own.

"A very fine fabric. Similar to this piece I have here, so you can take the sample to show her how the color will look. A white gown, with the border purple?"

"No. You know my mistress—fickle and constantly in need of something new. Especially for the gown she will wear before the Empress when she goes to Rome. She wants a pale blue, with a purple border."

"That should not be difficult. Indeed, if she wishes we can dye her silk in both colors here ourselves and guarantee the quality." In the workshop behind her the artisans were folding and hanging cloth and covering the vats of dye, preparing to close for the evening. She had no wish to rush as important a customer as the slave of a magistrate's wife, but she wanted the transaction concluded—or else put aside until after the day of rest. Concluded would be best. But she would not betray a moment's impatience—she did not glance back at her workers or out at the almost setting sun, but kept her attention entirely on her customer and the fabric samples.

"I wish I could convince my lady to let you do that," the man sighed, "but she is determined to have our own household slaves dye the fabric and make the dress. Which was fine in the old days, when Pollio was in charge, but now that he is gone, the younger ones don't know their work as your people do. She would be getting better quality if she bought the fabric from you, but she insists she wants only the dye."

Lydia nodded slowly. "Rachel," she called, "bring me a piece of that silk on the second shelf in the storeroom—yes, that's the stuff. Here," she said, holding out the fabric to the slave and noticing with an inner smile how his eyebrows lifted. "Is Flavia's silk similar to this? Yes? We could dye a piece of this—larger than these samples—for you to bring to your lady and show her. It will give her a good sense of how the color will look on a piece of silk—and also demonstrate to her our skills. And it may inspire her to trust her precious silk to my shop after all."

Lydia knew Rufus was impressed that she had pieces of silk ready to hand and could spare one to dye just as a sample. It was expensive, of course. But a merchant saved nothing by being too frugal—especially not when dealing with wealthy customers. Freehanded displays of luxury always reassured wealthy customers. Rufus was an old and trusted customer—or at least, his master and mistress were—and none of this needed to be said aloud between him and Lydia.

"So if I came—tomorrow evening, would you have this done?" Rufus asked. "No—forgive me. Your Sabbath, of course. The evening afterward?"

"Give us one more day," Lydia said, calculating the time needed in her mind. Simeon and Rachel could start dyeing as soon as the first day of the week dawned. He, she knew, was on the far side of the courtyard closing up the dye works, while Rachel swept the shop and put away fabric, readying everything for the quiet of Sabbath. This, too, her best customers knew about her, and were willing to accommodate.

After seeing Rufus to the door, she stood for a moment watching the setting sun turn the paving stones the color of fire. From across the street, Caius Memmius, standing in the doorway of his weaver's shop, waved to her. The retired soldier and his wife had been weaving fabric in that spot since Lydia and Philip had moved into their shop nearly 20 years ago.

Philip's establishment had in those days been only a dye-shop in which he traded in the common colors—indigo blue, madder red, safflower yellow. His great business success had come on a buying trip to Thyatira, where he traded with a wealthy supplier of Tyrean purple who happened to have a marriageable daughter. Access to the coveted and expensive purple dye, and the right to sell it in Philippi, was the dowry that Lydia took with her when she accompanied Philip, 15 years her senior, back to his Macedonian home. She brought more than that, though—Lydia quickly proved herself her father's daughter with a good head for business. It was her idea to purchase the land and the dye works on the far side of the courtyard behind their villa, and to buy two Egyptian slaves who were skilled dyers. When Philip was able not only to sell Tyrean purple dye but also to dye and sell the fabric, his business grew rapidly. His widow was now by far the richest woman on the street of weavers and cloth dyers.

That street was busy now as the afternoon shadows grew long. A handcart piled high with bales of wool clattered over the cobblestones as women carrying tall jars squeezed around it, hurrying back to their shops and workrooms. Small children ran barefoot along the edges of the street, play-fighting with sticks as their mothers and fathers showed off lengths of wool, linen, and silk to customers.

A tall, slim figure strolled down the street, his pace quickening as he drew closer to her doorway. Lydia watched him as if he were the only one on the crowded avenue. She smiled as her 15-year-old son drew close enough to say, "Home just in time for Sabbath, Mother!"

Reaching up, Lydia quickly touched Epaphroditus's cheek in a brief caress. He thrust several cloth-wrapped parcels into her arms. "I'll go wash before we eat," he said.

Before she could open her mouth to tell him to put the parcels on the storeroom shelves, he was already gone, running past Simeon and Rachel with a shout of greeting and up the stairs to the private apartments above the shop. Rachel, who was sweeping the shop floor, paused a moment to smile across at Lydia. "Our boy is almost a man," she said. Her eyes briefly filling with tears, Lydia smiled back. In many ways, Rachel and Simeon were like second parents to Epaphroditus. The boy had been away only a day, but it was his first time making the overnight trip to Neapolis himself. One step closer to manhood.

Lydia carried the packages to the storeroom herself—they were from her family and business contacts in Thyatira, jars of the purple dye that had made her wealthy. When shipments came in she would trust no one but a member of her own household to bring them from the port to her home, but she would not open them now until after Sabbath. The cook and house slave, Ariane, would have the Sabbath meal prepared, with the oil lamp ready to light as Lydia's household gathered in the atrium. The thousand and one cares and worries of the shop and business could be—had to be—put aside now.

Half an hour later, Lydia took her place on the couch at the head of the table. Epaphroditus reclined at her right hand, with her mother-in-law Helena at her left. Below the immediate family members, Simeon and Rachel shared a couch. The two artisans were the same Egyptian slaves Lydia's husband had purchased so many years ago. They had been a newlywed couple then, Alexandrian Jews forced into slavery after Simeon was unable to pay off his brother's debts. Their skill as dyers had led them here to Lydia's house, where they had started the dye works and become not only valuable employees but close friends, almost family. Lydia had freed them after her husband's death.

The two remaining slaves made up the rest of the household. The male slave Tacitus was well named, since he was a very quiet man who did much of the work around the house and shop without complaint or comment. Ariane took her seat last, laying a steaming bowl of lamb stew in front of the others before sitting beside Tacitus.

Often Lydia shared her meal just with her son and mother-in-law. Sometimes, in the middle of a busy workday, she might eat in the shop with Rachel and Simeon. But the Sabbath evening meal joined the whole modest household together: mistress, slave, and freedman.

Lydia lit the oil lamp in front of her and spoke the blessing aloud, the words Rachel had taught her so many years ago. "Blessed are You, Lord our God, Sovereign of the Universe, who has sanctified us with His commandments and commanded us to light the lights of Sabbath."

"Amen," they all chorused, bowing their heads for a moment before Ariane rose to ladle food into everyone's dishes. It was from Rachel and Simeon that Lydia had first learned of the God of Israel. She had encountered Jews back home in Thyatira when she was a girl—the city had its own synagogue. But Rachel and Simeon were the first Jews she had known well. Working alongside them in her husband's shop here in Philippi she had learned about their God and begun worshipping with the small community of Philippian Jews and God-fearers who met outside the city wall. Her husband had disapproved, and commanded her to stop going. Only after his death did Lydia become a God fearer and begin to worship regularly alongside the two slaves she had freed to become her loyal and indispensable employees.

Epaphroditus, who had been only 4 years old when his father died, had grown up with his mother's faith in the God of Israel, and now he attended Sabbath services along with her, Rachel, and Simeon. He had not chosen to become a convert, but numbered himself among the God fearers—a tiny number, here in Philippi. Philip's mother, Helena, had no interest in Lydia's beliefs. She maintained a small shrine of household gods in her room, paying special devotion to the goddess Diana. Ariane was also faithful to the Roman gods: she had been Helena's personal slave for many years and was very loyal to the older woman. What Tacitus thought about gods—or about anything—no one knew. But everyone participated in this one Jewish observance, the Sabbath meal, which drew all the household together for one night.

"So, what news from Neapolis, Epaphroditus?" Simeon asked as he scooped stew from the pot with his bread and ladled it over his couscous.

"Things were very busy at the port—a ship put in from Troas just yesterday. That's where I got your packages, Mother—a man on board had come from Thyatira. He said there was a letter from your cousin or uncle—he wasn't sure. I traveled on the road here with some of the men from the ship. They were Jews and wanted to know if there was a synagogue in Philippi."

"Perhaps we will see some of them tomorrow," Rachel said.

In the morning four of them—Lydia, Epaphroditus, Simeon, and Rachel—walked through the streets of Philippi's business district, already crowded as dawn touched the buildings, and took the main road that led through the city to the west gate. Once outside the city the road headed westward toward Amphipolis. Lydia and her companions turned off onto a well-worn path that led down to a stream not far from the city walls. The little building by the river had once been a temple to a Roman god, but it had long ago fallen into disrepair. Abandoned, a ruin with only walls and no roof, the site had been taken over by the tiny community of Jews and God-fearers who had no synagogue of their own.

They could not hold a proper Sabbath service there, for there were no longer 10 Jewish men in Philippi. The congregation that met there that Sabbath morning consisted mostly of women. Of them, only Rachel and two others were actually Jews. The rest were, like Lydia, God fearers who had learned to love the Scriptures and the God of Israel. Simeon was the only Jewish man there that morning. Old Solomon, the tanner, had been the mainstay and leader of the congregation for years, but his health was poor now and many Sabbaths he could not make the long walk to the meeting place by the river.

Lydia greeted Solomon's daughter Sara with a warm hand-clasp. "How is your honored father?" she asked.

"Very weak, very tired. And your mother-in-law?"

"Helena's cough is better, but her bones still ache, and she finds it hard to move around." Lydia turned to acknowledge a few of the other women who had just arrived. They all greeted her not only with warmth but also with respect. Most of the Jews and the God fearers in Philippi were artisans, many of them freed slaves like Rachel and Simeon. As a well-to-do merchant trading in a luxury item such as purple dye, Lydia was wealthier than most, and they honored her status in the community.

Now she looked around at her fellow worshippers as they took seats. Simeon and Epaphroditus, the only two men, sat near the front and just behind them Lydia and Rachel with 10 other women. Just 12 people here today to worship the God of Israel. A few years earlier, Rachel and Simeon had fulfilled a lifelong dream—made possible by Lydia's generous gift—and made the long journey to Jerusalem for Passover. When they returned, they held Lydia spellbound with their tales of an entire city dedicated to the God of heaven, of the vast Temple complex where people crowded together to worship.

She wished she could go there, just once. As a Gentile and a woman, she would be allowed only in the outer courts of the Temple, but it would be enough. Just to see it, to hear the voices raised in song, to witness so many others worshipping the God who had touched her life, the Lord who had healed her broken heart after her infant daughter's death, and who had brought Rachel and Simeon into her home. Lydia had much to be grateful for, and gathering with this tiny group here on Sabbath morning to pray and read Scripture hardly seemed a large enough act of worship to encompass the gratitude that she felt to her God.

Male voices outside the open door made her look over her shoulder. Four men stood in the doorway of the roofless building, peering in as if not sure whether they should enter. "Is this the meeting place of the Jews?" one asked.

All the worshippers sat silent and motionless for a moment, nobody sure who should take the lead. Finally Lydia stood up.

"This is where we worship the God of Israel. It is not properly a synagogue, for we are mostly women and God fearers. But you are welcome to share the Sabbath with us."

One of the men—not the one who had spoken, but a younger one, only a few years older than Epaphroditus—caught sight of Lydia's son sitting beside Simeon, grinned, and stepped forward. "This is the place of prayer by the river that you told us of, isn't it, Epaphroditus?"

Suddenly shy in the presence of the strangers, Epaphroditus nodded. The man who had asked if it was the place where the Jews worshipped turned back to Lydia. "My name is Paul, of Tarsus, although these days I call no place home, but travel the world telling good news to all people, Jews and Greeks. My companions are Silas, of Jerusalem, Luke, a physician from Antioch, and Timothy, of Lystra." The last man he indicated was the youngest of the three, the one who had spoken to Epaphroditus.

"You are Jews, then? Or God fearers?" Lydia asked. She surveyed the four strangers as she spoke. They looked and sounded like educated men of some modest means, though their garments were worn with travel. The young man named Timothy was tall, broad shouldered, and handsome, with dark hair and vivid dark eyes. While the other men remained standing, Timothy sat down next to Epaphroditus, like an old friend.

"I am born a Jew, as is Silas," Paul said. He himself was the least impressive of the four, though he was obviously the leader. Short statured, he had wiry graying brown hair and keen gray eyes in a lined face. He looked to be in his late forties, but it was hard to tell. "My other companions are Gentiles," he continued. "But we are all followers of the Lord Jesus, the Anointed One of Israel."

"The Anointed One?" Sara repeated, and a few others around her echoed the phrase. "Do you mean then that the Messiah, the Deliverer of Israel, has come?"

Paul found a seat on one of the front benches, near Simeon and Epaphroditus, but sat facing the back of the room and the women. The other two men, Silas and Luke, took positions nearby as Paul said, "I would like to tell you about Jesus of Nazareth, the Lord, the Anointed One and the Son of God. Will you hear me?"

Again the little group of worshippers were silent until Lydia said, "We will listen." She had no idea what the men could be talking of. Occasionally she had heard Rachel and Simeon speak of teachings in the Scriptures that promised a deliverer, a new king of Israel like King David of old, who would drive the Romans out of the land of Israel and restore it to its old greatness. As a Gentile who lived far from Jerusalem and had never even seen the Holy Land, she had no idea what this Anointed One had to do with her.

"Jesus of Nazareth lived in Galilee and followed a carpenter's trade," Paul began, his voice slipping easily into the rhythms of a storyteller. He leaned forward and his hands made quick darting gestures to illustrate his words. "But He was no ordinary man. Though those around Him did not know it at first, He was God's own Son, sent from heaven to save humanity. When Jesus was about 30 years old, he began preaching that God's kingdom was at hand. He performed many mighty miracles, healing the sick and even raising the dead. Many people in Israel believed in Him and thought that He was the Anointed One whom God had promised to send."

Paul paused, and Lydia noticed her friend Sara frowning. "I think I have heard of this Jesus of Nazareth," she said. "My father had word of Him from the Jews in Antioch. A false deliverer, they called Him. He is dead, isn't He?" Simeon and Rachel nodded as though they, too, had heard of the tale, though it was all new to Lydia.

Although he looked a little irritated at the interruption, Paul nodded gravely toward Sara and Rachel. "Jesus of Nazareth was, indeed, crucified on a Roman cross." Lydia caught her breath. Crucifixion was a punishment reserved for the worst kind of rabble-rousers and thieves. Who could believe in a crucified deliverer?

"His death was at the hands of Rome, but it was ordained by God," the visitor continued. "Jesus died for our sins, to reconcile humanity with God. But on the third day after His death, He rose again. He came back to life!" Seeing the disbelief in the faces around him, Paul insisted, "It's true! I saw Him myself, in a vision, when He called me to be His messenger and bring His story to the Gentiles!"

"But did you see Him in the flesh, after He supposedly came back to life, or only in a vision?" another of the women asked. "This is like a fable, a story of the pagan gods."

"None of us here saw the risen Jesus," the man named Luke replied, "but we have spoken with many of His followers in Jerusalem who did. He walked among His people there for some weeks after He was raised, and then He returned to God in heaven. He will come back to the earth again to set up His kingdom and rule the world with peace and justice forever. But first, we who are His followers must tell everyone about Him, to prepare the whole world for His coming."

Luke wasn't the speaker that Paul was. His voice was that of a cultured man, but his face flushed as he spoke, and his words tumbled over each other in their haste to get out. He looked to be about Lydia's own age, younger than Paul but much older than Timothy. His dark wavy hair framed a strong profile and a long straight nose. His looks were unassuming, but sincerity shone in his eyes. The man might never have seen this risen from the dead deliverer, but he truly believed.

Taking up the thread of the story again, Paul told them more about Jesus' message, about the kingdom of God, and about his belief that Jesus was God's Son, equal to God Almighty and now sitting beside Him on the throne in heaven. The message was so new and strange that Lydia could barely grasp it.

The little group of worshippers fired questions at Paul and his companions. "How can you say that God has a son?" Sara asked. "The Lord our God, the Lord is one God. We do not worship a score of gods and goddesses like the pagans around us."

"I am a true born Jew of the tribe of Benjamin, and I know that God is One God," Paul asserted. "But I have seen and heard the Lord Jesus, and I know that He is one with God."

"We heard of this when we were in Jerusalem a few years ago," Rachel declared, looking at her husband Simeon for confirmation. "People there told us that many men have claimed to be God's Anointed One, seeking to lead people against the Romans. They all die and are forgotten. We heard, too, of this one whom some claimed had risen from the dead. But He is gone now, like the others. Gone and forgotten."

"Not gone, and not forgotten!" Paul said, leaning forward, his eyes bright. "He sent His Holy Spirit—the Spirit of God—to fill His followers when He had returned to heaven. Thus He is still with us, alive in our hearts, giving us the power to spread this message all over the world. I myself have traveled throughout Asia, and now my friends and I have come here to Macedonia to bring the Good News of Jesus. For it is good news, people of Philippi! Our sins are forgiven in Jesus. We can have a new life— an eternal life—through His Spirit. All He asks is that we accept Him as our Lord and follow Him."

"I cannot believe this talk of a man rising from the dead," Lydia said. "This is like the stories we all heard as children—the tales of the pagan gods. A god coming down to earth in human form, a god dying and rising again—the heathen have many such stories. But we know they are only stories. All of us who are God fearers have joined with our Jewish brothers and sisters because we no longer believe such stories. We believe in the God of the Scriptures."

"But the Scriptures foretell the coming of Jesus!" Paul stated. "If you allow me, I will open the Scriptures with you and show you how they speak of Him. Jesus Himself loved to quote from the words of the prophet Isaiah: "The Lord has anointed me to preach deliverance to the captives." He told His followers that He had come to fulfill that Scripture. And there are many others . . ." Rising, Paul crossed the room to stand by the table where their Scripture scrolls rested in a basket. He drew one out as if to unroll and read it.

Lydia sensed the restlessness, the shifting of the women in their seats, the suppressed words of some who wanted to question or to speak out but would not interrupt a formal meeting. Some seemed intrigued, others appeared bewildered. Sara looked angry, offended by Paul's words. Having no wish to see a quarrel break out in the place of prayer, Lydia stood. "Paul, you have told us much that surprises us, and I know we all wish to hear more, but it will take time to absorb such new teaching. I would love to listen as you tell about how the Scriptures reveal Jesus, but the hour grows late, and we have not yet finished our prayers. Will you worship with us, then return to my house in the city for the noon meal? You and your three companions may come, and any others of our number who wish to hear more about this Jesus. After the meal we will sit in comfort and hear your teachings."

As Paul frowned, Lydia sensed the man's impatience, his urgency to have his message heard *now*, with no interruptions. But he nodded and resumed his seat, and the service continued as it had before the strangers entered. The atmosphere was different, though. They repeated the same words, sang the same psalms, bowed for the same prayers as every Sabbath. But the visitors had introduced something different, creating a tension that vibrated in the room like a plucked harp string. Lydia felt it as excitement, a challenge, the possibility of something new.

She tried to explain the feeling to Paul later, as they prepared to leave the meeting place and walk back to the city. "So much of what you say is strange," she told him, "and yet I feel drawn to it. I want to hear more about this Jesus—it's as if I've been waiting all my life for someone to tell me his story."

His earlier impatience gone, Paul smiled. "That is the Spirit of God in your heart, Lydia. He is drawing you toward Jesus, convicting you of the truth. I have seen it happen again and again, in every place I have preached. I speak the words, but the Spirit touches hearts. Already you belong to Jesus."

Lydia said nothing. This intense little man presumed so much, was so sure of himself. Yet she could not say that his words were untrue. Whether it was the Spirit of God or not, something was pulling at her heart, or at least tugging at her curiosity. She remembered first coming to Philippi as a new bride, seeing the city spread out before her when they rode up the Via Egnatia from Neapolis, entering by the east gate under the eyes of the carved images of the gods. All that sense of possibility, of hope, of opportunity—she had not felt like that in years. Now, approaching Philippi's gates from the opposite side, she experienced it again. Something new was happening here, and Lydia was ready for it.

CHAPTER 2
EUODIA

The voices woke her early. The sun had not yet risen, and she lay on her pallet on the floor, staring at the gray walls. She wanted to sleep—to shut out the voices, though they followed her into dreams.

Now they clamored in her head, one ordering her to get up, another to stay in bed. There was always one, a thin voice piping away behind the rest, telling her to take a knife and kill Demos. She struggled to ignore it. It would get her in trouble. Finally, she sat upright, hugging her knees, begging the gods for silence. But of course the gods would not answer. The voices were theirs.

Rising, she walked outside. She slept in the main room at the front of the house, while Demos and his woman occupied a private back room. Once they had to keep her tied by the ankle to a ring set in the wall. Back when she used to try to escape. But she hadn't attempted that for a long time. There was no escape.

While she might run far enough to leave Demos behind, the voices would come with her.

Outside, the predawn air was fresh and cool. Demos's house faced on a courtyard shared by several other houses. The courtyard was quiet at this hour, with only a few other slaves going about their morning work. After hugging her bare arms and shivering a little, she lifted the water jar and filled it from the cistern. Drawing a dipper of water from the jar for a quick drink, she then brought the water jar back into the house and began rolling up her bedding to place it in a tidy pile in the corner. Next she went into the small dark kitchen in the back of the house, beside the room where Demos slept. She would get an early start on the fire and begin making bread.

The other slave, the manservant Calvus, still slept, huddled in a pile of clothes at the opposite end of the main room. As she passed he stirred and mumbled in his sleep. He was a gross, fat, dirty man and she hated him. Once he had tried to force himself upon her, but Demos put a stop to that. She had told Demos that she was a virgin and must stay that way, for if a man touched her the gods would silence their voices. Demos would not risk that. Although she didn't know if it was true or not, it was something her mother had told her to say, like a charm that might protect her a little.

Kindling a fire in the brick oven, she began mixing and kneading the dough for bread. Sometimes—on good days—she liked such simple tasks. They filled her mind and kept it quiet.

Today was not a good day.

The bread dough oozed between her fingers and she thought of squeezing someone's throat. Not Demos. Someone else—a stranger. One of the men who had sold her, took her from her mother.

You deserved it. You were a bad girl. You are a bad girl. Your mother didn't want you anyway. Yes—she did. She cried when you were taken. She cried and then she died, alone, in terrible pain.

"Quiet!" she hissed aloud. "Leave me alone."

We never leave you. We are around you, above you, within you. We will follow you all your life. Don't think of trying to escape through death—you will be ours forever then.

Pressing the dough flat on the platter, she laid it on top of the glowing coals in the oven. Then she took grapes and honey from the storage shelves to carry out to the table. Simple tasks, repeated daily. But they made no difference. She felt taut as a drawn bowstring. A touch might break her.

"Bring me my sandals, crazy girl!" Calvus shouted. He was only a slave, but he could give her orders. Anyone could. She was theirs to command.

When the bread was done, Demos and his woman ate. Arsenios joined them partway through the meal. He lived in a rented room, not far from here, but he didn't have his own slave to cook for him, so he often ate at Demos' house. The two men talked loudly about business. Their voices fought with those in her head. None of them wished her well.

"Girl, we have customers this morning!" Demos told her as she swept out the main room. "Get yourself ready—call up the python and see what it has to say!" He and Arsenios and the woman laughed harshly.

She didn't want to, hating to open her mouth and let the python spirit speak through her. Sometimes she had tried to refuse, to run away, but it did no good. When the gods wanted to use her, she could not keep quiet. And when Demos and Arsenios brought paying customers, she could not say no.

Now she sat at the table across from the client—the usual type, a wealthy older woman. With the part of her mind that was still her own the slave girl made guesses about her. She was old and would be grieving for someone. You could not live to have white hair without losing a loved one. As always the girl could make things up, platitudes that would please the woman.

"You are thinking of someone who has passed beyond," she began in her own thin voice, holding the woman's plump hand in her own. "They are at rest—they are at peace, far from this world's troubles. Do not worry, do not lie awake at night crying . . ."

The woman did, indeed, look relieved, and a small smile began to play around her wrinkled lips. If she could end it here, the woman would pay her and leave happily. Demos and Arsenios would have their money and also be happy. The slave girl would be—not happy, but at least she would be torn apart by messages from the python spirit, messages she could not control.

It was coming now—pictures in her mind, clearer than the woman who sat in front of her. She saw the images, felt the sensations before the words came. Then they rolled out of her in a loud, rough-edged voice, a voice not her own, a voice that spoke through her. She could not stop it. If she tried, the effort would destroy her.

"Wait! There is more!" the harsh voice said through her. "Someone else you love will die—your son. He is a soldier, far away in—in the north. Fighting with the legions. He is—there will be a battle. He will fight bravely, but he will die alone, in terrible pain and suffering."

Then, as her vision cleared, she saw the woman's stricken face. "I'm sorry," she wanted to say. She wished that she could tell her "It isn't true," but she knew it was.

Demos was there now, smooth and slippery. "An offering at the temple of Isis, lady, will perhaps ensure your son a peaceful death—perhaps even avert his fate, move the goddess to protect him and preserve his life." Her owner was friendly with the priests. She knew money changed hands. When she gave people bad news he was always quick to suggest an offering.

Other clients came and went. Some received good fortunes, some bad. Always the voices took her over, speaking words that she could not have known or willed. When the last customer left she felt drained, limp as a piece of wet cloth.

"Now, girl," Arsenios said, "follow me to the marketplace. We'll drum up some business there."

Clients coming to the house were bad enough. But going to

the marketplace was terrible. The light assaulted her eyes. People's eyes stabbed like daggers. The sights, sounds, and smells pressed into her, leaving her faint and weak. Arsenios prodded her with a stick to keep her upright and moving through the ocean of people.

They passed across her vision: a beggar, a rich man, a child, a thief, a widow, a young girl in tears. Her hearing caught laughter, a scream, a man hawking his wares from the back of a cart, a child crying. And she smelled fish gone bad, spices, cheese, horses, unwashed people.

She felt terrified. Alone. Hunted.

They all hate you. Someone here today might kill you. Keep your eyes open! Don't let anyone get close.

Ahead, she noticed two men in worn travelers' robes, talking intently to each other. They looked unremarkable—common workmen or scribes, perhaps.

When she met their eyes she felt a bolt of raw power like nothing she had experienced since childhood when in the temple the gods spoke directly to her mother and the other priestesses. No—greater than that. A power she could not touch or name shone round the two men like an aura.

It slammed her to her knees in the street in front of them.

Arsenios stepped aside as the men stumbled to a halt, startled. Guessing that she might tell a fortune, attract some attention and some business, he waited.

When she opened her mouth the words were not her own: the voices spoke through her, as they did when she was in a trance.

"These men are servants of the Most High God! Listen to what they have to say!"

Her voice was loud, commanding. A few passersby stopped to stare curiously at the kneeling girl and the two men she addressed. The men frowned at each other. One looked as if he might speak to her, but the other grabbed his elbow and led him away.

Struggling to stand, she started to follow them. The voices would not stop shouting.

"These men are servants of the Most High God! Servants of the Most High! Listen to them, hear what they have to say! They will tell you how to be saved!"

The men hurried away. Arsenios pulled on her arm, saying something, but she saw only his lips move. The voices were too loud.

Anger. Fear. The gods had forced her to acclaim these men, to name them servants of a higher god, a deity they all must recognize. But her voices were not happy about these men. *They will destroy us. We will never worship them. We must destroy them. Pull them down. Tear them apart before they tear us apart!*

The next few days were the worst that she had ever known. Every time Demos or Arsenios forced her out of the house, she saw the strangers. The same men, and sometimes one or two others with them. They were everywhere. As she watched them talking to people in the marketplace she tried to hold herself back, to look away. But the words burst out of her. She had no power over her own speech. An urgent need to warn everyone that these newcomers were dangerous overwhelmed her, but the words she actually uttered were the same as those she had spoken that first day:

"These men are servants of the Most High God! Hear them. Pay attention to their words!"

The torment she felt inside grew worse with every passing day. She could feel the awe, the terror, and the anger of the python spirit inside her. The voices were going to tear her apart.

It wasn't always like this, she reminded herself one night as she lay curled into a ball on her sleeping mat, trying to protect herself from the relentless waves of pain and anguish that tore through her body. Her memories were faint and fragmented. She had always known the voices. But they had not always attacked her like this.

When she was small she had lived in a temple. Her mother, a priestess, had heard the voices, too. But her mother, and the ring of white robed priestesses who were like her family, had known the voices as part of their worship, their community, their carefully ordered and measured rituals. The voices of the gods were controlled and understood.

If she had stayed there, she would have grown up knowing how to control and serve the spirits, too. First she would have been an acolyte, then a python priestess like her mother. She would have belonged to the gods, and they would have cared for her.

But then came war and bloodshed. She didn't remember much, except the soldiers taking her from her mother. And her hands tied, and traveling somewhere. Far away. Frightened, she had lost everything, except the voices. They remained with her. But now they were confused and angry, and there was no mother, no priestesses, to help.

Knowing only that she had been a slave since childhood, she had no idea how long Demos and Arsenios had owned her. Time flowed together like drops of water in a river. Months and years had no meaning. Time was punctuated by dark, endless nights like this, and the raging clamor of voices.

When she saw the men in the marketplace, the gods spoke through her and said, *They are telling you how to be saved.* But that was the very thing she could not learn. How to be saved. She needed someone to save her from the torment that was her life.

Unable to silence the voices, she could not escape her fate. Instead, she realized that she would be haunted, and a slave, till she died.

But she could die. If she could figure out how to make herself die, maybe it would all stop.

That's right, foolish girl. Death is all you deserve. But when you come to Hades, you will find us there. Don't imagine you can escape. When you leave this world, you fall into our hands. We are waiting for you in Hades.

"No!" she cried aloud.

"Shut up!" Demos's voice rang out from his back bedroom. "I swear, girl, you useless pile of flesh and bone, if people didn't pay good money to hear your ravings I'd have thrown you out in the street years ago!"

Morning came again. It always did. This time Demos took her to the west gate of the city, where travelers on the Via Egnatia arrived in Philippi or went out on their way to the next city. People going on journeys often wanted their fortunes told.

Then she spotted them again, just inside the gate. The servants of the Most High God, the same two men—the short gray haired man and his taller, balding companion. Breaking free of Demos's grip on her arm, she threw herself in the dust at their feet. People turned to stare as she cried out. "These men are servants of the Most High God! Listen to them—they will tell you how to be saved! These men are servants—"

Always before, they had turned away or ignored her. Now the smaller man, the one she had seen first in the marketplace, stopped and turned in his tracks. She recognized the anger in his face—that he had had enough. His eyes gripped her far more tightly than Demos's hands ever could. They were stormy and gray like the sea. His hand was upraised, cutting off the words still in her mouth.

"In the name of Jesus Christ!" The words rang with command. "I order you to come out of her!"

Out. Of her.

Silence. A vast emptiness, as if a crowd of people had rushed from a room. As if water burst from a water skin that had been slashed with a knife. It left her empty, deflated.

Collapsing on the ground, face down in the dust, she felt exhausted, as if she had run a race and then been whipped and beaten at the finish line. But the voices said nothing. They were silent. More than silent—they were gone. The gods had deserted her. Finally she was alone.

Hands reached for her, helping her to her feet. She staggered against the man holding her, felt another pull at her arm. The voice was Demos's. "Leave this slave alone! She's my property—don't interfere with her!"

Somehow she could stand on her own, she realized, though her legs shook. Demos still held one arm. She brushed hair away from her face. The voices were still silent. The gods were really gone. For the first time in her life she could speak her own thoughts in her own mind and hear herself.

"She is no one's property, but a child of the living God," the other man said. When she turned to look at him, his gray eyes that had been so angry were now calm and even concerned. A small man, he was not much taller than she was. She smiled at him. Her lips mouthed the words, "Thank you," though she didn't have the breath to speak aloud.

He nodded at her. Turning to Demos, she saw him clearly for the first time. A little fat man with a red face. He had wielded such power over her. But everything he had—his wealth, his fine clothes, his place in the community—he had because of her. Because people paid silver and gold to hear the gods speak through her. And now the gods had departed.

"It's finished, Demos," she said, wondering at her own courage. "The gods have left me. Their voices are silent."

"Liar!" he said, slapping her across the face. But she had been struck so many times that she barely noticed.

"Set her free, and let her come with us," the small man told Demos. "She's no good to you anymore. The girl can't tell fortunes any longer—the evil spirit has been cast out of her."

Demos laughed harshly. "You fool, why should I give you my valuable slave? Get out of here before I make trouble for you! What are you doing here, stirring up our people? If you're going to pray with the Jews, go on—don't make trouble for Roman citizens." He pulled her roughly away, back toward the city.

"What is your name?" the small man asked, his eyes still fixed on her.

My name? It had been so long since she had been called by a name, had called herself by a name. Yet she heard it in her mind now, in her mother's clear tones. She had memories now, and the space in which to see and hear them. *Euodia.* A pretty name, like music.

"My name is Euodia," she told the man who had set her free.

"My name is Paul. When we meet again, I will tell you about Jesus, your deliverer." Then Demos, still cursing, pulled her too far away to hear the little man, back toward the marketplace and the crowds of people.

But it did no good. When they found a customer and brought him before her, she took his hand as she'd always done, but saw nothing there except work hardened lines and ingrained dirt. In his eyes she recognized fear, and hope—the hope that the gods had a word of advice or a promise or good fortune for him. But she heard no voices, felt nothing besides pity for the man. "I'm sorry," she said simply. "I have nothing to tell you. The gods no longer speak to me."

Demos flew into a fury. Arsenios came and tried to reason with her. "If you can't hear your voices, then make something up," he insisted. "You have a few tricks, you know how to read people. Tell them what you think they want to hear. Pretend it's a god speaking."

"I won't do that."

"You *will* do it!" Demos ordered. "It's what I bought you for." He took her back home and beat her, then tried again with another customer. "You can beat me all you want," Euodia told him after the disappointed would-be client had gone home. "But I cannot pretend. And if I did, people would know. They would recognize the difference."

"She may be right about that," Arsenios said, laying a hand on Demos's arm to stop the blow about to descend. "The girl was mad, and she's sane now. Anyone can see the difference. Why should the gods speak through a perfectly sane slave girl? There's nothing special about her anymore. She's common—and worthless."

"She may have other uses, then," Demos growled. Euodia guessed what he might mean—that he would find ways to sell her body if he could no longer sell her spirit. She was frightened, of course. The fear hurt, just as his beatings did. But neither fear nor pain tore her apart any longer. There was something inside, at the core of her, that was strong. A calm place that she had never suspected existed until the gods went away. Maybe it had never been there before. Perhaps it was something the man named Paul had put inside her.

She had to see him again. She had to know about this Jesus he had spoken of, about what her life would be now that she was no longer the plaything of the gods. But how could she ever get free from Demos and Arsenios?

"It's the fault of those men—those Jews," Demos complained. "They're up to no good, and they've turned our valuable property into a worthless piece of trash. I'll have them hauled before the magistrates."

"I know where they're staying," Arsenios said.

"You do? Where?"

"In the street of the weavers and dyers. They live in the house of Lydia, the purple dye merchant. One of them is a physician, another is a tentmaker. They take in a little work and support themselves on that. There are three or four of them—it shouldn't be hard to find the two who caused the trouble."

"Fine, then. Guard her—I'm going to see the magistrates."

"No, I'll come with you." Arsenios pulled on his cloak as Demos laced up his sandals. Demos' woman was nowhere to be seen, but the other slave was chopping firewood behind the house. "Calvus!" Demos called. "Keep an eye on the girl—don't let her get away."

She heard his low, throaty chuckle as he entered the room with a bundle of wood. "Don't worry, master. I won't let her go far."

Euodia turned her face away and sat on her sleeping mat, hugging her knees. They would not let her escape easily. Instead, they would watch her now, realizing that with her mind once again her own, she would be clearheaded and eager for escape. She would not try tonight—nor perhaps tomorrow. Rather, she would keep her head down, cook their meals and clean their house, try to be a good slave even though she could no longer be a fortune-teller. But before long—before they found another use for her—she would find an opportunity, and she would escape. This time she would succeed.

CHAPTER 3
CLEMENT

"Give me that! Chara, he took my shawl, tell him to give it back!"

"Here! I don't want it anyway, stupid thing! What would I want a girl's shawl for?"

"You took it just to make me angry. Chara, he's *always* bothering me!"

Clement paused in the doorway, not really wanting to enter the house where chaos reigned as Chara, the elderly slave, put the evening meal on the table. "Hush now!" her soft voice entered the fray. "You children don't want to trouble your parents with your quarrels. Sit down and be polite when they come to the table."

"I would, if *he* would leave me alone," Julia hissed under her breath.

"It's *your* fault," Lucius said in the same truculent tone.

"Hush now," the old woman repeated. She had been a wonderful nursemaid when the children were small but now that they were growing so fast they seemed to be slipping out of her control. Clement took a deep breath. They needed a firmer hand. He had no trouble keeping criminals in line but an 8-year-old boy and a 9-year-old girl were a different matter. Still, it was his duty, as their father—

"Lucius, stand still and be quiet. Julia, move to the other side of the table and keep your hands and feet to yourself. Not a word from either of you except 'Good evening' when your father comes in. Ah, here he is—good evening, my husband." Syntyche's crisp tones had transformed chaos to order in a matter of moments. As Clement entered the small atrium of his modest home, the scene in front of his eyes was a perfect demonstration of harmonious family life. The table was set— fresh bread, hot bowls of *puls*, figs, olives, honey, fish sauce. His wife and two children stood respectfully waiting for him to come to the table, then lowered themselves to their seats as he took his place. The faithful family slave hovered in the background, waiting to serve. No evidence remained of the chaos that had reigned just a moment earlier.

Julia looked demure and quiet as befitted a young girl, her eyes downcast toward her food, the offending shawl arranged neatly over her shoulders. Lucius was quiet too, but when his father asked what he had done that day, the boy darted a quick glance at his mother and reported he had cut and stacked the pile of firewood behind the house. "Good work for a lad your age," Clement said, impressed not just at the boy but at Syntyche's ability to teach the children to work.

His wife presided now over this quiet domestic scene, passing bread and pouring wine, occasionally summoning Chara to bring something from the kitchen, then telling the slave to get something to eat for herself from the kitchen. Clement watched her with the same quiet amazement he felt every time he looked at the woman.

Syntyche was a small person—when he stood beside her he could look right down at the top of her head. Her round face and plump body made her look deceptively soft and gentle, but under her pretty dark curls she was a woman of iron, strong willed and unshakeable once she made up her mind. When they had first met he had been entranced by her beauty but a little scared of her. Her allure had won him over, and it was the best decision he'd ever made. Syntyche had been his partner for more than 10 years—though his wife in the eyes of the law for only five since he had finished his military service, as soldiers could not marry.

She had traveled with him, borne his two children, lived the hard existence of a soldier's woman. Then she had made a home for him here in Philippi, his last post, where he received his pension—a job as chief jailer, with a residence adjoining the jail. She kept the little house running smoothly on their modest means and had the children clothed and educated and reasonably well behaved—and made Lucius Julius Clement a happy man.

He knew he was luckier than he deserved. Some might say the gods had been good to him.

That was a thought that made him less happy, so he shoved it aside and asked his wife what she'd bought at market that day.

"I made a very good bargain on some wool," she told him. "Chara and I are going to begin spinning it tomorrow. It will be a good opportunity for Julia to learn, too. We could buy the cloth already woven, of course, but we save so much this way, and there's plenty of time to spin and weave it before the children will need new tunics. And every girl should learn to spin as soon as she's able."

"I already can spin, a little bit," Julia said, but a frown from her mother silenced her as she knew better than to speak at the table without being spoken to.

Syntyche laid a hand on her husband's arm. "What of your day? Was it quiet at the jail?"

"Quiet enough—we've only a dozen or so prisoners at the moment. Two new ones this afternoon—foreigners brought before the magistrate on charges of disturbing the peace. I don't know what it was all about—they looked harmless enough. But the magistrates wanted them flogged and kept in secure custody, so they're chained and in the stocks."

Again Syntyche briefly touched his arm as she reached for the water jug. She knew without him saying it how he hated whipping prisoners. Being a jailer was no easy job, though it was better than being a soldier. "I had to find another man to watch the night shift along with Varro tonight," he added, to change the mood. "Alexander is still not better of his cough."

"Alexander has had that cough a long time." His wife said no more. She didn't need to.

The past winter Clement's brother Durio—a soldier like Clement, but still on active duty here in Philippi—had taken ill with a cough like that. It dragged him down, pulled the strength out of his young, active body. Clement had loved his brother very much. Their parents were both dead, and they had no other family.

When you were a soldier you knew death was a constant possibility. He had been prepared for his own death on the battlefield, or his brother's. But they had both survived many battles, and now he was retired and Durio was in a peaceful posting. He had looked forward to the day when his brother, too, would have finished his 20 years' service, married, and started a family. They would watch their children grow up together, turn old together.

His brother's illness, steadily worse no matter what remedies were tried, had not been part of the plan.

Lucius Julius Clement was a devout man. Not devout like a priest, but devout as a soldier was. Loving his gods, he believed that they cared for him. He had worshipped Mithras when he was a young man. Now, settled here in Philippi, he was more devoted to Apollo, and he joined his wife in her worship of Isis. But when Durio got sick, Clement prayed to them all—to every god and goddess he could find a temple and a ritual for. He gave offerings—far more than he could afford. Careful Syntyche never said a word about his extravagance. She knew what his brother meant to him.

But all the prayers, all the offerings had done nothing. The gods were deaf, or had gone away. His brother grew worse and died. In pain, begging for relief. Well, he had his relief now—in Hades.

Clement pushed the thoughts away again. He had been doing that for a year now, since the worst of his grief had passed. While he was glad for his job and his home, his good wife and fine healthy children, he didn't thank the gods for them. Why would they care? As for the empty space inside where he had once loved his gods—that would have to stay empty.

Joining the army at 16, he'd worked hard during his 20-year term of service, waiting for the day when he'd be able to settle down with his army pension and a wife, raise his children, and live a simpler life. He had all that now. There was no point in wondering what he was working for, what he had to look forward to.

After dark he went back across the small courtyard that separated his house from the jail's guardhouse and gave an army salute to Varro, one of the men on duty. "All quiet?" he asked as he entered the small room that served as the entrance to the jail. The cells were all underground. A dark narrow staircase led from this room down into the two dungeons.

"Nobody's giving any trouble," Varro said. "Those new prisoners—the Jews—are quiet enough."

"Good. The magistrates will probably send word in the morning about their sentence, but I imagine they'll be held for a few days and then thrown out of the city."

It was what usually happened to that kind of troublemaker. Strange that the two men should be Jews, though. He'd run across them when he had served in Asia, but only a handful existed in Philippi, and he'd never heard of them preaching or raising any kind of fuss in the streets. Quiet people with a quiet God, no temples or priests or sacrifices except far away in their own country. "Whoever they are, they're not likely to give trouble tonight."

He saw them when he took a torch down to check on the prisoners. The two Jews sat against the back wall of the inner dungeon, their feet locked in wooden stocks, shackled at the wrists to heavy iron rings set in the stone walls. Their torn bodies and bloody clothes showed evidence of the flogging that his men had given them earlier. Their voices, as they talked quietly to each other, sounded cultured and well educated.

Clement paused and leaned on the wall near the two men. "You two all right? Will anyone bring you anything—blankets, or food?" The jail supplied nothing for its prisoners, and nights could get cold down here. Part of his job involved receiving the prisoners' families and friends with food and extra clothes for the men incarcerated here.

"We have friends in the city who will send us food if we're here long," one man replied. "But we hope to be released soon."

"I'll have to admit, you don't look dangerous," Clement said with a grin. The prisoner smiled at him.

"Only dangerous as the truth is dangerous. We have come to Philippi to preach the good news of Jesus the Anointed One, the one who came to set men free. Today we set a slave girl free in his name—a poor, tortured thing possessed by demons. Her owners weren't happy—they said we had ruined their business."

"That's odd. You'd think most people would rather have a half sensible slave than a mad one," Clement mused. Clearly her owners didn't care much about their slave's well-being—but then some people were like that.

"She was a fortune-teller," the second prisoner explained. "Without the demons tormenting her, she has nothing to tell."

"Ah. That'd be Demos and Arsenios's fortune-teller—everyone knows her." Clement didn't add that he'd gone to see her once himself, hoping that she had a message from beyond the grave for him. The visit had disturbed him profoundly—both the girl's message and the fact that he'd been desperate enough to even attempt a thing like that. In fact, he hadn't even told Syntyche about it. He cleared his throat. "That Demos is a shifty character—too bad you had to cross him."

"We had no choice," the first man said. "We could not let a human being suffer such torment when Jesus has the power to set her free."

Clement shrugged. The prisoner was clearly crazy for his god—Clement had seen that type before. He felt sorry for such individuals. If they weren't completely insane, then they were bound to have a shattering disappointment.

A few minutes later he left to check on the other prisoners, none of whom were as cheerful or as talkative. Then he climbed the steps again to the guardroom, where the two guards were sitting on a bench playing a dice game. He was about to go back to his own house for the night when he heard voices drifting up from the cavern below. "What's that? One of the prisoners starting trouble?"

The door at the top of the stairs was locked, but a barred window in the heavy door allowed the guards to hear the men below. "It sounds like—singing," Clement said, shaking his head in disbelief.

"Singing? Who'd have any reason to sing down there?"

"The new prisoners—those foreign Jews." He knew it had to be them. The men were definitely not average captives.

Opening the door, he took a few steps down. Sure enough, two voices were singing—one a strong, clear bass, the other rougher, less polished. Another step down and he could pick out the words.

"Praise the Lord, O my soul;
    all my inmost being, praise his holy name.

"Praise the Lord, O my soul,
    and forget not all his benefits—

"who forgives all your sins
    and heals all your diseases,

"who redeems your life from the pit
    and crowns you with love and compassion."

Clement went to the corner where the two men were confined. "You're the most cheerful prisoners I've seen here in a while," he said, interrupting their song.

The smaller man, the one with the less practiced singing voice, smiled. "The truth is, we were getting a little discouraged. Silas suggested that we sing praises to the Lord."

"This is your god? Forgives all your sins, heals all your diseases, hauls you out of the pit? He sounds worth worshipping." Clement couldn't hold back a mocking grin. "Too bad he's left you down here in prison."

"He allows us to suffer trials, yet He always works everything for our good. My name is Paul, by the way—Paul of Tarsus. We are singing songs of the God of Israel, for we are Jews—but we are also worshippers of Jesus, the Son of God."

"Well, maybe you'd better sing a song about him," Clement suggested. "His father doesn't seem to be doing much about getting you out of those chains. Maybe the son can do better." Laughing, he turned to walk away. He was barely at the steps before the men started singing again. He expected to hear the other prisoners yelling at Paul and Silas to shut their mouths, but they were all strangely silent as the new song began.

"Let this mind be in you
  Which was also in Christ Jesus,
  Who, being in the form of God,
  Did not consider it robbery to be equal with God.

"He made Himself of no reputation,
  Taking the form of a bondservant,
  Coming in the likeness of men.

"Being found in appearance as a man,
  He humbled Himself
  And became obedient to the point of death,
  Even the death of the cross."

Some moments later Clement realized that he was still standing at the foot of the stairs, listening. What kind of crazy god did these men worship? One who could heal all diseases and save men from the grave, yet whose own divine son died on a cross like a bandit? He shook his head and went back up the stairs and across to his own house, leaving Varro on duty. Lying in bed beside his sleeping wife, he tried to put aside all thoughts of gods and mysteries.

Clement was almost fully asleep when he felt the ground tremble. Not sure if he was dreaming, he snapped fully awake. As he found his footing and stood upright, the room shook. Syntyche sat up beside him, gripping his arm. "What is it?" she cried, her composure cracking for once.

Before he could reply, the next tremor came, more violent. Clement tried to get out of bed and found himself on his hands and knees on the floor. Chara and the children were awake now, shouting, and Syntyche rose to try to go to their bedchamber. "Stop!" he shouted as the floor and walls heaved again, but she was already out of the room, clinging to the walls for support. He staggered out behind her. Far off he heard a crash as if a wall somewhere had fallen.

By the time they reached the frightened children sitting up in their beds, the tremors had stopped. Clement could hear voices from the street outside, but after a few minutes of calming and soothing their son and daughter it seemed that the earthquake had stopped. Only then did he think of the prison and wonder if the quake had caused any damage there.

His house, as he passed through the main room, seemed safe and whole. But across the courtyard he saw a chilling sight. A piece of the guardhouse wall had fallen into the courtyard, leaving the interior exposed. Inside, the guardhouse was empty—the guards must have fled in terror. The door at the top of the stairs had been ripped away, leaving the entrance to the dungeons gaping like a dark wound.

As Clement stood there, staring down, he heard someone entering the ruined building behind him. It was Varro. "Have you seen any prisoners? Have they escaped?"

"I haven't gone down to look yet, but it's quiet down there. With this much destruction, their shackles might have torn loose from the walls. They probably all ran when they could." His heart felt heavy as a stone, realizing that he had failed in his duty to secure the prison. "Is there much damage in the rest of the city?"

Varro shook his head. "Hardly any. The quake seems to have hit right here, right around the jail—people a few streets over barely felt a tremor. My wife said the dishes rattled on the kitchen shelves. I ran home to see if they were all right," he added, shamefaced.

Clement nodded. It didn't really matter; Varro had a duty to guard the jail, but the ultimate responsibility was his. He was the one who would be blamed if the prisoners had escaped.

Suddenly he realized that he was shaking all over. Perhaps it was delayed shock from the quake, the brief moments of terror he'd suffered at the thought of his family in danger—but mostly, it was fear of what would happen next. The prison cells below were deathly silent. He didn't want to go down there, to see the empty cells he knew were waiting.

A jailer could be executed for failing in his duty. Just like a soldier. He'd been an army man all his life. If the prisoners were gone, he could be sentenced to die for his dereliction of duty. Syntyche and the children would suffer the shame of seeing him arrested, charged, and executed.

As he took a hesitant step through the yawning doorway into the darkness below he heard nothing, saw nothing. The quake had extinguished the lights that had been burning there earlier, and the blackness of the dungeons was complete. As was the silence. There was no one down there.

Drawing his short sword, he held it, trembling, not sure what he was protecting himself against. It was possible the prisoners, if any were left here, might attack him. But the room remained dark and still.

A wave of despair overwhelmed him and he turned his dagger toward his own chest. He was a fool, and the gods were laughing at him. "I can't bear it!" he said aloud to the empty dungeons. "I'd rather die on my own blade than be sentenced and disgraced."

"Who's there?" called a familiar voice. "Is that you, jailer? No need to harm yourself—we're all here."

Slowly Clement lowered his sword. He recognized the voice from the darkness—the Jewish prisoner, the more talkative of the two. Paul of—Tarsus, wasn't it? Clement realized he was shaking all over.

"Who's here?" he called back.

"All the prisoners." He heard other voices now, confirming what Paul had said. The clatter of chains began as the prisoners started to move around. Clement called Varro to bring a torch. What the light revealed amazed him. The door gaped wide, all the shackles had come loose from the walls, and the stocks were broken open. Yet he counted 12 prisoners—the same number that had been there earlier in the night. At the head of the little group was the small man Paul, who seemed to have somehow convinced a group of unshackled prisoners not to escape. Clement had no idea how, but he already had a sense of the power of the man's personality.

Above, he heard Varro talking to someone—the second guard had returned to his post. "What happened to the prisoners?" the man asked.

"They're all down here," Clement called up. "They could have escaped, but—they didn't. I'll need to report that to the magistrates." If they knew the prisoners had had a chance to flee but had stayed in jail, the magistrates might be impressed enough to lighten some of their sentences.

None of that seemed to matter much now. As Varro began to lead the prisoners back to their cells, Clement kept his eyes fixed on Paul and the man's companion, Silas. That the earthquake had centered directly on the prison was no accident, he was sure. These men claimed to worship a god who could save them from prison, who could rescue and heal them—even though his own son had died as a criminal. This god of theirs not only made them cheerful enough to sing in a jail cell, but had done something—sent an earthquake—to rescue them.

All Clement's old longing for the gods, all the worship and adoration he had choked down since his brother's death, came rushing back. The world was a lonely place if you believed the gods didn't care about you at all. He had tried so hard to hang on to that. But then these men came, and their god *did* care, did act and change things, and he had to know more about such a deity, this Jesus. What was it Paul had said? That Jesus had the power to save people, to set them free.

He didn't even realize he was on his knees. "What do I have to do to be saved by your god?" he asked, his eyes never leaving Paul's face.

"Believe on the Lord Jesus, the Anointed One," the man said.

Clement stared at him a moment, wondering what that meant. He wanted to know, to understand, as much as he'd ever desired anything before in his life.

"Finish securing the prisoners," he called to Varro. "I'm taking these two to my house for the night—I'll guard them there. They were responsible for keeping the others from escaping—they deserve special consideration."

"That's kind of you," Paul said. "My wife and servant will clean and dress your wounds properly, and give you something to eat," Clement announced. "And in return, you will tell us about your Jesus."

CHAPTER 4
LYDIA

A pounding at the door wakened Lydia for the second time that night. The day had been turbulent, with the arrest of Paul and Silas that afternoon. When she finally got to sleep, the earth tremors had awakened her and half the household. She had just gotten back to sleep and now it sounded as if someone were trying to break down her door. Sitting up, she pulled a shawl about her shoulders. Downstairs the slave Tacitus answered the door, and she heard a young boy's voice.

"I have a message for Lydia," the lad said as she came into the shop.

"I am Lydia—you may give me your message."

"My father, Clement the jailer, says to tell you that he is coming with Paul and Silas."

"They are released from jail?"

"No, mistress. They are—I don't quite understand it. He just said to tell you they were coming."

By the time the jailer arrived with Paul and Silas—and his wife, daughter, and slave—Lydia's whole household was dressed and in the courtyard, speculating about what could have happened to the two men. Her usual family had greatly expanded. The four Christians had moved into her home soon after their arrival in Philippi. Luke and Timothy were there now, eager to see their friends again and hear about their night in prison.

"So our good friend Clement brought us to his house," Paul said, concluding the story of the earthquake for the circle of fascinated listeners sitting on benches and on the ground in Lydia's small courtyard, "and while dear Syntyche cleaned and bandaged our wounds, we told their family about Jesus. Clement has expressed a wish to become a follower of Jesus and be baptized as soon as possible. I strongly suspect this morning will bring either a return to prison, or an order to leave the city. So we want to go to the river and baptize Clement and his household now, before dawn breaks, then return to his house to await further news."

"Praise the Lord!" Timothy said, his eyes glowing with excitement. Luke was already checking the bandages on Paul's and Silas's wounds. "Well done," he said with a nod to the jailer's wife.

"It is a very sudden decision," Lydia said to the jailer. "I heard Paul teach and discussed the scriptures with him for many days before I decided to be baptized."

"What is there to discuss?" the man called Clement replied with a smile that lit the room. "Jesus, the Son of the God of heaven, sent an earthquake to the prison to free these men, and to set me free, too. I've never felt as sure of anything in my life."

The jailer's wife slipped beside him. She looked like a tiny, plump, bright eyed bird beside her tall, muscular husband, but her face was clever and thoughtful. Syntyche said nothing, and Lydia wondered how the woman felt about her husband's sudden allegiance to a new religion.

As everyone put on cloaks and walked through the predawn grayness out through the gate to the meeting place by the river, Lydia thought about the differences between her household and that of Clement the jailer. As a husband and father, Clement had the right to command his wife, children, and slaves to worship as he did. During her own husband's life, Lydia had obeyed his order to worship the Roman gods as he did, and had kept her interest in the Jewish faith quiet until after his death. Clement's family would likely all become Christian now, because the *paterfamilias* wished it so. Paul had told her that in the churches he had raised up throughout Asia that was the usual pattern—men would come to the Christ and bring their families with them. Women who were convicted of the truth of Paul's good news were often baptized without their husbands' consent, dividing the family. Indeed, that had happened already here in Philippi. Two of Lydia's friends among the God fearers had been baptized although their husbands had no interest in Christianity.

But though head of her own household, Lydia did not have that same power and authority. Helena, her mother-in-law, remained as remote and disapproving of the Christians as she had been of the God fearers, and the slaves still followed the older woman's lead. As for the freedmen, Simeon and Rachel, Lydia knew they were torn. Simeon had spent long hours with Paul discussing and debating the Scriptures. He was inclined toward believing in Jesus, but had not chosen to be baptized when Lydia had been, partly because of Rachel, who had a great struggle accepting that Jesus of Nazareth could really be the promised Messiah. The few other Jews in Philippi—especially old Solomon and his daughter Sara—firmly opposed the Jesus followers. As for Epaphroditus, he had accepted the truth of Jesus and spent many hours with Timothy and Luke, but he too held back from making the decision to be baptized. "I want to be sure, Mother," was all he would say when Lydia pressed him on it.

"You are deep in thought, Lydia," Luke the physician said as he fell into step beside her.

"I am thinking of how this good news so often brings division to families and households," she replied with a sigh. "I hope it will not be so for the jailer and his family—he truly seems to have been touched by the Spirit of God, and I hope his family will be glad to follow Jesus too."

"Jesus spoke about this," Luke said. "I have heard His words from the lips of His own disciple Peter—that Jesus said He came not to bring peace, but a sword; that families would be divided, father against son and mother against daughter, because of Him."

Lydia shivered. "That's a harsh prophecy. Yet Paul talks about the peace of Jesus."

"He did speak of peace too, but I think He had a different kind of peace in mind," Luke commented thoughtfully. "Perhaps He meant that following His Way would bring us into conflict with others, yet we would have peace in our spirits."

Luke was the quietest of the four missionaries, yet he was the one Lydia felt she knew best. Paul was the preacher, and Timothy followed in his footsteps, matching the apostle's passion with even greater skill at rhetoric. Silas was no great preacher, but he was outgoing and sociable, always to be found talking to people one-on-one, quick to raise his voice in song or laughter. Luke, the skilled physician with his steady brown eyes that seemed to miss nothing, watched and listened a great deal. In their quiet talks Lydia felt that she had really gotten to know the man and sensed how keenly she would miss him when they all left Philippi.

"Have His sayings been collected and written down by any of His followers?" Lydia asked Luke now, thinking of what he had said about the words of Jesus. "It would be good to have them to study."

"Some collections of His sayings and stories of His deeds have been compiled among the believers back in the land of Israel. They will become more and more necessary as we bring His message further into the world, and those who knew Him in person grow older and forget His words. I would like to travel there again, talk further with those who knew Him and see what they have written—perhaps make a collection of His sayings and deeds that we could send to the new churches." He, too, sighed as they drew near the bank of the stream. "That would be the work of a lifetime. Someday, perhaps."

The sun was just rising over the horizon, spilling a pale gold light on the water, as Paul lowered the jailer below the waters and then brought him out again. Lydia's own baptism just a few weeks earlier had been a strange experience, here in this same stream, bending low in the shallow water till it completely closed over her head. It was meant to be like dying and rising again, Paul had said. Dying to her old life and beginning the new life in Jesus.

There was so much she still did not understand. So much yet to learn about what it meant to be Jesus' follower. But her new life had begun. She just wished that those she loved—Simeon, Rachel, her other Jewish friends, even Helena—could make that same decision.

The small group on the riverbank watched in reverent silence as the rest of the adults in the jailer's household entered the stream and were baptized. Lydia searched Syntyche's face again after she came up out of the water, seeking for a clue to the woman's feelings. But her expression was as enigmatic as it had been earlier.

"Now we must return to the city before Clement gets in trouble with the magistrates for escaping with his prisoners!" Paul announced.

The streets of Philippi were already beginning to fill with people as the first light of morning accompanied the little group of believers into Lydia's street. Merchants began opening their shops, slaves hurried on their masters' errands, handcarts and horse drawn carts rattled along the street. Lydia decided not to go home with Epaphroditus, Rachel, and Simeon, but to continue to the jail with Paul and Silas. As a respected merchant who had taken the traveling preachers into her home, she hoped she would have some influence with the magistrates. Yesterday she had not even known of their arrest and beating until it was too late and they were already in jail. Today she had a second opportunity to change the outcome of the situation.

At the jailer's house Syntyche and her slave Chara busied themselves preparing a meal for the guests. Luke and Timothy had come with them, so it was a large party that met around Clement's table for a morning meal of bread, honey, grapes, fig cakes, and olives. Throughout it Clement plied Paul with questions about Jesus. Paul, of course, never seemed happier than when he had a chance to talk about his favorite subject, and everyone listened eagerly. Lydia wondered if she was the only one worrying about what the day would bring. What would happen when the magistrates heard about the earthquake at the prison, and learned that their two newest prisoners were staying as honored guests at the chief jailer's own home?

They didn't have long to wait. A heavy knock at the door sent Chara scurrying to answer it. "Message for you, master," she told Clement as she led a man into the atrium.

"The magistrates have commanded that the two Jews, Paul and Silas, who were arrested yesterday are to be released today," a round faced man with a rather pompous manner announced to Clement.

The jailor nodded, but before he could speak, Paul rose to his feet and addressed the messenger. "The magistrates had us publicly beaten without a trial, even though we are Roman citizens, and then threw us into prison. And now they want to get rid of us quietly? No! Let them come themselves and escort us out."

The man's round face turned several shades paler. "You—you are Roman citizens?"

"Yes. I am a citizen by birth. In fact, we are both Roman citizens, and we have been treated like common criminals. We deserve and expect better treatment from your city's leaders."

"I—the magistrates may not have been fully aware of all the facts in the situation," the man stammered. "I will return at once with your message. Remain here. You are—you are being well treated here?"

"Very well indeed," Paul assured him. His face was somber although the glint of a smile lurked behind his sharp gray eyes. "Much better than we were treated last night, with our feet in the stocks and our wrists shackled to the wall of the prison."

"I will return at once. . ." As he backed out of the room in his haste to leave, Clement followed him to the door. Lydia couldn't overhear the words of the quiet conversation the jailer had with the messenger just before the man left.

No sooner had the door shut than Silas burst out laughing, quickly followed by Paul. "You are always quick to reveal your Roman citizenship just when it will cause the most embarrassment," Silas commented.

"I am always glad to suffer for my Lord when I am called to

do so," Paul said, "but sometimes He summons me to demand respect for His messengers. If He could send an earthquake to the jail last night, I'm sure He won't mind if I shake the magistrates up a little more."

Before all the breakfast platters had been cleared away, another knock came. The messenger returned with word that Paul and Silas were to go at once to the forum, where the magistrates would meet with them personally.

"Let us face them, then," Paul said. "Friend Clement, you must accompany us to testify to what happened at the jail last night—and Lydia, my dear yokefellow, won't you come too? You are well respected in this city—perhaps we will look less scandalous in your company."

So Lydia went with Paul, Silas, Timothy, Luke, and Clement to the forum, where a servant brought them directly into the magistrates' audience chamber. One of them, Aulus Gabinus Sidonius, greeted her warmly. He and his wife Flavia were Lydia's long-standing customers, though their slave Rufus conducted most of their business.

"We deeply regret the way you were treated," Aulus Gabinus told Paul and Silas. "We were not aware you were citizens—those who complained to us painted you as foreign rabble-rousers from the provinces, here to stir up our city with Jewish superstition and strange teachings contrary to the laws of the gods."

"All the more reason, good magistrates, why you should make every effort to learn the truth about prisoners before sentencing them," Paul suggested. Lydia could barely stifle a gasp. His confidence bordered on insolence. But she knew that it was simply that he had no fear: he believed so strongly in his calling from God that no earthly authority cowed him, even though kings and magistrates had the power to put him in prison.

Amid the flurry of apologies and diplomatic talk, Aulus Gabinus turned to Lydia. "I did not expect to see you in this company, good merchant."

"But Paul and Silas and their companions have been staying at my home, as my honored guests," she said smoothly. "They are no rabble-rousers, but respectable men who have come to bring light and truth."

"Ah yes—about this light and truth," the other magistrate said, turning to Paul, "while we sincerely regret your beating and imprisonment, we do not wish further trouble. The fact remains that there have been complaints, and we wish to hear no more. How soon can you be gone from Philippi? We have an order for you to be banished from the city, but we wish to avoid unpleasantness in carrying out this sentence."

Paul smiled. "My companions and I can be away by this time tomorrow. Give us but time to wind up our affairs and say goodbye to our friends here, and you can assure those who complained to you that we are on our way out of Philippi."

"With pleasant memories of the city, I trust," one of the magistrates added, which made Paul smile again.

"Some more pleasant than others," he admitted.

The rest of the day was busy. The four missionaries, who had hoped to have several more weeks in Philippi, now had to get ready to leave at once. They returned to Lydia's house, spreading word among the Jesus followers in the city that they would gather that night for a final meeting and a meal together.

The house was busy as the men packed their things. Visitors came and went throughout the day. As Paul, Silas, and Timothy gathered their belongings, Luke came quietly up to Lydia in the dye works behind the courtyard. She was inspecting a batch of dyes recently arrived from Thyatira—for the work of her business had to go on at the same time as God's.

"Lydia, I have spoken to Paul of this, but I would discuss it with you too before I make a decision," he said. "I wish to stay here in Philippi when the others leave. The magistrates' sentence does not apply to me or to Timothy. Timothy is eager to continue on with Paul and Silas, but I am weary of travel for a while. I want to return to practicing as a physician, and I would like to help you and the believers in Philippi become established in the faith. Paul thinks it a good idea, though he's kind enough to say he will miss my company."

She smiled. The thought that at least one of the missionaries would stay behind soothed the knot of fear that had been growing in her all day—the fear that her newfound faith, and that of her friends and family, would falter without Paul and the others here to teach and support them. "I would be so glad if you did. And you would be welcome to remain here as part of my household. We like having you—even Helena listens to you, when she seems to have little time for anyone else. Please stay!"

By late afternoon work in Lydia's shop had come to an end and people began to gather in the courtyard. All her own household, all Clement's household, and many other people who had heard Paul's teaching and chosen to follow Jesus, packed themselves into what usually seemed a large and open space. Right now it felt crowded. As Paul spoke to the crowd, Lydia counted heads. Nearly 40 people—men and women, young and old, slave and free. Several of her good friends from the little group of God fearers who met on Sabbaths had joined them, having accepted the message of Jesus. She was sad that Solomon and Sara had not come, and hoped that they would someday learn to know Jesus. But who would preach and teach his message when Paul was gone?

It will be our job, now, she suddenly thought in wonder. *All of us, here, gathered in this courtyard. We will be—what does Paul call it? We will be Jesus' body on earth, now. His hands, His feet, His voice—just as Paul is.*

It seemed a calling at once exciting and frightening. Again she looked at the nearly 40 faces turned eagerly toward Paul, drinking in each word, crowded together in her house. A shiver traveled up her spine.

"So be of good cheer, brothers and sisters!" Paul said, his words at odds with her solemn feeling. "You are Jesus Christ's family, children of His heavenly Father, brought to new life through His Spirit. When He returned to heaven from earth, He promised that He would not leave His people abandoned. I promise you the same thing. He is with us, here and now, at all places and in all times."

Paul gestured, and Lydia's slave Ariane came from the kitchen carrying a large basket filled with several loaves of flat bread. Lydia had planned a meal for later in the evening, but it looked as if he had made some private arrangements with her slaves, for Tacitus came behind Ariane carrying a jug of wine.

"On His last night before His crucifixion," Paul continued, "Jesus ate a Passover meal with His disciples. Those of you who are Jews and God fearers know what the Passover is—God's reminder that He once delivered the Jewish people from bondage in Egypt. Today He has delivered all of us from bondage to sin through His Son Jesus, and Jesus gave us a new Passover meal to share in remembrance of that." He tore off a piece of bread and handed the rest to Silas, who tore off another piece and passed it on. All around the room the bread went from person to person as Paul spoke. "He commanded us to eat this bread in remembrance of His body, which was broken on the cross for us." As the wine also made its way around the room, he said, "He told us to drink this wine in remembrance of His blood, which was poured out for us, to redeem us from sin and death. He told us that we should come together and eat this special meal to remember Him, and He is present with us whenever we do it, even if only two or three of us are gathered there."

Again, as she swallowed the bread, a shiver went down Lydia's spine. But it no longer felt sinister. It felt like the presence of God's Spirit.

Into the holy silence that had fallen Paul announced, "Silas, Timothy, and I are leaving tonight. Luke has chosen to stay here with you. Along with our kind hostess Lydia, he will be a guide and leader to you as you learn to follow the Way of Jesus together. Before I go I must ask if there are any others who would like to join this family of God? Anyone else who wants to die and be buried and rise again in Christ? We can go right now, before dinner, to the river, and I will baptize anyone who asks."

After a moment's hesitation someone moved. Lydia pressed the back of her hand against her mouth as she saw Rachel, sitting just a few feet away from her, stand. Next to her, Simeon quickly scrambled to his feet, then a few others. Lydia reached across to squeeze Rachel's hand. "Now we will be sisters," she mouthed to her oldest friend.

"And not only us," Rachel replied. As she followed the direction of the woman's gaze, Lydia received a far greater shock. Her mother-in-law, Helena, was standing too, clasping her elderly hand firmly around that of Doctor Luke. The old woman had showed no more interest in Paul's preaching than in anything else she had heard about the God of Israel through the years. But it seemed her long talks with the quiet physician had done something no preaching could do. Helena, too, was going to join the family of Jesus. Lydia noticed that her slave Ariane, loyal to her mistress as always, was also in the knot of people now gathering around Paul.

Her household would truly be united in Jesus—save for one. Lydia looked at Epaphroditus and saw her son's eager young face fixed, as always, on Paul's. The boy leaned forward as if he were about to get to his feet, yet something kept him on the ground. *Please, Lord Jesus, Holy Spirit, convict him that this is the time. Let him give himself wholly to You,* she prayed. As if he could feel her prayer, Epaphroditus shifted his gaze away from Paul and met her eyes across the crowded space. He smiled, but shook his head very slightly before turning away to watch Paul again. No, this was not Epaphroditus's time. She didn't understand, but she had to accept it. All her household, save the son she adored, would be united in the family of Jesus.

As they prepared to leave the house for the place of prayer by the river, a young woman—a girl, really, dashed into the street in front of Lydia's door. She stumbled against Rachel's shoulder and drew back as if expecting to be struck, cowering in front of the small crowd of people. A slender, black haired girl dressed in a ragged and dirty tunic, she might have been pretty if not for her wild, frightened eyes. Then the girl saw Paul and fell to her knees in front him.

"You are still here!" she said. "They told me you had to leave the city—I needed to see you!"

Paul reached out a hand to pull the girl to her feet. "No more kneeling before me, Euodia. You know I am not a god to be worshipped, and you no longer speak with the voices of evil spirits. Speak to me in your own voice and tell me what you want."

"You remember my name."

"I am good with names."

"I ran away from my masters. I want to know this Jesus whose name you called on when you set me free."

Smiling broadly, Paul waved a hand at the people gathered around him. "I will tell you what I can about Jesus tonight, before I have to go. I will even baptize you in His name, if you wish it. But you will *see* Jesus, touch His hands and hear His voice, in these people around you. They are His followers here in Philippi, His family. They are not perfect, but they have all had their lives changed by Him just as you did. They will welcome you into their family, and help you learn about Him." He took the girl's hand and placed it in Lydia's. "Lydia, this is Euodia, who I think would like to become your sister in Jesus."

The older woman looked down at the thin, calloused hand in hers. It was dirty. The girl was obviously distraught, troubled, possibly had been beaten. She had never imagined clasping such a person's hand, claiming her as sister. It was one thing to welcome her own friends, the members of her household, even the city jailer as members of the same family. But this girl?

Yes, she is a child of God too, one for whom Jesus died, Lydia told herself and made herself grip the dirty little hand. She could foresee all kinds of trouble in taking a runaway slave under her wing, perhaps into her household—for what would happen to the girl unless some kind Christ follower bought her from her masters? As she fell into step with Paul and the rest of the crowd, Euodia's hand still tucked in hers, Lydia sighed. Thinking of what Paul and Silas had endured in the past two days, she realized that following Jesus would probably bring all kinds of troubles. Yet, strangely, her heart was light and she didn't mind the thought at all. She smiled again, more warmly this time, at the slave girl as hand in hand they walked through the west gate toward the river.

CHAPTER 5
SYNTYCHE

"Are we almost there?" Julia asked, her voice rising almost to a whine on the last word. Syntyche looked at her daughter sharply. "Sorry, Mother," the girl said quickly. She was panting a little. Taking pity, Syntyche slowed her pace. She wanted to reach the shrine on the hill in time for the morning rites, then get back home before Clement returned from duty at the jail. And she still had the morning's marketing to do.

"Almost there," she replied as they climbed the final steps of the hill. Other worshippers joined them on the rocky path that led to the shrine of Isis overlooking Philippi. The goddess had always been popular with the people of Philippi, but in Syntyche's grandmother's time the emperor of the day had opposed the worship of Egyptian deities and urged people to return to the gods of Rome. Worship of Isis had declined for a time, though a core of people had always remained faithful to the mother of all creation.

But times were changing. The last emperor, Caligula, had been an evil man and a fool in many ways, but he had brought back the worship of the gods of Egypt and introduced a festival in Rome dedicated to Isis. Here at Philippi, the shrine Syntyche had attended as a girl with her mother and grandmother was larger and busier now, with more priests and priestesses than it had had in years gone by. Some talked of building a bigger temple. *Perhaps not in my time,* Syntyche thought, *but Julia will worship there. Maybe even be a priestess?* It had been her own dream for a while—to be a priestess as many of the women in her family had been.

Meeting Clement had changed her path in life. She had chosen to be a soldier's woman and eventually his wife, to bear his children and make a home for him. In that role, too, she honored Isis the Mother. Still, she sometimes wondered what her life might have been like as a priestess: living at the shrine, singing the hymns and worshipping the goddess every day.

Inside the entryway of the temple Syntyche washed her hands in the basin of holy water drawn from the faraway Nile River, and Julia did the same. Mother and daughter joined the small cluster of worshippers and the larger group of white robed priests and priestesses around the veiled image of the goddess.

As the choir of priestesses began their morning hymn, one of the priests stepped forward and reverently removed the veil that covered Isis's image. It revealed the mother goddess on her throne, her infant son Horus suckling at her breast. Syntyche never saw the image without thinking of her own children as infants, remembering the tug of a small mouth at her breast, the flood of joy that rose in her when she could give them food and life from her own body. She had never felt as close to her goddess as in those years when she nursed her babies.

Her oldest child now stood on tiptoe at her side to see above the heads of the worshippers. Julia watched with her mouth slightly open and her eyes aglow as two priestesses brought Isis's garments and carefully clothed the goddess. All the while the words of the hymn echoed and reechoed through the pillared room of stone:

"I am the wife and the virgin
I am the mother and the daughter. . ."

Syntyche divided her attention, observing the image of the
goddess and the rites of the priests, but also studying the way
Julia watched, remembering how she, too, had gone with her
mother and grandmother to the temple of Isis, how she had
been trained in its mysteries. Even before her own initiation, Isis
had been as much a part of her as her blood and her bones,
something born in her. Her mother had been a year priestess before her marriage, and two aunts had remained priestesses for
life. Even now Syntyche could see her grandmother's hand
raised in worship, hands as veined and carven as the stone walls
and pillars of the temple. *I am a part of this place, and this place is a
part of me*, Syntyche thought.

As she lifted her voice in the hymns, Syntyche took Julia's
hand to join in the dance as the priests moved through the
group, sprinkling the worshippers with Nile water.

The splash of cool water on her skin, when her turn came, reminded her as it always did of her immersion when she was initiated into the mysteries of Isis. But now that memory was
layered with another, more recent one: her immersion in the
stream on that predawn morning a few weeks earlier when
Clement had so suddenly decided to dedicate his entire family
to the worship of a new god, Jesus the Christ.

Compared to the long period of preparation for initiation into
Isis's mysteries, Jesus seemed to require very little of His devotees, Syntyche thought. At sunset that evening Clement had
never heard of Jesus, but by dawn he was immersed and had become part of the "body of Christ," as Paul of Tarsus called it.
And it was no fleeting thing either. Since that morning, Clement
had talked about little but Jesus the Christ and his newfound devotion to this god man, even though he had no temple of Jesus
to visit, no rites to participate in. The whole situation was very
strange, and as she stood in Isis's temple and looked up at the
goddess, Syntyche almost felt as if she owed Isis an apology. One

might worship many gods, of course, but a devotion such as the women of Syntyche's family had to Isis was special, and allowing herself to be immersed and initiated into the mysteries of another god's cult seemed like a lack of loyalty. If Syntyche prided herself on one virtue, it was loyalty.

Julia's thoughts must have run in the same direction, for on the way down the hillside after the service she said, "Mother, will I be initiated someday like you were?"

"If Isis calls you to be an initiate, you will." It relieved her to hear Julia ask the question: she didn't want her daughter's loyalty to their goddess to waver.

"How will she call me?"

"She will come to you in a dream. At least she did to me, when I was not much older than you."

"What about Jesus? Will I be baptized like you and Papa and Chara were?"

"I . . . don't know." All that seemed to be required to become Jesus' follower was a desire to accept Him. "I suppose if you decide so, when you are older."

"But it might be easier if I belonged to only one of them. Two gods seems like quite a lot to be baptized for. I don't think I'd have any time left over for anything else!"

Syntyche laughed and touched her daughter's shining brown hair, still threaded with highlights of the golden color it had been in early childhood. "You have many years to learn about such things, daughter. Papa will tell you about Jesus, and I will tell you about Isis, as my mother and grandmother told me."

They went back into the city then, to the market, where they jostled though the morning crowds to buy fish, olives, figs, cheese, and flour. Syntyche kept up a constant running dialogue with Julia. "Now, if the fish cost 10 sestertius a pound, how much can we buy for five denarii?" she asked, making the girl stop and figure. She knew women who made their children walk beside them in silence, never speaking in public, but in Syntyche's opinion Julia could learn to manage a household only if she took her part in the marketing at an early age. "These figs or these? Which look fresher to you?" she asked, and nodded as Julia pointed at a bundle.

At home, the house was quiet. Chara took the marketing from Syntyche and went to the kitchen while Syntyche and Julia settled to work at their looms. Clement was still on duty at the jail, while Chara had kept Lucius busy all morning helping with small tasks around the house.

Clement arrived home about noon, tired from guarding the jail throughout the night and morning, ready to go to his bed. He stood for a few minutes in the courtyard, watching his wife and daughter work, asking about their morning. Syntyche told him about the market, but Julia, waiting politely for a break in the conversation, added, "You forgot that we went to the temple, Mother."

Clement frowned. "The temple of Isis? You went there?"

Syntyche glanced up from her loom. "Yes, for the morning services." She wondered at the sharp tone in his voice. Even last year, when Clement had lost all faith in the gods and avoided the temples himself, he understood her devotion and the role it played in her life. He never questioned how often she went to worship, or what offerings she brought. Now he looked angry.

"Syntyche, we are Christ followers. We have been baptized into the Lord Jesus."

"Yes, I know. I was there, remember?" she said tartly.

"Followers of the Christ do not go to worship pagan idols at their temples."

"What?"

"Isis is not a goddess. There is only one true God, maker of heaven and earth. Isis is a painted statue, nothing more. You cannot worship her any longer."

"Julia, take this cloth to the storeroom. Fold it away neatly, then go to the kitchen and help Chara make fig cakes." As the girl left the room, Syntyche turned back to her husband. She would not have one of the children hear her question their father's authority, but she also would not allow such outrageous statements to pass without a challenge.

"What are you talking of?" she demanded. "What is that about only one god, and pagans and idols? That is Jewish talk—no one else speaks such nonsense. I never heard Paul say it."

"Paul was here only a short time," Clement said, sitting on the low wooden bench opposite Syntyche's loom. She kept her hands moving as they talked, the thread flying through her hands in practiced motion. "There were many things he could not teach us, but I have been learning more—from Luke and from Lydia. The One God, the God of the Jews, is the Father of the Lord Jesus. We are to worship Him and no other."

"Worship who? The Father or the Son?"

Clement hesitated. "Both. But they are one."

Syntyche shrugged. "So these Christ following Jews worship only one God, but He is really two? That makes no sense, Clement! Anyway, you have not made us all into Jews, have you? Lydia the dye merchant may be a Jew lover, but we have always worshipped the old gods, and I don't see why this Lord Jesus should change that. You are my husband. If you wish the whole family to bow the knee to Jesus I will bow with you, but why should I abandon my goddess?"

"She is *not* your goddess!" he exclaimed, jumping to his feet, his face growing red. "I've told you, she is no goddess at all, just an idol, a statue, a block of stone. Do you really believe Isis was the wife of Osiris and bore Horus who died and rose and died and rose again and again, like the songs the priests sing? Do you really think that stone thing up there in the temple can hear your prayers, or heal your sick, or care about you?"

He was shouting now—he had always been an excitable man. Not violent. She didn't fear, as many wives would, that he would punctuate his words with a blow. But she knew he was past reasoning with. She could argue all day about one god who was both father and son—she knew as well as he did that the same god could take many faces, many names—but this was not a reasoned argument between scholars and priests. Rather, it involved something that they both felt passion about: their gods, and the bond between the two of them as husband and wife. She would hate it if the one passion severed the other.

Slipping away from the loom, she walked across the room to stand in front of him, spread her hands wide, and gentled her tone. "I am but a woman, my husband—not learned, not even a priestess. I do not know what Isis is or what Isis cares for. I only know that my mother and my grandmother, and their mothers before them, worshipped at the temple of Isis, and I hope that my daughter will do so too." As he started to open his mouth to interrupt, she held her hands out toward him as if pleading to be heard. He kept his silence, and Syntyche went on.

"We are mothers, and we need to worship a mother like the mother who bore us. Has this Jesus of yours ever borne or suckled a child? Of course not. How can a woman worship such a god alone, without any goddess at all? Worshipping Isis is what the women in my family do. No—more than that. It is not just what we do—it is who we are."

She thought she had won him over. His eyes were softer, and she could see his love for her written there as plainly as it had been when she was a girl of 16 and he had first kissed her. That first kiss had been in Isis's temple, during her festival, when young men and women often came together. As she took his hands his touch was gentle, and so were his words, but she sensed the iron behind them.

"Syntyche, it cannot be," he said, his voice almost breaking. "I would not take your goddess from you if it were up to me, but the God of heaven demands that we worship no other."

"The god of the Jews, you mean."

"The God of Jesus the Christ, God of all the world. Not just for Jews, but for us too—Jesus is Lord of Jews, Greeks, Romans, anyone who will hear and follow Him. Syntyche, this is what I have searched for all my life—a God who knows me, who hears me, who cares for me. I can never go back to praying to a thing of wood and stone, and I cannot allow my wife and children to do so either."

I cannot allow. He had made his decision, and it was final. Syntyche searched for a way to accept it, to make her own peace with the unexpected change.

She looked at Clement again. His words were stern, but his face told a different story. He looked as he had when she first met him—a young soldier, head over heels in love with a pretty girl, begging her to notice him, to accept his love. Only now he was head over heels in love with his new god. He still needed her, though—he needed her to accept this new loyalty, to make it her own, to put this Lord Jesus at the center of their family's life and worship.

It wasn't hard to remember what he'd been like last year, those long horrible months while his brother Durio was dying. Syntyche had brought offerings to Isis the Healer, had even paid for priests to visit the house with both their prayers and their healing wisdom. Clement had given offerings to the temple of every god in Philippi. And she remembered her husband's grief and loss when Durio died—loss not just of his loved one, but of his faith.

Now, that faith was back. Could Jesus the Christ have healed Clement's brother if her husband had prayed to Him then? Syntyche had no idea. Her private thoughts were cynical. Though she honored Isis with her worship and loyalty, she believed that if a man was going to die, the gods would do little to change that. But Clement demanded a deity who was more than just a symbol of family stability and loyalty. He wanted a god who knew him and cared for him personally, and he believed Jesus the Christ was that being.

As for Syntyche, what did she love more than Isis? That was easy. She loved Clement, and their children, more than anything. For her husband's sake, she would offer more than just obedience. She would do the hard thing he asked—turn her back on the goddess her mothers had worshipped, and turn her face toward his new god. Putting her hands back in his, she bowed her head.

"I will honor Jesus the Christ and his Father God just as I honor you, my husband—with all my heart."

His smile, for that moment, was all the reward she needed. A picture of the statue of Isis nursing her infant flashed into her mind, but Syntyche forced her thoughts away, like a woman saying good-bye to a loved one that she knows she will never see again.

CHAPTER 6
EUODIA

Euodia struggled with the heavy dye-pot, staggering toward the fire to lay it in the iron ring that hung suspended above the flames. "Careful," Rachel said, watching her. "You don't want to slip and burn yourself, or catch fire to the sleeve of your robe. It's easy to do—I did it often when I was first learning."

With the dye pot in place, Euodia stepped away from the fire and turned to face the freedwoman who was teaching her the dyer's craft. She wondered when Rachel had first learned the craft, whether she had been a child or a grown woman. Euodia had no need to know, only curiosity. Asking questions simply because you wanted to know the other person better—it was a new concept. She was learning many new things in Lydia's house. This was one. People might ask questions, not to hurt you or get you in trouble but just to know. It had been hard to get used to. Their questions had frightened her at first. Lydia's questions, Rachel's questions, the old woman's questions. Scary.

Now she knew it was all right. They just wanted to know her. And she wanted to know them, too. Wanted to learn about

Rachel, about dyeing, about the past.

She wanted to know, but she wasn't ready to ask yet.

Rachel must have guessed, even without any questions. She went on talking. "It was Simeon's mother who taught me dyeing, back in Alexandria."

"Where—is that?"

"In Egypt." Rachel sounded a little surprised. She could not guess what Euodia's life had been like: how narrow, how closed. Though Rachel, too, had been a slave. "The best dyers come from Egypt. It was Simeon's family trade. It's in Egypt that they know the secrets of the mordant, all the tricks of the trade. How to get different colors, different shades in the cloth, from a single color of dye, just by saturating it with mordants of different strengths. All right—this is the time to plunge the fabric in." Following her gestures, Euodia took the fine linen, hooked it on a stick, and thrust it into the pot of bubbling purple dye. It seemed a risky thing to do to such fine fabric, but she had already seen how lovely the pieces looked when they emerged. This was her first time trying it herself.

The dyeing absorbed both women's attention. No more time for questions. Euodia wanted to know more—especially how Rachel had gotten here to Philippi. How did she become a slave, and then free? How did people move through the changes in their lives, to become something altogether different?

She didn't have the words to ask, to talk about such things. Only her wonder, the empty spaces where she didn't understand. Like the empty places inside her where the voices of the gods had once spoken. She was glad there were many people in Lydia's house, many voices to listen to. It wasn't that she missed those other voices—she just didn't want the silence where they had once been.

She felt Jesus, then, warming her from the inside, as warm as the dye in the vat. Close to her, almost as if His arms were around her. She never heard Him as a voice. He was not a replacement for her old gods. Rather, He was something different, a Presence beside and inside her, reminding her without words that she was not alone—would never be alone.

"Praise to You, Lord Jesus Christ," she murmured softly in reply. Luke had taught her the prayer and told her that she could repeat it anytime and add any words of her own that she desired. She wanted to add her own words, to talk to Jesus. Like she wanted to talk to Rachel, to the others in Lydia's household. But she wasn't quite ready for that either.

"You are praying to Jesus," Rachel observed.

"Yes."

"It still seems strange to me," Rachel continued. "I believe what Paul taught us about Jesus, but I am so used to my own prayers that to think of the One God having a Son who can hear us and plead for us is—something new. But I suppose it would be different for you, since you have never prayed to our God before."

"I had other gods," Euodia replied. Rachel shrugged and turned her attention to hanging the latest batch of fabric to dry. The task occupied both women. Across the workroom, by the built-in cistern, Simeon and Epaphroditus were mixing dyes. Euodia saw the two of them between the bands of colored fabric—Simeon stocky and dark, with flecks of gray in his hair; Epaphroditus tall and slim and (she could not help admitting it to herself) very handsome. Lydia's son would follow his mother into the business and do what she did—make bargains with customers and sell their dyes and dyed fabrics, while the slaves and workers managed the dye works. But while Lydia went out into the markets and to customers' homes to meet with them, she wanted Epaphroditus to know the business from the ground up. So he was a pupil here, as Euodia was, though one with a far better understanding of the work since he had grown up surrounded by it.

Euodia had spoken little to the young master, who was about her own age, since his mother had purchased her from Demos and Arsenios. She avoided Simeon too, and Tacitus—all the men except Luke, who reminded her a little of Paul.

But she watched, though. The girl knew that while Epaphroditus dutifully learned his mother's business from his mother's freedman, he spent all his free time lingering in corners while Luke treated patients, mixing up remedies for the doctor. Somehow she guessed that was the trade Epaphroditus really wished to learn. But a son, especially an only son, could not choose his own path. He would be what he was destined to be, even if his heart inclined a different way.

The door to the street opened, and Lydia entered, greeting her household, sweeping around the room to examine the morning's work. "Very good, excellent," she said to Rachel when she saw the linen dyed purple.

"It was Euodia's work. She did it all herself."

Lydia turned her glowing smile on the slave girl. "You learn fast, child."

"No—Rachel showed me, she told me everything . . . " Euodia bowed her head and clasped her hands. She felt such a surge of gratitude every time she stood before Lydia that she was in danger of drowning from it.

"That is how we learn, Euodia," Lydia said with a smile and a nod. "We watch and listen, then we try it for ourselves with the guidance of our teachers. Rachel is a good instructor, and you are a good pupil." She turned away, her attention already somewhere else. "Simeon, what of my son? Is he dyeing or daydreaming?"

"A little of both, Mother," Epaphroditus responded. The hint of laughter in his voice softened any sting her words might have had. There was something between them—something between everyone in this house—that puzzled Euodia with its unfamiliarity. Something in the air that made every exchange gentler, easier, more pleasant. It was not a quality she had encountered before, and she did not know what to call it. *Nobody gets hurt here,* was the closest that she could come to finding words for it. *At least, nobody tries to hurt.*

She had not known what to expect when she ran from Demos's house seeking shelter with Paul and the other Christ followers. Paul had been on his way out of Philippi, in trouble for what he had done for her, and she barely saw him before he left. But Lydia took her into her busy household, paying Demos generously enough that he stopped grumbling about his lost income and his now worthless slave. Euodia had not seen him since that day. She hoped never to see him again.

And now she was Lydia's slave, part of this household in which people treated each other with such strange kindness. Treated her that way, too. And here they all, like her, were learning about Jesus. They had all been baptized into Jesus, as she had been, that morning before Paul left. Dying in the water, rising to a new life. Discovering this new life together.

"Praise to you, Lord Jesus Christ," she whispered again, then took the pot off the fire and carefully poured the purple dye back into its vat.

She was learning the rhythm of a life without fear, without voices, without anger and pain. People were sometimes cross in Lydia's house, sometimes careless, but always apologies and forgiveness would follow. She watched like the outsider she was, trying to learn their strange ways.

Most evenings the whole household sat to eat together—family, freedmen, and slaves—and Lydia or Luke led them in prayer. And on the Sabbath day all the work ceased at sunset, and the other Christ followers in Philippi gathered at Lydia's house in the evening and the next morning and afternoon. Lydia fed them all, and they read from the Scriptures and sang songs and talked about Jesus. Sometimes Luke and Simeon would debate about something in the scrolls, some prophecy or old story. Occasionally people who weren't Christ followers, but who wanted to know more about them, or ask questions, would come too. They would talk and listen and eat together. When just the believers were gathered, they would share the meal that Luke called the Lord's Supper, the bread and wine they ate in memory of Jesus' death. Then there would be another meal, for everyone, with meat and fruit and fish sauce. Euodia carried baskets of bread and poured cups of wine and helped Ariane in the kitchen. And she watched. And listened.

It had been summer when Paul had been here. Now autumn approached. The days were cooler. Time passed. Euodia learned to be a dyer of cloth. She learned to ask questions. She learned to add words to her prayers. She still liked best to say, "Praise to You, Lord Jesus Christ." That simple prayer answered many of her needs.

One day in the market with Ariane, arms laden with baskets and packages, she bumped into a wealthy woman. Euodia apologized profusely, picking up the woman's packages as well as her own, afraid of a harsh word or a raised hand.

Instead, the woman met her eyes, as few wealthy people would do with a slave, except among the Christ followers. But this woman was not one of Jesus' people. Euodia had never seen her at Lydia's house.

But she had met her before. In another house. In another life.

"You're the fortune-teller," the woman gasped.

Then Euodia remembered. One face among many—hundreds perhaps. One hand among many, held in hers. The voices speaking through her.

"Do you remember what you foretold for me?" The woman's eyes were hard and glittering, like polished gems.

The girl shook her head. "I remember none of it. I'm sorry, mistress. The spirits spoke through me."

"But your owners told me you had gone away," the woman said. "No more prophecies! I went looking for you, and they had some other girl playing your part—clearly a charlatan. She made it all up. You were—the real thing. You told me that my son would die in battle, and he did. I made offerings, but the gods did not turn aside from their prophecy."

"I—am sorry, mistress."

"But you have not gone away."

"No. But I tell no more fortunes."

Euodia was dimly aware of Ariane at her elbow, of the busy market around them, of the rich woman's manservant taking his mistress's packages from her. But it was as if she and the woman stood on an island in the middle of a swirling river. The things around them didn't matter.

"Why no more fortunes?" the woman said. "I have great need of a word from the gods."

"I am sorry, mistress. Those gods—those spirits—no longer speak to me. I serve the One True God now."

"Which god?" The woman sounded hungry, as if she wanted a deity as badly as a starving beggar wanted bread.

"The God of heaven, who created all the earth, and His Son Jesus." She was repeating words, parroting what Paul and Luke and Lydia had told her. Then she felt as if Jesus stood beside her, nudging her gently with His elbow. Suddenly she had words of her own after all, and it was time to speak them. "Jesus the Christ is the One who set me free from bondage," she added. "I was driven mad by the spirits—I believe now they were demons and not gods, sent to torment me and deceive those who listened to me."

"But what you told me was no deception! It was truth!"

Euodia took a deep breath. "It was *true*," she admitted, "but I don't think it was *truth*. I don't think I ever spoke truth till I knew Jesus." Her heart was racing. She had never planned, never thought of these words. It was as if Jesus, or His Spirit that Paul talked of, were speaking through her. But not as the old voices did. Not using her as a dumb tool, but teaching her to say what was in her heart. Suddenly she felt joyful, and smiled at the woman.

"If you want to know truth, come to the house of Lydia the dye merchant, in the street of dyers and weavers," she said. "Come on the seventh day, when we do no work but only learn and teach about Jesus. Do you know what Jesus said?" she added, remembering something that Luke had once told her. "He said that the truth will set you free."

"Lydia, the dye merchant?" the woman repeated. "I know the place. You say to come on the seventh day?"

"We call it the Sabbath, the day of our Lord." As the woman turned to go, Euodia added, "You will be very welcome there!"

To the girl's amazement, the rich woman did come to Lydia's house the next Sabbath. Her name was Flavia, and she and Lydia seemed to be acquainted, as Lydia was with all the better people of Philippi. Her husband was apparently a great man, the magistrate Aulus Gabinus. Flavia's slave came with her, a redheaded man aptly named Rufus, who also seemed to know Lydia. Rachel said that he often bought dyes for his mistress. Both of them sat and listened to Luke, to Lydia, to Clement the jailer as they talked about the message of Jesus. But afterward Flavia took Euodia off into a corner of the courtyard and asked to hear her story in greater detail.

Silently she listened as the slave girl explained what had happened to her, then went on to ask a great many questions about Jesus. "I'm sorry," Euodia kept saying as she tried to explain. "There's so much I don't know. Mistress Lydia or Doctor Luke could answer your questions better."

"No, it's you I want to hear it from," Flavia insisted. "You once brought me the words of the false gods. Now teach me those of the true God."

"All I know is that He changed my life, and I have given it to Him. Paul said it is because Jesus died and rose from the dead. I don't understand anything about that, but I know that I was changed, and I believe you could be, too."

The day that Luke baptized Flavia, she came up out of the water, dripping and smiling, and embraced Euodia before she turned to any of the other people on the riverbank. "You are the one who brought me to the Christ," the woman said, holding her in her arms. The feeling that flooded Euodia was the strongest sense of God's presence that she'd ever felt, the greatest joy. At once she knew: *This is what I want to do. Tell others about Jesus, lead them to Him. This is what my life is meant for.*

After that, she didn't wait for chance encounters. She began to seek people out when she saw them in the marketplace. Sometimes they came into Lydia's shop—people she had once told fortunes for. It was a little frightening the first few times, but soon it became second nature to walk up to a man or woman and say, "Do you remember me? My name is Euodia, once the fortune-teller and slave of Demos. You came to my master to have your fortune told, and I gave you a message from the false gods. Now I have a message for you from the true God. Will you listen for a moment?"

Some shook their heads as if she were still insane. Others backed away a step or two, excusing themselves with polite apologies. But many listened. Her strange greeting tugged at their curiosity. And of those who listened, a few would come back again to learn more about Jesus.

At first, when they returned, Euodia would tell them to talk to Lydia or Luke. "They are our leaders," she explained, "and they know all about Jesus the Christ." But soon she realized that wasn't true. She couldn't read the Scriptures as they could, as even Rachel and Simeon did, but she was learning, and what she learned, she could explain to others.

One afternoon she slipped into Lydia's room where Lydia, Rachel, and Helena sat at the loom, weaving woolen cloth from already dyed wool. "Forgive me for being late," Euodia said, taking her place at the loom. She had received permission to take a break from her work during the midday hour to meet with a young woman who wanted to know more about Jesus.

Lydia smiled tolerantly. "You are a hard worker, Euodia. Both for our business, and for the Lord. I can excuse one late arrival, when I know you are doing the Lord's work."

"So, how did the girl respond to what you had to say?" Rachel inquired. Euodia had met the young woman, a slave like herself, when she spoke to the girl's master in the marketplace. Though the man had once been glad to hear Euodia predict wealth and good fortune for him, he had no interest in the story of Jesus. But the slave girl who looked after his young children wanted to hear more, and she had arranged for Euodia to visit the house at a time when her master and mistress were absent and she was alone watching the children during their midday rest. They had had nearly an un-interrupted hour to talk—luxury for two slave women!

"She wanted to hear all the stories of Jesus I knew," Euodia explained. "I only wish I knew more—Doctor Luke must hurry and write his book so that we can all have more stories to tell! She loved the stories about Jesus caring for children and women and servants. 'Did he really care about people like us?' she asked. And I told her that he not only cared for us, He died to bring us into His kingdom, and in that kingdom the lowest slave girl is equal to the empress herself!"

"Good for you, Euodia!" Lydia said. "Do you think she will come to worship with us on the Sabbath?"

"She would like to, if she can get permission to come. I think she would like to be baptized."

"Doctor Luke is right about you," Helena said suddenly. The older woman seldom spoke during the hours when the women worked together, and the other three all turned to look at her. "Right about what, my lady?" Euodia asked.

"He says that you have the same missionary spirit as Paul him-self."

Euodia felt the color rising in her cheeks. "Oh, surely he did-n't mean that, my lady."

"Yes, he has said it more than once," Helena insisted. "He said he's seldom seen someone with such a passion for spreading the gospel, and that the Spirit had given you the gift of teaching."

The girl didn't know what to say. But she realized that she was seldom happier than when she was telling someone about Jesus, especially if the other person was eager to hear it and to respond. But she'd never imagined placing herself on the same level as the great apostle.

"It's true that we all have different gifts from the Spirit of God," Lydia said. "I can lead in prayers and reading Scripture, but to talk to people about Jesus as you do, Euodia—it doesn't come as naturally to me. Yet I think that being able to open my home to others, to welcome people here and create a place where they can come to worship and learn—perhaps that's a gift in itself."

Rachel spoke for the first time, a bit tentative as if she didn't want to challenge Lydia's authority. "If Euodia really has such a gift, we must be sure she has a chance to use it. Surely doing the work of Jesus is even more important than dyeing cloth and selling the dyes?"

Slowly Lydia nodded, and Euodia could almost see the sharp-minded businesswoman at war with the leader of the Christ followers. "Don't hesitate to ask, Euodia," she said after a moment. "If you have the chance to teach someone about Jesus, and it conflicts with your work here in the shop or the house, we will be glad to let you go. Service to God must always come first."

Euodia said only, "Thank you, mistress," and watched the wool flying through her fingers. The changes in her life in a few short months were too much to grasp sometimes. She no longer felt like the same person who had been haunted by voices, tossed about by angry spirits like a rag doll. Yet that girl was still inside her. That Euodia was part of this one, this one who lived and worked in a house of people who cared for her. Who treated her with—dignity. That was a word that fitted the feeling she had, though not completely. She belonged to another God now, a God who gave her gifts, who used her in a different way. The changes were hard to put into words, but they were weaving themselves into the fabric of her life, making a pattern she could never have imagined just a short time ago.

CHAPTER 7
LYDIA

"Here, take this," Rachel said, laying a folded piece of coarse wool on top of the already heavy basket. "There's enough there to sew a little tunic for each of the children so that they don't have to be going about in rags."

Euodia appeared in the workroom, tucking a bunch of figs into a similarly laden basket. "Would it be all right if we bring her these figs?" They would be a luxury item for a woman such as Nerissa who almost every day struggled to feed her family just with bread and water with a little fish sauce. She had always been poor, but with the sudden death of her husband in a building accident she and her three small children were on the point of starvation.

"We'll go to the landlord first and pay her rent, so we can put her mind at rest," Lydia said as they walked along the Via Egnatia, the broad road that bisected the city. She knew the landlord who owned the apartment building south of the Forum, near the public baths. The man had often done business with her. His own house was on a broad street shaded by trees, not far off the main road. When they arrived, a slave brought Lydia a cool drink of date juice in the atrium while she waited for the master to appear. The same slave invited Euodia to the kitchen, where, Lydia imagined, Euodia would probably have half the man's slaves worshipping Jesus before their short visit ended. Nearly two years had passed since Paul's visit to Philippi, and while Luke and Lydia were the official leaders of the Philippian Christ followers, without a doubt Euodia was their most enthusiastic evangelist.

The landlord, Agricola, joined Lydia in the atrium a few minutes later. "How may I help you, Lydia?" he asked as he took his seat on a bench facing her. He looked a little surprised when his visitor explained that she had come to pay rent for one of his tenants in the building that was little more than a slum.

"The simplest thing, if you wish to help this widow, would be to give her the money herself so that she can continue making her rent payments as she did when her husband was alive," he pointed out.

"I think that sort of charity might be harder for her to accept," Lydia replied. She knew that Agricola didn't even know the family in question. Probably he was not even aware that a worker had been killed on the new arena building site or that the man's widow was a tenant of his.

"Also, you will want to ask yourself how long you can continue this," Agricola pointed out. "It is a kind gesture, but once this month is over the woman will be as destitute as ever and still unable to pay her rent. No matter how you help her, the result will still be the same—she will have to sell herself and her children as slaves. It may be better to do it sooner, before she becomes accustomed to the idea that she can live as a free woman with no husband to support her."

"Nerissa is a Christian," Lydia explained, and the man nodded.

"So, then, your community is prepared to accept the responsibility of paying for her accommodations and feeding and clothing her children for life?"

"Until her sons are grown and can work to support her."

Agricola shook his head as he reached out his hand for the small bag of coins Lydia proffered. He dug the money out, counting it expertly without even looking as he spoke. "I do admire the way your people look after their poor. There's no doubt it's a wonderful thing you do. Some people speak against you, say you bring ill fortune on the city by not honoring the gods, but I always defend you. Say what you will about the Christ followers, I always say that they look after one another. They treat the whole lot of them, rich and poor, slave and free, as if they were all one family."

"Exactly. We believe we are all brothers and sisters, and no one could leave a brother or a sister to starve."

"Yet as good as you are to each other, some believe that you do not show the same respect for the city as a whole," he commented. "What is good for the Christians may not be good for Philippi." He raised a hand as if to forestall further question or comment. "Just a word of warning, nothing more. A word in your ear."

Lydia reported the conversation to Euodia as they walked together to the tenement. "I think he is trying to let me know that some of the magistrates and the leading men of the city disapprove of us," Lydia said.

"But what can they do? We have broken no laws," Euodia protested.

"Laws come and go. We do not honor the gods or the emperor as the pagans do. Apollo or Isis may care little who visits their temple, but Claudius is more attentive. When things go badly, people want a scapegoat. Last year's harvest was bad and there was an outbreak of plague in the city. If that were to happen a second year in a row, people might begin turning against those whom they see as different."

"But didn't the Lord Jesus say we should expect persecution and troubles? 'Blessed are those who are persecuted for My sake.'"

"Your memory amazes me, child." The slave girl could not read or write, but her mind was like a sponge and soaked up every bit of Scripture, every report of the words or deeds of Jesus that she had heard during the years since Paul and his companions had visited Philippi.

Their little Christian community was still growing. The original converts—Lydia and her household, the jailer Clement and his wife Syntyche, and a few other families—still formed the group's core and leadership, but there were now about 50 or 60 people in Philippi who had been baptized into the fellowship of Jesus the Christ. They worshipped together each Sabbath, and often met at other times throughout the week as well. The Christian believers pulled together to support one another in times of sickness, death, and need, as now with the death of the laborer Petros which had left his wife and children penniless.

When they climbed the steps to the fifth floor one-room apartment where Nerissa lived with her children, they found the woman bent over a barrel of water, scrubbing clothes. "Mistress Syntyche helped me find work doing the wash for people," she explained. Her oldest son watched the younger child at play, while the baby slept in a basket in the corner. Nerissa was grateful for the gifts Lydia and Euodia brought and for the news that her rent had been paid, but Lydia could see she was also glad for honest work to earn a few coins of her own.

Syntyche, as always, had seen clear to the heart of the problem and thought of the best solution. It was unfortunate that the jailer's wife had such an abrasive manner. Lydia wasn't sorry when she learned that she and Euodia had missed Syntyche's visit by a few hours. Being sisters in Christ was one thing, but even the love of Jesus didn't make it possible to actually *like* everyone.

"We're so grateful for your help, Mistress Lydia, me and the children," Nerissa said as she laid aside the laundry and unpacked the basket of food with Euodia's help. "If only poor Petros could see all that you've done for us. I worry so much about where he is, whether he knows what's happening to us and if I'll see him beyond this life. What do you think happens to the souls of Christians? Do we go to Hades, or to the land of the blessed? I thought the Lord Jesus would return and bring in His kingdom before any of us had to die. My Petros went before his time." The tears spilled over and she turned away, wiping her face with the back of her hand.

Lydia slipped an arm around her, but it was Euodia who spoke. "Paul and Luke teach that there's no going to Hades, but that our dead will sleep in the grave until the Lord Jesus returns with the kingdom. Then our dead will be raised again, just as the Lord Himself was. He went to death and came back to show us all that the power of death was broken." Now she, too, crossed the room to place a hand on the woman's arm. "You will see your husband again, Nerissa, when the Lord comes back. He'll hold you and the children in his arms and thank you for taking such good care of them while he was asleep."

Nerissa threw herself into Euodia's arms, her tears a flood of release. In the corner the baby stirred, and Lydia went to pick up the infant, wrapped in a length of thin cloth. She cuddled the boy as she brought him to his mother.

The little apartment was a happier place when they left it. Lydia and Euodia had two other visits to make—to some of the poorest members of the Christian community who lived in this squalid building. Lydia couldn't help thinking of Agricola with his spacious house and cool shaded atrium. Was it right that he lived in such luxury when his tenants lived in a building that was on the verge of falling apart? She could imagine the expression on the wealthy magistrate's face if she had dared raise that question with him.

Euodia would have said it, she thought, hiding a smile. The slave girl was fearless, ready to speak out to anyone about anything in the cause of Jesus. Lydia felt such love and admiration for Euodia that it sometimes overwhelmed her. Her household, always close-knit, had become a true family when they had chosen to worship Christ together, and when both Luke and Euodia had come to live with them. If Rachel was like a sister to her, Euodia was the daughter Lydia had never had. The girl had no idea how old she was, but she looked to be about Epaphroditus's age, 16 or 17. It was time to think of marriage and her future, though Euodia seemed content to leave everything in the Lord's hands.

Lydia had thought of giving Euodia her freedom, but she was unsure what would be best for the girl. As a freedwoman, if she left Lydia's household she would be expected to earn her living, at least until she married. But as Lydia's slave, she worked in the house and in the business, but Lydia left her free to devote a large part of her time to the work of the Christian community. She had an extraordinary gift for teaching others about Jesus, and

Lydia did not know whether slavery or freedom would give the girl the best opportunity to use that gift.

"Mistress Lydia, I want to speak to you of something," Euodia said, a little hesitantly, as they walked back through the streets of the poorer district. Lydia thought of her own street in the business district as crowded, but here in the slums the two women had literally to push through the throng of people, brushing against beggars, peddlers, and most likely pickpockets. The stench of unwashed humanity was strong, and Lydia clutched her purse close.

Euodia's tone suggested the matter was something important, and Lydia wondered if the girl's thoughts had been traveling the same paths as her own. Marriage, freedom, the future—did Euodia want to speak of these things?

"There is nothing you need to fear asking me," Lydia said with a smile.

"Master Epaphroditus asked me—he asked if I would like to learn my letters. He and Doctor Luke said they would teach me, so that I could read the Scriptures. I think it might take too much time from my work, but Epaphroditus says he is sure I could learn quickly." Her cheeks colored a little. Lydia guessed that the girl had received so little praise and so much ill-treatment in her previous life that she was embarrassed by the frequent words of commendation that she earned from her Christian family.

But Lydia had no hesitation in her answer. Teaching a slave girl to read was an uncommon thing to do and most people would see no purpose in it. Christ followers, however, were people of the Book, students of the Jewish Scripture—and someday, Luke assured them, the words and deeds of Jesus Himself would be written onto scrolls for everyone who could read. Such a skill was hardly essential for Euodia, but someone with such a quick mind and so gifted by the Holy Spirit could only be helped by being able to read Scripture.

"By all means, Euodia, you should learn." She wondered briefly if it would be more appropriate for another woman—herself, perhaps, or Rachel who was also literate—to teach Euodia. But the barriers between a man's place and a woman's were far less rigid within the family of Christ followers, and Euodia's reputation would hardly be tarnished by allowing Epaphroditus to teach her her letters, especially if Luke were overseeing the process.

She watched them together a few days later, two dark heads bent over a scroll at the table in Luke's workroom as Epaphroditus sounded out words for Euodia and she repeated them. Lydia felt a quick swell of pride at her son. Imagine a busy young man who was learning to run his mother's business as well as the art of medicine from Luke, taking an hour to teach a slave girl to read!

It did occur to Lydia as she returned to the workroom that Euodia, as well as being intelligent and a gifted speaker, was also a most attractive young woman. Lydia wondered if she should have a quiet word with her son, a reminder to keep his behavior appropriate. In many wealthy families it would be far from unusual for the son of the house to have a brief dalliance with a slave girl, perhaps leaving her with child before finding someone to marry her. But the followers of Jesus allowed no such things. Lydia was sure Epaphroditus knew that, but it couldn't hurt to remind him.

Still, she worried about him, well aware that her business did not interest him, although he did everything she asked him to. If she had had another son, then Epaphroditus might have pursued another path—but that was not an option. He was by no means rebellious, but she sensed a disquiet in him that he kept well below the surface. While he attended Sabbath services, prayed, and read Scripture with the family, he still had not chosen baptism. When Lydia asked him about it, he said only, "I will be baptized when the time is right, Mother." Luke had cautioned her not to press him. Apart from not having gone through the water of baptism he was to all appearances a devout follower of Christ. Just as he was, to all appearances, a dutiful and devoted son. Yet there was always that discontent, never voiced, that she saw in his eyes.

He was a young man with a young man's desires, and the question of his own marriage had not even been broached yet. Lydia was sure she could count on him to treat Euodia as a sister in the Lord—but still, she would speak to him.

One always had to consider the question of how things appeared to the outside world. As the little Christian community grew, some of their neighbors in Philippi looked with suspicion and hostility on the new religion, and wild rumors flew. Because the Christians did not visit the temples or sacrifice to the gods, some said they were atheists, worshipping no god at all. Others said that the Christ followers ate human flesh and drank blood in secret midnight meetings, that they were sexually immoral, or that they taught slaves and women to reject their natural places and tore apart the fabric of society. And it was becoming more and more common, when any misfortune befell the city, to point an accusing finger at those who did not honor the gods and the emperor.

Lydia could understand where the roots of all those suspicions came from—even the ridiculous accusation of cannibalism sprang from the innocent ritual of the Lord's Supper, in which the bread and wine represented Jesus' body and blood. Superstition and ignorance fueled such talk, yet she felt it was important to do everything they could to prove that Christians were decent, law-abiding citizens.

It wouldn't hurt if the rest of the community was as concerned about appearances, she thought a few nights later as her courtyard filled with people sharing a meal at the close of the Sabbath. All day her house was full of people. They began gathering for the Lord's Supper at sunset on Friday, returned to study the Scriptures and pray together the next day, and had a meal of fellowship at sunset. It was after this final meal, when the sacred hours were over, that discussion about the business of the community often arose. Discussion was one thing, but outright quarrels were inappropriate. Listening to the strident voice of Syntyche, the jailer's wife, Lydia cringed and thought it was little wonder that Christians had a bad name in some parts of Philippi.

"It's a disgrace!" Syntyche was saying, standing amid a group of seated women and a few men. "It's all very well to share what we have with our own poor, but we're only patching a leaking ship. Some of our men should go to the city magistrates and tell them what conditions are like in the tenements! Surely our Lord never intended for the rich to grow fat on the backs of the poor. Can't we do more to make their lot better?"

"But that's not our task!" another voice objected, and Lydia saw her own son Epaphroditus standing to challenge Syntyche. "We are only travelers in this world, moving on to the next. The Lord Jesus will return soon to establish His kingdom. Our job is to tell people about Him so they'll be ready, not to attack the rulers of this world."

"So we go on bringing baskets of bread to apartments where the children share their beds with rats, and hope that the Lord Jesus will return before the rats bite them?" Syntyche shot back. "We collect a tithe from every working man and woman here, and we could be putting that money to use to make things better for the poorest among us!" Syntyche was in charge of distributing money to help the poor. She was, Lydia had to admit, a genius at organization, and nobody doubted that the money was being fairly distributed. But she was so passionate about her work that she often spoke with little concern either for appearances or for the feelings of others. To argue down a man as she had just done with Epaphroditus—who, though young, was well above her in status—was hardly appropriate. Lydia found herself glancing about for Syntyche's husband to see if Clement could restrain his wife a little, but he was deep in conversation with a group of men at the other end of the courtyard.

"We have too many quarrels among us," Euodia said, standing. As always, she spoke softly and with dignity, her tone never becoming shrill or scolding like Syntyche's. Though she was both a woman and a slave, everyone quieted to listen to her. Something about her commanded respect. "As Doctor Luke has told us, the apostles themselves who knew the Lord Jesus in His life on earth quarreled in just this way, and He rebuked them for it, and said that there should be no fighting, no struggling over who was the greatest, but that they should all be servants to each other. Yet here we are quarreling and fighting among ourselves, each trying to take control and set out how we think things should be done. Is this the Spirit of Jesus?"

Nobody said anything, but heads were shaking all around the courtyard, and even Syntyche managed to look shamefaced. The knots of private conversation ceased and everyone turned toward the center of the courtyard as Luke came to stand beside Euodia and lend his voice to what she was saying.

The missionary physician had become a fixture of life both in Lydia's household and the wider community of Philippi. Although he had a busy medical practice, he was even more respected as a leader among the Christians. He alone among them had traveled with Paul, had even been to Jerusalem and met the apostles of Jesus themselves. The man knew more about the life and words of Jesus, the teachings of Paul, and the practices of the other Christian communities, than anyone among them. Luke was their link to a wider world in which other people also followed the Christ and tried to live according to His teachings.

"Euodia is right," he said now, stroking his beard as he talked, a gesture that always meant he was worried or troubled. Lydia noticed streaks of gray in his brown beard—he must be nearing 40, as she was herself. Odd that she sat with him at her table every day yet did not notice that he was aging till she saw him standing in the midst of a crowd of people. He was no great orator like Paul or Timothy, yet every day she thanked God that Luke had chosen to stay behind in Philippi to teach them more about Jesus.

"In other places, as the church grows, the people have chosen leaders," Luke said, his clear voice carrying throughout the courtyard. "Even in Jerusalem, after Jesus Himself returned to His Father, the apostles led the church and chose seven men to be servants of the church, to meet the daily needs of the people.

Other communities have done the same as their numbers have grown—selected one or two to be overseers and others to be deacons and deaconesses. Perhaps it is time we do the same here in Philippi. God has given us all different gifts, and perhaps it is time to decide how best to order our life here so that everyone can use their gifts to do His work."

A silence greeted Luke's words. Lydia tensed, looking at Syntyche, almost expecting the woman immediately to propose herself and her husband as overseers. Luke was right—they did need leadership, yet the attempt to choose leaders might quickly turn into the very kind of struggle that Euodia had just spoken of—a contest over who would wield the greatest power. To her own surprise, Lydia found herself on her feet, raising her hands before anyone else could speak.

"Euodia and Luke have spoken well," she said, "and we must indeed select leaders from among ourselves. But we must not do it in our own strength. Before we speak more about it, let us pray and ask the Spirit to be among us and guide us."

She led the company in prayer, and then they prayed together in small circles, pleading with the Lord to guide them until Lydia could feel the presence of the Spirit in the darkening, lamp lit courtyard like a physical entity. Suddenly she remembered the story of Pentecost, of the tongues of fire that had settled on the apostles and given them power. No fiery tongues fell from the sky, but as the wind stirred the dust beneath their feet and made the lamp flames flicker, she could almost hear the voice of the Spirit.

As a result, she did not attempt to argue when the community almost unanimously appointed herself and Luke as the overseers. Luke was the missionary who had brought them the good news of Jesus, and Lydia was the first convert whose home was now the center of worship and community. It was not a role that she had ever imagined for herself but it had become hers, and she felt right about accepting it, though she wasn't sure what it might mean for the future.

The deacons, the servants of the church, created more debate, but finally they had decided on seven, the same number chosen in Jerusalem during the first days after Pentecost. The seven included Syntyche and Clement, Rachel and Simeon, Euodia, and two others. They knelt in the center of the courtyard while Lydia and Luke placed hands on their heads and prayed once more, this time that the Spirit would give the church unity and power under their new leaders. Again, as the prayer ended, Lydia felt a wind that seemed more than a night breeze touch her garments and send a chill down her spine. They were just ordinary people, weak and fallible and sometimes contentious, but the Lord was with them and in them. She could hardly wait to see what He intended to do with them.

CHAPTER 8
EPAPHRODITUS

"I think you'll find this compound soothing to your throat," Doctor Luke said to his patient, a young woman in the simple dress of an artisan. Epaphroditus was grinding licorice root with mortar and pestle as Luke examined the patient. "However, I cannot lie to you—while it will make you feel better, it will not shrink the growth. That will continue to grow, unless there is a miraculous healing."

The woman put a hand to her neck as if to feel the deadly growth that was swelling inside her throat, one that would someday choke off her breath and end her life. "I brought offerings to the temple of Isis, and one of the priests attended me there," she said. "He gave me something for the pain, too. But I don't think Isis will heal me. That was—two months ago, I believe. I wondered if your god . . ."

Hope and despair mingled in her voice. Epaphroditus felt sorry for her and wished that the young woman had lived during the time when the Lord Jesus had walked the earth and healed with a word and a touch. Even the touch of Paul was said to be powerful to heal, and Epaphroditus himself had seen things he could only describe as miracles among the Christian community here in Philippi. Christ followers had laid their hands on people who were sick and even dying and prayed for them, and they had been restored to health. But it seemed the Spirit did not pour His healing power out in the same way as in the days of Jesus.

Luke was said to have the gift of healing, and he always laid hands on patients who were willing to have his prayers. But he combined those prayers with the ministrations of a skilled physician, and Epaphroditus wasn't always sure which it was—prayers or potions—that healed a particular sick person. The physician said it didn't matter, that God worked through many different channels. But then there were those who didn't recover. The young woman looked as if she might belong to that group. Having given up on physicians and on her own gods, she was now seeking out the Christian God's healer as a last resort. He saw many patients like that.

"Would you like me to pray for you?" he asked.

"I have nothing to bring for an offering."

"My doctor's fee is for the medicine, which you already know will only help your pain, not cure you. There is no additional fee for God's grace. That He gives freely, though I do not pretend to understand why some receive healing and others die. All we can do is ask."

He motioned Epaphroditus to put down the mortar and pestle and join them in prayer. Together the two men put their hands on the woman's head as Luke prayed that the Spirit of Jesus would heal the woman. Then she left, tears that had never fallen still filling her eyes.

Epaphroditus cleared up the workbench after she left, washing the mortar and pestle, carefully putting away the licorice root, the ginger, all the herbs he had used to mix the compound. Since he and Luke had had such conversations many times, he did not raise any difficult questions about prayer or healing or God's will. They worked in a quiet and companionable partnership, like master and apprentice.

Which they were not, Epaphroditus reminded himself. Although they had labored together for two years, he was not the physician's apprentice and never would be. Instead, he was the heir to his mother's business, the future seller of purple dyes and purple cloth. As a result, he would spend his life mixing dyes to adorn people's garments and flattering them on their choice of color, rather than preparing compounds to bring relief to the sick and praying for God's healing power to transform their lives.

Although he tried every day to be resigned to God's will, a slow anger burned inside him. His happiest hours were spent in Doctor Luke's consulting rooms, either assisting the physician to treat patients or learning the art of medicine from the older man. Though lately, he had to admit, the few hours—or minutes— that he could spare to help Euodia with her reading and writing were pleasant ones, too.

It wasn't that he disliked the work in the shop, or the business of trading and selling. But it seemed so unimportant. If the Lord Jesus was returning and bringing His kingdom, what difference did it make whether the tint of this week's batch of dye was a little too harsh, or whether they could make a lighter color for the gown a magistrate's wife would wear at a formal dinner? Was he really going to spend his life pandering to rich people's vanity when there was work to be done—work that glorified God and also interested and challenged him?

Yes, he thought, *it looks as though that is exactly what I'll spend my life doing. And as the law says to honor my mother, I had better be pleased with it. Or at least not complain.*

"You are getting a very quick and sure hand with mixing this compound," Luke said as he joined Epaphroditus at the work bench. "The licorice root will soothe the pain and help with her cough, which will get worse as the tumor grows."

"Unless God heals her."

"She is in His hands now," the physician agreed.

"Do you have anymore patients for today? I am to oversee the dyeing of the new linen, but it will be an hour before that is ready. If Euodia is free I would like to bring her up here to read—it has been a few days since we've had the chance."

Luke smiled. "By all means, find her and bring her here." Fond of the young slave girl, Luke often told people that she was as gifted a missionary as Timothy or Silas. He also understood Epaphroditus's promise to his mother—that he would not meet with Euodia privately, but always have an older person present when he taught her to read. The young man had kept that promise scrupulously since his mother had spoken to him about it. It was very important to do nothing that his mother might disapprove of where Euodia was concerned.

Epaphroditus knew that Luke guessed his feelings, though he hoped they were hidden from the rest of the household and the others in the household church. He was sure that not even Euodia herself sensed them, since he had taken great care to behave with extreme propriety around her. But sometimes he caught the little smile Luke gave when he saw the two of them poring over a scroll together, and he knew the doctor shared his secret.

"In fact, we may be able to help each other today," the doctor added. "I received a scroll along with some letters on that last ship to make port at Neapolis. It comes from a fellow believer in Jerusalem. He has copied for me some of the sayings of Jesus written down by the church there, and I intend to make a copy for the believers here. I'll keep the other for my own collection—for the book I intend to write someday. You and Euodia can help me read the scroll, then do the scribal work of copying it."

"A scroll with the words of Jesus? Amazing!" Epaphroditus responded. He knew Euodia would be as excited as he was.

That was the thing about her he found especially interesting, he decided as they sat together half an hour later looking at Luke's scroll. Sometimes her very nearness was distracting. She was beautiful, her black hair gleaming in the afternoon light that fell through the window, her low soft voice reminding him of music. Her dark brown eyes glowed in an olive skinned face that rarely broke into a smile, and her hair smelled of lavender. He tried hard to concentrate as she leaned forward, her slender finger pointing out the words. "There once was a man . . . who . . . had two sons. The younger son said . . . to his father . . . " What's this word, Epaphroditus? I don't know this one."

"Give me the . . . portion . . . that falls to me," Epaphroditus continued, then glanced up at Luke. "Have you heard this story before?"

"Never. It sounds like one of the Lord's parables, but not one that is familiar to me. The apostles say there are hundreds of such stories. Those who knew Jesus have memorized a great many of them, but it is good that some are being written down, too."

"How can you be certain it is a story Jesus really told?" Euodia questioned. "What if someone else wrote it and circulated it in the name of Jesus?"

She's so clever! Epaphroditus thought. Her mind was as keen as a sword, cutting straight to the heart of things. If she had been a boy and born into a good family, she might have become a great scholar. Just then she shifted her weight a little on the bench next to him, moving closer as Luke thought about his answer to the question. Epaphroditus was very glad she wasn't a boy.

"I think the Jerusalem church takes great care with the words and stories of Jesus, to make sure they are passed on correctly," Luke replied after a moment. "I trust the man who sent this to me, and of course I trust that the Spirit of God watches over these words, which are as precious as the Holy Scriptures. But someday, when I return to Jerusalem myself, I will take all these stories and sayings I have collected and talk to the people who knew Jesus Himself, asking them what they remember. I will try my best to make a faithful collection, so that if our Lord does not return before the apostles die, those who come afterward will have a true record that they can trust."

"But surely the Lord Jesus will return to the earth long before His apostles die!" Epaphroditus protested. He knew that Jesus would come back to the earth very soon and that he himself wasted far too much time thinking about his own future, about his career and who he would marry, when in reality he would probably never have to worry about those things, for the Lord would establish the kingdom of God long before then.

The same thoughts chased through his mind later that night as he lay on his bed, staring at the moonlight streaming through the window. He tried to calm his mind by reciting to himself the story from the scroll, but though it was a beautiful one that assured him of God's love for the lost sinner, his own concerns were still the same. If Jesus returned soon, all that mattered was spreading the Good News and remaining faithful. But He had already delayed His return to earth for nearly 20 years. What if he waited 20 more? What would happen to Epaphroditus of Philippi, son of Lydia?

He recognized that everyone around him wondered what held him back from taking the final step of baptism. Others were baptized as soon as they heard the message of Jesus. His own mother, Euodia, Clement the jailer—they had leaped across that gap from unbelief to full-blown faith so easily. Epaphroditus believed—he knew he did. His long talks with Luke only deepened the certainty he already had. But indecision about his own future tore at the fabric of his faith. If he was baptized, he wanted to come up out of that water ready to serve Jesus with his whole heart, his whole life. How could he do that, trapped in a dyeshop, bound by the life of a merchant? Until he could give his future to God with a whole heart, he couldn't step into the river and be baptized.

After tossing and turning for another half hour he got up and crossed the courtyard to the dye works, dark and silent at this hour of night. He walked among the covered dye vats, the skeins of fabric hanging to dry, the neat shelves stacked with the supplies of his mother's trade. His trade.

Try as hard as he might, he could not truly imagine a life spent dealing in dyes when there was so much better, more worthy work to be done. Nor could he imagine disappointing his mother, telling her that her only son would not follow her into the family business, that it must pass to strangers when she died. Rachel and Simon could continue to run the workshop, but they were artisans, not businesspeople. His mother needed a merchant to inherit her life's work. She expected him to become that person.

And she needed him to marry well. It was true that Christ's followers spoke about Jew and Greek, slave and free all being one. Paul had told them that in the churches he had raised up, slaves served as deacons and overseers, working alongside their free brothers and sisters on an equal footing. Lydia claimed Euodia as her sister in Christ—"almost like a daughter to me," she said. But as a real daughter? A daughter-in-law? Epaphroditus knew that possibility would test even his mother's Christian faith.

One thing was certain—he could not speak to her about both these things. A career away from the dye business, a marriage to a slave girl of no family and dubious background—Lydia, fine and intelligent Christian woman though she was, would not be able to tolerate two such shocks. *One or the other*, he thought. He was 17 years old, and if the Lord Jesus did not return soon, he had a life to make for himself. Epaphroditus could present his mother with one request or the other, but not both.

A choice, then. He looked around the room again, tried to see himself there as a grown man with a wife and children, overseeing his artisans, directing the business. Their home might continue to be the center of the Christian church in Philippi and he would still be a deacon, perhaps even someday the overseer as his mother was. With Euodia by his side, it would certainly be a center of missionary activity, of learning, of help and hope for those who came to Jesus. In the end, it was more important that he serve Jesus than that he become a physician or a missionary or anything else. He could be baptized and dedicate his life to serving the Lord even as he managed the dye shop and trade. If—if Euodia were by his side. If God would grant him that one thing, then he would find a way to bear all the rest.

Better to be a dye merchant with her than a doctor without her, he thought. If he could only speak to his mother about one of his dreams, he knew which it had to be.

Hearing a step behind him, he turned to see Lydia framed in the doorway, as if his thoughts had wakened her. She smiled. "Are you sleepless too?"

"Yes."

"It must be the warm night—though everyone else seems to be sleeping soundly. I just went to check on your grandmother, but she is resting well. Then I was going to get some water—come with me."

He followed her to the kitchen, where she poured the water with a little honey in it for them both and sat across from him on a bench pulled up to the worktable. "Did Luke tell you about the missionaries who are coming?" Lydia asked.

"Yes. Did he tell you about the scroll they sent?"

"He said you and Euodia were fascinated by it, that you are planning to work together on transcribing it. He hopes you will read some of it for the believers when we gather on Sabbath."

Epaphroditus nodded. "Euodia was able to read most of it herself. She learns very quickly."

Lydia smiled. In the dim light of the single lamp Epaphroditus could see the lines in his mother's face and the gray in her hair. She was still a handsome woman, but she sometimes looked careworn. When she spread her hands on the table and stared at them, he looked down at them too, placing his own larger hands beside them.

"She's a wonderful girl," Lydia said. "In many ways she has

filled that need I have had for a daughter, ever since your baby sister was taken from me. And you have treated Euodia with the respect due to a sister in Christ—I'm proud of you for showing her that respect, Epaphroditus, for I can see that you find her attractive."

His face must have registered surprise, for she chuckled. "A mother is not blind, my son. Euodia is not only a brilliant girl and one filled with the Spirit, but she is also a very pretty young woman, and you spend a great deal of time with her. It will be time soon to think about her future, as we must do with yours."

Thank You, Lord, Epaphroditus thought, running his fingertip around the rim of his goblet. *You have spoken to my mother as well as to me—this truly is Your will.*

"I'm glad you've spoken of it, my mother. You are right—I do think a great deal of Euodia, and I have tried to treat her as a sister. I would like you to think of her as a daughter—not just as your slave and a sister in Christ, but as my wife. If Euodia wishes it, would you be willing to accept her as a daughter-in-law?"

He knew he had miscalculated as soon as the look of shock—perhaps even horror—crossed his mother's face. "Euodia? Your *wife?*" she repeated in a sharp whisper. He knew she had dropped her voice so that no one else who might be sleepless in the house would overhear. "Epaphroditus, she is a fine young woman, but she is a slave. I have talked about how it is inappropriate for a Christian young man to dally with a slave girl, but you can't truly think that she would make a suitable wife for you."

"Why not?" The words rushed out of his mouth before he had time to think. "We say that we are all one in Christ's kingdom—how then can we say a slave girl is no fit wife for me?"

Lydia was shaking her head, but in disbelief this time. "Epaphroditus, you're very young. While I admire your spirit and your sincerity, you must realize that although we are citizens of Christ's kingdom, that kingdom has not yet come on this earth. We are also citizens of Philippi, and you will be a merchant and a man of position in this city. I want you to marry a

Christian girl, of course—I have already spoken to Andrew, the linen merchant, about his daughter Rhoda."

"Rhoda is 12 years old, Mother!"

"Yes, but she will not always be 12 years old. She will grow up, and you need not marry for a few years. In four or five years a marriage between you might be very suitable—a good match, in fact, for us."

"I hate this kind of thinking!" he said, slapping his hand on the table. The water in his cup shivered from the blow. "Is this what your kingdom of Jesus is about—making good marriages and moving up in society and building a fortune? Surely we are above all that. Together Euodia and I can work for Him—as true partners, like Clement and Syntyche or Rachel and Simeon. What difference does our station in life make?"

"You may think it does not matter, and in the eyes of God perhaps it does not. Nor in the eyes of a young man in love. But in the eyes of the world—no one will look at you as true partners. You will be seen as a man who married beneath him, and Euodia as a grasping girl who does not know her proper station. I cannot imagine she would—" Lydia looked up sharply. "You have said nothing to her, have you? There is no—understanding between you?"

"No, Mother. I would never have approached her without speaking to you."

"Good." She set down her glass and sighed. "But I feel that this will not be easy for you to forget. You will not simply lay aside the thought of Euodia just because I forbid it, will you?"

Epaphroditus shook his head. "I think not, Mother." It might have been the moment to say, *I will lay aside Euodia if you allow me to be a physician rather than following you in to the business.* In her relief, she might well have agreed. But he found that he could not do it. His love for Euodia was not something to bargain with.

"No, I do not think I can forget her so easily, Mother."

"Then perhaps it would be best if you were to go away for

a while. You are eager to do the Lord's work. What if these missionaries—this man Barnabas and his companions—were willing to take you with them? You could do the Lord's work, and there are people you could see—my own family, back in Thyatira—who could teach you more about the business. After a year or two you might return with a very different view of the world."

He couldn't deny that the thought of leaving Philippi, of seeing the world, had its appeal. But he knew what she was thinking. "While I am away, you will arrange Euodia's marriage to some nice Christian freedman, and I will return to find her settled, and Andrew's daughter a little older, and you think I will forget my youthful infatuation with a slave girl."

Lydia's smile was very faint. "Yes, I suppose that is what I hope. Things change—the way you see the world changes, as you get older. Love that seems as if it will last forever does fade with time. Epaphroditus, Euodia is not only a slave girl, she is also a girl who was demon possessed for most of her life, who has no family background or upbringing. She knows a little about the work of a dye shop and a great deal about the service of the Lord Jesus, but nothing about being a wife—perhaps very little even about being a woman. I would not marry her to anyone just now without giving her time—but I do not think having you here, loving her silently, will help either you or her grow up to be the people you should be."

He nodded, not really meaning the nod to say yes. Just that he would consider it. Then he dropped his eyes so that she couldn't see the anger he was sure burned in them. For so long he'd kept that resentment covered, told himself that his duty was to do God's will and obey his mother. Now, having come so close to believing that he could actually have what he wanted, that anger was ready to flare into life, and he had to excuse himself quickly before he lashed out at her. Yes, she was doing what she thought best, of course. But she was wrong. And he couldn't keep back what even he realized was a childish thought: *She will live to regret this.*

During the weeks that followed he longed to speak to Euodia, to let her know what was in his heart. But she was so dedicated to the Lord, so dutiful. Surely she would just tell him to obey his mother. Perhaps he would, after all. And perhaps he would go away just as his mother wanted him to do. In the wider world he might find a different path that would lead him out of his anger and pain and frustration.

Barnabas and John Mark arrived as winter began to close in. Unlike Paul and the other missionaries who had come, they brought their wives, and John Mark wanted to stay at Philippi through the winter because his wife would soon have a child. She was absorbed with the coming baby, but Barnabas's wife, Mary, was as active in ministry as he was, spending much of her time teaching women and girls.

It was a new realization for Epaphroditus to learn that many of the missionaries and apostles traveled with their wives. If only his mother would relent, someday he might go with Euodia and preach the Good News. It wouldn't matter, then, what Philippian society thought of the dye merchant's son marrying his mother's slave. They would be a missionary couple, tied to no home and community except the kingdom of God.

He accepted Barnabas' invitation to join their party in the spring when they left Philippi. Then he would travel with them to several cities in the area before he stayed with his mother's family in Thyatira for several months studying the dyer's trade.

Euodia was never far from him that winter, as he counted their days together dwindling. They copied Luke's scroll, and by the time that was done she was confident in reading and writing and eager to explore the Scriptures for herself. Epaphroditus watched her graceful form as she lifted a child into her arms, her serious face as she read Scripture with a group of women. Once or twice that winter he even teased laughter from her: she was always so sober, as if afraid to be happy, but her slow smile when it came warmed the whole room.

When Epaphroditus saw that smile, he knew it was best for him to go away. If he could not marry her, it might destroy him to remain near her.

His mother, Luke, and even John Mark all urged him to be baptized before he left Philippi. Epaphroditus began avoiding such conversations. "The Lord will tell me when the time is right," he told Luke, shifting his eyes away from the doctor's knowing gaze. In fact, Epaphroditus felt further than he ever had from hearing God's voice. He was angry not just at his mother, but at God for not granting the one prayer of his heart.

On the night before their party left to take ship at Neapolis, the whole Christian community gathered in Lydia's house, though it was not a Sabbath day. Barnabas preached, and there were tearful goodbyes. Epaphroditus embraced his grandmother Helena, Rachel and Simeon, Luke, and last of all his mother. He knew that the distance and coolness between them over the winter had hurt Lydia, but she had not pressured him. Now she looked at him with steady eyes and said, "Thank you, my son. I do believe you are doing the right thing. God go with you."

It was hard to find words, so he just inclined his head. He was tall enough to touch the top of her head with his lips. "God bless you, Mother. Pray for me."

Euodia was nowhere around when he said his goodbyes—in fact, he could not see her anywhere in the courtyard. At last he found her in the kitchen, mixing bread for next morning, though that was normally Ariane's task.

"We leave in less than an hour," he said, standing in the doorway, trying to keep his tone light. "Were you not going to bid me farewell?"

She looked down at the bread dough beneath her hands, rather than up at his face. "You know that you are in my prayers always, master."

He crossed the floor in two steps to stand beside her. "Is that all, Euodia? Only in your prayers, as a brother in the Lord?"

She flattened the dough beneath her palms, pressing it into

large round circles. "I think we have been friends, but it seems—presumptuous—to say so." Her large dark eyes darted up at him just for a second, and their depths reminded him of how little he really knew of what her life had been.

"I have thought of you as both a sister and a friend, Euodia—and—perhaps as more than that. If things were different—our stations in life, perhaps—"

Just then he heard voices behind him, people drifing from the courtyard into the atrium.

"Hush," she said. "You . . . should not say such things, Master." She glanced up at him again, very quickly.

"I mean no disrespect."

Euodia nodded. "I took no disrespect from your words. But all that matters is—we must both do the Lord's will."

"Is that all that matters? Not our own desires, or our happiness?" He wished his words didn't sound so bitter.

"What happiness can we have, apart from His will?"

"I don't know. Perhaps I'll find out when I leave here."

She took a hesitant step toward him. "Don't speak that way, Master—brother. I do not want to think of you turning aside from the Way when you are far from here."

Epaphroditus turned to leave. The room seemed small and hot and he was afraid he would cry or say something she could never forgive. "Do as you said you would. Pray for me," he managed. "I will need your prayers."

CHAPTER 9
SYNTYCHE

"I need to buy wool to make tunics for 10—no, 11 children, food for three families for a week, and—enough to pay the laborers for the repairs to Arius's roof," Syntyche said, sliding a written list across the table toward Lydia. The dye merchant sat in a tall chair, the Christian community's moneybag at her right hand, perusing Syntyche's list with a faint, single frown line creasing her forehead.

"Pay for repairs? Have we not enough men to do the work ourselves?"

Syntyche had expected this objection and was prepared for it. "Lysander and his brothers can do it, but Clement and I believe it is only fair to pay them for their work. They have to take time from their own jobs to repair Arius's house, and they are poor themselves, with families to feed."

"But that is not the purpose of the collection. We are all to give what we can of our time and goods to help one another, and the collection is for the spread of the gospel."

"For the spread of the gospel and the needs of the poor," Syntyche countered. "It makes sense, Lydia. Think about it. Men like Lysander can give of their time and labor, while those of—us—who are wealthier, like yourself and Flavia, can give of your wealth. Arius's roof gets repaired, and the other men's families don't suffer for their kindness."

Lydia sighed heavily, and Syntyche hid her smile, knowing she'd won. She still didn't really like the older woman, and it galled her to come before Lydia with her hand out, needing approval for every copper coin she spent on behalf of the Christian poor. But their roles had been chosen—Lydia was the overseer of the community while Syntyche was a deaconess, a servant. And of course as a merchant Lydia was skilled in handling money. *If only she wasn't so tightfisted,* Syntyche thought. *But then, I suppose that's how merchants get rich—watching every penny.*

After Lydia counted out the coins Syntyche turned to go, but the older woman tapped the table with her forefinger—another annoying habit she had—and said, "While you are here, we should talk about the Feast of Tabernacles."

"All right—what did you want to discuss?" Syntyche knew

that she was being churlish, but she had had enough of Lydia's officious manner, and with so much work to do today, the last thing she wanted was to discuss another obscure Jewish feast.

"I will build a sukkot and host the feast here, as I did last year, of course," Lydia began, "but I worry there won't be enough room for everyone, now that our numbers have grown so much. A good complaint to have, but I often think we may need to split into two groups since we have no larger place to meet."

"What about Sister Flavia's house?" Flavia was by far the wealthiest member of the congregation, and her home was huge.

"It's not possible—her husband has returned from Rome, and he does not approve of her holding Christian gatherings while he is there."

Syntyche shrugged. "Perhaps not everyone will want to come for the feast. Surely it matters a great deal to only the Jews and the God fearers."

"How can you say that? Scripture commands the Feast of Tabernacles—and there are no Jews, God fearers, or Gentiles among us now. We are all—"

"All one in Christ Jesus, I know," Syntyche repeated the familiar words along with Lydia. It was a favorite formula of Paul's, and Luke used it often too. Sometimes Syntyche thought it was more of an ideal than a reality. Her fellow Christians might pretend to erase the divisions between Jew and Gentile, slave and free, man and woman, rich and poor—but they were still there. They seemed to be branded into people's skin, marks so deep that mere baptism couldn't wash them away.

She put the collection coins into the purse at her belt, her mind already busy with how she could best spend the money to help the ever growing group of poor Christians who depended on the rest of the community to help them feed and clothe their children. "Do what you think best about Tabernacles, Lydia," she said finally. "Clement and I will help with whatever you need done." The feast mattered little to her, but she was far too busy to argue with Lydia just now.

Out in the courtyard behind Lydia's house she found her daughter Julia helping the slave Euodia to fold a large piece of purple linen. They were talking intently—about fabric and dyeing, Syntyche assumed, until she got closer and heard Julia ask, "What do I do, then, if someone mocks me for being a Christ follower?"

"You know the words of Jesus that Luke has told us," Euodia said.

"To turn the other cheek, yes, but what does that mean? Am I really to let someone strike me in the face?" Julia pursued, her eyes wide.

"Has anyone offered to strike you?" Syntyche asked, breaking in. She knew other children sometimes questioned Julia and Lucius about the Christian way, and everyone in the congregation had suffered some small inconveniences because of their faith. But it was the first that she had heard of anyone being unkind to her daughter. If such a thing had really happened, why would Julia choose to confide in Euodia rather than her own mother?

"No, Mother. But—a girl I know—said some unkind things. I only wondered what it really meant to turn the other cheek."

"That would be Paula, no doubt." Paula's father was an old army friend of Clement's, and the two families had been friends for years. Their daughter was the same age as Julia and the two had grown up playing together. Her parents had suggested a match between Julia and Paula's brother, Marcus. Since Clement and Syntyche had become Christians the friendship with the other couple had cooled considerably, and Paula and Marcus's mother had told Syntyche plainly that she would not marry her son to a Christian girl. Offended, Syntyche had been reserved toward the woman ever since. She had not thought much of how it might have affected the friendship between the two girls.

Syntyche and Julia walked home in silence. She could hardly ask the girl, *Why would you confide your troubles to Euodia and not to your own mother?* The question answered itself. She felt a little curl of anger inside: anger at the new religion, at this Jesus who demanded so much of them, who had turned their lives upside down.

Julia's question to Euodia was only a foretaste. Worse was to come. As Syntyche entered her own home, she heard men's voices raised in the atrium.

"It won't do, Clement. A man's beliefs are his business, I don't try to interfere, but once you go making it public business, setting yourself up as a leader in this cult and drawing attention to your practices, I can't turn a blind eye."

"I'm sorry, sir." Her husband's voice was deferential, his respect for authority honed during his many years of army service. She recognized the man speaking to him as the city official in charge of the prison. He had given Clement the position as chief jailer after Clement's retirement from the army, and since then he had had little reason to interfere in the running of the prison. Clement did his job well, and Caius Livius had many other concerns. Syntyche could not remember the man ever visiting their house before.

Their house. She remembered suddenly that it was not—that it belonged to the city and went along with the position of jailer. If for any reason her husband lost his position, they would be without a home.

After shooing Julia to her room, she went into the kitchen where Chara was making bread. Syntyche hovered near the door, close enough to hear the conversation in the atrium without intruding on the men's business.

"I have tried to do my job the best I can these five years, sir," Clement said now. "But the truth is, it has troubled my conscience since I became a follower of the Christ."

"Your conscience?" Livius repeated, an incredulous tone to his voice. "Are you Christ followers opposed to punishing criminals, then? Do you think there should be no laws in society?"

"Not at all, sir." She could hear the tremor in her husband's voice, imagine the slight shaking of his hands as he addressed his superior. "Law and order must be kept, sir, but some of our punishments are—cruel, and followers of the Christ are taught not to use violence. I cannot flog a man, sir."

"Not even one who richly deserves it?" Clement didn't answer right away, but Caius Livius didn't wait for one. "Well, soldier, it seems your conscience and my convenience have the same idea. It doesn't suit you for a Christian to do a jailer's proper work, and it doesn't suit me for my chief jailer to be a—a *Christian*." He spat the word "Christian" with contempt. "As of today, you are relieved of your duties and ordered to vacate these premises to make way for the new chief jailer."

Syntyche felt fear and anger twist together like twin snakes in her stomach. How dare Livius dismiss Clement just for being a Christian? And how dare her husband toss away his family's livelihood so lightly? What would become of them now?

"It's for the best," Clement tried to soothe her after the official had gone. "I've known for some time now this job isn't right. How can a follower of the Christ hold a whip in his hand and flog men? I should have made the decision to leave, but I lacked the courage. Caius Livius was only God's instrument, forcing me to do what my own conscience should have made me do."

His arms were around her, and she buried her face in his shoulder. As he gently rubbed her hair and back, she assumed that he was probably thinking that she was overwhelmed with emotion. She was, but what shook her was rage, and she hid her face so that he wouldn't see it.

"What will happen to us, Clement?" she said finally. "Where will we go?"

He laughed—actually threw his head back and laughed, and she could hear in his laughter no fear or pretense at all.

"I don't know, wife. I have no idea what to do or where to go. Do you know how that feels? I've been an army man since I was a boy. I've never had a day when I didn't know where I was supposed to go and what I was supposed to do. Now I'm taking orders from a different Master, and He hasn't told me where my next post is."

"I don't know how you can laugh! We have two children, Clement! Not only do we need to feed and clothe them, we need to prepare Lucius for a career and find a husband for Julia. How are we to do that? How are we to live?"

As he pulled her face away from his shoulder and looked into it, his eyes were serious now but still lit with that strange joy she did not understand. "Syntyche, my wife, since we joined ourselves to Jesus we have been working for Him. Now we have a new task—trusting Him. We trust our God, we trust that our brothers and sisters in Christ. Jesus and His family will care for us."

His wife could see that the thought excited him. Clement had never been a gambler, but he looked like one now, thrilled to risk everything on a roll of the dice. She could barely grasp his excitement and could never share it. Working for Jesus had been easy. Making sure the Christ followers cared for the poor and needy had been a task Syntyche found herself well suited for. But to become one of the needy? To be dependent on her "brothers and sisters in Christ," people like Lydia and Euodia, for shelter and daily bread? Clement might talk about trusting Jesus but this was what it came down to—trusting the other Christ followers.

Syntyche didn't like the idea one bit.

CHAPTER 10
EUODIA

Euodia woke an hour before dawn on the preparation day before Sabbath. She anticipated a busy day of cooking and cleaning in between her regular work in the shop.

But more pressing than all those activities was the need to spend time in prayer, time with her Lord. For that reason she rose when it was still dark, folded away her bedclothes in the workroom corner where she slept, and knelt alone in the still, silent workroom between the dye vats and the fabric samples hanging to dry.

She recited a psalm from memory. Thanks to Epaphroditus who had so patiently taught her, she could read now. But she rarely had opportunity to sit down with a scripture scroll, except sometimes during the Sabbath. However, she had memorized many psalms and said one aloud now.

"O God, you are my God,
   earnestly I seek you;
   my soul thirsts for you,
   my body longs for you,
   in a dry and weary land
   where there is no water."

In her morning prayers she felt closer to God and more at peace than at any time during the day. Sometimes, as the words of the psalms themselves repeated in her head, she felt filled with the Spirit. It was nothing like the days when she had been possessed by those other spirits—and yet there was a similarity, she had to admit. The same sense of being in touch with something greater, something outside herself. But the Spirit of Jesus was filled with love. Love, she knew now, was the strange quality that filled the air of Lydia's home.

Now, though, something uneasy edged at the corners of that peaceful love. She tried to turn her mind away from thoughts of Epaphroditus and back to God, but it was impossible. Finally she put aside the words of the psalm and said simply, "Lord Jesus, I am troubled by my feelings for my mistress's son. I know it is not my place to love someone who is so far above me, and I should behave toward him as a sister in Christ. Please take these unworthy thoughts away from me, so that when Epaphroditus returns I can be at peace. Guard him and keep him following in Your Way. Please find him a good Christian wife, and please give me contentment in a life of solitary service to You."

She knew she was not destined to marry and have a family. The Lord was coming soon, and Euodia was certain that He had called her to give all of herself—all of her time and effort and energy—

to doing His work. It left no place in her life for love, except for the brotherly love she shared with all other Christians.

But that didn't explain why the house had seemed so empty since the young master's departure, or why his face so often appeared in her dreams. She was sure that he, too, felt attracted to her, but also certain that he was honorable, would never have taken advantage of a sister in the Lord just because she was his mother's slave.

By now he had been gone for half a year. He had left with Barnabas and John Mark and their wives, traveling on through Macedonia and Greece to expand the missionary work that Paul had begun on his journey two years ago. The missionaries had stayed the winter in Philippi, and during their time there many more people had come to know Jesus. The Christian community now numbered nearly 100 people—far too many to crowd into Lydia's house every Sabbath. They often met at the old place of prayer by the river, but with cooler weather coming no doubt some would meet in smaller groups at each other's homes.

In the spring Barnabas and his wife Mary had departed, taking Epaphroditus with them, along with John Mark, his wife Lucia, and their new baby. Watching Lucia with the baby, Euodia reflected it was a difficult life for a woman with a child, traveling in the Lord's service. Of course, few women missionaries journeyed alone—the roads and inns were hardly safe for an unaccompanied woman. Many missionary couples went from place to place together. Some of the men, like Paul and his companions, did go alone, often leaving their families behind.

Euodia thought with a wry smile of the years when she had told other people's fortunes. Now her own future was clouded. She knew she would serve the Lord all her life, but whether she would stay here in Philippi or take to the road to spread the message farther, she had no idea. Two things she was sure of, though. First, that her future was in God's hands, and second, that it had no place for daydreams about her mistress's handsome young son.

She was glad Epaphroditus had gone—she really was.

Prayers finished, she unfastened the shutters of the workroom to let the dawn light in, then checked the dyed fabrics to see which were dry and ready to put away. Ariane greeted her as she came through on the way to the kitchen, ready to prepare the day's bread. Rachel and Simon next entered the workroom, and they began at once preparing the dye vats.

The door to the street opened and Euodia went to greet the newcomer, thinking it was much too early for customers. Clement the jailer stood there. Euodia welcomed him in—she liked the friendly official, even if she found his wife difficult at times.

"Good morning, Euodia. I know it's early, but I was wondering if Lydia might have time to see me today. It's a matter of—some urgency."

"Of course, I'm sure she would." Her mistress made as much time for dealing with the church's business as she did for her dye works.

Lydia invited him to take the morning meal with her, while Euodia and the others went about their day's duties in the workroom. A wealthy customer came in and looked through samples, waiting for Lydia to join him. "The mistress is seeing someone else right now, but will be with you soon," Rachel told him.

"Hmph," the customer grunted. "Is she seeing another customer, or one of her Christian friends? I've bought my dyes from Lydia for years, but I don't mind saying I've got my doubts about doing business in a nest of Jesus followers."

Ignoring his slurs, Rachel only said, "I will send a message to her at once to tell her you are here, sir."

"I'll go," Euodia said immediately.

Her heart beat a little faster as she went to find Lydia. She knew many people in Philippi were unhappy with the fact that the Christ followers were growing in number. But except for her former owners, Demos and Arsenio, who still cursed her whenever they passed on the street, she had encountered little hatred or prejudice. A casual remark such as Lydia's customer had made reminded her just how unpopular her new Christian family was with many of their neighbors.

But she quickly learned that that hostility had touched them far more intimately than just the comments of a rude customer. When Lydia excused herself to see to the man, she directed Euodia to clear away the remains of the meal that she and Clement had shared. A few minutes later Clement said, "I am afraid my family and I may be making more work for you, Euodia. Lydia has kindly invited us to share her hospitality for—for a time. A short time, I hope—we do not wish to be a burden."

"But why? What has happened?"

"I have been relieved of my post as chief jailer. The magistrates do not want a Christ follower in such an important position—and to tell the truth, I do not find the work suitable for one who follows our peaceful Lord. But with my occupation gone, my family has no home for now. I need time to find out if I can still have my army pension in some other form, or if I am homeless and must seek a new occupation."

"Of course, Lydia would invite you to stay here while you sort out your affairs. It will not be a burden—this is what we do, isn't it? What we're supposed to do—to care for one another in times of need?"

But later that day, when Clement's family arrived at Lydia's house, Euodia knew it wasn't as simple as it sounded. In theory, yes, it was nice to believe that all Jesus' followers were one family and would share what they had whenever one of their number needed food, shelter, or clothing. But reality was something else, she realized as she watched as Clement's wife led her children through the courtyard into a storage room beside the dye works. That room had harbored other needy Christians in the past two years—but they were always poor, always people used to receiving charity. Euodia knew Syntyche was a proud woman. A deaconess like herself, Syntyche went far beyond the call of duty in serving the poor. Surely she had never imagined herself as one of the poor, in need of food and a place to live.

In fact, Syntyche and Clement and their children were hardly destitute. They brought with them their own stores of food to help with the expense of feeding them. Also they brought so many of their own goods that storage was as much of a problem as finding beds for everyone.

The house was often crowded, but Euodia reflected that having Syntyche under the same roof made any building seem twice as crowded. No, that wasn't fair. She tried hard to be impartial in her attitude to her fellow deaconess, but as soon as she heard Syntyche's loud voice, giving orders to Tacitus just as if she were the lady of the house, it was hard to be charitable.

They had endured a whole week of living in tight quarters when the Sabbath arrived again. On the evening of the sixth day as the sun set, believers from all over Philippi gathered at Lydia's home to begin the day of worship together.

As the deacons and deaconesses prepared to serve the bread and wine of the Lord's meal, Luke spoke to the gathered believers. "This has been a difficult week for some of us. Our brother Clement and sister Syntyche and their family have discovered that there is a cost to being a follower of Jesus—just as many of the rest of you are learning each day as our neighbors grow more suspicious of those of us who teach and practice this Way which is so different from the manner of the world. But when our brothers and sisters suffer hardship, it is an opportunity from the Lord Jesus to show that we are all family, and that we can care for one another. Before we eat Jesus' meal tonight, I want to tell you a story about Him and His disciples. Some of you have heard it before. John, who was one of Jesus' apostles, told me it himself when we met some years ago. On the night Jesus gathered to eat His last meal with His disciples, there was no slave present to wash their feet. The disciples wondered which of them would lower himself to the humble task of foot washing, but none was willing. Then Jesus himself wrapped the towel around his waist, took up the basin, and knelt at His disciples' feet to wash the dust of the road from them. He said that we should do the same—we should be willing to wash each other's feet.

"Here in our little community in Philippi, we have masters and slaves, rich and poor, but we meet together as equals. Nobody washed your feet when you came into Sister Lydia's house tonight, but let us now follow the example of our Lord. Let us each take a basin and towel and wash our neighbor's feet as a sign of our willingness to serve one another."

Euodia had noticed Ariane carrying a large pile of shallow clay bowls and folded towels of coarse fabric into the courtyard before the meeting, but she had not known of Luke's plans, nor indeed had she heard this story of Jesus before. She tried to imagine the humble yet dignified Man of Galilee—as she pictured Him in her mind—kneeling at another's feet like a servant. For her, surely it would be no great stretch to wash the feet of her fellow Christians. As a slave she had washed feet before. But perhaps she should seek out Syntyche and wash her feet as a gesture of Christian love.

She was about to get a basin when she realized that the woman was standing in front of her, holding a basin and towel. "Euodia, may I wash your feet?" Syntyche's lips were tightly compressed, and she sounded as if she were being choked. But she was there, holding the towel, kneeling at Euodia's feet. At least she was trying. *I'll try, too*, Euodia promised the Lord silently, as she sat down on a bench and allowed the jailer's wife to wash her feet.

CHAPTER 11
CLEMENT

Clement dressed in his best tunic and trimmed his beard before going to see the centurion. He knew even without his wife's constant reminders how important the interview was. But that didn't stop her from coming into the tiny, cramped room, straightening his belt, and tidying his hair as if he were Lucius' age. "Remember, don't presume anything. Come to him as a supplicant—he'll react better that way . . ."

"How on earth can you know how the man will react, Syntyche, when you've never seen nor spoken with him?" Clement allowed a little of his fear and worry to tinge his voice with annoyance, hard as he tried not to.

He saw her anger and the hurt that lay behind it. After all, he knew her so well—every expression of her face, every tone of her voice. Even when she was at her most shrill and bossy, she too was hiding fear. The past two weeks staying in Lydia's house had been hard on her, a strong willed woman used to running her own home. To soften his harsh words, he touched her cheek with two fingers.

"You know what you can do to help me, Syntyche? Better than any advice, better than combing my hair or tying my belt, what can you do?"

Her eyes dropped. "Pray," she said, her voice barely audible. "But it does not come as easily to me as to you."

This, too, he realized. Clement respected the way that his wife had embraced the new religion. He had ordered her to abandon her devotion to the old faith of her mothers, and he recognized that had cut her deep. She might easily have obeyed him and become a Christian in outward form only, going through the motions without real devotion. But no, not his Syntyche. She had thrown herself into the service of Jesus with a whole heart, finding it easier to show her love of the Lord through caring for the poor and doing acts of mercy than through prayer and worship. Today, though, prayer was what they needed. No actions of Syntyche's, no matter how well intended, could lighten the burden that lay on their family. They must have the help of the Lord Jesus and His Father, the Almighty God of heaven.

"You think you cannot pray, love, but the Lord Jesus hears even your simplest words. Paul told us that when we could not find the words, the Spirit of Jesus would help us to pray."

"All I can do is ask that He will move the centurion's heart to mercy and give you a pension so we can live," Syntyche said, glancing away.

"Then ask Him just that, while I go and speak to the centurion."

He didn't say so to Syntyche, but he didn't hold out a great deal of hope for this appointment. The centurion had already kept him waiting a fortnight to see him, though by now word of what had happened to his position at the jail must have reached the army command. The job and the house that accompanied it had been his army pension—many men received a grant of land, but Clement was no farmer and wanted a city life. Now, if the government did offer him a little land, he would accept it gratefully and be a farmer for Jesus' sake. But he had no trade, no skills. He didn't know what else he could do, having given his whole life to the Roman army.

Centurion Titus Cassius Placidus, of the Philippi garrison, didn't seem to know what to do with him either. "The magistrates gave you a choice," he said. "If you'd been willing to give up your religion, you could have kept your position at the jail and your house along with it."

"That is correct, sir," Clement replied, standing at attention as he'd done for so many years.

"But you chose not to do that."

"No sir. I cannot give up my faith, sir."

"Why not?"

The question threw him. Clement didn't know why not—he only knew that he couldn't. He searched his mind for a moment. "I've given my allegiance to the Lord Jesus," he said finally. "I cannot change that now." He would not speak to this man of love, or joy, or the Spirit of Jesus alive in his heart. Loyalty and allegiance—those were concepts a soldier understood.

"The purpose of religion is to make men better citizens, better soldiers, better subjects of the empire," the officer continued. "Do you worship the emperor?" he asked abruptly.

"I respect and obey the emperor, and all the rulers and authorities that God has set over us."

"No god set the emperor over you. The emperor Cl—the emperor Nero *is* a god." Placidus caught his error and smoothly corrected himself. Claudius, the emperor they had all honored and served for most of Clement's years in the army, had died less than a month ago and his adopted son and heir, Nero, was now emperor. Nobody knew what kind of ruler the 17-year-old boy might become, but gossip from Rome was rife with rumors of power struggles and even the possibility that Agrippina, Nero's mother, had murdered Claudius. It was hard to imagine such people as gods, Clement thought—hard not to contrast the decadent imperial court with the simple life of Jesus of Nazareth. Wisely, he said nothing of this as Placidus repeated, "The emperor is a god, and he was born to rule over you. Do you acknowledge that?"

"I acknowledge that the emperor rules over me."

"And that he is a god, to be worshipped by all true Romans."

"No, sir."

The centurion didn't look shocked. His name, Placidus, suited him well. No ripple of emotion showed on his smooth round face. Clement knew the centurion had expected such an answer, had introduced the mention of the emperor just to elicit this particular blasphemous answer. "You refuse to worship the emperor," he repeated, as if making sure.

"Yes, sir. I worship only the one God, Father of our Lord Jesus Christ."

"Stop talking nonsense, legionary. If you were a younger man and your 20 year's service not yet done, would you take up your sword and fight the enemies of Rome as your commanding officer and your emperor ordered you to do?"

Clement felt a cold hand clutch his heart. "No, sir."

"Do I hear you right? Why are you wasting my time here today?" Irritation crept into Centurion Placidus's tone.

"Permission to state my case, sir?"

The centurion nodded once.

"While I do not worship the emperor, I respect and obey him. I did my 20 years' service and received an honorable retirement from the army. I was given a job and a house as my army pension and I did that job well for five years. Now that that job has been given to another veteran, I respectfully request that I receive my pension in another form, either in money or land, so that I may continue to support my family."

The centurion fixed him with gray eyes as hard as the glint of an enemy's shield. "Now let me state my case—Rome's case. Lucius Julius Clement, you have said openly that you do not offer the emperor the homage due him, that you would not obey his orders if you were still in his service, and that you freely and willingly gave up your position and your home rather than renounce this degenerate religion of yours. I see no reason at all why the Roman army owes you a pension or anything else. We are finished with you. You are not, and never were, a soldier of Rome or a true servant of the empire. Get out of my quarters and out of my sight."

"Yes, sir," Clement said, saluting the officer. The centurion did not return his salute. Clement turned and left the room.

As he walked back down the hill toward the busy streets he realized that he could not go back to Lydia's house empty-handed, refused, with nothing to offer Syntyche, no hope and no future. Words of Scripture that he had heard someone recite—Lydia or Luke, perhaps—drifted into his mind. "I know the plans I have for you, says the Lord; plans to prosper you and not to harm you, plans to give you hope and a future."

He knew that his hope and his future resided in the coming kingdom, when the Lord Jesus returned and everything would be peaceful and prosperous. But until that happened, Clement of Philippi, once a jailer, needed a place for his family to live, bread to put in their mouths, and work that would enable him to earn that bread. "If you have plans to prosper me, God our Father, if you have plans to give me hope and a future, then please reveal them to me now," he prayed. "Give me something to take home to my family."

Instead of going back to the street of the weavers and dyers, he turned in the other direction, to the villa of Flavia, Christian wife of the magistrate Aulus Gabinus. Gabinus disapproved of Flavia's new religion and her new friends, but he was often away in Rome.

The lady of the house was at home. She received him in her spacious courtyard with a warm greeting and a cool drink of date juice and a plate of fig and nut cakes sweetened with honey. Clement reminded her of his situation—she knew what had happened, of course, as all the Christians did. He told her that his attempt to get back his army pension had failed. "I wondered, sister Flavia, if you might have any work you need doing about your house. I know you have your own servants and slaves, but if there's anything—I can bend my back to any task, I just need to earn enough to keep my family."

She frowned, but in thought rather than in refusal. "We are having a new barn built on our property outside the city," she said finally. "I need laborers, but that will be quite a change in status for one who has been a soldier and the chief jailer. Are you sure you are willing to work with your hands?"

"Every soldier has to be able to turn his hand to building when the job requires it, my lady. I've done my share in the past, and I'll do it again. I'll labor for you till your barn is completed and look for other work afterward—I won't leave you in the middle of the task even if a better job comes along. I must have food for my family and a place for them to live."

A smile tugged at the corner of her mouth. "You are staying at Lydia's home for now, aren't you?"

"Yes, my lady. It is—quite crowded there. We need our own space."

"And your wife needs her independence, I'm sure. There are too many strong willed women in that house as it is. I love Lydia and Rachel and Euodia dearly as sisters in Christ, of course, but. . . yes, I quite understand why you want a home of your own again."

The problem was, Clement reflected as he walked back to Lydia's street, it wasn't likely to be much of a home at first. He'd do better if they stayed on at Lydia's and saved up his wages for a while, but he suspected Flavia was right. Too many strong willed women lived in that house already.

That suspicion was soon confirmed. At this time of day he would expect to find the artisans and slaves working at the dye works, but Lydia herself was often in the shop meeting customers. Today the large shop room was deserted, and he heard raised voices coming from the courtyard beyond. With a sinking heart he recognized one of them as Syntyche's.

He found her embroiled in an argument with Euodia, both women almost shouting at each other. At first he assumed it involved some domestic matter until he noticed a third woman standing between them and clutching an infant. It was Tulla, one of the poorest members of the Christ followers, with the baby she had just given birth to a few days before.

"Don't listen to her, Tulla!" Syntyche said. "Her words make no sense to you because they *are* nonsense. There's no need to bind yourself to a Jewish custom—we are not Jews, but followers of the Christ, whom He calls from all nations."

"Calls to become children of His heavenly Father!" Euodia shot back, just as hotly. "His Father, who gave His chosen people a sign by which they would be known. Why would we not have our sons bear this sign if we truly belong to the God of heaven?"

"But it will hurt him, surely?" the poor woman said to Euodia, clutching her baby even closer to her chest. Clement understood now what they were quarreling about. The men of the community had had several lengthy discussions about the issue of circumcision, with Simeon and others who came from a Jewish background arguing that the special symbol of commitment to God was for all His people, at all times. Luke had countered that Gentiles who became Christ followers did not need to be circumcised—it was a sign for Jews only. Until now he had not heard of the issue coming up among the women, but of course it would arise when a woman gave birth to a baby boy. And, he thought with resignation, his wife would naturally be in the thick of it.

"Yes, it will hurt your baby, and for no purpose," Syntyche said. "The Lord Jesus does not demand this of us. Our teacher Paul tells those who come to Christ that God is interested in marking their hearts, not their bodies. You don't have to do this to your child, Tulla—and don't let anyone tell you otherwise."

Clement hated the thought of intervening in an argument among women. Besides, he knew his wife was in the right. There was no point trying to keep his wife in line when he agreed with her—and no need to take her part, since she was doing just fine on her own.

"It is the God of Israel we worship!" Euodia protested, her thin dark face flushing a little. "The Lord Jesus sent Paul to call us Gentiles *into* Israel, not to take us out of it!"

Tulla was almost in tears, and the infant caught the woman's mood and began to whimper. "I don't understand any of this— I just don't want to cut my baby!" she moaned. "But I don't want to disobey the Lord either!"

"What's going on here?" Clement hadn't even seen Lydia brush past him as she came into the courtyard, but she was there now, and the three younger women all looked a little abashed as the mistress of the house, overseer of the Christian community, caught them squabbling in her courtyard in the middle of the day.

"Sister Lydia, she says I need to have my baby—what is the word? That I have to cut him, to prove he is one of God's chosen people!" Tulla burst out, pointing at Euodia.

Lydia merely raised an eyebrow. Clement was reminded that despite Euodia's position as a deaconess, despite the fact that

Lydia treated all the members of her household as family, Euodia was still her slave. But she said nothing directly to the girl—she spoke to Tulla.

"Euodia's words to you were well-meant, but mistaken. It is true that many Jews and God fearers choose to have their boys circumcised, but our leaders have clearly said that those of us who follow Christ do not need to do this. I think it is best left to each person's conscience. If you and your husband see no need to have your baby circumcised, you don't have to do it." She laid a hand on the young mother's shoulder. "Go in peace, Tulla. Your baby is part of God's family because he is being brought up by parents who fear God and love the Lord Jesus. You don't need to do anything else."

"Thank you, sister Lydia!" Tulla gathered the skirt of her robe in the hand that wasn't clutched around her baby and almost ran from the courtyard. Syntyche, too, turned to go, but Lydia's voice was sharp. "Both of you stay a moment."

"Yes, mistress," Euodia said. Syntyche said nothing, but remained. Clement did not move from where he was, watching the three women. Lydia, gray haired and regal, well dressed, assumed command as if she were born to it. Euodia, tall and slim, her long black hair striking against the rough dun fabric of a slave's robe, looked at Lydia gravely, her thin face stern and sober except for the snapping dark eyes. His own Syntyche, short and plump beside the other two, wisps of brown curls escaping around her flushed face, looked like a small hen whose feathers had gotten ruffled.

"I know that you two have different views on this matter, as you do on many others. In this case, it is Syntyche whose opinion accords with that of Paul and the other apostles, so—"

"But mistress, should we obey even the apostles above the scriptures?" Euodia said, the words bursting out of her. "Forgive me, but—surely our conscience owes a duty to God alone?"

Lydia fixed her frown on Euodia. "Indeed, but we must be guided by our leaders—by overseers and by the apostles. As your overseer I say that here in Philippi we will follow the leading of the apostles, and no one will be forced to circumcise a child. If and when you have a son of your own, Euodia, you will of course be free to follow your own conscience, with the guidance of your husband."

She turned back to Syntyche. "Regardless of the issue, or of who was right or wrong, it does the believers no good to see two of our deaconesses quarrelling publicly. If you disagree, come discuss it with me or with Luke in private. Do not confuse and upset the believers with displays like this. It is not seemly. Euodia. I believe you have work to do."

The slave woman nodded, bowed, and hurried off across the courtyard toward the dye vats. Lydia turned to Syntyche. While she obviously wanted to dismiss her too, she didn't have the kind of authority over her that she had over Euodia.

Clement saved the moment. "Syntyche, come with me," he called, and for the first time the women noticed him standing there. "We have much to discuss."

"I will leave you," Lydia said. "I, too, have work to do." She swept out of the courtyard and back into her house without further comment. Clement saw that Syntyche's cheeks still burned with anger as she watched Lydia leave.

"Did you see that, Clement? She knew I was right and Euodia was dead wrong, but did she take my part? No, she blamed both of us, as if we were both equally wrong—"

"Wrong to make a quarrel of it," Clement pointed out. "She did acknowledge your position was the right one. I am sure that she is trying her best to be fair."

"You may be sure, but I'm not! The way she favors that slave girl, treats her like a daughter, lets her put herself above her position—it makes me furious. We may be all one in Christ Jesus, but we're not all one in the household—you can't order a household that way, and Euodia doesn't know her place. And these Jewish laws and customs—she gets all that from Rachel and Simeon, you know. They'd have us all make Jews out of ourselves!"

"Hush, hush," Clement said, attempting to fold Syntyche in his arms. It was like trying to stroke a spitting cat, but he was used to dealing with his wife's anger: he'd never have wanted a meek, timid girl with no spirit. Syntyche's rage was the price that went with her passion. When she cared deeply about anything she was roused to anger, and he was glad that she cared so much about following Christ, enough to get angry when she saw others teaching falsehood. She just had to learn more appropriate ways to express it. He was sure that if it wasn't for her personal dislike of Euodia and the strain of staying in Lydia's house with no home of her own, this little issue of circumcision would never have caused her to speak so harshly.

"I have tried, Clement—you and the Lord know how I've tried to get along here . . . " As she settled into his embrace her anger subsided into tears.

"I do know, and the Lord Jesus knows. I have good news, love—we won't be here much longer. I can't get my pension—the army won't allow it. But I do have some work, and while it's little enough, I think we can make it stretch to rent two rooms for us and the children."

"Yes! Yes! I don't care if we all have to live in one room, so long as we're on our own again!" Syntyche wiped her eyes with the edge of her sleeve. "Oh, I'm terrible, I know. We should all be living together in Christian love and unity, but it's so hard, Clement! So hard to be the one taking charity, and always having to be grateful, and living by the rules of someone else's household. I'm afraid I suffer from the sin of pride."

He kissed her on the forehead. "Confess that sin, then, and ask the Lord to soften your proud heart—and thank Him for taking care of us. I'm proud too, my wife—proud of you for taking care of me and the children so well in this hard time. You could have complained that I've let a good position go for the sake of my faith. Even today, the centurion suggested I might get my pension back if I could forsake my faith in Jesus and promise to worship the emperor like a good Roman soldier should. But you've never uttered a word of criticism or doubt—you've stood by me all the way."

Syntyche nodded, and he could see that her quick mind had already moved on to practical matters. "Clement, I think we're going to have to let Chara go. Give her her freedom."

"Chara? Do you really think so?" The elderly slave had come with Syntyche into the marriage, having belonged to Syntyche's parents, who were no longer living. She had been the first care-giver for both their children and had done all the household work alongside Syntyche all these years. "I can see that we can't afford to keep a slave, if we're going to live in two rooms on a laborer's pay. But where would she go—what would she do? Wouldn't it be cruel just to cut her loose after all these years?"

"Of course I wouldn't do that, Clement." Syntyche's forehead creased in thought. "I'll find a good place for her—we could make a little money if I sold her to someone, but I don't feel quite right about that. I'd like at least to offer her freedom, to see if that's what she wants. My sister might have a place for her, or if she'd be more comfortable in another Christian home then perhaps someone in the community could take her in. Lydia may know someone. I'm sure she'll help—oh, she's a good woman, Clement, really she is. I don't know why I'm so cross and impatient—she really is a good woman."

He smoothed his wife's damp hair back from her face. "So are you, my love. So are you."

CHAPTER 12
LYDIA

A ship from Thyatira had arrived at Neapolis. It had been months since Lydia had heard news from the city where her family lived and where Epaphroditus had gone to stay with her relatives. As soon as word began to spread on the street that a ship was in port, she found it hard to keep her attention on her work. Surely, this time, there would be a letter?

When a messenger from the port finally came, he brought more than a letter. He presented her with several carefully wrapped parcels from her brother—new dyes she had ordered for the shop to trade here in Philippi. And there were two letters—one for her, and one for Luke.

The messenger arrived in the middle of the day when the shop was busy and two customers waited to meet with Lydia. She glanced at her letter to be sure it was from Epaphroditus, then put both letters aside for later and quickly toured the dye works to see that everyone was busy about their tasks. She had given Euodia and Rachel permission to finish work early today, to meet with a group of Jewish women who had newly arrived in town and wanted to know more about the teachings of Jesus. The women's husbands had already had several long discussions with Luke and Simeon, but Euodia and Rachel were eager to study Scripture with the wives.

Lydia noted with approval that both the slave and the freed-woman were working quickly and efficiently, trying to get through a day's work despite leaving the shop early. Now that her home was not only a business but the headquarters of the Christian church in Philippi, those two roles sometimes competed for her attention. Lydia knew business had suffered a little during the past several years, but she was sure that was because of the prejudice some people held against Christians, not because her shop was less efficient or that her dedication to her customers had lessened.

She met with the two clients, then went to her private chamber with her letter. As she unfolded it, the sight of her son's familiar handwriting sent loneliness breaking over her like a wave. She missed him so much. He had been gone for more than a year and a half now, and in that time he would have grown from the tall, long limbed, slightly awkward youth of 17 into a man.

His shoulders and chest were no doubt broader, his beard fuller, his voice deeper. And she had seen none of those changes. Her son had sent only a handful of letters in that time—this was only the fourth. Each letter was polite and dutiful, but left her lonelier and more worried than before it arrived, as if the words on paper only underlined the fact that he himself was not there.

She stared at the handwriting a little longer, trying to picture Epaphroditus penning it. Then she sighed, shook her head, and began to read.

"To my gracious and revered lady mother Lydia, greetings from Epaphroditus your son. I hope you and all our household are well."

In his earlier letters he had used a greeting common among Christ's followers—"May the grace of our Lord Jesus Christ be upon you and all our household." The fact that he had dropped that formula made her uneasy. She shook herself a little, realizing that she was probably worried over nothing.

"I write to you from the house of your brother Alexius, who greets you with brotherly love and affection, as do all his household. They care for me well and I have learned much of the dyer's art and the merchant's skills from Alexius and Jason.

"During the winter I went on a journey with John Mark and his wife, who are on their way to Rome to work with the apostle Peter. I went with them as far as Assos and Troas, and saw Mark and Peter preach and many were baptized. They invited me to go on with them but I chose to return to Thyatira. I did some business for Alexius my uncle on the journey too, trading his dyes in those cities, so it was a valuable journey in many ways."

Lydia knew already that her son had journeyed with John Mark, because the apostle and his young family had passed through Philippi on their way to Rome weeks ago. Mark had been evasive when she asked about Epaphroditus. Although she didn't know him well enough to press him on the subject, she had the sense that Epaphroditus had not been the asset to their ministry that Mark had hoped. "But I was his age myself once, and irresolute, and not much help on a preaching tour," he had told her. "Paul grew irritated and refused to travel with me, but my cousin Barnabas had more patience, and kept working with me. Under his guidance, I grew up. Your son is but a young man. He, too, will grow up and will be of great value to the Lord's work, I'm sure."

Now Lydia scanned her son's letter looking for something that would bolster that certainty, but she found nothing. He had once spoken of how he longed to travel as the missionaries did, bringing the Word of Jesus, but she detected no sense of joy or a dream fulfilled when he wrote about his trip with Mark, only a dull recitation of the fact that he had come and gone. Perhaps letter writing simply wasn't one of his gifts.

That was far from being her only worry about her son's future. It was high time he was betrothed. Yes, the Lord's return might be near at hand—but it might also be a lifetime away, and Epaphroditus must marry and have sons of his own, if Jesus did not return. She had written to her brother when she sent Epaphroditus to Thyatira, suggesting that he look about for a likely bride for the boy. She had mentioned that although Alexius was not a Christian, she would prefer a Christian bride for her son, and if Alexius knew some of the families in Thyatria who were Christ followers he might be in a good position to judge which of their daughters would be a marriage prospect. She repeated the suggestion in a later letter, and in his reply he had agreed to make enquiries.

Lydia realized that her brother would wonder why she made such a point of this. While matches were sometimes made between very young people, it was far more common for a man to wait till he was older and then be bethrothed to a girl still in her late teens. There was no hurry to marry Epaphroditus off—no hurry, at any rate, as far as age was concerned.

She guessed that Alexius was perceptive enough to recognize that if she had mentioned the matter of a bride for her son twice, there must be some reason for urgency. The most obvious reason, he would probably asume, was an inappropriate attachment back home in Philippi—one that had worried Lydia enough for her to encourage her son to leave the city for a time.

If Alexius suspected that, he would be right, of course. If her son did stay away for a year or two, his infatuation with Euodia would fade. A suitable match might be made for him in Thyatira, or a marriage might be arranged for Euodia here in Philippi. Either, or both, would suffice to put the matter aside forever. While she loved Euodia, almost as a daughter, the fact that they were sisters in Christ did not change the reality that the girl was a slave, her family background unknown, her past murky. Nothing could make her an appropriate bride for Lydia's only son.

Again Lydia picked up the letter. She knew that she had glimpsed the word "marriage" in the closing words of the letter and that it had led her thoughts down this byway. Now she looked more closely to see what Epaphroditus had to say.

"My uncle has lately suggested that I consider two young women as possible brides. He assures me that he acts with your permission and will guide me in my choice. One is a relative, the daughter of your cousin Leandros. She is about my age and in good health, but I will confess truly I do not find her company pleasant. The second girl is the daughter of a family of Christ followers. The family is of good repute as the father is a spice merchant, but the girl herself is very young, only 14 years old and, in my opinion, not truly ready to consider marriage, though her father is prepared to make a betrothal and wait two or three years for the wedding.

"Truly, my honored mother, I do not wish to enter into a marriage contract with either of these young women. Perhaps it is best that I wait until I return home and can be guided by you, rather than make an arrangement I might later regret. I desire in all things to be a loyal and faithful son to you."

She sighed. If her son truly wanted her guidance, he would marry either one of the two girls his uncle had selected—both, it seemed, quite appropriate. One was a Christian, the other a close relative, but obviously neither one pleased Epaphroditus. An unhappy, unwilling marriage would be almost as bad as an unsuitable one. The boy needed time, but Lydia guessed that two years had not been enough to erase the thought of Euodia from his mind. Indeed, it was probably not Euodia herself he was now in love with, after all this time, but an image of her that he had created in his thoughts.

But there was a hastily written note at the bottom of the letter, still in Epaphroditus's hand but apparently done later and in a hurry.

"Dear Mother, while I awaited a ship to send this message to you, a vessel arrived in port with the apostle Paul on board! Paul and his companions Silas and Timothy are here in Thyatira and will travel on to Macedonia when their work is done. I hope you will approve my returning with them, for I am so eager to see you and all the family again. Further news is in Paul's letter to Luke, which I wrote for him. I remain, your loving son, Epaphroditus."

Lydia glanced at Luke's letter and saw that it was, indeed, in Epaphroditus's handwriting. She knew that Paul, like many people, preferred to dictate his letters rather than write them himself, and Epaphroditus had such a clear hand he could easily be a scribe. "Tacitus? Ariane?" she called, going to the door of her chamber. When Tacitus appeared a moment later, she said, "Please go to Doctor Luke's rooms and ask him to attend me as soon as he is free—I have a letter that he will be eager to read."

The letter, when Luke finally opened and read it, confirmed what Epaphroditus had written. Paul was embarking on another journey into Macedonia, believing that God had more work for him to do there. He hoped to take a ship for Neapolis in the spring and spend some months in Philippi before moving on into Greece.

The man's eyes shone as he read the letter aloud to Lydia. "I will read this again tonight, when all the household has gathered—and then again on Sabbath," the physician said—for Paul had written not just about his plans, but a few words of encouragement to share with the believers. His letters, copied and circulated from one church to another, were regarded as precious as gold. "Everyone will be so excited to know that Paul is coming to us again."

"You are the most excited of all, I think," Lydia commented with a smile.

He nodded. "It is true. I love the home you have made for me here, my work and our church in Philippi—but I have missed Paul and our other companions. I've missed preaching the good news from town to town—even though those times were often hard. There's a thrill to it—I can't explain."

"You will go away with Paul when he travels on from here, won't you?"

After a moment's silence, he admitted, "I don't know. I want to—at least, a part of me wants to. I seem to be torn in two— half a man who wants a quiet life, to be a physician, live in a comfortable house with a family, heal the sick and teach the gospel to a little group of believers like we have here. The other part of me longs for the excitement, even the danger and hard- ship, of walking the roads with nothing to rely on but my cloak, my staff, and the grace of God."

"Well said."

"But it doesn't really matter what I want—either part of me. What does matter is what God calls me to—and I don't yet know what that is. Perhaps by the time Paul returns, my way will be clear."

"Perhaps." Epaphroditus would return with Paul, and she would rejoice to see him. But she hoped that her son's way, too, would become clearer by the time he reached home. And that meant the problem of Euodia would have to be dealt with.

CHAPTER 13
EUODIA

She was expecting a summons to talk to her mistress alone. The household buzzed with news that Paul was returning to Philippi, bringing Epaphroditus with him. Sure as darkness followed sunset, Euodia knew a request for a private conversation with Lydia would accompany that news.

It came after the evening meal, three days after the arrival of Epaphroditus's and Paul's letters. Euodia and Ariane were clearing platters from the table. Rachel and Simon had already gone to their own room, and Tacitus was busy with his work, but Luke, Lydia, and Helena remained at the table, reclining at their couches though they had long finished their meal. They were talking, of course, of when Paul and his companions might arrive and of what Epaphroditus would do upon returning home.

"It's time you give him a larger part to play in the business since he's a grown man now. He can meet with customers, make decisions about what to buy and whom to sell it to. After all, the business will belong to him soon enough," Helena said, her aged voice still ringing out clear.

"Of course, of course," Lydia agreed. "He's learned a great deal working with my brother in Thyatira—still, I don't know how much responsibility he's ready to take on his own."

Euodia listened, as slaves always did when their masters were talking, she and Ariane as silent and unnoticed as the pitchers and bowls on the table or the hangings on the walls. And she knew everyone here well enough to hear the words that weren't being said. She realized that Helena had always regarded Lydia as nothing more than a caretaker for her late husband's business and looked forward to the day when the man of the family was ready to take over again. Lydia longed to see her son again, but wasn't quite ready to give up running the business she loved. Luke looked forward to the return of Epaphroditus and Paul because he was eager to take to the road again. After five years in Philippi he felt called to rejoin Paul in his missionary travels.

It would have been nice, Euodia thought, if she were just an observer, if none of the business of the family touched her personally. But she recognized that was not the case. Lydia talked to her mother-in-law and her friend without regarding the silent and efficient slaves, but Euodia wasn't fooled. She knew the woman would ask to speak with her alone. Sure enough, as Helena rose from the table and summoned Ariane to help her to her room, Lydia signaled Euodia. "Just stay a moment, will you?" She said good night to Helena and to Luke, then waited on her couch, gesturing Euodia to take a place on a stool across from her.

"Euodia, we are so busy here I scarcely have time to speak to you unless it's about the business of the house, the shop, or the church, but I must take a moment to commend you. Since you've come to us, your work in all three has been excellent. I feel I can rely on you fully, and it's a delight to me to see how gifted you are and how hard you work."

"Thank you, mistress." The servant girl still remembered the rebuke Lydia had given her after she had quarreled with Syntyche about circumcising Tulla's baby, and the discussion she and Lydia had had later about following the Jewish ceremonial laws—one that had not ended in perfect agreement. But Euodia remembered those conversations simply because rebuke and dispute were so rare in Lydia's household. She knew she was well treated. In many ways, when they worked together for the good of the Christian community, Lydia treated her almost as an equal. She had no complaint here, but she knew why her mistress was strangely distant and formal with her now.

Lydia must have seen that there was some attraction between her and Epaphroditus. When he was still at home, and teaching her to read, Euodia had often seen his mother watching the two of them together. The woman missed nothing. Two years had passed since the young master had gone away, and Lydia had never said anything to her about Epaphroditus. She had made hints and suggestions about her future—about marriage—but that was as far as it had gone. Now, with Epaphroditus returning to the household, Lydia would be determined to make sure that such an attraction would not blossom.

Privately, Euodia was sure it was not worth Lydia's trouble. Epaphroditus was a pleasant, friendly, good-looking boy of good family. During his two years away he had no doubt met many young women. Even if he hadn't yet contracted a marriage, she was sure he wasn't still thinking about her. For a moment she had a vivid memory of her last awkward conversation with the young master—a memory that she usually kept buried. Time had not changed *her* feelings toward him—yet she hoped it had altered his toward her.

"I have often said, Euodia, that I think you have a bright future ahead," Lydia began. "I believe the Lord has given you many gifts and laid His hand upon you, and I want to do everything I can to help you along His path for you."

"Yes, mistress."

"You know Sergius, the linen weaver's apprentice, don't you?"

"I know him, mistress." Only about 100 Christ followers lived in Philippi, and they worshipped together weekly. Of course she knew the young man, a freedman a couple years older than herself. He had been baptized about a year ago and was very active in telling others about the Christ and helping out in any way he could in the community. His name had been suggested as a possible deacon, and Euodia though him a good choice. But she was quite sure Lydia had not called her here to discuss his suitability as a deacon.

"He has asked if he might make an offer of marriage for you," Lydia continued.

In fact, Lydia didn't even need to ask. As a slave, Euodia was her property, and if Lydia wished to marry her—say, to another slave within the same household—Euodia could not legally refuse. She wondered just how desperate the woman was to make this match. Euodia herself had only one good reason for refusing the offer, and she intended to use it. Perhaps it would put Lydia's mind at rest about Epaphroditus as well.

"Mistress, you know you have the right to make this choice for me, but my own wish would be to refuse it," she said, looking down at her hands knotted tightly in her lap.

"Why? I think Sergius would be a very suitable match for you.

He is a Christian, a freedman, and he is learning a good trade. He is of a good age for marriage and seems to be a very pleasant young man. And . . . if you were to accept his offer, I would give you your freedom, so that you would be free to marry."

"Ah." That was a generous offer. Euodia was not entirely sure whether she wanted her freedom or not, but she knew it was no small gift. While she might almost see it as a bribe, it was uncharitable to think Lydia intended it that way.

"All that you say is true, mistress. If I wished to marry, I doubt I could find a more suitable husband. But I believe God has called me to a life of service as an unmarried woman. I think that is how I can serve Him best. Unless you order me to do it, I will not marry."

Lydia picked up a goblet that still sat upon the table and lifted it as if to drink, then, realizing that it was empty, lowered her hand. She did not set the goblet down, but turned it around in her hands as she spoke.

"You don't know how old you are, do you, Euodia?"

"No, mistress. I know I am a woman full grown. Perhaps 18 or 19 years old? I don't know. I was still a child when I was taken from my mother—from the temple. That's all I know."

Lydia nodded. "It seems very noble and at the same time very easy, when you are 18, to dedicate yourself to a celibate life. I have known people who did so—priests or priestesses to one or another of the pagan gods who demanded that of their servants. Maybe if you lived out your life in a temple, it would be—easier. But you may have a long life ahead of you—we don't know how long it will be before the Lord's return. It's natural for a woman to want to marry, to have children. You may make this decision now and regret it in years to come."

Euodia shook her head even though she knew, in fact, that Lydia was right. She would regret her decision as soon as Epaphroditus returned. But regret didn't mean a decision was wrong. She was absolutely sure that this was the life that God had called her to.

"I plan to be wedded to the Lord's work, and to have no children but those who are born again in Jesus through my witness."

"Fine words, Euodia. A nice little speech. I don't doubt your sincerity, but I wonder if this is really God's calling—or your own pride."

"Pride, mistress?"

"I'm not speaking to you now as your mistress, but as your sister in Christ, the overseer of this church. God has given you great gifts. I am quite sure He has called you to work for Him. But don't make the mistake of assuming that He has summoned you to an extraordinary sacrifice just to set you apart from others."

"I don't think that, sister Lydia."

"So will you consider Sergius's offer of marriage?"

Again Euodia shook her head. For the first time her composure broke and she felt her throat tighten. "I cannot. Please . . . do not ask this of me."

Lydia nodded again, just once, slowly. "You may go, sister Euodia."

The younger woman started to leave, then turned back for the goblet Lydia still held. "Are you done with this, mistress?" Placing it on the tray she was carrying along with the other goblets and cups, she left the room.

She washed out the platters and bowls and everything else in the big basin in the kitchen, pouring jugfuls of water heated over the fire, scrubbing at the platters with a coarse sponge. And as she did she thought of the words she and Lydia had exchanged, of the offer of marriage, of Lydia's accusation of pride, and of Epaphroditus's return.

Show me Your way for me, Lord Jesus, she prayed, her words matching the rhythm of her sponge on the wooden platters. *Lead me in the right path.* An hour ago she had been so sure she was on that right path. Now, all her certainty was gone, washed away with the water she poured down the drain in the stone floor. Without certainty, she had nothing to hold to but faith.

CHAPTER 14
EPAPHRODITUS

Sunlight glittered on the water like a handful of gems carelessly tossed on a tablecloth, dancing so brilliantly that Epaphroditus had to shut his eyes for a moment. When he opened them again, the faint green line of the shore was just visible across the shining water. Macedonia. Home, at last.

He had enjoyed his time in Asia, but he longed for home, for the familiar streets of Philippi, for the sounds of voices speaking Greek with his own accent. Longed to see his mother and grandmother again, to see Rachel and Simeon. To see everyone . . . old friends, family, neighbors. Yes, he longed to be in Philippi again—and dreaded it, too. His heart beat a little faster as the shore drew nearer.

"Eager to be back?" a voice said behind his left shoulder.

"Yes, of course. There's nothing quite the same as going home, is there?" Epaphroditus said to the short, wiry man who had just come up behind him.

Paul's keen eyes squinted at the shoreline. "I wouldn't know—everyone calls me 'Paul of Tarsus' but the truth is I haven't returned to my home city since I was—about your age. My parents are both dead, and I have no reason to go back there. Most of my journeys are to where I've never been before, rather than returning to familiar places."

"Is there no place that gives you this feeling—the feeling of coming home?"

The apostle thought a moment. "Jerusalem, perhaps. But I think that is true for every Jew—no matter where we were born, Jerusalem is our true home. I remember so well the first time I saw the Temple. It seems strange now to think that the Temple seemed the greatest thing I could see, the purest evidence of God's presence on earth—and yet all that time, the Lord Jesus was working in a carpenter's shop in Galilee, and I didn't know it. If I had known, I could have seen Him in the flesh. Perhaps He was even in Jerusalem, attending one of the feasts while I was there. I lived among Pharisees in Jerusalem when Jesus was preaching and healing in Galilee—but never even heard His name till shortly before He died, and even then thought little of it. I never saw Him with my own eyes. But if things had been just a little different, I could have met Him, could have journeyed with him as Peter and James and the others did." A wistful longing in his voice was so sharp that it sounded almost hungry. That surprised Epaphroditus. He imagined Paul as a man who wasted no time on regrets or thoughts of what might have been. But for the man who had dedicated his entire life to spreading the good news of Jesus, the realization that he might have narrowly missed meeting Jesus in the flesh must have been frustrating.

"You regret it very much—that you didn't have that opportunity?"

Like a man trying to dislodge a fly that had alighted on his hair, Paul shook his head vigorously. "No, no—I mean, yes, it would have been wonderful, but it would not have made me any more of an apostle than I am. What I was granted—seeing the Risen Christ in vision, being touched by His Spirit as I was—that is just as real as anything Peter or James or John experienced in Galilee. Just as certain."

The note of regret still sounded faintly behind his words, but Epaphroditus did not pursue the subject. Anyway, Paul didn't give him a chance.

"What matters is not that I might have seen Him in the past, but that I will see Him in the future—soon, I hope, when He returns to establish His kingdom. All that matters to me now is spreading the word so that the world will be ready when He comes."

Epaphroditus was silent. When Paul spoke of regret, of missed opportunities, he felt some connection to the man. But the apostle was so quick to hurry on to certainties, and these days Epaphroditus had few of those.

Both men were quiet for a few moments, then Paul spoke

again. "At least that is what matters most to me. I hope it does to you, too. But you have changed since we last met in Philippi, my young friend. I think you have lost your first love for Jesus, and that is a terrible thing."

The younger man glanced at Paul, who was not looking at him but toward the shore ahead. Epaphroditus was glad—he didn't think he could bear the piercing gaze of those eyes right now. He had not been able to put into words, even for himself, what had happened to him in Thyatira, but Paul had phrased it well. Yes, his love for Jesus—an infatuation, perhaps—had faded. Strange that it had proved so fragile, when that other forbidden love for his mother's slave girl remained so tenacious.

Yes, he had tried—he really had—tried both to forget Euodia and to remember Jesus. He had gone through the motions of being a good Christ follower in Thyatira, even though his mother's family had little respect for the new religion. It was easy after a while to stop meeting with the believers, to live as a pagan. When John Mark came to Thyatira and invited Epaphroditus to accompany him on a missionary journey, he had gone, hoping the experience would rekindle his faith. But the sermons, even the faith of the newly baptized, seemed empty and hollow to him. Maybe, he told himself, it was because John Mark was not the preacher Paul was. Perhaps being around the apostle again would make him fall in love with Jesus once more.

"It was harder, there—in Thyatria," was all he could find to say to Paul.

"You were never baptized, were you, lad?"

"No. Do you think—is that why? I mean, if I had been baptized, would I have —?" Unable to frame his question, he stumbled to a halt.

Now Paul looked at him directly. "You mean, does baptism keep a man from losing his faith? No. The Holy Spirit does that. But we must be vigilant. It is always possible, even after you have preached to others, to fall away yourself. Still, you should be baptized."

Epaphroditus shook his head. "Not now."

"We'll make port in about half an hour," a passing sailor announced to Paul and Epaphroditus. "Make ready."

Paul could be like a dog with a rat in its jaws when he latched onto a conversation, especially about someone's salvation, but to the younger man's surprise he let the subject drop after that interruption. He gave Epaphroditus a quick grin, though, as he turned to go below decks. "Don't think I'm done with you. We'll talk more of this later."

They landed in Neapolis as evening fell and spent the night at an inn there, sending a messenger ahead to Philippi to inform Lydia that they would be arriving the next day. In the morning Epaphroditus, Paul, Silas, and Timothy set off along the Egnatian Way to Philippi. As they drew nearer to the hills that sheltered the city, the place where he had been born, Epaphroditus felt the knot of tension inside him grow tighter. He should be simply happy about returning home—but things were rarely simple.

As they passed through the city gate, a small group of people came toward them from the busy crowd in the street. Epaphroditus recognized his mother first. Before she was close enough to touch, he saw in a moment that the passage of even a few short years had changed her. More gray filled her hair, more lines creased her high forehead than he remembered. Then she was in front of him, struggling to greet everyone formally while obviously longing to take her son in her arms.

He stepped forward to embrace her. "Mother, it's so good to be home."

She looked up at him, and he could see her eyes were brimming with tears. "You're a man," she said. "You look so like your father."

With her were Luke, Rachel, and Simeon. Epaphroditus greeted them all, as did the other men, and he tried not to glance behind them or over their shoulders. It was foolish to look for her—she was long gone, married and perhaps moved away, he reminded himself.

He didn't see her till the evening meal, when they were all seated in the courtyard of his mother's home. The place was bursting with people. Half the Christians in Philippi had shown up to see Paul and the other missionaries as well as to welcome him home. Among them he saw many familiar faces as well as those he didn't know, or people he recognized as ones who had not been Christians when he left. Paul was delighted with the way the community had grown. "There are twice, perhaps three times as many followers of Christ here as when I went away!" he said as they broke bread, leaning past Epaphroditus to address Luke. "This is wonderful! Do you know how many places I've been where the church we planted has dwindled away to almost nothing by the time I returned? Or where the same group of believers is faithful, but they've done nothing to spread the message—just remained like a stagnant pool. What has happened here in Philippi is wonderful!"

"We have nearly 100 baptized members now, and their children of course," Luke said, "and several more who are ready to be baptized. I'm afraid that when they heard you were coming they wanted to wait so that you could baptize them."

Paul frowned, a moment's irritation clouding his happiness. "That's no good—that won't do at all. We can't have people thinking they're better quality Christians if they were baptized by this apostle or that one—that's the way to create division. You should hear them back in Jerusalem, talking about belonging to the church of Peter or the church of John. There's only one church—the church of the Lord Jesus! Tell people that if you hear any fools bragging about who baptized them," he added, sweeping a glance around the table at those near him.

"Brother Paul, you will not believe who one of those converts is—the last man I ever thought would hear the message! If you will not baptize him, you must at least give him your blessing."

They all glanced up to see the speaker, a slight young woman in a simple gray robe. Epaphroditus felt as if his heart had stopped beating for a moment as Paul stood to take the girl's hands in both of his.

"Euodia! What a pleasure, what a delight to see you again, my dear sister!" The apostle leaned forward and kissed her cheek. "But who is this unlikely convert you've won to Christ?"

Her grave dark eyes sparkled a little, and she allowed herself a tiny smile. Epaphroditus thought she had never looked lovelier as she said to Paul, "One of my old masters, Demos. The very one who had you beaten and sent to prison for setting me free."

"No! Really? Praise the Lord, He does keep surprising us! It will be my very great pleasure to greet Demos as a brother in the Lord. Speaking of my time in jail reminds me, is my brother Clement here? And Syntyche? I have not seen them yet—"

Luke led Paul away to find the couple. Euodia remained standing in front of Epaphroditus and the others who were still eating. She held a tray with more bread and a bowl of fish sauce, tucked between her elbow and her hip to free up her hands when Paul had reached out to her. Now she took the tray in her hands again and offered it to Silas and Timothy. It could only have been a few seconds that she stood there, but it seemed forever before she dragged her eyes toward Epaphroditus and their gazes locked. He saw her cheeks flush and hoped his own face didn't give as much away.

"Welcome home, brother Epaphroditus, my master," she said formally.

Rising, he held out a hand, then realized her hands were still full. "It is good to see you again, sister Euodia."

"Thank you. The Lord has been gracious to me."

"And to me." He couldn't think of anything more to say, and even those words felt like a lie. In the little awkward silence Euodia inclined her head briefly and then turned away. He had to say something, do something—anything to make her look back at him again. "You will remember before I went away—I promised I would pray for you."

She did look back, though her dark eyes were unreadable and the blush had vanished from her cheeks. "I do remember."

"I did. Every day. I never forgot to pray for you." That, at least, was true. Even when he had found it nearly impossible to pray at all, he had repeated, "Lord Jesus, bless Euodia," before sleeping every night.

"Nor I for you, master," she said, then offered the tray to someone else.

Epaphroditus sat back down. He knew that if he looked up he would see his mother's eyes watching him closely. He could no more hide this from her than he could the color of his hair or his skin.

It was hopeless. Two years away had done absolutely nothing to make him forget. If he'd thought he was over this madness, it was only because he wasn't seeing her every day. Now, back in the house where she lived, sharing work and prayers and meals with her, there was no escape. If anything, his feelings were stronger than before. Time had passed, neither of them was married, his mother would still never approve of him marrying a slave—and he was hopelessly in love.

Somehow he bore the unbearable situation for a fortnight before he found a chance to speak with Euodia alone. She was working by herself in the dye works, struggling with a heavy vat. Taking it from her, he set it down near the fire, then reached out for her wrist before she could turn back to her work.

"Euodia. We must talk."

She looked so cool, so calm. Apart from that first evening when he had seen her blush, she had never betrayed any discomfort in his presence. Although she was so much more in control of her feelings than he was, he was sure those feelings were there.

"As you wish, master."

"Not as slave and master—nor as brother and sister in the Lord either, Euodia."

"How else can I speak to you?"

"Don't play the fool with me. You know what's in my heart. I spoke to you before I went away—and nothing has changed. I would still marry you, if I could."

She dropped her gaze to the ground. "But you cannot. You know your mother will not allow it. And I—I believe the Lord has called me to remain unmarried."

"So that's why you have not wed? Rachel told me that my mother tried to arrange a marriage for you and that you refused." He had hoped Euodia had rejected the match because she loved him, but it seemed that she loved Jesus more. "Why would God want you to stay unmarried?"

"I believe I can serve him better that way. It is His will." She started to turn away again, but this time he grabbed her upper arm and pulled her toward him.

"Is that the most important thing—God's will? Or my mother's will? What about your will, Euodia, or mine? What if we desire to be together? I know I desire it. What about you?"

Now she met his eyes with a clear steady gaze. "None of that matters. Our will is irrelevant. I am a slave to your mother and a slave to Jesus. You and I cannot be—together, as you say—without disobeying both of them. All we can do is put it out of our minds."

Her composure finally broke on those last words, and she said them more as a plea, as if she were begging him to forget. Tears brimmed in her eyes.

"I cannot put it out of my mind, Euodia. And I cannot accept a life of servitude to a God who won't even allow us the happiness of loving each other."

"Master, you cannot reject our Lord." Real fear flashed in her eyes.

"Perhaps I already have. Or perhaps He has rejected me." Now it was Epaphroditus who turned to go, striding out of the dye works, away from her, blinded by pain and anger. He paused once in the courtyard. "Please, Euodia?" He held out a hand, waiting.

She shook her head. Although he was too far away to see her face clearly, her hand brushed her cheek, perhaps wiping away tears. Epaphroditus again started toward the house. He was almost inside before he saw his mother standing in the shadow, watching him. While he didn't know how much she had seen, he could tell from her face that she must have guessed something of his purpose in seeking out Euodia.

"Epaphroditus—my son —" she said, reaching to touch him as he passed.

"Let me go, Mother." Continuing on through the house, he walked out into the street, not sure where he was going, only longing to be away from this house, his mother, Euodia, Paul, Jesus—everything that held him here, everything that stood between him and his desire. He couldn't believe that he had ever wanted to come home to Philippi.

His steps took him through their own district, through the busy commercial streets he knew well, through the bustling marketplace. On the south side of the market was a neighborhood Epaphroditus had never visited. Taverns, gambling dens, and other places of ill repute lined the narrow streets. He felt in the purse at his belt for a few coins as he hesitated at one low, dark doorway. Everything he had been taught, all his life, held him back for one moment. He thought of his mother and of Euodia—how disappointed they both would be to see him go down those steps into that place. Then he hardened his resolve. It was his mother and Euodia, both of them, who had set his feet on this path. If his mother had allowed him to marry Euodia— if Euodia had agreed to stand beside him—then he would have followed the Lord's way dutifully. But the two of them, together, had cut him adrift, and this was where he found himself.

He went down the stairs.

For the next few months Epaphroditus felt as if he was living a double life. At home he worked beside his mother and her household, learning to take his place in the business that was his by right. Although he had no more love for the dye shop than he ever had, he accepted now that he would be a dye merchant and made up his mind to be a wealthy and successful one.

He avoided Luke's room, where he had once enjoyed helping the physician prepare remedies and consult patients. He avoided Euodia. And he avoided Paul and Timothy and all the various church gatherings that centered in his mother's house. During the Sabbath hours he was seldom found at home. He had other friends now, in the city—some of them young men he had grown up with, who were able to introduce him to a whole world of pleasures that he'd never known. While he knew it pained his mother that he no longer worshipped with the Christians, he refused to speak with her about it.

Luke and Timothy both sought out opportunities to talk with him, but Epaphroditus grew skilled at evading such conversations. That hurt him a little, too, since he and Luke had once been so close, and Timothy, only a few years older than him, had been a good friend. But he did not have the strength to listen to rebukes or to be told he was living a sinful life.

The one person who didn't seem to bother him or badger him was, to his surprise, Paul. The older man never pulled him aside on the afternoon of the sixth day to ask if he were coming to worship with them that evening. Paul never gave him a stern look when he returned home late at night, drunk and disheveled. In fact, the apostle hardly seemed to notice him at all. Epaphroditus supposed that he was so busy preaching to the large groups who gathered to hear him all across the city that he had little attention to spare for his friend Lydia's son, now straying from the narrow path.

So he was taken quite off guard one afternoon after he had finished selling purple dyed linen to a customer to see Paul enter the shop with the wealthy noblewoman Flavia clinging to his arm. "Brother Epaphroditus!" Paul said. "Sister Flavia brings me some interesting news. You know that her husband, the magistrate, is ill?"

Epaphroditus had heard but thought little of it. But whatever Flavia was, she had been a valuable customer of his mother's for many years, and he had no desire to offend her. "I was very sorry to hear of your husband's illness," he said politely.

"He is dying," she said flatly. "So his doctors say—I've asked him to have Doctor Luke to see him, but he won't allow a Christian doctor into the house. I wish someone from the church could speak to him—to pray for his recovery, but also to tell him about Jesus. I have tried to be a good wife, even though I've defied his wishes by being a Christian. But oh, how I wish he could be saved before he dies!"

Unclear why they had come to him, Epaphroditus glanced from her to Paul. "You know how Aulus Gabinus set himself against Christ's followers," the apostle said. "But Flavia tells me he has had something of a change of heart."

"Not entirely," Flavia said. "I was sitting with him last night—I go every night to sit beside his bed for a few hours, and I try not to talk about things that will upset him. But he brought it up—he said someone had told him that preacher Paul, the troublemaker who got me baptized in the first place, was back in town. At first I thought he was going to say you should be thrown in jail again," she added apologetically, "but he said the strangest thing. He said, 'I don't want to listen to any of those Christ following friends of yours, but if I were ever to allow a Christian in the house it would be that man Paul. I'd like to see for myself the man who could cause so much trouble, all for the sake of his god.'"

Paul laughed. "And you have decided that's as good as an invitation to visit, is it not? Epaphroditus, I am going with sister Flavia now to speak to her husband. I want you to come with us."

"I? But—I have work to do here."

"Your mother says she can spare you for the rest of the afternoon. Please, I would like you to accompany us."

Everything in him wanted to say no, but when Paul gazed at him with those gray eyes, he felt paralyzed. Epaphroditus could not refuse the man. He didn't understand Paul's power, but he felt it unmistakably. "I'll get my cloak."

They rode in Flavia's carriage to her spacious home on the grandest street in Philippi. She and her husband had another home outside the city as well, Epaphroditus knew. It was the finest villa he had ever been inside, and he couldn't help staring a little wide-eyed at the wall hangings and furnishings. He knew that by the standards of many of the poor Christians of Philiippi that his mother's household was rich indeed, but he had never seen luxury on the scale that Flavia and her husband enjoyed.

Aulus Gabinus, magistrate, lay on a curtained bed in a quiet room that was hot and airless. His breathing was slow and labored, but his dull eyes brightened when his wife led Paul and Epaphroditus into the room.

"So this is the famous Paul of Tarsus, the great troublemaker," the man said with a wheezing laugh.

"I have been called worse things," the apostle answered with a smile, sitting down by the bed. Flavia left the room, and Gabinus gestured vaguely to Epaphroditus to sit down as well, without asking who he was or why he was there.

"Your wife hoped I would pray for you," Paul continued. "You do not believe in my God, but do you wish me to pray to Him for your recovery?"

Gabinus shrugged. "It makes no difference, does it? Pray to anyone you like—it can't hurt. I'm not sure I want to recover, anyway. I'm old and in pain. Dying is difficult work, and if I recover now I'll go through it all again in a few years. I'm sorry to leave my Flavia—she's a good woman, and our only son is dead, so she'll be all alone in the world when I'm gone. Apart from that—I wouldn't mind a rest."

So Paul prayed, in the simple, everyday language he always used for prayer, that the Lord's will might be done in Gabinus's life, and that whether he lived or died, God would be glorified. When Epaphroditus opened his eyes he saw the old man was smiling.

"Do you not have enough faith, then, to ask your god to heal a dying man?"

"I have great faith," Paul answered. "I would ask Him to raise the dead if needed, and I believe He would do it. He has done it before, as He Himself was raised from the dead. But I do not think healing of the body is what you need most. I think your spirit needs to be reborn before your body falls asleep. Then you will be ready to wake again on the morning when the Lord Jesus returns to call the dead from their graves."

"Your Jesus is coming back to wake up the dead? That's quite a claim, Paul of Tarsus."

"I believe He will do it, because He rose Himself, the firstfruits of all those who would die and rise again. And on that day, you will not be raised only to grow old and die again. You will be raised in a body like He had after His resurrection—perfect, glorious, immortal, incorruptible."

"You speak in dreams and myths," Gabinus sighed. "I've heard such things all my life."

"But this is no myth—not like those of your Roman gods," Epaphroditus said suddenly, breaking into the conversation. He hesitated, not sure he should go on, but Paul gave him a nod. "I've talked to men who saw Jesus Himself, before and after His death. They believe it was more than just a story—that He died and was raised again in the flesh."

"This young fellow speaks well," Gabinus said to Paul, with a nod at Epaphroditus. "You Christians train your acolytes well."

"He is not my acolyte. We believe the Holy Spirit speaks through people as He wills—sometimes when even they themselves are not sure of the power of their words."

"My wife would be very happy if I became a Christ follower on my deathbed," Aulus Gabinus said, drawing a long and shuddering breath. "I've had no use for your cult, as you know, but I would like to make my wife happy. Tell me what I would need to do."

For the next hour Epaphroditus listened, sometimes putting in a few words of his own, as Paul explained the Way of Jesus to the dying Roman. He thought the apostle would dismiss the man's motive as insincere or cynical—surely he couldn't pretend a deathbed conversion to Christianity just to make his wife happy? But Paul talked to him quite seriously until finally Aulus Gabinus said he was tired and needed to rest.

"You'll have to go away now. Bring my wife in before you go—you can say a prayer over me, and we'll hope that your Jesus will recognize me if He really does come back to call the dead from their graves. I'm afraid I'm not in any condition to be hauled down to the river and baptized."

"In the circumstances, I think Jesus will understand," Paul said. A moment later Flavia came into the room, dabbing at her eyes with a fresh handkerchief.

"Aulus Gabinus Sidonius, do you truly repent of your sins and wish to live a new life?" the apostle asked.

A ghost of a smile flickered across the old man's face. "I truly repent. If I had more life left to me, I would wish to be a better man."

"Do you believe Jesus died to give you forgiveness for sin, and rose again to give you freedom from death?"

"I suppose I do."

"Do you accept the Lord Jesus as your Savior, and His Father in heaven as your only God?"

Gabinus looked about the room till his eyes rested on Flavia. He heaved a heavy sigh and closed his eyes. "I do."

"Our God, Father of our Lord Jesus and our Father, this man Aulus Gabinus Sidonius lies here today as a sinner in need of forgiveness. Unless you choose to heal him today, he will soon face the darkness of death, but I pray that you will go with him and assure him that because you conquered death, he can too. Forgive his sins and call him to you when you come again to establish your kingdom, when all the righteous dead will be raised. In the name of our Lord Jesus Christ, Amen."

When they were walking home, Flavia's house well behind them, Epaphroditus waited for Paul to say something—to explain why he had brought him along, to comment on what had happened, perhaps to ask why Epaphroditus had spoken out in defense of the Way of Jesus when he no longer followed it himself. But the man continued on in silence, and finally it was Epaphroditus who asked a question.

"Was he sincere? Did he really believe in Jesus, or did he just pretend in order to please his wife?"

Paul smiled. "I don't know. No one on earth can know, only the man himself and our Lord Jesus. And perhaps the man himself doesn't truly know what his motives are. He is a cynical old pagan, and his heart is divided. But I believe there is one part of him that truly wants to believe and trust Jesus. With that one part he made his confession of faith, and we trust God to the rest."

"And you think there is value in that? For that much faith, you would baptize a man?"

"Jesus said with faith the size of a mustard seed, we could move a mountain. If we're talking of small faith and sincerity, what about yourself?"

"What do you mean?" It was the very conversation he had hoped to avoid with Paul, but now that it was here it seemed as inevitable as sunrise.

"You said that Jesus was raised in the flesh, that His story was not just a myth. Is that what you truly believe?"

"I—don't know. Anymore. Sometimes I believe it. But I don't want to—live as if I believe it."

"So there is, somewhere within your soul, a little seed of faith still springing through the dirt of rebellion and anger." Their eyes met briefly, and Epaphroditus nodded—it was all he could do. "Today you have seen what God can do with even the smallest seed of faith. Did John Mark ever tell you the story about the man with the demon possessed son?"

Epaphroditus nodded. "Wasn't he the one who said to Jesus, 'I believe ... please help my unbelief?'"

"Yes, that was the one. Aulus Gabinus might have prayed the same prayer today. It's a prayer Jesus always hears—and always answers."

They went the rest of the way home in silence through the crowded busy streets of Philippi, each man lost in his own thoughts.

CHAPTER 15
SYNTYCHE

It was a warm morning that promised a hot day ahead. Syntyche relished the splash of cool water as she offered a towel to a dripping wet woman who climbed up out of the river, her face radiant.

"God bless you," Syntyche said, kissing her on the cheek. "We are sisters now in Christ Jesus."

The woman responded by throwing her arms around Syntyche. A poor woman, she was a neighbor in the apartment building where Syntyche and Clement lived. Her husband was a laborer. *Like mine*, Syntyche reminded herself. She wished she didn't think in terms of such distinctions, that she could accept this woman as her sister in poverty just as readily as she accepted her as a sister in Christ. But the line from comfort to poverty was proving a hard one to cross.

But today she had little time to dwell on it. Clement helped the woman's husband out of the water, and another woman came behind him, grabbing Syntyche's outstretched hand as more people waded into the river.

Thirty people were being baptized today, and it wasn't the first such baptism they'd seen since Paul had returned. The community of Christ followers was twice the size it had been before his arrival, and many more people were coming to hear the Word, though they had not yet chosen to be baptized.

Syntyche kept busy all through that Sabbath morning, helping people into the water, greeting and welcoming them as they emerged from it. Nobody seemed to mind the chilly air. All up and down the riverbank the deacons and deaconesses assisted the new believers, while Silas, Luke, and Timothy stood waist deep in the water baptizing people in the name of the Father, the Son, and the Holy Spirit.

The best moment, for Syntyche, occurred near the end when she and Clement led their own son and daughter, Lucius and Julia, down into the water to be baptized. She could hardly believe how quickly her children were growing, but now that Julia was 14 and Lucius 13, they were both truly eager for baptism. It thrilled her to see how happily they followed the Way of Jesus. As Syntyche led a dripping Julia up out of the stream she caught sight, for a moment, of Lydia on the shore helping the other new believers, and she felt a moment's sympathy for the older woman. Who would have thought that Lydia's son, always such a good boy in his younger days, would reject the Lord and turn away from the church? It was a pity, and Syntyche felt sorry that the woman could not know the joy and pride she felt at this moment.

When the baptism concluded, the crowd on the riverbank began to sing. Syntyche loved singing. The hymns of praise to God reminded her of those she had once sang in the temple of Isis. She had a sudden sharp memory of watching the priests clothe the image of Isis in the dawn light as the worshippers chanted her awakening hymn. That worship—that temple—seemed very far away now. Syntyche had grown accustomed to worshipping a God she could not see. But she still loved the tangible parts of worship best: the songs, the water of baptism, the bread and wine of the Lord's meal. Never did she feel closer to her fellow believers than when they shared the broken bread and drank from the cup together.

That meal was being laid out now, on cloths spread out on the grass, and she hurried to help. In baskets and barrels behind it waited the second meal, less sacred but eagerly anticipated by hungry people who had been at the riverbank since early morning—fish, cheese, olives, and dates. Before they began that meal, Syntyche and the other deacons and deaconesses carried around the baskets of flat bread. Syntyche passed a piece to each of the small groups of people sitting in circles on the ground. In each circle one person tore off some bread and handed the rest to the next person. Behind her came Rachel bearing a jug of wine, which she poured into one common cup for each small group to share. Lydia's voice led them all in the ritual of the meal: "As the Lord Jesus said, Take, eat, this is my body which was broken for you."

Her duty of serving others finished, Syntyche took her own piece of bread and chewed it slowly, thinking of this Jesus, a Man she had never met but who had changed her whole life. Mostly for the better, she thought, although it was because of Him that four of them now lived in two rooms, that their beloved family slave had been given to Syntyche's sister, and that Julia had lost the prospect of a good offer of marriage. Put that like that, it didn't sound as if following Jesus had been such a wonderful blessing. Suddenly Syntyche laughed out loud in the middle of the sacred meal.

Fortunately, no one noticed except Clement, who turned to her curiously. "What is it?" he mouthed.

"I'll tell you later," she replied. But how to explain, really? They had been stripped of everything she depended on, every thing that had once made their lives worthwhile. Though she had mourned and protested, in the end she was surprised how little difference it made.

Oh, she still hated to think of herself as one of the poor, someone in need of charity rather than able to give it. But she had learned to make do with less, and in the process she had finally grasped the joy in the Holy Spirit that she heard others talking about. He really was with them, sustaining them through everything. Once she had heard Paul say, "If God is for us, who can be against us?" Finally she understood his meaning, now that she was sleeping in the same room where her family ate, now that she was washing her own laundry and watching her husband come home exhausted from a day's hard labor. In some strange way, letting go of security had set them free.

Somehow she couldn't help adding a silent prayer. *So, Lord, if You think I have learned what You had to teach me in this trial, and You are now ready to give us back some security, I will accept it gladly!*

Little did she realize how close her prayer was to being answered.

Flavia approached Clement and Syntyche together. The rich woman's husband, the magistrate Aulus Gabinus, had passed away a few weeks earlier. Although Flavia wore the dark garments of mourning, her face looked serene. Syntyche knew that Gabinus had accepted Jesus as Lord before his death, and though he had not been able to be baptized, Flavia's mind was more at peace with the certainty that her husband would be restored to her in the Resurrection.

Grief had obviously not blinded her to more practical matters. She seized each of their arms and said, "I've been waiting for a chance to speak with both of you together—I could have just discussed it with Clement, of course, but I would so like for both of you to consider this. With my husband gone, there will have to be many changes in my establishment. My steward, Rufus—" she nodded toward her slave, who was also a deacon and was currently talking to some of the new converts as they finished their meal— "will have even more work to do, now. I need to hire an under steward to oversee my villa here in the city. At the same time, my housekeeper is far too old and ill to work anymore. Rufus and I have discussed hiring a couple, husband and wife, who could share the work. I know what hard workers you both are—would you be willing to consider the position? You and your children would have rooms in my house, of course—which might be a more satisfactory arrangement than you have now."

How tactfully she put it. Surely she knew quite well that anything would be a more satisfactory arrangement than their present situation. Well, anything except moving back into Lydia's house.

Now she was considering living in another woman's home

again—but this was quite different, and with a glance at Clement, Syntyche could see how much the idea appealed to her husband. He had worked hard to feed the family since losing his position at the prison, but he had the ability to be more than a laborer. She knew he would enjoy the dignity and responsibility of being Flavia's under steward, and she had often heard him mention his respect for Rufus. As for herself, she was sure she could learn to manage a large household. After all, it was the work that she had been trained to do, except on a larger scale. In the widow Flavia's home they would not be receiving charity, but earning their keep. The woman could certainly have bought a couple more slaves to fill the roles she needed, but finding slaves who were sufficiently well trained and good workers was not always a certainty. She knew Clement and Syntyche and no doubt saw advantages to having a free couple in her service.

Syntyche barely needed to pause for thought or consult with her husband. In fact, Marcus Rufus had joined them quietly and was explaining to her husband about what the under steward's duties would involve. She turned back to Flavia. The magistrate's widow was not like Lydia—not a leader, not a manager. While she would provide them with work and a home and pay their wages, their lives would be their own. "My husband will have the final decision, of course," Syntyche said, "but for myself, I will say that I would be pleased to serve as your housekeeper, and would be honored to live and work in your home."

"Oh, wonderful!" Flavia exclaimed. "It will be a good thing, too, because—no, I'd better let Paul talk to you about that part. He said he would do it today, but of course he's always so busy with people, isn't he?"

Syntyche glanced at Paul standing in the middle of the crowd and wondered what he was supposed to discuss with her and Clement. But she didn't have long to wait. Before the meeting on the riverbank ended he led the couple aside.

"I understand sister Flavia has already made you an offer of employment and lodging in her house?"

"She has, and we have accepted gratefully," Clement said.

"Excellent. That will be most suitable. Let me tell you what I am thinking," Paul continued. "We have more than 200 Christians here in Philippi now, along with children and others who wish to attend services and who may someday become members. Even before these new converts were baptized, we had far more people than could meet comfortably in Lydia's house—you will know that yourselves, having lived there for a time."

Syntyche and Clement both nodded. "In most of the places where we have raised up churches," the apostle explained, "the believers meet in two or three different homes, but until now, here in Philippi, there has been no one except Lydia whose house was large enough to accommodate more than a few individuals. Flavia's villa was always an obvious choice, of course, but while her husband lived and was so bitterly opposed to Christ, we could hardly expect her to have a church in her house. The situation is different now. Flavia is quite willing to open her home to the believers for Sabbath worship and other services, but she does not see herself in the role of a leader as Lydia does. Rufus is a deacon and is glad to go on serving in that role, but a new congregation will need its own overseers as well. Since you two will be living in Flavia's home, and you have been such tireless workers for the gospel here in Philippi, I am asking if you will be the leaders of this new church."

For the second time that day Syntyche found herself taken completely by surprise. Were she and Clement really going to go in a single day from being impoverished to being comfortably employed and housed as well as the overseers of a new church? The reversal was as stunning as the loss of their home and livelihood had been nearly two years before. She felt unprepared to deal with so much change.

This time Clement said, as he had not done with Flavia, "My wife and I will need time to discuss this, and to pray together." Taking new employment, moving to a new home—those were small things compared to accepting such a position of responsibility in the Lord's work. Syntyche knew that she loved being a deaconess, and she dared to believe she was fulfilling her duties well. But an overseer? In a way, she would be representing Christ to the new converts—being their shepherd, as Paul often said. She wasn't sure she was ready for that. Clement—yes. Her husband was filled with the Holy Spirit. He was good enough to be an overseer, surely. But Paul had asked them both.

All around them people gathered up baskets of food, dividing the leftovers among the poorer members of the congregation. Syntyche thought she should be helping, but there were plenty of hands to share the task, so for once she just sat, next to Clement and Paul, watching.

"You have heard the story of the Lord Jesus and the miraculous meal of bread and fish, haven't you?" Paul asked. "How He fed 5,000 people with just five loaves and two fish?"

"A mighty miracle indeed," Clement said.

"And afterward, just like today, there were baskets full of leftovers to give to those who needed it most," the apostle observed.

"But this was no miracle," Syntyche said. "We brought all the food we needed, and ate most of what we brought."

The apostle smiled at her. "Dear sister Syntyche, don't you see that everything that has happened on this riverbank today is a miracle? Don't you recognize the true meaning of our Lord's act? It was not to show that He could multiply bread—He could make bread from stones, if He willed. No, it was to demonstrate that He will always have enough to supply our needs. No matter how little we bring Him—our courage, our faith, our talents—His grace is sufficient. We give Him our little, and He multiplies it."

Could Paul read her thoughts? She hoped what he said was true—that God's grace could multiply her gifts, however little. Because if she and Clement accepted the task of being overseers, she was going to need all the divine grace that she could get.

CHAPTER 16
LYDIA

She sat in her chamber tallying her business and household accounts, half listening to the sounds from the rest of the house. They were those of men preparing for a journey, packing their bags, saying goodbyes. Spring air drifted through the window. After leaving Philippi last fall, Paul and his companions had spent the winter traveling through Macedonia and Greece. Luke had remained at Philippi, but now the others had returned on their way back to Asia, and Luke was going with them.

Tonight they would eat the Passover meal together, and Paul would preach a farewell message to the whole assembled community—not here, but at Flavia's villa, where even there they could barely fit everyone unless they squeezed in tightly. Tomorrow morning Paul and Luke would leave to join the other members of their party at Troas.

Lydia knew Luke was torn over this decision, and he still spoke of returning to settle in Philippi someday. But his greatest desire was to return to Jerusalem, to talk to the apostles and others who had known Jesus and to peruse the stories written down about them. His goal was still to write the definitive account of Jesus' life, something that could not be done in Philippi.

Although she didn't like to admit to herself, Lydia realized how much she would miss the physician. He had become as close as a brother to her during the years he had lived in her home, as close as Simeon or Rachel. Her mother-in-law Helena had died during the winter. The older woman had been fond of Luke, and the doctor truly grieved for her passing. Luke was very much a member of the family, and Lydia relied on him in a thousand ways. Even with the other members of her close knit household around her, she had the feeling that with him gone, she would be, in some sense, alone against the world.

She relied on him most, these days, for guidance about her son. When Luke had first come to them, Epaphroditus had looked up to him, and the physician had at least partly filled the role of the boy's long dead father. In the months—nearly a year, now—since Epaphroditus had returned from Thyatira, it was clear that he no longer saw Luke in that role. In fact, he avoided the older man as he did many of his mother's Christian friends.

"He is afraid I will lecture him," Luke said once when Lydia pointed it out.

"And would you?"

"Why? He gets enough of that from you," Luke smiled. Then his face grew serious. "Lydia, I know your fear for the boy, and I would not belittle it. But lecturing him will do no good now. He is a young man and cannot be ordered to follow Jesus. The Holy Spirit must convict him, and I do not think scolding will help with that."

She tried hard not to scold. But it had been a difficult year. In some ways Epaphroditus was a model son. He was polite and respectful to her, and his former lack of interest in the dyeing business had transformed into, if not wild enthusiasm, at least an adult competence. As the days passed he took on greater responsibility, overseeing the dye works, dealing with customers. In business affairs she trusted him. And she could not complain of his behavior at home.

But when working hours ended he left the house as swiftly as possible, never lingering to spend time with her or Luke or even with Rachel or Simeon. As for Euodia, he ignored the slave girl completely, paying even less attention to her than he did to the other slaves. He had a group of friends now, other young men from merchant families who were at the threshold of adulthood, and who used their newfound freedom and wealth for an endless round of entertainment. Lydia knew these boys—many of them had grown up with Epaphroditus, but before he had gone to Thyatira she had seen him drifting away from them, avoiding their foolishness, choosing friends from among the Christ followers instead. Now he had thrown himself into this group of reckless boys with abandon. The sad tales of wayward sons that she had always heard from her neighbors—of drunken brawls and gambling debts, of young men who took actresses and dancers as their mistresses—such tales now included *her* son. In vain she had tried to talk to him, sought to make him see sense.

Usually he avoided such conversations, but the last time she was able to make him sit and listen to her—a few weeks ago, now—he was blunt, though not rude. "Mother, what have you to complain of?" he asked reasonably. "You don't like my friends. Well enough, but I don't bring them into this house. I drink too much wine—but I don't come home roaring drunk and beat the slaves and tear down your wall hangings. I gamble—but only with my own wages that I take from the business. I have never lost or endangered your money, nor will I. I haven't settled down to marry the good Christian wife you dream of—but I am young yet, half my friends aren't married either, and in the meantime I have dishonored no girl of good family or brought shame on your name. Truly, mother, as reprobates go I must be one of the best in Philippi!"

His laughter was so hearty that she almost wanted to join with him, but it was too serious a matter for joking. "What you are saying, then, is that as long as you keep your activities within limits, as long as it does not threaten my money and my business and my reputation and my peaceful house, I have no cause to complain?"

Epaphroditus grew solemn too. "No cause to complain, and truly, Mother, no right to give me orders, for I am a grown man now. I respect you and I love you, but I don't have to obey you. The only thing you really have to complain of is that I am not a Christ follower like you."

That was when her composure broke, and she began to cry. "The *only* thing, Epaphroditus? But that is *everything!*"

He gently laid a hand on her shoulder. "That is where we disagree, Mother. And there's no point in discussing it further, is there?"

Since that day she had made no more attempts to speak to Epaphroditus about anything other than business and household matters. Usually he disappeared during Sabbath hours, and his absence from worship services was an ache that she could never get over. But she knew that both he and Luke were right— Epaphroditus was a man now, almost 20 years old. If anything was going to win him back to Jesus, it would not be nagging from his mother.

She prayed for him now and of course asked the others to pray as well, but she was beginning to accept that that was all she could do.

Her short-lived illusion of acceptance shattered when Epaphroditus himself walked into her chamber. He looked cheerful and full of energy and gave her a warm smile as he said, "Mother, may I see the accounts? Tertius Antonius has sent his steward with payment for the dyes I sold him, but I'm sure it's only half what they owe. I told him I'd look it up."

Lydia began sifting through the pages in front of her, searching for Antonius's accounts, but when she saw her son leaning over the table she pushed the sheets toward him. After all, she had to begin trusting him to do these things on his own.

"There! You see?" he said a moment later, passing the account back to her. "This is twice they've underpaid us."

"Be cautious," she warned him. "It may seem foolish to say the man is a valuable customer when he regularly fails to pay his bills, but he is well respected and someone of influence. The challenge is to get him to pay without angering him and losing his business."

Epaphroditus's smile broadened. He was turning into a handsome man, warm and pleasant and likable, and at moments like this Lydia could almost convince herself that everything was well, that she need have no worries for his future. "That is the skill I need to learn," he agreed. "You have such a gift for dealing with people—they all like you, but they respect you and pay their bills promptly as well. Perhaps it would be best if you dealt with Antonius?"

"No . . . I think you should do it. We learn by doing, after all.

I will pay a visit to the man myself as a last resort, but I think that if you negotiate with his steward, you will learn a great deal—and you may get the money as well."

Her son looked at her for a long moment, the sheet of parchment in his hand. "Thank you for trusting me, Mother. It means more than you know."

While there were so many things she could have said in that suddenly intimate moment, what she did say was, "You know that tonight is the Passover feast."

"Yes. Yes, I remember that. In fact," he added before she could say anything more, "that reminds me of something. Tacitus spoke to me—he and Ariane wish to marry. Apparently—did you know this?—Ariane promised Grandmother she would never marry while Grandmother lived. Now that she is released from that vow, they would like to marry. They have wanted to do so for years."

"Really?" Lydia had had no idea there was any particular affection between the two slaves. It surprised and troubled her to realize that such a thing could go on in her household without her knowledge. She'd always thought of herself as being aware of everything that affected her family, but this had passed her by completely. But then, Ariane was a reserved woman and Tacitus rarely spoke at all. No doubt they had carried out their romance with utmost discretion.

"They have served me faithfully for many years now," she said finally. "Do you think that along with granting them permission to marry, I should free them? Would they wish that?"

"That was the very thing I was about to suggest. They are very loyal to us, and I think they would wish to remain in your employ, but freedom would be an appropriate reward for their long service. And an appropriate time to do it, too."

"Passover?"

"Yes, Passover. I have not forgotten everything you taught me. I know the slaves are freed at Passover."

"All the slaves? Should I free Euodia, too, then?" She had

wrestled with the thought on and off throughout the years. Once, she had feared that if she had manumitted the slave girl, Epaphroditus might again talk of marrying her. It seemed unlikely he would want to do that now, and certainly Euodia, devout and dedicated to the Lord's work as she was, would have little interest in marrying the man her son was becoming. If anyone in her service deserved freedom, it was certainly Euodia—yet something still held Lydia back.

The light went out of Epaphroditus's eyes and his smile disappeared behind a blank mask. "I do not know what might be good for Euodia, Mother. Discuss it with Luke, or ask Euodia herself what she wants."

So he still cares for her, then, she thought. She had wondered if he had become indifferent to the girl he had once loved, but now she knew better. This was not indifference. Talking, or even thinking about Euodia, was still too painful for him. No parade of actresses and loose women could change that.

"Come with us tonight—to Flavia's," Lydia said impulsively, even though she knew it was the wrong moment for that invitation. "Let us eat the Passover together as one family. And it will be your chance to say farewell to Luke and Paul. Who knows if we will see them again in this life?"

"Who knows, indeed? And who knows if there is any life beyond this one in which we will see them? I will say goodbye to them today, in private. Go eat your Passover with the other believers. There's no place for me at that table." Turning, he left the room.

Lydia sat alone, staring at rows of names and figures on pieces of parchment, seeing nothing through the blur of her tears. When she heard a footstep in the doorway she looked up, hoping against hope that he had come back to soften his refusal, perhaps even to agree that he would attend the feast. Instead, her visitor was Paul.

She was amazed the apostle was even in the house, much less that he had time to slip into her chamber for a quiet conversation with her. He spent his last days in Philippi visiting among the new converts and the would-be converts, doing the work that mattered more than anything else to him. But he sat down on the bench across the table from her and said, "Why is my loyal yokefellow crying?"

She smiled through her tears. "I feel—overwhelmed, I suppose. You are going away again, and Luke is leaving, and I have to carry the burden of this church here alone without his help. And my son—I wish he were ready to stand beside me, to take his place in leading the congregation just as he is assuming his role in our business. But instead he is turning his back on our faith, and I think my heart will break."

Paul reached across the table and took her hand. "Dear Lydia. What a tower of strength you are for all around you, for everyone here in Philippi. What this little company of believers would have done without you, I do not know. But please don't think you're bearing the burden all alone. The burden is not ours, but the Lord's. It is in His strength, not our own, that we stand. Indeed, His strength is perfected in our weakness. When you feel least able to manage, that is when you must rely on Him."

"I try. I really do," she said, wiping away tears with the back of her hand and straightening. Really, it was most unlike her to indulge in tears and self-pity.

"I will keep lifting up Epaphroditus in my prayers, as I pray for you all," the apostle continued. "Leaving Philippi makes me feel both sadder and happier than in any other city where I've said goodbye—sadder because I leave so many good friends behind, but happier because I know the church here is built on a firm foundation of faith and has strong leaders who will keep it in the Way of Jesus. You will keep doing that, won't you, my yokefellow?"

"I will," she promised. "Come, let's get ready to go to Flavia's and prepare the feast."

CHAPTER 17
EUODIA

"Where are you going?" Rachel asked as Euodia slipped past, pulling a cloak around her shoulders.

"To the marketplace. I promised to meet some people there— a group of women who have been learning about the Scriptures and the Lord Jesus." Everyone in the household was used to her comings and goings. When she finished her work in the house and in the dye shop she usually went off to someone's home to study and teach. But today Rachel gave her a sharp glance.

"In the marketplace?"

"They chose the meeting place. I suppose it's convenient for them," Euodia said, trying to keep her voice light.

Rachel wasn't fooled. "Who are these women, exactly?"

Euodia was tempted to continue being evasive, but it wasn't in her nature. She rarely hid the truth, no matter what the consequences. "They are priestesses of Cybele."

"You are going to teach Jesus to priestesses of the Great Mother? On the steps of her shrine, no doubt! Are you a fool, Euodia? You'll be arrested again!"

"If that is the Lord's will for me, so be it. His servants have been imprisoned before and will be again. These women sought *me* out, Rachel. Would you have me ignore a call to preach for Jesus?"

"No, of course not." The harsh lines of the older woman's face softened a little, and she placed a hand on Euodia's forearm. "I would only have you be cautious. Meet with them in secret, as most of our leaders have been doing since the city officials began issuing fines." The benign ignorance that Philippi's rulers had once held toward the cult of Jesus the Christ had begun to shift. Times had changed since Paul had made his last visit to Philippi nearly four years ago. The Emperor Nero might be far away in Rome, but his every move and decision rippled throughout the Empire, especially here in this very Roman city. Nero was capricious and Rome under his leadership was unsettled. During such times people liked order and stability—and that meant allegiance to the old gods. New religions—especially one that forbade its followers to worship the traditional gods and the emperor—were unwelcome.

Several Christian leaders in Philippi had been arrested and given fines or warnings for preaching about Jesus in public. Euodia herself had been warned once, then on the second occasion the authorities had brought her home. Lydia had paid her fine, and the city officials had told her to whip her slave and keep her in better order. Of course Lydia had not punished Euodia, but she had told her to use more discretion in the future.

"Jesus warned His followers that persecution would come," the young woman had replied.

"Yes. But I don't think He told them to go out looking for it, though. No one is saying we should stop preaching or teaching, but preaching in the marketplace is borrowing trouble. No one will prevent us from going to people's homes, or inviting them to ours."

"I've never known Paul to avoid trouble," Euodia had protested. "Is he not in prison in Judea even now?"

Lydia gave her a long, thoughtful look. "I've spoken to you before about the sin of pride, Euodia," she had said at last. "You are not Paul. And you would do well to remember that."

The slave knew her duty to her mistress. She did not argue back, not then or ever. She held her tongue, being good at controlling her emotions and keeping silent even when waves of anger or indignation rolled over her. Sometimes she felt that her whole life since becoming a Christian had been an exercise in learning to keep quiet, choking back anger when she felt it, stifling the desire to argue or criticize. While she hoped it was the work of the Holy Spirit, making her more gentle and loving, the feelings raging inside her didn't change. When she cared passionately about anything, it was hard to keep silent.

After the fine and the second arrest she had tried to stay within the boundaries of the law, to obey both the city officials and her mistress. She spoke about Jesus only in private as she taught the scriptures to groups of women as she had always done. And she enjoyed her role as deaconess of the church that still met in Lydia's house. The church was growing, with many new converts, including a number of Jews who had moved to Philippi and converted to the Way of Jesus. With this group at their center and Rachel, Simeon, and Euodia in positions of leadership, the church in Lydia's house remained faithful to the scriptures and to the God of Israel, observing Jewish law along with their worship of the Lord Jesus Christ. It angered Euodia to see the other church, the congregation in Flavia's house, drifting away from those laws and traditions, rejecting Scripture. But that was one of the many things about which she tried to swallow her anger. Lydia had often said that dissent and quarrelling between the church groups was a far more serious matter than allegiance to the law. Euodia didn't agree, but as Lydia was both her mistress and overseer she tried, for now, to keep quiet.

But keep quiet about Jesus? When these priestesses had sent word to *her*, asking her to teach them? Of course she knew it was risky. She had met with them twice before in private, but it was they who had suggested she come publicly to speak to them before the shrine of Cybele. They wanted to attract attention, to make a public statement about their new allegiance to Jesus. How could Syntyche possibly reject such an opportunity?

"Rachel, sister, I am in God's hands," she said now to her friend and sister-in-Christ. She was glad it was Rachel and not Lydia who had intercepted her. Rachel was gentler, more inclined to let things pass. Lydia probably would have ordered her to stay at home, and that would have led to a confrontation Euodia did not want to have. But Lydia was busy with a customer in the shop, and Rachel and Simeon were both in the dye works. Leaving Rachel with the assurance that she would take no unnecessary risks, Euodia hurried through the courtyard toward the front entrance of the house, sure there was no one else now who could question her.

But she was wrong. Just at the door she met Epaphroditus, gorgeously dressed in a striking new toga, also on his way out the door.

Lowering her head, she slid her gaze away with a quick, "Greetings, master," and waited for him to leave before going out herself.

But he paused and turned back in the doorway. "Look at us— both ready to go out into the streets of the city." His voice had a mocking edge that she was used to hearing—not that he spoke to her often, but it was his habitual tone when addressing anyone in the household. "I am off to get roaring drunk with a crowd of fellows, as one of our number is about to be shackled to a wife—and you, I suppose, are off to preach a sermon. Quite the contrast, aren't we?"

Euodia cursed the blood that flowed to her cheeks as she tried to meet her master's eyes. "No one would think of comparing us, sir—slave and master as we are."

"No, of course not. Everyone would think I'm better off by far—but you think differently, don't you?" His smile had an edge like a knife blade. "You think you're walking in the narrow path of righteousness, and I'm on that slippery broad path to perdition. Isn't that right?"

She wondered if he had been drinking already, though he was usually very scrupulous about observing the proprieties in his mother's house. Certainly this was the longest conversation he'd had with her in many months. Usually he ignored her, and if they spoke at all his comments were as flippant as they were today, but much briefer.

"Forgive me, master, but with your permission I must be going."

Epaphroditus lounged in the doorway, one hand on each of the doorposts, leaning slightly toward her. He looked as though he had no intention of letting her pass.

"In such a hurry? No comment at all about the state of my soul? You seem very eager to go off and save the souls of others, Euodia. Have you no care at all for mine?"

She took a step backward—there was still an arm's length between them, but it felt much too close. This, of course, was the other feeling she had fought to keep contained all these years—her powerful attraction to him, still alive even now when she ought to feel nothing but disapproval and pity toward him. It had always been an impossible match, even when he was a follower of Jesus. Now, she knew, the feeling that drew her toward this man was a snare and a temptation. It was purely sinful for her to notice the long dark lashes fringing his gray eyes, the high sculpted bones of his face, the breadth of his shoulders as he stood in the doorway, blocking out the late afternoon sun. *Lead me not into temptation,* she prayed.

"I do care for your soul, master. You asked me once to pray for you. I have never once failed in that duty."

"Your duty. Well, I suppose I deserve no better," he said, and she saw a flash through those mocking and flippant gray eyes of something that lay beneath. *He is lost, in more ways than one,* she thought. But Euodia knew that she was not, could not be, the one to save him, not without losing herself.

His gaze held hers for a moment, and her cheeks burned even hotter. Although he said nothing more, his look reminded her that he was her master. Most men did not trouble to respect the virtue of their female slaves. For a moment she felt a shiver of fear. Epaphroditus had made it quite clear that he had rejected Christ and the values the Christians held. Could this sudden interest in talking to her have a more sinister motive? She took another step backward.

But he did not pursue her. "Pray on, then, Euodia, for all the good it does." He turned to go, then looked back over his shoulder. "You are not going to make a nuisance of yourself preaching in public so that my mother will have to pay a fine for you again, are you?"

The question was unexpected, but once again she found herself unable to lie. "I will do as God calls me to do, master."

"Don't be a little fool—we can't afford to be always paying

your fines," he snapped. Then, in quite a different tone, he added, "Have a care for yourself, Euodia." With that he left, and she watched his long easy stride down the street for longer than she would have cared to admit to anyone.

She was late, now, for her appointment with the priestesses, and she hurried through the crowded streets. If all went well she would bring them back with her to Lydia's house—but she was by no means certain that all would go well, despite her brave words to Rachel about being in the hands of God. She had observed that those divine hands seemed not to mind placing their loyal servants in the middle of trials.

The women were there, three of them, dressed in the robes of their office and waiting on the steps outside the small shrine, which was on a street corner in the busy marketplace. Worshippers went into and out of such buildings regularly to make offerings and say prayers. Already the sight of three priestesses standing outside on the steps had attracted a few curious onlookers.

"Sister Euodia, we thought you had forgotten us!" one of them said as she approached.

"Never. I was delayed at my mistress's house. But now I am on the business of my heavenly Master, my Lord Jesus. That always takes first place."

The uncertainty, the tumble of confused emotions that had roiled inside her since her conversation with Epaphroditus—all that dropped away. What did her feelings matter, anyway? Epaphroditus had chosen his path—though she still prayed he might turn aside from it—and she had chosen hers. This was hers—to do God's will. He had called her here today, and she was sure He had not summoned her to whisper His name in back rooms, but to shout it from the rooftops.

"Now you have called me sister, my friends, but I wish you would become my sisters in truth by being baptized into Jesus Christ!" She spoke to the three women, but she had pitched her voice to carry, and sure enough the few onlookers drew closer as she spoke, and a few more stopped to listen.

"What does Jesus require of his devotees? What do we need to do to become His followers?" another of the women asked.

"Only repent of your sins, believe that He has forgiven you and will grant you eternal life, and be baptized," Euodia answered.

"But any god will forgive my sins if I bring the right offering!" a male voice from the growing throng of people nearby cried out. "Why should I follow yours, and reject all the others?"

That was it, then—Euodia launched into a sermon, retelling the familiar story of Jesus and explaining to her hearers about His life, death, and resurrection, and His promise to come again.

More people gathered in the street around her and pressed closer to hear. Some were attentive and eager to listen to her message, but in the back of her mind as she scanned some of the faces in the crowd, she realized that some were there to criticize and condemn. "I know you!" one voice called out when she paused for breath. "You're the slave of Lydia the dye merchant. Can't your mistress keep order in her own house?"

"A woman and a slave, preaching about this Jewish superstition here in front of the shrine of Cybele! It's a disgrace!" someone else added.

Paying no attention to them, Euodia went on with her message. But it was harder to ignore the delegation of priests and priestesses who soon emerged from the shrine to see what the commotion was. A man in priestly garments approached and grabbed Euodia by the upper arm in a painful grip.

"Who are you, woman, and what do you do here?"

"She's preaching about this Jesus of the Jews!" someone shouted. "And your priestesses are listening to her."

"She's telling us not to worship the gods of Rome or the emperor!" another added.

"Is this true?" the priest demanded. "Are you spreading your vile Eastern superstition on the very steps of the Great Mother's shrine?"

"I am preaching the good news of Jesus of Nazareth, the Son of God," Euodia replied clearly.

"There are laws against this!" the priest exploded. "Will you people never learn? I'll have an example made of you!"

He dragged her down off the steps and into the street. Euodia wanted to tell him that she would go willingly. But he enjoyed the show of force, shouting at her all the way. The same crowd that had gathered to hear her speak now followed along as the priest led her through the streets.

She remembered how Paul and Silas had been arrested and jailed all those years ago—had it really been nearly 10 years?—for setting her free from the evil spirits that possessed her. Euodia had not been there when the two missionaries had been taken away, but she hoped she was showing a little of their spirit, facing the magistrates as they would have done.

But, she remembered, Paul had gotten them out of that mess eventually by revealing that he and Silas were Roman citizens. After that, they had to be treated with more respect. She was a female slave, as low in society as it was possible to be. And when the magistrates saw her and she gave her name, they would remember—or find in the records—that she had been twice warned against preaching in public. Perhaps she might get away with only another fine. But she might just as well be whipped or imprisoned.

Go with me, Lord, she begged as her captors approached the hall where the magistrates sat. She had spoken many brave words today, but words were easy. Now her courage was about to be put to the test.

CHAPTER 18
SYNTYCHE

With the midday meal cleared away and her morning responsibilities finished, Syntyche allowed herself a few moments to relax. She sipped a cup of lemon water and thought over her mental list of things she had to accomplish in the marketplace that afternoon. Even with her body at rest, her mind could never truly be quiet.

Along with her usual duties of overseeing the kitchen and household slaves to make sure Flavia's villa was clean and everyone in it well fed, and of her responsibilities to the church, she had the added burden of planning her daughter's wedding for the following day. Not that it was really a burden. She was glad her Julia, now a young woman in her late teens, was making a good match.

Syntyche had worried for years about Julia's marriage prospects. For a time there had been no families in the church of suitable social standing with sons of the right age. Andreas, a young cabinetmaker, had become a Christian just two years before along with his parents, and Clement had not waited long to speak to the young man's father about a match. Fortunately the young people liked each other, which made matters easier. The marriage was now to be celebrated tomorrow.

On top of all that busyness there was the problem of Flavia's illness. Their wealthy patroness had had four healthy years of widowhood, mourning her husband but also enjoying the freedom her new status gave her. She relied on Clement, Syntyche, and Rufus for the practical details of running her city villa and country estate and managing her husband's large fortune. Through their efforts she was able to entertain a steady stream of guests in her home and open her doors to Christ followers in Philippi, as well as those who traveled through the city on their way to other places, which often included itinerant preachers. Paul and his companions had not come again since their last visit in the spring after Gabinus's death, but now many Christian evangelists made the journey from Asia into Macedonia and beyond, bringing the gospel to new territories. Flavia, with her gift for hospitality, enjoyed welcoming such people into her home.

All that had changed in the past few months as her health began to fail. She experienced frequent fevers and coughs, and her formerly plump frame grew wasted and thin. During the past few weeks she had spent most of her time in her sleeping chamber, confined to bed. Someone always had to sit with her, for she grew lonely and fretful if left alone. Syntyche was grateful to Julia for taking this responsibility much of the time, but now, busy with her wedding preparations, the girl had few moments to sit with the old woman.

In her mind Syntyche ran through the plans for the morrow. Julia's gown, woven by the bride herself, and her flame colored veil waited for the morning. Andreas would arrive accompanied by family and friends, including many of the members of the church that met in Flavia's house. Others would already be here at the villa, helping Julia prepare for the marriage. After the couple had stated their intent to marry and Clement led them in the prayers and blessings that would replace the traditional offerings to the pagan gods, the feast would begin. Syntyche and the slaves had planned its every detail. But although she had checked her lists several times, again she found herself worrying about whether everyone would have had enough to eat before they all left, later in the day, to accompany the new couple through the streets to Andreas's house.

Clement came into the bedchamber just then, stretching and sighing. He looked as tired as she felt. Both of them had worked hard for the nearly four years they had been employed here—harder than they had done since his army days, Syntyche thought, and they had been 20 years younger then. But it was good work in return for a very comfortable home, and Syntyche would not complain.

"I'm just ready to go to the market," she said, getting to her feet. "Can you think of anything else we need?"

"Not unless you find a lot of experienced laborers standing around looking for work," he said with a smile. "Two of the men we hired to repair that courtyard wall didn't show up, and I had to put two of the household slaves onto the job with them. I don't know if we'll have it finished for tomorrow—they aren't experienced in that kind of work, and I've ended up doing a good deal of it myself. I just have to wash and change now before I go negotiate with the mosaicist again—it's ridiculous, what that man is charging for his work!"

"I know!" Syntyche had tried to dissuade Flavia from having a new mosaic laid in the floor of her courtyard. "Clement, think of the hungry people who could be fed with the money she's putting into that floor! She could have plain tiles and give the rest to the Lord's work—we have church members practically starving down in the tenements. How can we justify paying a mosaicist just to make the floor look more attractive? It's only for people to walk on!"

He smiled, as he often did, at his wife's fervor. "We couldn't, my love. But she can, and it's her house and her money. You know she has often argued that things made with skill and beauty bring honor to God."

"A hollow argument." Syntyche had never believed it for a moment, though some in their congregation—both rich people and the craftsmen and artisans who served them—would agree it was so. "Look at the pagan temples—the gold, the statues, the mosaics! Then look at our Lord Jesus, who had no house, no fine things, nothing but the shoes on His feet and the clothes on His back. What would he have had to say to a mosaicist—or a seller of fine dyes—or to our mistress Flavia? You know what He would say—leave it all behind, sell it and give to the poor, and come follow me!"

Clement was frowning now. "Remember all that Flavia has done for the poor, for the church—for us, even. And her generosity is not yet finished."

"What do you mean?"

"She has spoken to me and to Rufus about her will. As she and her husband had no children, she wishes to leave her entire estate—both houses and all the land—to the church."

"To the church?" Syntyche had heard nothing of this. With the old woman fading so fast, the disposition of her property after her death was a real concern, but Syntyche had given it no thought except to wonder what she and Clement would do when their employer died. She had assumed the property would pass to some male relative.

"Yes, that is her desire. I think what she would like is for the country property to be sold and the money distributed among the needy in our community, but for the church to retain this villa in the city and continue to use it for meetings and to house Christians in need of a place to stay."

"What a wonderful idea!" she exclaimed, her annoyance at the thought of the mosaic entirely forgotten. "But—can she do that? Legally?"

"Ah, that's the question. I doubt she can. There are many laws about who can own property, and the city magistrates will no doubt look for some relative in the male line of Flavia's husband to inherit. It's not unusual for people to make gifts of their property to the temples of the gods, but the magistrates will hardly recognize the Christian church as a body that can own property."

Indeed, the city magistrates barely tolerated the local church congregations these days. Philippi had nearly 300 Christians now, meeting in four different house churches. While in the early days the worst anyone had endured was ridicule or the loss of a position because of being a Christian, the fear of greater reprisals hung over them. During the past year several Christians had been fined for preaching in public places and warned against doing it again. Clement had himself been one of them.

Syntyche herself was no preacher. Her service for the Lord kept her busy working among the poor, the sick, those whose need of help and encouragement was greatest. As she found her purse and began counting out coins for the market, she thought how glad she was that Clement was a cautious man. He had changed his tactics after receiving a fine and a warning though he still went to people's homes to preach and teach the gospel, as did most of the other church leaders. But most of them had stopped preaching in public places, except for a few foolhardy ones like Euodia, who seemed determined to court trouble.

Considering it folly, Syntyche had no respect for that kind of courage. What was the good of courting trouble? How would it serve the cause of Jesus if Clement got himself thrown in the jail he had once guarded? Perhaps it was different for Euodia—an unmarried woman and a slave, with no family or responsibilities to protect.

Long ago Syntyche had come to the conviction that Euodia was actually trying to get herself arrested. The woman simply loved drama and attention. Syntyche's fondness for Euodia hadn't grown over the years. She had softened toward Lydia, now that the dye merchant was growing older. And she liked Rachel and Simeon well enough, even though she disapproved of the way they clung to Jewish customs and encouraged the Jews in their church to do the same. But she still couldn't warm to Euodia. Although she had tried hard enough to be courteous through the years, to act like a sister in the Lord, she had eventually concluded that it was best if they just avoided each other.

Fortunately, that was easier to do these days. Since the local Christian community had divided into several smaller house churches, it met together as a whole only on rare occasions— at Passover and a few other celebrations or when a visiting missionary came through the city. At such times they assembled at the old place of prayer by the river outside the city walls—once the site of a pagan temple, then a gathering place for Jews and God-fearers, now a Christian place of worship, celebration, and baptism.

But most Sabbaths, smaller groups met at each of the four house churches, and each congregation had its own deacons, deaconesses, and overseers who took care of their own business. The leaders of each house church came together as a group from time to time to make plans for the church in Philippi as a whole. During such occasions Syntyche tried to avoid Euodia and concentrated on not letting the other woman irritate her too much.

Syntyche brought herself back to the present and said farewell to Clement as she left her chamber. The bride-to-be was busy with last-minute preparations for the wedding, so Syntyche went by herself to the marketplace.

The afternoon hours flew by as she pushed her way through the busy and crowded stalls looking for the items she needed for the next day's feast. She encountered several people she knew and paused to chat with each, inviting them all to share the wedding celebration—and worried after each encounter whether she was asking too many people, whether there would be enough to feed them all.

The afternoon sun was slanting low and the shadows long when the basket she carried over her arm was full and heavy. She paid several of the merchants extra to deliver larger items in boxes and barrels to the villa, and began to make her way back home. The homeward path brought her past the place where she and Clement had once lived—the jail and the house attached to it. Syntyche glanced over to see the building that held so many memories for her. How bitterly she had once resented her husband's loss of his position, the price they had paid for his loyalty to Jesus. Yet it had all worked out for the best in the end—as Paul used to say, all things worked together for the good of those who loved the Lord.

A crowd had gathered in front of the jail. Syntyche knew what that meant. She well remembered the eager crowds that showed up whenever a prisoner was being flogged in the yard outside the prison. Struggling to overcome curiosity, she kept her gaze in another direction. It seemed wrong to enjoy watching someone else suffer, even if they had deserved it.

"Sister Syntyche! Do you see what's going on?" A sharp hiss from the crowd drew her attention and she turned to see Doris, a deaconess in one of the other house churches, frantically waving to get her attention. Syntyche drew near enough to hear her say, "It's Euodia—from Lydia's house! She was arrested for preaching in public—on the steps of a temple!"

Doris kept her voice low now that she had Syntyche's attention, and Syntyche was glad. Today was obviously not a good time to declare oneself a Christian in public. She peered through the bodies ringing the prison courtyard. Sure enough, the slight figure tied to the whipping post was that of a woman, stripped to the waist. As Syntyche watched, the prison guard brought the whip down on her slender back, already streaked with blood. She saw the woman shudder and slump against the whipping post as the sharp pieces of lead embedded in the leather thong bit into her flesh. No doubt she groaned, but the chatter of the crowd drowned out her voice.

". . . slave woman, so they say," she heard a man just ahead of her comment to his companion.

"Ah . . . a runaway? But why not have her master beat her in private?" the other replied.

"Not a runaway—she's one of those crazy Jews, the ones who follow the god Jesus, you know?"

"That's a crime now?"

"Preaching about it is—and they say this wasn't her first offense."

The other man nodded. "Making an example of her, I suppose."

Syntyche stared in horror, unable to take her eyes off the scene. True, she was no friend of Euodia's, and she didn't mind sharing with others her opinion that the slave was a fool to court trouble by preaching in public. But nobody would wish such a fate on any woman. The lash was cruel, and Euodia's body, sagging now against the straps that tied her wrists to the post, did not look as if it could take much more. "What will happen to her?" Syntyche mouthed to Doris.

"Jail, I think. I wonder if Lydia knows?"

"She should have kept Euodia in the house," Syntyche whispered back. "But I don't imagine it's easy to stop Euodia from getting her own way, even if you were her mistress."

A shriek pierced the air. This time Euodia's cry rose above the voices of the crowd, and for a moment it silenced them.

They had all seen floggings before, but women were rarely flogged in public, and an unease spread through the crowd rather than the usual hearty approval when people watched a thief or other troublemaker flogged. Some people obviously agreed with the punishment, but others, such as the man in front of Syntyche, clearly thought it was a matter better dealt with in the home.

"Twenty!" roared the guard as he brought the whip down for the final time on Euodia lacerated back. Her body lay against the pole, unmoving except to slump slowly toward the ground—as far as the straps that tied her would allow. "Someone should send word to Lydia," Syntyche said to Doris. *I suppose I could send someone when I get home*, she thought. But Doris said, "I'll go—I hope I find her at home. Even if she can't bring the girl back at once, she'll want to tend to her. You know how fond Lydia is of her—she treats her almost as a daughter."

"Too fond," Syntyche said, edging away from the crowd a little as the guard dragged his unresisting prisoner away. "Euodia needs a firm hand—what she's done today will mean trouble not just for her, but for all of us."

A frown creasing her forehead, Doris said, "God's blessings on your family—you have a wedding tomorrow." Then she turned to cross the marketplace toward Lydia's house.

"Yes, thank you. And I will pray for Euodia," Syntyche promised, "and I hope she will be released swiftly."

As she made her way home through the gathering dusk she couldn't blot out the image of the flogging. Pity, horror, anger, and resentment all mingled in her mind. Because it was true what she'd said—Euodia's disobedience would draw the attention of the city authorities to the Christians. They would be seen as rabble-rousers, disturbers of the peace, undisciplined people who could not keep their slaves and their women in check. Syntyche was more than ready to stand up for truth—but she did not want a target painted on her by this foolish girl who was driven by her own vanity.

Almost like a daughter, she thought, remembering Doris's words about Lydia and Euodia. She thought of Julia, happy and radiant, ready to be married on the morrow. If real persecution began—if the city officials began a campaign to silence Christians—then any of them might be tied to that post. Even her own daughter. That was a thought too terrible to bear. *Be with Euodia, and forgive me my lack of charity,* Syntyche prayed as she turned into the street where Flavia's villa lay. As she prayed she tried to forget what she had seen.

CHAPTER 19
EPAPHRODITUS

The music was loud, the food excellent, the wine free-flowing. Epaphroditus reclined on his couch and raised his goblet. "To Gaius Fabius . . . and his lovely bride-to-be! May they live long and happily together, and may she never be inclined to ask too many questions!"

A hearty roar of approval greeted his toast as all the guests raised their glasses. They were all young men, about a dozen of them, the intimate friends of young Fabius who would wed on the morrow. If the bride was celebrating the wedding eve at all, she was with her own friends on the other side of the city, and doing so in a discreet and appropriate fashion, one would hope. The only women present in the room, apart from the slaves serving the meal, were a group of female dancers brought in for the further entertainment of Gaius Fabius and his friends. Their performance over, they were now getting to know the guests a little better. One, in fact, was draped over the same couch on which Epaphroditus reclined, resting her head on his chest and gazing up at him with an adoring expression.

"Speech! Speech!" the young men shouted as the bride-groom-to-be rose unsteadily to his feet, a dancer draped around him also. He set her gently back on the couch before he raised his glass to his fellows.

"No, no worries there, my fellows—my Cassandra is a fine girl, a good girl, she'll be a model wife and you needn't worry, I won't be chained to the house once I've a wife, not a bit. Where would I be without you fellows?" He gazed at them with owlish affection, though it seemed he had a little trouble focusing. "The scrapes we've gotten into together—I won't soon forget it—Kleitos, Alexander . . . Epap—Epaphroditus." He stumbled a little over the name and waved his goblet vaguely in Epaphroditus's direction. A slave hurried up to refill the almost-empty glass. "No, you mustn't think it's all coming to an end just because I'm the first of our lot to get married—plenty of good times ahead. . . . " His voice trailed off, and he stumbled back onto his couch amid a round of hearty applause.

Epaphroditus lifted his own glass for a refill. As no slave was forthcoming the dancer took it herself for him. "Thank you, my darling." She really was awfully pretty, with artfully dyed scarlet curls and a lovely figure beneath the flimsy swirls of her gown. That was how a woman ought to be—soft and gentle and eager to please—not harsh and unyielding and righteous as a steel blade . . .

He shook his head to clear it, as if he could get rid of the memory of Euodia in the hallway of his mother's house, ready to go out about the Lord's work. It wasn't fair that anyone so stern, so severe, so holy, should also be so beautiful. Yes, it was totally wrong, and he refused to give her another thought. After all, he'd been a fool to strike up conversation with her this afternoon—it was beneath him, really, to banter that way with a slave girl. But he really, really was not going to think about her anymore. At all.

The dancer brought back his goblet and he took another long drink.

The evening blurred as it went on, individual moments merging into a mosaic of wine and laughter and dancing and bawdy jokes. Sometime later he threw an arm around Gaius Fabius's shoulders and said, "We should go out! You shouldn't stay at home on your last night of freedom!"

Everyone agreed it was a wonderful idea. "Let's go to Publius' tavern—that's the place!"

"No, no, no," another voice protested. "He said he'd have soldiers drag us out if we ever showed our faces there again—don't you remember?"

"That's only because you owe him money!" Epaphroditus said, to which his friend Alexander replied, "More likely because you almost burned the place down last time you were there!"

"That's a lie, I deny it absolutely—cat—categorically," Fabius said, grasping a wine bottle in one hand and a dancing girl—a different one this time—just as firmly in the other.

They reeled out into the darkened street together, a loud and merry party as they stumbled from Fabius's wealthy neighborhood, through the quiet marketplace and into the narrow streets where their favorite taverns and gambling dens awaited.

"You know a funny thing, a very funny thing," Gaius Fabius said, slinging an arm around Epaphroditus shoulder as they lurched along. "I'm getting married tomorrow, of course, and do you know who else is getting married tomorrow? Funny thing, but the fellow who's been putting in the cupboards in my new villa—he's getting wed tomorrow as well. Fancy that, eh? Rich and poor, high and low, we all get wed. Perhaps our marriage processions will cross in the street. Wouldn't that be funny?"

"How on earth do you know when your cupboard maker's getting married?"

"Oh, one gets to talking, you know. I've got rather a way with workmen—I like to chat to them. I'll tell you what else is peculiar about it—he's one of your mother's lot, the Christers or whatever they call themselves."

"Christians," Epaphroditus corrected automatically. "That's nothing to do with me, anyway."

"No, no, of course not—we don't hold it against you," Fabius said, squeezing his friend's shoulders a little tighter. They were at the tavern now, pushing into the torch lit room. The tavern keeper did indeed look less than happy to see them, but the large bag of coins Fabius tossed on the bar seemed to mollify him a little.

"Drinks for all my friends!" he proclaimed as Alexander leaned in to ask, "What is it we don't hold against you, Epaphroditus?"

"Hold anything against me, as long as it's not a dagger to my throat," Epaphroditus replied, but Fabius leaned around him to say, "The Christians! His mother being—you know, one of their priestesses or whatever. We don't blame Epaphroditus for that, do we?"

"No . . . ," Alexander replied, but his eyes narrowed a little. His father was a linen merchant and a neighbor of Lydia's. "But the whole house is a nest of them, the slaves and all—I know you don't like to give orders to your own mother, Epaphroditus, but you are the man of the house and you might, I don't know, regulate them a bit. I mean, it's not right, is it?" His drunken gaze was sincere. Epaphroditus knew that Alexander was an ardent devotee of the cult of Mithras.

"No, doesn't look good, not good at all," Fabius said. "My father-in-law to be says something's going to have to be done about that lot, they cause so much dissension and disorder. Not just here, but all over the empire—in Rome itself, even . . . "

"Rome perhaps, but they cause no trouble here in Philippi," Epaphroditus said, squirming away from his friend's wine-soaked embrace. The gods knew his mother's religion caused him plenty of embarrassment and he'd made it clear to all his friends that he disapproved. He went along with them to the temples of their deities on occasion—indeed, it was likely they'd end up in a shrine before the night was over. With a wedding on the morrow, somebody would surely suggest an offering and a prayer. A lifetime of belief was not easily abandoned, and after years of his mother's teachings he could never see the gods of Rome and Greece and Egypt as anything but witless statues. But he would never say so. Still, the conversation made him uncomfortable and he wished talk would turn to other matters.

But the tavern keeper had overheard them and leaned over the bar to talk. "These Christ followers, you mean? Cause trouble in Philippi? I'm here to tell you they do. Right here on this street, in front of the temple of Cybele, there was one of them preaching today—a woman preacher, if you can fancy that, talking about this god Jesus, and the priests had her hauled away to the magistrates. I hope she got the flogging she deserved."

All around him the men nodded drunken approval. For Epaphroditus the hot crowded room had suddenly grown chilly. "A woman preacher? Was she a slave woman, do you know? A dark haired woman, young, bit on the tall side?"

"Oh no! Not one of your mother's crowd, is it, Epaphroditus?" Fabius groaned, while on the other side Alexander said, "It's as I said—you need to keep them in better order. Less time out drinking with us and more time home beating your slaves, that's what you need, my friend."

A clatter of dice on a tabletop nearby caught the attention of Fabius and Alexander, who turned to join the game, leaving Epaphroditus at the bar with his drink and his thoughts. The tavern keeper had neither confirmed nor denied his guesses, and now he questioned him again. "I didn't see the woman myself, young sir," the man said. "I couldn't say if she was young or old, tall or short, dark or fair—but I think I did hear someone tell that she was a slave."

"Taken before the magistrates, you say?" Epaphroditus repeated. "When was this?"

"Oh, before sunset, I think—yes, I remember, because there was an awful commotion in the street. A few hours ago, now, I'd say."

Epaphroditus turned abruptly from the bar toward the table around which his friends sat, all their attention focused on a pair of dice and a pile of silver coins. Fabius slid over to make room for him on the bench, but Epaphroditus shook his head. "No, I have to go. Got to go—take care of something!"

"Can't it wait till tomorrow? Don't be a fool, I need you here!"

"Tomorrow's your wedding and you'll need me then too. I just have to go—see about this one thing. That's all. I'll be at your house in plenty of time tomorrow, I promise."

The night air hit him like a slap in the face as he left the tavern. A slap . . . Euodia had looked, this afternoon, as if she half wanted to slap him. He certainly deserved it, the way he'd spoken to her. If she had been taken and flogged—

Odds were good that she had. The civic authorities had already warned and then fined her. His mother had been strictly ordered to keep Euodia under control, to stop her preaching in the streets. Epaphroditus knew that, had known that she was walking into trouble when she left the house this afternoon. He should have ordered her to stop, forced her to stay home. Although he had no confidence that she would have obeyed, he could have—

Well. That made no sense, thinking about what he could have or should have been done. He stood alone in the street, wondering what to do and where to go. Should he go home and see what news they'd had of Euodia? Whether she had been returned in disgrace? Even if she was being held in jail, he couldn't go to the magistrates and buy her freedom in the middle of the night. Though he'd left the tavern claiming he had urgent business, the fact was that now, out in the street, he had no idea what that business was. Only that if Euodia was in jail, bleeding from a beating, he had no desire to be drinking and gambling in a tavern with his friends.

Blindly he followed his own aimless feet through the streets of Philippi, not so much going toward anything as trying to escape, to run away from—what? Himself, perhaps. This life he'd made for himself, this existence of meaningless work and mindless pleasure that left him with nothing but bitter regret when he woke each morning. There had to be something more—more point to life than this. After all, he lived around people who woke every morning with a sense of purpose and hope and joy. But where did that lead? To a whipping post and jail, it seemed, and was that what he wanted for himself?

Eventually he found himself at the steps of a temple: the temple of Jupiter, he realized as he looked up and saw the carving over the door. He stumbled to his knees on the steps, driven by an urge to go inside, to pray, to ask for guidance. But not Jupiter—no, there was no one in there. The temples were empty, the statues were just that, the gods were all false and hollow. And the true God, the one he'd been raised to worship, had no temple where he could go, no place he could seek Him out. The God of the Jews, the God of the Lord Jesus, would live inside his heart if he desired—but that was the last place Epaphroditus wanted to look.

He stayed kneeling on the temple steps for a while, his face in his hands, and was surprised to find his hands wet with his own tears. *Heaven help me, I'm more drunk than I thought I was,* he told himself as he staggered to his feet. *Must get out of here before anyone notices. I should go home—see if she's there . . .*

But the jail was much closer than home, and he couldn't resist—it drew him like a magnet. He'd been there once before, when his friend Kleitos, more drunk and disorderly than usual, had been incarcerated for a night before being brought before the magistrates and fined. Now he greeted the guard on duty and said, "Do you have a slave woman in the jail?"

"Yes, sir, she was brought in this afternoon and flogged. For preaching some vile superstition, they said."

"She was flogged? How many lashes?"

"Twenty, sir. What's your concern? Is she yours?"

"She is—or my mother's, anyway. I don't know if my mother's been informed."

"I don't know, sir. There's been no one here about her tonight."

"May I take her with me now?"

"Oh no, sir. I've got no orders to release her. You'll have to talk to the magistrates tomorrow."

"Can I—can I see her, at least?"

The guard gave him an odd look. "No reason why not, I

suppose," he shrugged, then led Epaphroditus down into the dungeons.

She was there, slumped on the bare ground, her hands and feet chained. The upper part of her gown, back and front, was stiff with dried blood that had soaked through the coarse fabric. Her dark hair lay matted and tangled across her face. For a long time he stood looking at her. Twenty lashes was a brutal beating for a woman to withstand. Euodia might well be unconscious, rather than just asleep. The guard moved a foot toward her as if to nudge her awake.

"No—no, let her sleep." Surely it was no good to wake her now when he could not set her free or even offer her ointment and blankets to make her more comfortable. Remembering their conversation just that afternoon, he thought that if she woke now, his would be the last face she would want to see. He wanted to reach down, to touch her face, to brush the hair away from her nose and mouth, to take her in his arms—

Horrified to realize that he was trembling and tears had again sprung to his eyes, he backed away a few steps. The sane thing, the sober and sensible thing, was to go home and tell his mother and Rachel and Simeon what had happened. They could come to the jail and clean Euodia's wounds and make her comfortable, while he—changed and sobered and calm—would go to the magistrates in the morning and arrange for her freedom. As he backed toward the stairs he could not tear his eyes from her slight form, lying wounded and exhausted on the stone floor.

In the square outside he stood still again, listening to the night sounds of the city—dogs barking and far-off voices quarrelling. Then he turned his steps toward home, feeling as lonely and desolate as he'd ever felt in his life.

CHAPTER 20
EUODIA

She came to consciousness in the prison dungeon—as dark a place as she'd ever been. Her eyes fluttered open but she saw only a faint flicker of torchlight. Far more real was what she felt: searing pain in every muscle and joint. Her back burned with raw wounds. It took a few moments to notice that her hands and feet were shackled and that she lay on bare cold stone. Pain blocked out all other sensations.

Now sound began to filter through—the moans and cries of the other prisoners. She could hear but not see them. When she tried to sit up pain radiated out from her lacerated back, down her legs, and up into her head. She fell back again onto the stone pavement.

The events of the day swam in her memory. Tentatively she reached up to touch her face. Her face, at least, seemed whole and unscarred.

Then she began to remember the beating—at least, she remembered being tied to the post, remembered the circle of the crowd and the voices all around. The actual touch of the lash— she had no memory of that. But she could feel it now, as if the whip were still cutting into her flesh.

A soft moan escaped her lips and she tried to turn it into a prayer. *Lord Jesus, You were beaten too, for me. I am glad to share a little of Your pain.* Then she tried a more honest prayer: *Make me glad to share your pain.* That wasn't really the case—not yet. But perhaps the Holy Spirit would descend into this dark place and give her peace and joy.

Or just stop the pain. She wanted to think of better things, loftier things. But there was only the pain gnawing at her.

A new feeling, distinct from the pain. Someone kicking or nudging at her foot. "You have visitors, slave."

Again she tried to sit upright, or at least to look up, but the effort was too great. But whoever it was, was beside her now, talking in low soothing tones, cradling her.

"Euodia, my poor girl, can you hear me?" Lydia's voice, husky and soft in the darkness. Hers hands, and someone else's—Rachel's, no doubt—lifting her, turning her. "No, don't try to talk—I'm sorry I didn't come sooner. It was the middle of the night before I heard, and the guard would not let us in until daybreak—I couldn't bear to think of you alone here. Hush now—this will hurt a little, but we're going to take off your robe and wash your wounds."

Carefully Rachel and Lydia bathed her back and sides as gently as possible. Even then, each touch of the cool water caused her to cry out. Rachel sang a psalm to a haunting tune while she washed and then rubbed oil on the wounds. Euodia tried to relax into the gentle touch and Rachel's soft voice, tried to block out the waves of pain. *Jesus, I would be glad to die for You,* she prayed. But she was surprised how stubbornly she clung to life, how unwilling she was to die.

She drifted into and out of consciousness, but every time she woke Lydia and Rachel were still there, holding her.

Then they left her alone, finally, dressed in a clean robe, with a blanket rolled under her head and another one covering her, and a basket of food nearby. If family and friends didn't bring food and clothes and blankets, prisoners might starve or freeze down here.

They had prayed with her, recited psalms, and assured her that she would be free soon. "Epaphroditus has gone to see the magistrates, and if they will not agree to release you, then I will go myself. We will give them no peace till they let you go," Lydia said. "Tonight you will sleep in your own bed, I promise."

It was a hollow promise, Euodia knew, for the authorities could hold her as long as they wanted—but perhaps, having made a public example of her, they would be willing to release her to her mistress's care. And her master's. She thought of Epaphroditus bargaining for her freedom. He barely spoke to her, often acted as if she didn't exist. Yet there seemed nothing strange in the idea that he would be the one to ask for her freedom. The thought drifted into her head that his indifference to her was all pretence, that he still felt what he had always had, just as she did. She tried to banish that thought as sternly as possible, but there was nothing stern left in her. Her thoughts flowed like newly dyed silks, slippery and multihued, and then she slept. A real sleep this time, peaceful and without dreams, though when she woke again it was still to pain.

"Hey, crazy woman! More of your crazy friends!" The jailer's voice cut through the dull cloud of pain that enveloped her. She had no sense of how much time had passed since Lydia and Rachel had left, but now here was her mistress again, this time accompanied by Euodia's old master Demos and his wife Hermia.

"We are all praying for you, all the Christians in Philippi. We have taken up a collection to pay your fine," Demos said, settling himself on the floor beside her. Strange that a man who had once used her so harshly was now a brother in Christ, lifting a flask of water to her lips and urging her to drink a little.

"*Almost* all are praying," Hermia said. "I went to Flavia's house today, to wish Julia and Andreas blessings on their marriage, and of course Syntyche had to declare how foolish you were for preaching in public, how you brought your troubles on yourself. I told her just what I thought of that, I did—"

"Hush now, Euodia doesn't want to hear of quarrels and trouble," Lydia interrupted. "How are you feeling, my dear? Any better?"

"I can move about a bit more, and I've eaten a little. It's much better since you came."

"Before I go, I'll bathe your wounds again and put more ointment on. I'd hoped we could bring you home today, but Epaphroditus has been all day arguing with the magistrates. Finally they told him they had it in mind to keep you here a while, and if he kept protesting he'd find himself chained alongside you."

"Can you imagine?" Demos's wife said. "They said such a thing to your son—and him not even a Christian!" She was not a woman known for her tact.

Euodia looked around herself. Her eyes had adjusted to the torch lit dimness now, and she could see detail in the rock walls, even make out some of the other prisoners—there were only a handful—each chained in his own place. She was the only woman in the prison, she was fairly sure, but as all the men were shackled securely she did not fear then.

"Ten years ago, Paul and Silas were chained in this same dungeon," she said. "For the crime of setting me free. Remember Clement telling how they sang in prison?"

"What courage!" Lydia said. "I don't know if I could sing."

"I can't—not here alone. At least they had each other."

"But we have each other now," Demos said. "Let us sing a hymn together before we leave you."

Euodia gratefully raised her voice with his, and the other women joined in. They sang Paul's own favorite hymn, one he had taught them: "Let this mind be in you, which was also in Christ Jesus . . ."

That is what I need, Euodia prayed. *The mind of Jesus so that I could suffer with more patience and courage. But thank You, Jesus, for giving me the other members of Your Body to sing with me and lift my spirits in this terrible place.*

"We have had news of Paul," Lydia said.

"Is he still in prison?"

"He is going to Rome. As a prisoner." Demos filled in the details he had heard from the travelers who had arrived that day from a ship at Neapolis—how the authorities in Caesarea had been ready to release Paul, but he had appealed to Caesar himself so that he might have the chance to travel to Rome and witness for Jesus as a prisoner there.

"Now *that* is courage!" Euodia exclaimed. The apostle had not sought to be released. He was more than willing to suffer for Jesus. *God, give me the strength You gave Paul,* she prayed.

After Demos and Hermia departed and Lydia had again washed and anointed Euodia's lacerated back, the two women prayed together. "Tell Epaphroditus thanks for me," Euodia said.

"It is—good of him, to do all this for me. Especially when he is—not one of us."

"If there is one good thing to come out of your suffering, Euodia, I pray it would be a softening of his heart. It's his place, of course, as man of the household, to go before the magistrates if our slave is put in prison. But he did not do it just because it is his place. I think the Spirit is speaking to him, Euodia. I only wish you didn't have to suffer so, just for him to hear that voice."

"If he could—it would be worth it." Euodia tried hard to mean it, to believe that her imprisonment was worth it if anyone's faith was stronger as a result. And surely it would build up the faith of others to see her suffer bravely—just as her own courage became stronger by thinking of Paul on a prison ship, headed to Rome.

But that faith wavered a little the next day, when the jailer came to drag her out into the prison yard again—not for release, but for a second beating.

This one was worse. She remembered that when she was first arrested, she had walked tall and proud to the whipping post and stood upright as they bound her hands. At first she had tried to be strong and not cry out, though that resolve had quickly broken down.

This time she had to be half carried to the post, as she was still unable to walk upright and unaided. When her hands were tied, her body slumped against the ropes, pulling at her arm sockets. *Jesus, this is so little compared to what You bore for me,* she prayed, trying hard to mean it, to be brave. But she screamed as soon as she heard the whip whistling through the air, before it even touched her scabbed and sore back, breaking open the wounds that had barely begun to heal.

Only 10 lashes this time. But each one was a fresh agony. Each time she was sure she could not bear another. She wanted to be brave and strong. But she screamed, she sobbed, she begged for mercy.

When the guard cut her loose from the post she lay in the

dirt. She was aware of falling but of nothing after that, until she felt someone picking her up and carrying her. Back into the prison, she guessed, but the arms were gentler than a guard's would be. Somehow she felt cradled, safe, as she had been when she woke to Lydia and Rachel's soothing touch. But neither of those women was strong enough to hold her, to carry her like this. *The arms of God*, she thought, before she drifted out of consciousness again.

When she woke again she was in the same spot as before her whipping, shackled in the same way, with fresh pain piercing her body. But she realized as she cautiously explored her own body and her surroundings that she had not been alone. Someone— probably Lydia or Rachel again—had changed her blood-soaked robe and washed and treated her wounds. And she had been unaware of it all. But she cherished the knowledge that her sisters in Christ cared for her even while she slept.

There was food beside her as well, and to her own surprise she felt well enough to eat a little as well as drink. She wondered how long she had been unconscious. Long enough to begin healing a little, though every movement was still agony.

Despite the pain, she felt a curious buoyant strength. She had survived two severe beatings and some days—she wasn't sure how many—in prison. *It's You I should be grateful to, Lord Jesus,* she reminded herself. *It's Your strength, not mine, that sustains me.* It felt good to know that God had brought her this far. She felt confident, for the moment at least, that she could endure whatever happened.

"One thing I'll say for you Christ followers, you look after your own—even your slaves," she heard the jailer say. When she looked up, trying to see him in the dim light, she saw him talking to a man, leading him toward the place where she was shackled. He drew quite close before she realized it was Epaphroditus.

The contrast between this meeting and their last could not have been greater. He was seeing her now at her worst and her weakest. Before, she had used her words and careful downcast gazes to protect herself from his mockery. Now she had no defenses, but she knew as soon as she looked at him that she would not need any. His dark eyes now held no hint of mockery or flirtation, only concern for her.

"You're awake. It's the first time I've seen you awake since you were arrested."

"You have—been here before?"

"Yes. I was here the night they brought you in, after the first whipping. I came again yesterday when you were being whipped the second time. I tried everything to stop it—you must know that. You fell into a faint again as soon as they finished beating you, and I brought you here and stayed a while, till my mother arrived to dress your wounds and change your clothing."

"That was yesterday? The second beating?"

"Yes. You've been asleep about 18 hours this time. It's nearly noon now—four days after your arrest. I've been to see the magistrates again this morning. They've agreed to accept a fine and promised that you won't be flogged again. But they want to hold you here a few more days—a full week in all, before they'll release you. They intend to make you an example to the rest of us—the other Christians, I mean."

She nodded slowly. "I can bear a few more days here. I'm glad they won't beat me again. But I'm sorry about the fine—I've cost you and your mother a great deal."

He smiled, finally, half shyly, like the boy he had been when she first met him. "You've given us a great deal more. Anyway, all the community contributed to pay your fine. Everyone is proud of you."

"That's wrong. Nobody should be proud of me—of anyone but Jesus. What I've gone through is nothing compared to what He did. It's a sin to boast."

He was quiet a moment, searching her face. "None of this weakens your faith, then?"

"How could it?" The idea that being in prison for Jesus, being beaten for His sake, might weaken her faith?—well, it only showed how far Epaphroditus was from understanding the followers of Jesus.

"I've often heard the apostles tell stories of how God has spared them from prison or floggings or even death. Yet He didn't for you. I would cut off my hand if it would have spared you this suffering—yet God did nothing for you."

"No—don't you see? He has done so much—He is doing so much, just to sustain me here. Sometimes He spares His children, but we are all willing to suffer for Him when the time comes. And this is my time."

"I wish it weren't. I haven't slept for three nights, thinking of you in here."

"You are—very kind, to concern yourself so much."

"You know it isn't kindness."

"I don't know what it is," she said, lifting her eyes to his again. His face looked naked—all the defenses he had built over these past years, all the barriers raised between them, stripped away. Except that one barrier, the most important of all. He reached out to take her hand and she gave it to him, but it was like reaching across a vast chasm. Epaphroditus did not believe, and unless he did he would never understand why she was willing to sit here in pain and in chains.

"I have spent—what, four years? Five? How much time have I thrown away?" he said, his voice low and urgent, aiming for some privacy in this cavernous prison where thieves and bandits sat chained nearby. "All these years, trying to run from God and from you. From what I felt for you. And here I am now with you in this terrible place, and these are the only two things that matter."

"One of them should not matter," Euodia said. Suddenly she felt as if she had been standing on swampy ground and then placed her feet on a ledge of firm rock—she knew what to do and say now. "What you say you feel for me—that is not important. But this running from God—you are right if you believe it's He who has led you here, right now. You say you'd cut off your hand to spare me this suffering. But if I could believe that one more flogging for me would make you stop running and turn back to Jesus, I'd let them drag me there again—gladly."

"You truly mean it, don't you?" he said almost in a whisper.

"Every word."

He still held her hand, and she was suddenly aware of it and wanted to draw it back, but he gripped it even tighter. "I don't know if I can separate the two, Euodia—what I feel for you and what I feel about Jesus. I only know that since you've been here, two thoughts have tortured me. The first is what I told you—that I hate to see you suffering like this. You know that. But the second is that if you were to die in here, at least your life would have been worth something. Unlike mine. I've tried every way I can to turn my back on God, on everything I once believed, to lose myself in this world and all the pleasures it offers. But every night I lie down on my bed as hollow as an empty bowl, Euodia. I look at you and despite your scars, the terrible pain you're in, I can see a kind of—peace, I suppose—in you. And I don't have that—not even a shred of it."

"But you can."

"I don't know if I can. It may be too late. Some say that if you ever turn away from Jesus, you are rejected for all time."

She had heard people say such things too—had even half believed it, but now she knew it could not be true. The conviction that Epaphroditus was feeling was more than just passion for her—it was the work of the Spirit. It had to be.

Suddenly she felt faint. The room spun around her, and she caught her breath. Epaphroditus was beside her in a heartbeat, his arms around her, lowering her back to lie down on the blanket and pillow his mother had provided. "You must rest. I cannot stay long—the guard gave me only a few minutes."

"Wait. First—let me pray for you." She reached again for his hand, blindly, unable to turn her head to look up at him.

He took her hand again and enfolded it in both his. "Please . . . if you can."

She didn't have strength for a long prayer. Just a few words, placing him in Jesus' hands, asking the Spirit to keep working on his heart. Epaphroditus touched her cheek gently before leaving, and she lay for a long time in the dark, wondering if he would finally return to Jesus.

CHAPTER 21
EPAPHRODITUS

Epaphroditus and Lydia went together to bring Euodia home on the morning of her release. She looked pale and shaken and said little as they walked home. As he remembered sitting beside her on the cold stone floor of the prison and how natural it had felt to clasp her hand in his, he wished that he could do that again now.

As they turned into their own street Euodia spoke at last. "I am sorry for the trouble I have caused you. I have been a most unruly servant."

"Unruly for Jesus," Lydia said with a smile, brushing back a strand of Euodia's hair and tucking it behind her veil. "No one who knows you would expect less."

"All the same, you must be more cautious now," Epaphroditus said. It was all very well to talk of courage and bravery and suffering for the truth, but after what she had endured the past week surely she would not be eager to repeat the experience.

Saying nothing, Euodia just bowed her head in a gesture that might have appeared submissive to one who didn't know her well. "Do you want to go inside and rest?" Lydia asked.

"Yes, thank you," Euodia said, slipping inside the house and leaving Epaphroditus alone with his mother.

"I am so proud of her," Lydia said as they, too, went inside.

"As you are not proud of me?" Instantly he regretted the words. He really hadn't meant to sound petulant or bitter.

His mother's face grew grave. "I have much to be proud of in you, my son. Forgive me if I don't always show it. You have taken charge of our business and proven a good and capable manager for one so young. I am proud of that."

"Thank you." He should have stopped then, he knew. But something was driving him to speak when he would better be silent. "What a pity those things don't really matter."

Mockery tinged his voice—that same hard-edged shell he'd used to protect himself in every conversation with his mother since—when? Years. But there was not a trace of flippancy in hers as she lifted her eyes to him and said, "These things matter, but not in the great scale of things eternal. I would rather see you penniless and living on the street, with your heart given to Jesus."

Now he really did laugh. "Yet when I was young and wanted to give up all this—" he waved his hand at the shop and the dye works—"to become a preacher or a healer for Jesus, you didn't want that, did you? Nor did you want me to marry a slave girl of no family, no matter how devout a Christian she was. You wanted it all for me—prosperity, the family business, a good marriage—and Jesus too."

"I did. Perhaps that was my folly. If nothing else, these past few years have taught me what really counts." She stood for a moment looking as if she wanted to say more, but then she turned away. "Excuse me. I must go see what Rachel and Simeon are doing."

Epaphroditus walked alone into the courtyard, empty for once. Although he had work to do, he didn't think he could keep his mind on it. He had seen Euodia, walked beside her, knew she was alive and safe at home. Yet the picture of her, bleeding and crying out under the lash, was burned into his mind. The slight weight of her body in his arms as he carried her back to the jail, her blood soaking his clothes—it was all that he could see or think of.

Entering the shop, he stared at the accounts, wrote a letter to a client, and started every time someone entered the room, thinking it might be Euodia. It never was.

Late in the afternoon he could no longer concentrate. Putting on his cloak, he left the house. In the street outside he saw his friend Alexander standing outside his father's shop.

"Hey, Epaphroditus! Coming out with us tonight?"

"I'm—not sure. I'll tell you later."

"Where are you off to now?" Alexander probed, falling into step beside him.

"Nowhere . . . I just want to walk. I needed to be alone." Since he had been alone in the shop for hours, it wasn't exactly true, but it was the closest he could come to explaining the feelings churning inside him.

His friend frowned. "You've been alone a deal too much lately, if you ask me."

"I didn't, actually."

"No. Well. Fabius is angry at you, by the way."

"Is he now." Epaphroditus quickened his steps a little.

"Well, be fair, man, he has reason. You missed his wedding feast and most of the days of the celebration afterward."

"I dropped in when I could. I had domestic troubles to see to."

"Very commendable, but too many people know about your domestic troubles. This wayward slave of yours—you've made such a fuss over her, anyone would think she was your mistress, or else that you were one the Christ followers yourself."

Epaphroditus allowed himself a twisted, grim smile. Both shots close to the mark, but neither dead center. "What of it? Even if either of those things were true, I don't see that it's your business, or Fabius's, or anyone's but mine."

Alexander stopped, evidently expecting Epaphroditus to do the same. But Epaphroditus kept walking as Alexander said, "It is your business, and you'd better look to it carefully, or you may have more 'domestic troubles' than you've bargained for!" His voice grew fainter as Epaphroditus continued toward the gate that led out of the city. "Watch yourself, that's all I'm saying . . . " were the last words Epaphroditus heard.

Seeing nothing of the beauty of the day or the people who passed him, he walked on. Soon he was outside the city, near the river. The place of prayer. He had come here with his mother every Sabbath when he was a boy. It was a spot laden with memory for him, and he found as he sat on one of the ruined stones of the old temple that those memories flooded back.

Here he had learned to worship the God of Abraham, Isaac, and Jacob. Here he had learned of Jesus, the Son of God. Here he had listened to Paul and Silas and Timothy. Here he had strolled and talked with Luke. And here he had watched his mother, his grandmother—all the people he cared for—led into the water of baptism.

What had held him back from making that final step? And why had he chosen to turn from the path of Jesus? It seemed to him that he had had no clear reason for what he'd done, only feelings that raged inside him. He remembered his anger at his mother for denying him Euodia. Anger at Euodia, too, that she would not defy Lydia and marry him anyway. Resentful that he had to be a dye merchant rather than a physician or a missionary. Stifled by the narrow rules of his mother's God and intrigued by the freedoms that his pagan friends enjoyed.

It seemed such a tawdry, boyish little collection of grudges, now that he looked at them all at once. So little, to lure him away from so much. And in all the drunken nights in the taverns, all the gambling and carousing and flirting with actresses and dancers, had he known one moment of true joy, of sincere happiness? He couldn't recall one.

"Forgive me, Lord Jesus," he said aloud. "I traded gold and pearls for dust and ashes. What a little fool I've been."

Sitting in prison beside Euodia, watching helpless as she was again bound and beaten, he had seen what the cost of following Jesus might be. Indeed, things might well get worse than they were. Someday, as Paul had often predicted, Christ's followers might find themselves summoned to die for their faith. It was not an appealing prospect. Epaphroditus was no idealist: he knew the blood and the pain were real. But he also realized that what he'd seen in Euodia's eyes, what he'd heard in her voice, was real. And it was worth everything.

His feelings for God were all tangled with his feelings for Euodia—he knew that. And while in one sense they were the same thing—for it was her devotion, her passionate commitment to God that he admired as much as her beauty—he knew he had to separate those twisted threads. If he were to be baptized, it could not be in the hope of winning Euodia back. That would be a false allegiance—how could he offer that either to God or to her? He had no reason to believe either his mother or Euodia would change their minds, even after all that had happened.

"The question is," he said, speaking aloud again, "am I willing to follow You for Your own sake—even if I can never marry Euodia, even if I can never serve you as anything but a dye merchant? Even if there's no glory, no grand passion, no great life's work—would I still choose You, and You alone?"

Epaphroditus knew the answer now. It was in the sun, in the air all around him, in the warm flow of his own blood through his veins. He found he could no more say no to Jesus than to the beat of his own heart. Too long he had wandered by the side of the road, poking around in rubbish heaps. It was time to continue the journey.

CHAPTER 22
LYDIA

"Let this mind be in you
Which was also in Christ Jesus . . . "
All around Lydia's courtyard the voices echoed, blending to-

gether in harmony on the first Christian song most of them had ever learned, the beautiful hymn about unity and humility that Paul had taught them so many years before.

If only it were true, Lydia thought. True it was, of course, that Jesus the Christ had taken on humanity and suffered and died—she believed that with all her heart. But that His followers were of the same mind—humbly willing to put others above themselves—for that she saw little evidence.

The voices sounded beautiful, now, but she knew trouble was coming the way she sensed a storm in the air. This gathering at the end of the Sabbath was not a meeting of all the believers who worshipped at their house church. It was a smaller group: the overseers and deacons of all four of the congregations in Philippi. They had washed each other's feet and shared the Lord's Supper and prayed and sung hymns together. When the sun set, though, they would turn to discussing the business of the church, and then the façade of unity would shatter.

Lydia had felt the tension in the air from the moment Clement and Syntyche entered, accompanied by Rufus and the other deacons and deaconesses from the church that met in Flavia's house. She and Rachel had greeted them warmly, but Euodia's welcome had been barely civil—she had turned away even before Clement was done saying hello. Syntyche had not spoken to her at all.

During Euodia's imprisonment Syntyche had spoken freely to others in the church, declaring that the slave should have had more sense, that it was her own fault and not God's will that she was in jail. Even before that, she and Euodia had never gotten along well, going right back to the days when Clement and Syntyche had lived in this house. But since her imprisonment, a month ago now, Euodia's resentment of Syntyche seemed to occupy her mind more than it should. She rarely mentioned the woman's name, but her tone was biting when she spoke of those whose commitment to the cause of Christ was halfhearted, those who chose to be cautious rather than risk imprisonment or beatings.

Since her release, Euodia had not returned to preaching in public, a fact that relieved Lydia. She had feared the girl would insist upon immediately preaching again, which would lead to more beatings and arrests. As Euodia's mistress and the overseer of her church, she was prepared to forbid her from preaching, to spare her further punishment. But she wasn't sure the young woman would obey her in either role: Euodia believed that obedience to God came before all earthly allegiance.

So far, no problem had arisen. Euodia threw herself once again into the Lord's work, but she worked quietly behind the scenes, teaching the Scriptures to the women and girls as she had been doing for years, meeting privately with would-be converts. But she did no public preaching. Perhaps suffering for Christ hadn't been such a privilege that she was eager to repeat it.

Despite simmering tensions, the first part of the meeting went smoothly as they discussed the needs of the poor members in the four congregations. One church could help another with money, food, clothing, even work and housing for the members in need. There had never been a problem with sharing resources, though Lydia noticed that more and more the four churches had begun dividing into two camps. The church that met in Demos's house was largely a satellite of their own church here in Lydia's house, and the two groups frequently collaborated and shared with each other as required. Meanwhile, the church in Nikolai's house attached itself to the larger and wealthier congregation in Flavia's villa. Lydia worried that if a conflict arose between church leaders, the four churches would split into two hostile camps, effectively dividing the Philippian believers in half.

Euodia and Syntyche were bickering already—something to do with the best way to help some poor family. "The Lord Jesus told us to feed the hungry, clothe the naked, and preach the gospel," Euodia said, her cheeks flushing with the controlled anger that so often simmered beneath her cool exterior, "not to spend our time finding work for people and teaching them to weave and spin, leaving no time for the preaching of the Word!"

"Not everyone is called to preach," Clement pointed out, and Syntyche added, in a quietly spoken aside but one obviously meant to be heard, " . . . and not all those who think they're called to preach should do so!"

"We are called to preach the gospel, in season and out," Euodia replied quickly, "to take no thought for tomorrow, but to trust in the Lord."

"Yet I notice you've not been so quick to raise your voice in the marketplace after 10 nights in the jail!" Syntyche shot back. For a moment the two women glared at each other, an expression of pure rage on each face. Remembering the song about having the same mind as the humble Christ, Lydia interjected, "Sisters and brothers, nothing is gained when we become angry at each other," cutting off Euodia's sputtered reply. "Let us not forget that we are all one family, though we may sometimes disagree. Only the devil is honored by discord."

"There is a time for discord!" Euodia protested. "Our Lord Jesus Himself spoke out against the rulers and religious leaders in Judea when they twisted the Word of God to change its meaning. When leaders are in the wrong and leading people astray, we must speak out. To talk of peace when we have real disagreements is cowardly—just as it's cowardly to talk of shutting our mouths when Jesus calls us to speak."

"Seems to me you've got a very convenient idea of what God calls you to do," Syntyche muttered. Putting his hand on his wife's arm, Clement said, "Sister Euodia, no one doubts your courage, nor do we deny that we should witness for Jesus as He calls us to. The question at hand is simply—are there times when one way of serving Him is better than another? If we defy the authorities, do we bring the church into shame and disrepute?"

"Does Paul bring shame on the church? On the name of Jesus? No! God is glorified when we are persecuted for His sake!" Euodia replied.

"Not if we seek out persecution when we could avoid it!" Syntyche again, rising to her feet now as other voices chimed in, some siding with Syntyche, others with Euodia.

Lydia, too, stood. She felt her own cheeks flush as she pitched her soft voice to rise above the babble. "What brings shame on the name of Jesus is strife and dissension such as we are hearing here this night! Yes, we may disagree, but disputes are settled by the Word of God and the guidance of the apostles—not by the brother or sister with the loudest voice."

Euodia and Syntyche both subsided, as did most of the others, and Lydia took advantage of the lull to move on. "In the meantime, we have other matters that must be settled."

She sighed, knowing that the storm they had just weathered was only a preparation for the one that would erupt in a few moments. "Next Sabbath we celebrate a baptism. Among those who have chosen to join our fellowship are Benjamin the leather worker, Joshua and his wife, and the household of Judah the grain merchant."

Simeon, frail from the illness that had ravaged him during the past months, pushed himself to his feet. He had taken little part in the leadership of the church recently and Lydia felt the loss—her house church no longer had a strong male leader. But this issue mattered enough to Simeon to bring him from his sickbed. "Why must we even raise this as a question?" he demanded, his voice sounding thin and old. "When did we ever vote on whether a person becomes a part of the body of Christ? The apostles baptized all who believed in Jesus. Why even discuss this?"

Already other voices were murmuring, some in agreement and some in dissent. Lydia looked steadily at her employee and dear friend. "You know quite well, Simeon, why these names are being brought before the leaders. It would be dishonest to pretend otherwise. These men have been here in Philippi, attending our services, for nearly a year now. They are devout Jews who say they are followers of Jesus, but the only baptism they ever received was by followers of John the Baptist many years ago.

Some here have questioned the sincerity of their beliefs and publicly stated these men should not be baptized." She shifted her gaze from Simeon to Clement and Syntyche.

"They are Judaizers, circumcisers!" Clement declared. "They have assumed the authority of teachers even though they are not yet baptized, and instruct others that all Christ's followers should be circumcised and obey all the Jewish laws!"

Lydia's own beliefs on the matter were far from clear. She had been a God fearer and worshipped with the Jews long before ever hearing of Jesus. Yet she had never made that final step of becoming a Jew, and she understood Paul as saying that Jesus had come to share the God of Israel with everyone, not to make Jews out of Greeks like herself.

Rachel, Simeon, and Euodia had embraced the new Jewish converts and their teachings with enthusiasm. In fact, it was Euodia who now shouted: "They follow the scriptures—*all* Scripture!"

Lydia couldn't accept everything the men taught, but neither could she reject the Jewish traditions and the teachings of Scripture as Clement and Syntyche and their church were so quick to do. She sought a middle way that was becoming increasingly narrow and difficult.

"We do not attempt to judge any man's conscience," she said. "If Judah, Benjamin, Joshua and their families want to follow the Jewish law, that is between them and God. But when they teach new converts that they must follow these laws if they are to follow Christ—when they pull aside a young father on his way home from Sabbath meeting and tell him that his family does not belong to Christ if his newborn son is not circumcised—yes, it happened, you know it happened—then we must intervene."

The argument raged on. The dividing lines she already saw so clearly were becoming sharper now. She felt weak, unable to counteract the influence of the circumcisers even among those of her own household. Demos and his deacons tended to agree with Simeon, Rachel, and Euodia in support of the Jews. The other two churches, with Syntyche as the most vocal of their leaders, declared passionately that binding themselves to Jewish law meant rejecting the freedom of Christ. "This is what Paul preaches!" Syntyche shouted at one point, and Euodia, almost in unison, shouted back, "This is what Scripture teaches!"

The meeting that had begun with footwashing, prayer, and the Lord's Supper dissolved into chaos. No one started an actual fistfight, but small individual shouting matches broke out all over the courtyard and Clement had to pull Syntyche away from Euodia, actually prying his wife's fingers away from their firm grip on the slave woman's arm. Lydia felt as if she alone was trying to stem the tide of disorder.

When it was impossible to be heard above the noise of the crowd she went from one person to another, asking, pleading for calm and quiet. Finally the worst of the arguing subsided. But there was no move toward harmony—people only began to gather their possessions and leave, ostentatiously refusing to speak to one another.

A haughty silence wouldn't do for Syntyche, of course. As Clement led her away she had to turn back for a parting shot over her shoulder at Euodia. "Those Jews are trouble makers, but *you* are the one leading this church astray—a madwoman setting herself up as a leader! You bring shame to the name of Jesus!"

For once, Euodia was speechless, and Lydia felt that was probably a good thing—she didn't want to imagine what her slave might have said in response to that. Lydia's own words came without thinking, shattering the careful illusion of calm she'd kept in place all evening. "Clement, take your wife home and teach her humility!"

Syntyche was still muttering as her husband practically dragged her through the house and into the street.

Several people still remained in the courtyard, but they were all from her own church or Demos's, none from the other two congregations. Dissent had vanished with the overseers and deacons who had left. Now there was plenty of unity—but it wasn't the unity of the Spirit. It was rather that of people united against a common enemy—complaining, accusing, repeating some unbelievable, terrible thing that a brother or sister in the faith had said.

Lydia dismissed them without prayer. How could she pray? Her heart was so heavy, and she had no words to offer God. She remembered how Paul used to laugh and call her his yokefellow. She had been given this yoke to bear and had now failed at it, having allowed division and strife to tear the Christian community apart.

For a long time she sat with her head in her hands on a bench, only Rachel beside her. "Tempers will cool with time," Rachel commented finally. "By the time we all meet for Passover, people will remember what we are here for."

"I will pray for that," Lydia said. As she rubbed her tired eyes she hoped that Rachel was right about time healing. It was just as likely that some would spend the period between now and Passover in gossiping and making accusations behind the backs of other church members.

"I should go to Simeon," Rachel said. "He ought not to have come tonight—this was too much for him. I fear his heart will fail him."

So Lydia found herself left alone, as she so often felt these days. Simeon was ill, Rachel was absorbed in caring for him, Epaphroditus had turned his back on Jesus, and Euodia was as much a problem as a helper. She missed Paul and Luke acutely. It all was too much to bear alone.

Help me, Lord, she prayed. *Forgive me for thinking this is mine to bear alone. It was You, not Paul, who raised up this church, and it is You who must heal the rifts and unite us by Your Spirit. Just—give me strength to carry on, please. Strength and wisdom.*

She found Euodia in the workroom, folding pieces of fabric into neat, precise squares. Lydia joined her in the work, glad to have something to do with her hands.

"I am sorry if I made your task more difficult tonight," the slave woman said, in that stiff tone she often used for apology—as if she were sincerely sorry to have caused trouble, but honestly would not have changed a thing. Which was probably the exact truth. "I know you try to make peace and keep us all unified."

"And I know you believe truth is more important than unity," Lydia said with a sigh. "Leadership is not easy, Euodia. I appreciate your fervor and your passion—you know that."

They worked together in silence for a while, till Lydia could keep quiet no longer. The thing she needed to say had nothing to do with tonight's conflicts or the troubles of the church. It was a personal thing, between herself and Euodia, and she had known this moment must come ever since bringing Euodia home from prison. The thing should have been done long ago.

"Euodia, I want to give you your freedom."

The younger woman looked up sharply, and Lydia saw that it had taken her completely by surprise. "Mistress—I—I hardly know what to say."

"You may thank me," Lydia said with a smile. "If freedom is what you want."

"I—do not know what to do with freedom," Euodia admitted. "If I was ever free, I can't remember it. But now . . . is this because you want me to go away?" she asked with her usual direct candor.

"No!" Lydia had not thought of that, though she knew that if Euodia were to take to the road as a missionary it would solve many problems here in Philippi. She could hardly go alone, though. "You are welcome to remain here and work for me, as Rachel and Simeon have done—but I know that you have a strong belief in following God's purpose for your life. If you have no earthly master or mistress, you are free to follow that purpose wherever it might lead you."

"Thank you," Euodia said after a long silence. "I may—remain here? At least for now?"

"For as long as you like. Until God calls you elsewhere." Lydia was relieved. Despite the problems that Euodia's strong will created in the community, she could not imagine the house without her. *I will be bereft if she goes,* she thought.

A step sounded in the doorway, and Epaphroditus entered the room. "Mother, you're working?" he asked incredulously. Lydia rarely set food in the dye shop these days.

"The meeting was very—unsettling. I needed something to calm my nerves before bed."

In the past her son had made gentle but pointed jests about the bickering among Jesus' followers, and she expected something of the same this time. Instead he said, "You were arguing over whether to baptize Judah and the rest of the Jews this Sabbath, were you?"

"Yes," Lydia said with some surprise.

A faint smile slowly spread around his lips. "I am not entirely uninformed, Mother. Simeon and Rachel do tell me a few things. In fact . . . that is I why I came looking for you tonight." He glanced down at the ground, as if suddenly shy, and he seemed much younger.

"What is it, Epaphroditus?"

"I—I wish to be baptized with the others this Sabbath, Mother." He looked up, the shy half smile again lighting his face. "I decided it was time to stop running from Jesus."

"Oh, Epaphroditus!" Lydia crossed the workroom floor in three steps and took her son in her arms. "Oh, my son, how I've prayed for this day."

"So you see, your prayers are powerful. Next you must start praying Paul out of prison, and of course praying for peace in the church. If God can soften my heart, what can He not do?"

Still in his arms, she felt his head lift and his gaze shift to the quiet girl behind her, and knew that Euodia had come up to offer him her own blessings. Lydia stepped away and saw Euodia's hand outstretched. Epaphroditus took it as a drowning man grabs a rope.

"I am so glad. So very, very glad," Euodia said.

Lydia felt a chill down her spine. Epaphroditus had returned to Jesus, and she herself had just freed Euodia. And her son was a grown man who did not need his mother's permission to marry.

Although loving them both as she did, she had no more desire to see them married than she ever had—call it family pride, call it a sin she needed to repent of, she still did not want this match made.

For all her prayers and hopes for Epaphroditus's soul, she had not really imagined this particular outcome when she decided to free Euodia. But she stayed back in the shadows and kept her mouth shut. This time, she would leave it to God's will. He obviously had His own ways of working things out. Her attention was better spent on the division in the church, upon which she could have some influence. The matter of Epaphroditus's future would better remain in God's hands—where her son himself had, at last, chosen to place it.

CHAPTER 23
CLEMENT

Flavia was dying. Clement went to her room at sunset on the sixth day of the week, the beginning of Sabbath. Her eyes darted around the room and rested briefly on him. "Gabinus," she said. Her husband's name.

"No, my lady, it's me, Clement. Your under steward and brother in Jesus."

She showed no sign of recognition when he said his own name and his position, but at the name of Jesus a light came into her dull eyes.

"Jesus," she echoed.

"That's right, my lady." Clement sat down beside her and took her hand in his. Once he had thought he would never see this—the death of a faithful Christ follower. He had expected that Jesus would return to set up His kingdom before even one of His saints died.

Now he was used to this duty, and in a melancholy way he almost liked it—sitting at the bedside of someone dying, praying with them, reminding them of God's promise that the dead would be raised to new life just as their Lord Himself had been.

I wish I'd seen Him, Clement thought, the desire so fierce for a moment that it stabbed at his heart. Then he remembered that even Paul had never seen Jesus. The only person he, Clement, had ever met who had known Jesus in the flesh was the missionary John Mark, and John Mark had few memories of Jesus—he had been only a boy when he'd known the Lord.

I never saw Him, never heard Him speak, and yet I know Him, Clement thought as he held Flavia's hot, dry hand in his. It was an amazing thing. He remembered as if like tales from distant childhood the prayers that he'd once prayed, the offerings he'd once brought, to the gods of Greece and Rome and Egypt. They seemed pale, dead things beside the living Christ whose spirit he felt inside him everyday.

"Are you still here? Don't go," the dying woman said, pressing his hand.

"I'm here. My day's work is done. This is the Sabbath, and I will sit with you as long as you want." The believers would not gather here tonight, though some would come to worship tomorrow morning. Thoughts of the church made Clement's heart heavy just now, and he tried to turn his mind back to Jesus. They should be one and the same—thinking of the Lord, and thinking of the body of believers that was now His Body here on earth. But it wasn't the same thing at all. The body of believers was fractured and quarrelsome, and he, Clement, was not without fault in the whole sorry mess. He wished there was a way to heal things, but he couldn't imagine what it might be, though he'd spent many hours in prayer about it.

"I feel so . . . tired," Flavia said, breaking the silence.

"That's all right. It's time to rest now." The physician had made his last visit two days before. He said there was nothing more he could do. Clement, Syntyche, Rufus, and a few other believers had anointed Flavia with oil and prayed for her. While Clement had seen marvelous healings in response to prayer, he knew that wasn't the kind of healing Flavia required now. She needed rest. "Soon you'll be asleep, sister—asleep in Jesus. Like a child going to sleep on his mother's breast. When He wakes you, you'll be young and strong and happy again."

"With Gabinus," she sighed. "And poor Gaius." Her eyes were closed and her voice was as faint as a summer breeze, but she seemed to be making sense now, to know what she was saying.

"Yes, with Gaius and Gabinus." Clement remembered that Aulus Gabinus had professed faith in Jesus before he died, though he had never been baptized. As for their soldier son who had died many years ago, long before Flavia had met Jesus— Clement was not sure of the fate of pagans who died without knowing Jesus. Some believed that if they had been good people and lived according to the best they knew, they would be in the resurrection. He recognized that that belief comforted Flavia in her last days, and he clung to it himself when he thought of his beloved brother Durio. "You'll be with your husband and son—and with Jesus," he assured her.

"Good. I'm tired. I want to . . ." She didn't finish the sentence. She was asleep, her breaths shallow and slow.

Clement stood when he was sure she was sleeping, and went to the window to look out. Twilight deeply shadowed the elegant and well kept grounds of the villa. Strangely, when she died, all this would belong to him—in name, anyway. Flavia's wish to leave her property to the church of Jesus could not legally be carried out, so instead she had willed her property to her stewards—the country house to Rufus, whom she had freed, and the city house to Clement. Her understanding was that they would hold these properties in trust, not as their private fortune but to do God's work.

The country property would be sold and the money used to feed the poor and send out missionaries. The city villa would continue to serve as a meeting place and would also provide shelter for those Christians in need of a home. Clement had never imagined being a man of property. Now all this was going to be placed in his hands--on the condition that he use it to God's glory. The thought almost frightened him. He'd never expected that much responsibility.

The door opened and Syntyche stood there. Years ago when he was a soldier and he'd first met this strong willed, hotheaded Philippian girl, he'd thought she was the most beautiful woman that he had ever seen. He still thought so, though there were threads of gray in her hair now and her face and figure were rounder than it had been in those days. She moved past him toward Flavia's bed.

"She's sleeping," he explained as Syntyche laid down the tray she carried. She had brought honeyed water for her mistress, who could no longer drink from a cup but would take a little liquid dribbled into her mouth by a patient hand.

"I'll sit by her," Syntyche said. "Demos and Epaphroditus are here to see you and Rufus."

"You could meet with them, too. One of the slaves can sit with the mistress."

Syntyche shook her head. "I can't talk to them, Clement. It makes me so angry just to think about them and everything they stand for. I don't even want to be in a room with them."

"They stand for what we stand for, my love. For Jesus the Christ."

She shook her head. "No, it's not that simple anymore."

"It should be. There shouldn't be factions and—different parties. We're no better than the pagans if we allow that."

"So we should let them go on teaching error, leading people astray?" Her firm strong hands plucked at the blanket covering the sleeping woman. She was smoothing it, as if trying to make Flavia more comfortable, but Clement could see how badly she needed to do something, to keep herself busy.

"They are our brothers—all Christians are," he reminded her.

"Brothers and sisters."

"Sisters." She said the word like a curse. "That's why they've come, of course. She sent them—Euodia. Everyone in Lydia's house dances to her tune. Ever since they baptized those Jews, those Judaizers—do you know what they've done? They made Petros the carpenter get circumcised before he was baptized. And a group of their women—led by Euodia, of course—went to Sulla's house and told her to have her son circumcised even though her husband was against it. They do nothing but set up rules for people, try to bind them to their ancient laws! Where is the Spirit of Jesus in all that? Where is grace?"

He knelt beside her chair and put a hand on her trembling arm. It sometimes surprised him to see how deeply such things moved her, how intensely she cared about the life of the church. Occasionally he wondered, even now, about the depth of her commitment to Jesus. She had never talked about feeling the Lord's presence, being filled with His Spirit, the way Clement himself had been. But Paul had told him long ago that people responded in different ways to God's touch in their lives. Some would be more vocal than others, and each would express his faith in a different way.

Syntyche's way had always been one of work. Since she had turned her back on the goddess Isis, she had thrown herself into the tasks of the church. Apart from their family, the church had become her whole life, and now she was seeing it torn apart. He hated how it hurt her, and yet he couldn't help feeling that her own stubbornness, especially her harsh attitude toward Euodia, was at least partly to blame.

The accusation Lydia had once made—that he couldn't keep his wife in check—gnawed at him. Surely Syntyche was subject to him and should be guided by him. But the feud between herself and Euodia was more than theological—it was personal, and it was hurting everyone. He didn't have a clue how to stop it.

In the atrium he found Rufus already talking to Epaphroditus and Demos. Rufus spoke in his usual measured, pleasant tone. The man had plenty of humor but not a shred of malice, Clement often thought. He knew Syntyche had made a wise choice in staying away. Perhaps without her, this visit could proceed in peace.

"Good Sabbath to you, brothers," he said, inviting the other two men to sit across from himself and Rufus. The pair of visitors made a sharp contrast—the short, rotund, graying Demos next to the tall, handsome Epaphroditus with his ready smile. Clement wasn't entirely comfortable with either man. He remembered Demos too well as a sharp but rather shady businessman, even though he had been an exemplary Christian leader in the years since his conversion. As for Epaphroditus—well, Clement had always liked the boy, shared Lydia's worry for him when he seemed to be headed down the wrong path, and rejoiced when he had finally chosen to be baptized a few months ago. Since then, he had stepped into the position of deacon at his mother's church that was vacant now that Simeon's health was failing, and Clement could see that Lydia was handing more and more responsibility for the congregation over to her son. Surely the lad was still too young in the faith, too untried, to be handling such weighty matters.

The men exchanged some small talk, asking about Flavia's health and about Clement's daughter Julia who was expecting a baby. But Epaphroditus soon brought the conversation around to business.

"We had a letter this week from Linus and Claudia, Christians in Rome," the younger man said. "They report that Paul has arrived there and is being kept under house arrest in a small apartment belonging to one of the church members while he awaits the outcome of his appeal to Caesar."

"He's alive, then!" Clement said with relief. Some months ago they had heard a tale of a shipwreck involving a ship that the apostle and his companions were supposed to have sailed on. Since then, they had received no further news. "Praise God! And he is kept in a house, not in a prison—that's a great blessing."

"It is indeed," Epaphroditus agreed. "Their letter says that the believers there are doing all they can for Paul, and he is comfortable, but it seems he has very little. They do not appear to have a great deal to share with him, for things have been difficult there." Everyone knew that the Emperor Nero's unstable rule was making life hard for both Christians and Jews in the great city.

"I wonder what we can do to help?" Clement said, and saw the other two men glance at each other.

Epaphroditus smiled. "Your thought is the very same as ours. My mother and—ah, some of our womenfolk—suggested we take up a collection of money to send to Rome to help Paul's living expenses while he waits there. He cannot work while he is under arrest, and I'm sure he has no wish to be a burden to the Roman believers."

"Yes, collecting money would be best—food and other goods would be too hard to send." Clement glanced at Rufus. "If Sister Flavia's country property were already sold, we would have a ready fund to draw upon—but that will take time. But I will speak to some of those in our congregation who can afford to give—and in Nikolai's church as well, of course. Within a week or two we should have some funds collected."

"And will you add it to ours, so we can make a single gift?" The question was significant. Once, there would have been no question that the churches should work together, but the recent strain between the various congregations meant it was by no means certain that the leaders of one church would have any confidence in the others when it came to money. Clement hoped he could trust Epaphroditus and Demos. But what really decided the matter was the thought of what Paul would say if he knew that quarrelling or dissension was involved with any gift they sent him. "Of course," he said quickly. "Will we find a believer willing to go to Rome to bring the money to Paul, or will we wait for one who is passing through?"

Epaphroditus's hesitation lasted only a heartbeat. "We will send someone with it on a special journey," he said. "That will be quicker than waiting for a brother or sister who just happens to be passing on the way to Rome." His spirits seemed to lighten at the decision, and as if this easy agreement made him bolder, he hurried on his second piece of business.

"The Passover feast is not far off now—only half a month away, and we have made no plans. Will all our believers meet together to observe the feast as we have done before?"

Clement shifted on his seat and glanced at Rufus, but the other man was silent, leaving it to Clement to reply. Which was right—he was, after all, the overseer. It was his duty to have this awkward conversation.

"We have talked this over among our leaders and our members," he said. "Our church will not celebrate the Passover this year." It had been Syntyche who had insisted, of course. She had gathered support from those who agreed with her and then convinced others—the women first, and through them their husbands, till it seemed like a decision that all had agreed on together. Clement believed they were right, but he wished there were another way to make this change.

Epaphroditus looked genuinely shocked. "Not celebrate the Passover? But we have always—"

"What we have always done is not to be our rule," Clement said. "Before our Lord Jesus came, the Jews always worshipped at the Temple and made sacrifices of animals, and did many things that were abolished with the coming of the true Anointed One. We are not bound by those traditions."

"Not every festival, not every law, no—but the Passover? Surely you would not abandon that—the Lord Jesus celebrated it Himself. It honors not only our freedom from bondage, but also our Lord's death and resurrection. How could we forget it?"

"Ah, you see? Hear yourself," Clement said, echoing the younger man's own words back to him. "You speak of 'our' freedom, when you mean the exodus of the Jews. You think of yourselves as Jews, even though you were born Gentiles. Christ did not come to make Gentiles into Jews, but to make us all one in Him."

"What's more," Rufus interrupted, "He never told us to celebrate the day of His death or the day of His resurrection. He gave us one memorial, one feast to keep only—to gather in His name and break the bread that represents His broken body. Why should we require any other feasts?"

Epaphroditus was speechless for a moment. Before he found words, Clement heard another voice behind him, one that made his heart sink.

"Even that feast is one we cannot join you for," Syntyche said, emerging from Flavia's private chambers. In the wake of her unexpected words the room was so silent that Clement could hear the fabric of her tunic swishing as she walked, the click of her sandals on the smooth marble floor. "We will no longer be bound to the dead feasts of a dead law, nor will we break the bread of Christ's supper with those who do not truly follow the Spirit of Christ."

Clement heard the other men gasp in surprise and was glad their shock covered his own. He knew how strongly his wife felt about these things—he did also, as did many of those they worshipped with—but he had never imagined making so bold a statement. To say they would not share the Lord's meal was as good as declaring that the members of Epaphroditus's church were not even Christians.

Epaphroditus turned at once toward Clement and Rufus, not even responding to Syntyche. "Is this your word as well? Is this what your congregation says to ours—that we are no longer one? You will no longer worship and break bread with us?"

Clement hesitated. He looked at Rufus, who was staring at Syntyche with an expression of horror. Rufus was as passionate as Syntyche was about freeing Christians from the bondage of the Jewish law. In private, he had said some bitter words against the Judaizers in Lydia's church. But he had never spoken of a division between the two congregations.

At any rate, it was not Rufus's place to speak here. It was Clement—Clement as the overseer and as Syntyche's husband—to whom the men looked. They could dismiss her words as the raving of an ill-tempered woman if her husband did not support her.

Drawing a deep breath, Clement clasped his hands tight to hide the fact that they were shaking. He was so angry at his wife that he could hardly keep still. But she was his partner in work, in life, in marriage, in faith. He would not rebuke her in front of these men. If she had come to him first—but she had not.

Slowly Clement nodded. "I support what Syntyche says," he said, wondering how he could smooth over her harsh words to prevent a complete rift. "Not that we reject you as our brothers and sisters—of course not. We are baptized into the same Lord, the same faith. But until you deal with these Judaizers in your midst, until you agree with the teaching of the apostles, we cannot worship together. You know, brother Epaphroditus, that if Paul were here he would urge you—he would urge you with tears—to stop these men from putting barriers between Jesus and His followers."

Silence again. Epaphroditus broke it finally. "These are hard words you've spoken, brother Clement. But Paul has spoken hard words to us. The apostles tell us that Jesus Himself spoke hard words. Just because a word is hard doesn't mean we shouldn't listen to it." He glanced at Demos, who said, "We will bring your answer back to our leaders and our people, and pray about it.

"I'm sorry we will not worship together at Passover," he concluded, holding out a hand as he got to his feet. "I hope the Spirit will work in our congregation and in yours so that we can again come together."

Clement felt the iron band around his chest loosen a little. The Spirit was, indeed, present in this very room, turning aside what might have been a most unpleasant moment. Rufus, too, shook hands with their visitors, and then Epaphroditus turned to Syntyche. After a moment she held out her hand stiffly.

That was when Epaphroditus made his mistake. "My mother, Euodia and Rachel send you their greetings, sister," he said, "and want to know if sister Flavia is well enough for them to visit."

"Your mother is welcome to visit. Flavia had great regard for her. It would be better if the other women stayed away. She is tired and cannot bear many visitors."

"It was sister Euodia who most wished to visit," he persisted. "Euodia was the one who first taught Flavia the message of Jesus. She still feels a great fondness for her and would like to see her and pray with her before she falls asleep in Jesus."

"It would not be wise," Syntyche snapped. "Euodia brings unrest wherever she goes. We need no trouble in this house. Tell your slave girl to stay at home, do her work, and mind her own business."

The air of calm that had descended on the house dissipated. Epaphroditus's polite smile disappeared and his face froze. He turned back to Clement. "God be with you, brothers," he said shortly, turning to leave.

When they were gone, Clement turned back to his wife, ready to give her the rebuke she deserved, to tell her that she had spoken out of her place.

But her whole demeanor changed with the departure of the other men. She looked drained, as if her righteous anger and her pride had flooded out of her body. Her hands were pressed together and her eyes brimmed with tears.

"What were you thinking, Syntyche?" he asked, shaking his head. "What possessed you to speak so?"

"I'm right, Clement. You know it." Her voice trembled.

"Right in your beliefs, perhaps. But in the way you present them? In attacking Euodia personally, forbidding her to see her old friend Flavia before she dies? Was it your place to say who can and cannot break bread with us?"

"You treat it too lightly!" she burst out, her tears spilling over now. "You think it an insignificant thing, but these disagreements will tear apart the body of Christ."

"What tears His body apart, Syntyche, is pride and anger such as yours! Backbiting and strife—those are the true enemies, not just the Judaizers."

She was really weeping now. "Why don't you see? Why won't you understand the danger?"

He gripped her shoulders, not hard but firmly. "Syntyche, we have always been partners, you and I. How often in our marriage have I given you an order—as a husband to his wife, an order that must be obeyed?"

He thought her answer would be "Never." She respected his authority, but every decision was discussed and shared between them—it had always been so. She was passionate and intense, but always reasonable. Now she seemed to be beyond reason.

"Once," she said, the word barely audible through her tears.

The answer caught him by surprise. "Once? When?"

"You ordered me to turn away from Isis and worship Jesus the Christ."

Suddenly he remembered. He had thought of it differently—had assumed that they had both come to Christ together. But he had forgotten that she had clung to her old goddess for a time, and that he had indeed given her an order.

"And are you sorry I gave that command?" he asked now.

She shook her head. "No. You were right."

"And I am right now. I order you, Syntyche, to put aside this quarrel with Euodia, to lay aside your anger at those who disagree with you. We may disagree, but we are still one family."

Covering her face with her hands, she turned away from his touch. A moment later she looked up, and he could see that she had composed herself, controlled her sorrow and anger. The tears were nearly dry, and she was calm again.

"I will promise you, my husband, that I will try. That is the best I can do."

"No. The best you can do is to pray with me, and ask God to change your heart." When he held out his hands, she reluctantly came to take them. Then he bowed his head and prayed for her, for them both, for their wounded church. He hoped that prayer was enough, because he had no idea what else to do.

CHAPTER 24
EUODIA

She pounded the dough flat with the heel of her hand, rolled it into a ball, and pounded it flat again. Again and again she repeated it until she forced herself to lay it aside and pick up another ball of dough, knowing the bread would be tough and hard if she continued to take her frustrations out on it.

When the flat rounds of bread were ready she took the platter and placed it on the coals in the oven and stepped back, brushing her forehead with her arm. The kitchen was hot, and she had been here for an hour already, preparing food for the day.

Ariane came in from the courtyard with a basket of clean laundry. "Hermia, the wife of Demos, is here to see you," she said briefly. Since Euodia had come to Lydia's house she had watched Ariane age 10 years, become a Christian and marry her longtime lover Tacitus—yet she seemed to have changed little. Her dark hair had more gray in it, but the face from which it was pulled severely back was as stern and unsmiling as ever. Neither her face nor her eyes gave many hints of what she was thinking.

"Sister Lydia will see them," Euodia replied.

"I brought them to her chambers, but they asked for you, and so did she."

Lydia was the mistress of the household and, along with her son, overseer of the congregation. Euodia deferred to her, but as Lydia grew older, more of the work that concerned the women of the church passed on either to Euodia or to Rachel.

She was glad that Hermia would bring nothing controversial, no quarrels to settle. Rather, she came with a donation of money that several families had collected to add to the funds the church was raising for Paul.

"Who is going to Rome to bring it to him?" Hermia asked as she turned over the small bag of coins to Euodia.

Euodia shifted her glance to Lydia, who was running a piece of fabric—a rich silk dyed with the latest blend of purple—through her fingers. They both guessed that Epaphroditus wanted to go. He had dropped hints as they talked about the mission to bring relief to the imprisoned apostle. Each woman had her own reasons for not wanting him to leave, but if he decided to travel to Rome, neither of them had the power to hold him in Philippi.

"That has not yet been decided," Lydia answered.

The women stayed a little longer, talking about their families and about the church—a conversation that quickly turned in the direction of gossip. "Have you heard that Syntyche turned away the widow Claudia and her sons, refused to give them relief from the church's poor fund, because her sons were circumcised before they joined."

Euodia pressed her lips together tightly. "I expect nothing better from that woman. Tell Claudia to come to us. We will give her and her family food and clothes, and they are welcome to worship and break bread with us."

"Did Claudia tell you this herself?" Lydia asked Hermia.

"Well, no—I heard it from. . . ."

"Perhaps it's better if we don't repeat what's been passed on by others," the older woman suggested. "Euodia is right, of course—we will help anyone who comes to us for help, circumcised or not."

"Two men from Nikolai's church were given a fine and a warning by the magistrates for teaching the Scriptures to a group of men in the marketplace," Hermia added eagerly. "And I heard that Clement and Syntyche rebuked them and told them not to teach in public anymore. And my brother went to Flavia's burial service, and they would not allow him to break the bread and share the cup with them."

"I was at Flavia's burial," Lydia said, "and so was Epaphroditus."

"And were you invited to share the Lord's meal?"

"No. But," she added, "we were not forbidden. There was no spirit of welcome or brotherhood there. To break bread with them would have been a deception."

"They are saying terrible things about you, sister Euodia." Hermia's face looked bright, almost avid, obviously eager to repeat the worst slanders she had heard. Lydia put a hand up.

"There is no need for us to repeat gossip and slander. That does nothing to honor the cause of Christ. Instead, let us pray for our brothers and sisters and do what we can to bring healing."

After the other women left, Lydia asked Euodia to stay. The two women sat on either side of Lydia's table, Lydia still idly playing with the strip of purple silk while Euodia piled the coins the women had brought into small towers on the surface before her. It was not much—the equivalent of a few days' wages, perhaps, painstakingly scraped together by a few families denying themselves small pleasures through a series of weeks. But the pile of coins in the locked chest collected by the whole community during the past few weeks was steadily growing.

"Soon there will be enough to take to Rome," Lydia commented. "We should not wait too long. Now, in summer, is the best time for someone to go, and Paul will surely be in need of the money."

"Yes." Euodia wished she could travel to Rome, to see Paul once more, to have a part in the work of the Lord in that great city.

"Epaphroditus will go to Rome for us," Lydia continued. "My son has made up his mind to take our gift to Paul, and see what he can do to help Paul and relieve his needs there. He plans to leave within the next two weeks and has already booked passage on a ship."

"Ah. I—didn't know that." Euodia felt her cheeks flush and wished that she hadn't said anything. Why should Epaphroditus make her party to his plans? "You will miss him very much, I'm sure."

Lydia sighed. "I will. But I no longer feel it is right to hold him back from doing the Lord's work. If I had let him follow the path he wanted to take when he was younger, perhaps he would not have wasted so many good years away from the Lord. Now that he is following Jesus again, I cannot restrain him from going wherever the Lord leads—and anyway, he is a man grown. I could not forbid him. I am sure there were times that Mary wished she could keep Jesus in the carpenter's shop in Nazareth." She smiled, no doubt thinking of the stories Luke had once told them about Jesus' mother.

"You are doing the right thing, I am sure."

Lydia's gaze held hers steadily. "I am growing old, Euodia. I find as I get older I have less time and less patience with talking in circles. There are things we have never spoken of, you and I. You know my son loves you."

Euodia's hand shook as she placed a denarius on top of the stack of coins. The head of Nero gazed impassively up at her from the metallic surface. As she laid the coin on top the pile toppled over, spilling across the tabletop with a clatter.

"He loves me as a sister in the Lord."

"Don't lie, Euodia. It's a sin, and it wastes time. I withheld your freedom for many years because I believed that as long as you were my slave, my son could not marry you. Even when Epaphroditus turned away from the Lord, when I would have given anything for him to fall in love with a Christian girl who might bring him back to Jesus—still, my pride could not bear the thought of him married to a slave. Even though I have loved you as a daughter, I always thought of you as. . . . " Her voice trailed off.

"As an unworthy wife for your son. As a slave with no family and no background."

Lydia looked hurt, but nodded slowly. "The words sound harsh when you say them like that. But of course, they are harsh. We preach and sing that we are one in Christ Jesus, but—do the words really mean anything?" She passed a hand over her fore-head and rubbed her eyes.

As she began painstakingly restacking the coins, one denarius on top of another, Euodia said nothing. She knew that Lydia

sought something from her—some kind of forgiveness or abso-
lution—but she could not offer it. The sting of being thought
less than others because she was a slave, or a woman, or an outsider in some other way was too much. "All one in Christ Jesus"
was a lovely ideal more than a reality.

After a moment's silence, Lydia went on. "I have tried hard to
do my best, Euodia—the best for you, and the best for
Epaphroditus. For so many years I prayed for my son . . . now
God has answered my prayers. And I realize that He was always
in control . . . I never was. It's time for me let go—to stop pretending that I always know what's best and can arrange everything for the best."

"Is that why you gave me my freedom? Because you are giving up control?"

"Yes, I suppose so."

Finished restacking the coins, Euodia folded her hands on the
table before her. "I have always known God was in control of my
life. It was His will that I should be your slave, and His will to
free me. And it is not His will for me to marry anyone—even
Epaphroditus. I told you that many years ago when you wanted
me to marry Sergius."

Slowly Lydia nodded. "I remember that you said that. But I
thought—I thought you might change with time. I thought that
perhaps you had some fond feelings for Epaphroditus too, and
that if you were free to marry, you might accept."

"He will not offer, and if he did I would not accept, sister
Lydia." Many months had passed since she had received her
freedom and Epaphroditus had been baptized. In all that time he
had said nothing of love or marriage. They worked together on
the business of the household and the church and were friendly
and pleasant to each other, but that was all. "He is my brother in
Christ, nothing more."

Lydia closed her eyes. "You don't have to make me any prom-
ises, Euodia. Only follow God's will."

"I always do."

"I hope so. Whatever happens with Epaphroditus—that is between you and him and God. But there is another matter on which I must speak to you. This division in our church grieves me. It has many causes, and perhaps there is right and wrong on both sides. But the heart of it is this bitterness between you and Syntyche. If you could make peace, the church could begin making peace. I have showed you the darkest corner in my heart so that perhaps you can do as I have done—confess that darkest corner to the Lord and ask the Lord for the courage to do what you must do to shed light in that darkness."

The tower of coins toppled again. This time Euodia did not rebuild it but she swept them back into the bag and crossed the room to dump the bag into the chest with the rest of the money Epaphroditus would soon carry to Rome.

"You misunderstand the problem," she said to Lydia. "I am sorry to disagree with you. You say I have been as a daughter to you—I don't know if you have been a mother to me, but I do not even remember my own mother, so how else can I think of you? What could a mother be, but what you are? I respect you, Lydia, as my mistress and my mother in Christ and my overseer. But I cannot be guided by you in this. Between myself and Syntyche the problem is not a dark place in my heart, but rather that of a misguided shepherdess who is leading the sheep astray. It is my duty to oppose her, and I will not stop."

Lydia smiled for the first time. "You are still very young."

"I am nearer to 30 than 20, I think."

"Still young enough to be sure you are right."

"It's not my age, but the Spirit that gives me conviction."

The older woman shrugged. "I have done what I had to do and said what I had to say. Pray about it—that's all I can ask you."

Later in the day, her work done, Euodia went for a walk. For 10 years she had gone out from this house into the streets of Philippi to preach, to visit people in their homes and teach the Scriptures to them, to bring food and clothing to the homes of the poor. Very rarely, even in these months since Lydia had set her free, had she walked anywhere simply of her own accord, to do no one else's bidding but her own. She was free to come and go as she pleased . . . free to do so many things. But the idea was still new to her.

Freedom. It was a two-edged sword, that was for certain.

Where was she going now? Where would she be led?

Her feet took her through narrow and twisted streets where she had told fortunes, possessed by pagan spirits. Also where she had preached the gospel, filled with the Spirit of Christ. She walked past people who called out greetings that she ignored because she didn't hear them. At last she came to the road that led through and out of the city, to the riverside place of prayer where the people of God gathered.

Weary, she sat down on the bank. She had been walking since the time of the morning meal and now the sun was noon high in the sky. When she tried to pray, for the first time in memory she had no sense that her prayers were being heard, no feeling that Jesus was standing nearby and answering. Maybe, like Lydia, He had taken a step back to allow her greater freedom.

She had sat there a long time before she saw anyone on the road coming out of the city. When he drew nearer she recognized his gait, the easy way he walked, before she could see his face. As he approached she rose to her feet, but he sat down on the bank and gestured for her to take a seat too.

"I thought I might find you here," Epaphroditus said.

"Your mother told me you are going to Rome."

"I am. My ship leaves in 10 days. We have a good collection to bring to Paul."

"What news will you bring him about us?"

Epaphroditus looked out at the river. "I will tell him that the church in Philippi is growing, that it is full of people who love Jesus, that we care for the poor, that some of our number have been persecuted but it has not dampened our faith or our courage. That I am glad to say I am part of this family now, rather than an outsider. He will be happy to hear that, I think."

"He will. And that's all you'll tell him?"

"No." He frowned. "If Paul is the same man he was, he'll know there's more to the truth than that. I'll confess the truth—that strife and anger have torn us apart. I'll tell him that we are two churches instead of one, that we do not have the unity of Christ."

"Will you blame me? Your mother does."

"I will tell him that you always do what you believe to be right. You are the most honest woman I know, Euodia. If you make a mistake, I know at least that it is an honest mistake."

Glancing up sideways, she saw him smiling down at her. The warmth in his eyes was so open it made her chest hurt. She pressed her hand against her ribcage as if she could mend a wounded heart that way.

"We shouldn't be alone here so long," she said, getting to her feet. "It will look bad. And I have work to do."

Taking her hand, he pulled her back down to sit beside him. "No one will think it wrong for us to be alone if I ask you to be my wife."

"This is a very sudden decision."

"Not sudden at all. I first asked my mother if I could wed you when I was 15 years old."

"Much has changed since then. You have. I have. Everything has."

"All that's changed for me is that I used to be a fool, Euodia." His eyes shone as he kept his grip on her hand. "And now I'm still a fool, but a humbler one, who wants to be a fool for Jesus. If anyone—anyone brought me out of my folly and pride it was you, by your example and your prayers. I went down into that water, there —" he nodded at the sparkling river—"to die to that foolish old life and be raised to Christ. And now that I am new in Christ, I want the same thing I wanted when I was 15. To be with you, to be worthy of you, to share my life and my work for the Lord with you. That is what I long for, Euodia, and every day of these past long months I've bitten my tongue to keep back these words. I wanted you to know—I wanted to be sure my-self—that my commitment to Christ was true, that it wasn't just a way to win you. So I waited. But I'm going to Rome now, and I can wait no longer. I have to say it. Marry me, Euodia."

She closed her eyes. The sunlight on the water sparkled so brilliantly that it actually hurt if she looked directly at it. "I have always believed I can serve God better if I do not marry."

"And you have served Him well. But do you think it's possible He may have a different plan for you now? If we marry, you can come to Rome with me. You can serve the Lord, preach the Word, do His work, and never worry about how to earn your daily bread. You will have wider opportunities for ministry than you could ever have as a woman alone, slave or free. And you will have my love—all the love I have to give you. Which, I can assure," he said with his old sly grin, "is a considerable marriage gift."

"God comes above any earthly love, brother."

"But God also comes to us through earthly love. Can't He? Isn't it true that Christ loves the church as a husband loves his wife?"

"Perhaps I would rather be married to Christ alone."

Now it was Epaphroditus's turn to get to his feet. "If that's the case, Euodia, then tell me so. Tell me you won't marry me, and I'll go to Rome, and you can stay here—with my mother, with your church work, with your endless feud with Syntyche. I think those are the things that really hold you here—not God's will."

"Ten days. Do you think I can go so quickly from being a single woman to a wife, from a woman who has lived all her life in Philippi to a missionary on the way to Rome? It's too sudden— I can't take it in."

He stepped closer to her now, his face above hers, too close for her comfort. Her heart pounded. But he did not touch her.

"It is very sudden. But I need an answer. What is your answer, Euodia—my sister and my love?"

Unable to trust herself to speak, she just shook her head and mouthed the word "No." Then she stumbled back onto the road that led to Philippi, blinded by her own tears. She didn't think he would hurry after her, catch up, try to persuade her. No, she knew him. He would leave her to walk alone.

CHAPTER 25
SYNTYCHE

The air was cool, with a hint of coming winter in the breeze. Syntyche sat in the garden with her daughter. Julia's baby was due any day now, and she sat awkwardly on the bench, her hands smoothing the fabric of her robe over her belly, moaning a little with discomfort as she shifted on the seat.

"Your back aches again. Do you want me to rub it?"

"Later, perhaps," Julia said. "I wish you'd told me how difficult it was to carry a baby! Have you told me the truth about how hard it is to bear one?"

Syntyche smiled. "As much of the truth as you can handle, my dear. If mothers told daughters everything they know about bearing and raising children, no one would ever have another baby. And where would we be then?"

Heaving herself to her feet, Julia began to pace. Syntyche watched her, still amazed that her little girl was going to have a baby, that she, Syntyche would soon be a grandmother. It truly did seem yesterday since Julia was a little girl herself, learning to walk. Last week they had made an offer of marriage on Lucius's behalf to a young girl named Aikaterine, of whom he was very fond. Her family were Christians, her father a leatherworker willing to give Lucius a job when his apprenticeship was done. It was a good match, but it was one more sign of how time was passing.

"When I was a little girl," Julia said, "when Paul first came to us and preached about Jesus, I used to think I would never grow up, marry, and have my own children before Jesus returned to set up His kingdom."

"I know. For 10 years we have been saying that the Lord is at hand. But time passes on."

Julia turned back and laid a hand on her mother's shoulder. "Don't be discouraged, Mother. I'm not. Whenever He comes, I'll be ready. But now my child will grow up in His kingdom too."

Syntyche shook her head. "Sometimes I think we're getting further from the kingdom instead of closer to it."

"What do you mean?"

"I don't know—don't pay any attention to me. I'm feeling old and tired—I'm going to have a grandchild. It's just striking me all at once."

Her daughter beamed at her. "You're going to have a grand-child—that's exactly why you can't get old and tired! I need you now, more than ever."

"Come along then." Syntyche took Julia's hand. "Come into the house, and I'll rub your back."

She still wasn't used to treating this vast house as if she were mistress of it, although legally it belonged to Clement now. Worship services still met here, as they had when Flavia was alive, and the house was now a busy center for the life of the church. Four poor families were living there at the moment—not just living but working together to earn their bread. Lucius's soon to be father-in-law was teaching some of them the leather trade, while others were learning to make baskets. They had planted a small garden and now were harvesting the vegetables they had grown. Whatever was made, grown, or sold went to the common fund, and out of that same fund everyone's needs were paid for. It was a busy place filled with the love of Christ, and Syntyche was as happy overseeing it as she had ever been in her life. If the Christian church in Philippi were restricted to the congregation that met here, she would truly have believed that they were living in Jesus' kingdom.

But another congregation—Euodia's church, as she now thought of it—lurked in the back of her mind like a sore on the roof of her mouth.

Epaphroditus had gone to Rome, and shortly after his departure Rachel's husband, Simeon, died after a long illness. Lydia and Rachel both seemed older and weaker with their menfolk gone, leaving the leadership of their church largely to Euodia. The very thought of the woman irritated Syntyche. She had had no direct contact with Euodia for a long time now, but the tales that came back from those who had left that congregation made Syntyche so angry it kept her lying awake nights.

She tried to banish the disturbing thoughts as she led Julia into the villa. Inside, the basket weavers worked in the atrium while several women cleaned the halls. Hearing Clement and Rufus in the dining room talking to another man, she glanced inside to see who it was. He was a stranger, a tall burly young man whose accent suggested he had come from far away, perhaps as distant as Rome.

She knew they would not welcome an interruption just now, so she took Julia to her own bedchamber and there massaged the girl's back and shoulders with fragrant oil. While she did, she told about when Julia herself was a baby, laughing with her daughter over the stories that she hoped would make her look forward to her own baby with happiness and without fear.

Later when she went down to the kitchen chamber to take charge of preparing the evening meal, Clement told her they had three guests. Urbanus, a believer from Rome, was traveling to Antioch with his wife and child.

"From Rome?" Synytche echoed. "What news does he bring of Paul?"

"He is well, but still under house arrest waiting to appear before Caesar. Urbanus says he has more to tell us, but he has people to see in the city this afternoon and will return to join us for dinner."

Three extra people would make little difference for dinner. The whole household ate together in the evening along with whatever other church members happened to be there—some just for the fellowship, some because they were hungry. Syntyche was used to directing the women in the kitchen to prepare meals for 30 or 40 people each night.

"Are you going into the city with him?" she asked.

"Yes." Clement shifted his weight from one foot to the other, his hands tucked under his arms. His awkward stance told her all she needed to know, but that didn't stop her from pressing to find out more.

"He wants to see—them—doesn't he?"

"Of course he wants to see 'them,' Syntyche—our sisters in Christ, Lydia, Euodia, and Rachel. He has come from Rome. He has news of Epaphroditus. In fact, he asked if my wife could accompany us, since he thought it would be best if a woman came along when he gave them some distressing news."

Syntyche snorted. "I hope you told him that was not a good idea."

"I told him that my wife was very busy today and that no doubt the women there would be a support to each other. He was not fooled—he has heard about our divisions. But I was ashamed to admit it, Syntyche—that you would not even go to comfort a sister in her grief."

"I have no quarrel with Lydia or Rachel, though we differ on many things. As for their slave woman, she is no sister of mine. What grief is this, anyway? Has something happened to Epaphroditus?"

"He is dying."

Syntyche paused in the middle of the kitchen, turning an empty bowl over and over in her hands. Whatever quarrels she had with Euodia and the others in that church, she had always liked Epaphroditus and been glad when he was baptized. A nice fellow, always with a ready smile and a laugh. She had found little fault in him once he abandoned his wayward ways and came to Jesus. And so young. Just a boy, really, only a few years older than Lucius or Julia.

"What is the matter?" she asked.

"He took a fever in the middle of winter and was at death's door for several days. He did not die then, but neither did he recover. The fever gave way to a wasting sickness, and he has been in bed for many weeks. At the time Urbanus left Rome, the physicians—even Luke—held out little hope that Epaphroditus would recover. Luke and Paul gave Urbanus the sad task of bringing the news to the family. It was the main reason he came to Philippi—had I not chanced to meet him in Neapolis, he would have gone straight to their house."

"Perhaps he would be better off staying with them," Syntyche said, turning her back to her husband as she laid down the bowl and ladled fish sauce into it.

"Syntyche. Stop this. Whatever you think of their beliefs, Lydia has lost her son. Rachel and Euodia and all the rest of them have lost a leader, a brother, and a dear friend."

"I know. But I still can't go there."

"Very well. I'll take Urbanus to Lydia's house and bring him back here for dinner. I'm sure she will be in no mood to entertain a guest after she hears his news."

The two men returned, as Clement had predicted, in time for supper, and their mood was somber. During the evening meal, which everyone ate together in the atrium, Urbanus related more about Paul's ministry from his guarded apartment, how he preached about Jesus to the soldiers sent to watch him, and how several had become Christians. The visitor told them about the believers in Rome and about the apostle Peter, one of Jesus' original disciples, who had ministered among them for many years. Finally, someone asked, "Is it true that brother Epaphroditus is dying?"

With a sigh Urbanus laid down the piece of bread he had just dipped in oil. "Most likely he is asleep in Jesus by now. Luke thought he would not last more than a week or two at the time

I left. That was a month ago." As voices up and down the table murmured surprise and regret, Urbanus turned to Clement. "I knew, of course, that there was some division among the church in Philippi. But it seems many of your people know Epaphroditus and wish him well."

"Yes," Clement said. "He is a fine young man. Whatever our differences we are all fond of him, and this is terrible news."

"How did Lydia take the news?" someone else asked.

"She was terribly shocked, and could not speak at all," Clement replied.

"I'm sure she is sorry she let him go to Rome," one of the women commented.

"What could she do? He is a man, he was free to make his own choice."

"Poor Euodia," said another in a voice so soft that it could barely be heard above the rest. Syntyche struggled not to respond, but when another of the women echoed the same sentiment she said, "If Epaphroditus wanted Euodia to grieve for him more than any other church member would, he should have married her. To have any other kind of relationship with her—with his mother's slave—is hardly fitting for a Christian."

"No one ever suggested they were lovers," Clement interjected firmly.

"But everyone knows he loved her," one of the men said. "And she is free now—Lydia freed her herself."

"Whatever was between them, they were not man and wife," Syntyche insisted. "Epaphroditus's death is a terrible blow, of course. But there's no reason to pity Euodia above anyone else. Save your sympathy for his poor mother."

After a moment's silence, Clement asked Urbanus about the persecution the Christians in Rome were experiencing, and talk turned in that direction, leaving the awkward subject of Epaphroditus behind.

Syntyche and the other women were clearing bowls and platters from the table when Julia's husband, Andreas, burst into the room, his eyes wide, his breath coming in sharp gasps.

"Mother Syntyche!" he shouted. Everyone stopped talking or moving. "Come with me now, please!"

"The baby? Is the baby coming?"

"Yes! I've already called at the midwife's house, but Julia wants you to be there."

"But it's too soon!" Syntyche protested, racing around the room as Clement handed her a cloak and bag. The baby was not due for at least a month.

Rain slashed through the streets as Syntyche followed Julia's husband, slipping on the wet cobblestones. Her heart raced. Julia had seemed well this afternoon, had not complained of any pain save her aching back. Perhaps she and Andreas, this being their first child, were just panicking. That must be it. The baby could not be arriving so soon.

She quickly changed her mind when she reached the house of Andreas's father, where Julia and Andreas lived in a single room behind the cabinet maker's shop. Her daughter lay on the low bed doubled over in pain, panting and whimpering, her pale face glistening with sweat. The midwife knelt beside her, but Syntyche didn't need to hear her professional assessment. She had seen enough women in labor to know that it was indeed the real thing.

Syntyche dropped to her knees beside the bed and gripped Julia's hands in her own. "I'm here, my love, I'm here. Don't worry. Everything will be all right." The lie slipped from her lips as easily as a prayer.

"She's in hard labor, but the entrance to the womb is still closed—the baby is not yet ready to come," the midwife explained. "I am going to make her a draught of milk and honey wine to ease the pain and hasten her labor. Can you keep this on her belly," she added, indicating a cloth soaked in warm olive oil. "Call me if you need me."

Glad the midwife had had the sense not to ask her to prepare the soothing draught, Syntyche nodded. Nothing could have pried her from her daughter's side now, no matter what the need. Outside, the young husband paced and muttered in the workshop, but this was a woman's world, and Julia needed her mother even more than she did the midwife.

The midwife's tea didn't seem to help matters much, though it dulled Julia's pain a little. But the labor continued on through the long hours of the night with no end in sight. "It's all right, love," Syntyche kept repeating, still crouched beside the bed, stroking her daughter's sweat soaked hair. "When you were born, my pains lasted all day and into the night. It takes many hours, but it's worth it all in the end. Lucius came much more quickly—so will your next one. But you will cherish your first-born all the more because you fought so hard to bring him into the world."

Julia's grip tightened for a moment. She spoke little now, all her strength focused on fighting the waves of pain. The midwife examined her once more to see if the baby was ready to come, then shook her head sadly at Syntyche.

Drawing her mother's hand close to her mouth, Julia involuntarily bit down on Syntyche's knuckles as the next contraction swept over her. Syntyche felt the sharp nips of pain from her daughter's small teeth and welcomed them, wishing that she could bear more of it.

"Pray for me, mother," the girl whispered.

Searching for words, Syntyche hesitated. She believed that Jesus could heal—she had seen so many miracles in her years serving Him. Then she remembered worshipping Isis before that, bringing offerings in hopes that the goddess would heal the sick. Sometimes her prayers seemed to be answered, sometimes they were not. But she had seen prayers to Jesus go unanswered, too—some claimed that the sick and those who prayed for them had too little faith, while others said it was a mystery why God would heal some and call others to sleep until Jesus woke them.

Syntyche poured every ounce of herself into her prayer. "Dear

God and Father of our Lord Jesus Christ, lend strength to Julia now. Help her as she bears her child and protect both her and her child in the loving arms of Jesus. Please, let them both live and be well, our Father." Silently she added, *Don't let my daughter die. I cannot live without her.*

Yet as night turned to morning and morning to full day, Syntyche struggled not to know what the midwife had already accepted. Julia was fighting a losing battle. Neither she nor the child could survive if it lasted much longer.

Someone must have called Ariston, the one physician among the community of Christians. He came into the birthing room and examined Julia, conferred in low tones with the midwife. "What are you saying?" Syntyche demanded. "Tell me, please."

"Her womb has finally opened to let the child be born, but she is exhausted. I doubt she can give birth to it—and I doubt the baby is still alive." He glanced at the midwife, who nodded her agreement.

Syntyche looked down at Julia, but her daughter was too far gone to hear what they were saying. "Never mind the baby," Syntyche said. "If the child is lost, so be it—she can have another. Or live without having one. But you must save her—you must!" She stared in disbelief as she saw them shake their heads. They had already accepted that Julia, too, would die.

The ordeal lasted throughout that day and nearly till night. The baby emerged at last, a tiny, still, blue creature. Julia lay amid her bloody, sweat stained sheets, breathing in shallow breaths. Syntyche had not let go of her hand. She didn't think she could remember how to let go.

Still she prayed through her tears. "Lord our God, in the name of Jesus, save my child," she repeated again and again, like a chant she might have once made to Isis, and so desperate was she that she might have called on the goddess or any deity, any power at all that could have saved her daughter. But she remembered how strongly Julia had trusted in Jesus. Even though it seemed that faith was not to be rewarded, Syntyche found that she could not betray it.

Without ever opening her eyes or speaking again, without even knowing her son had been stillborn, Julia took her last breath at dusk. Her husband and father came into the room before the end. Syntyche would not let go of her daughter's hand until, finally, Clement pried her fingers free. Julia's hand was already growing cold, her body taking on the stillness of death.

Clement held out his arms for his wife, but she turned away. For more than 20 years she and Clement had been partners in everything, but now she was in a dark cold place where no comfort, not even his, could touch her. She headed toward the door alone, turning back for one last glimpse of Julia lying on the blood stained bed. Syntyche had no idea how she was going to live beyond this moment.

CHAPTER 26
LYDIA

"Dear sister, you must get out of bed. I've brought you some honeyed water to drink, but Euodia and Ariane have dinner ready downstairs. It's been days since you ate with us. The table is not complete without you."

Lydia buried her face in her pillow, shutting out Rachel's gentle voice. "The table will never be complete again," she said, her voice muffled by the fabric. She pulled the covers over her shoulders.

As she felt Rachel's hand rubbing her back, Lydia felt ashamed of herself. Six months had passed since Rachel had lost Simeon. Her grief had been bitter: the childless couple had been married more than 30 years, since they both had been 15 years old. They were each other's world, yet Rachel had carried on bravely through her tears. She had not given up, taken to her bed, collapsed under the weight of sorrow as Lydia had done.

Two weeks had passed since Urbanus had arrived from Rome with the news that Epaphroditus was dying, perhaps already dead. Rachel was somber and sad. Euodia was agitated, desperate for more news from Rome, hoping against hope that he might still be alive. Lydia had no hope and no strength. As she lay in bed she remembered again and again the day her son had informed her that he was going to Rome. She had told him she did not want him to go, that she feared some danger would befall him at sea or in the great city.

His announcement had filled her with a sick dread. Even then she had feared that she was losing him, that he would never come home to Philippi. Yet she had also been so grateful that he had been baptized, that he wanted to serve the Lord again, that she had at last reluctantly given him her blessing for the journey. Now she wished she had not. She could have, should have fallen to her knees and begged him not to go. She could have prayed to God right in front of him that He keep her son at home, safe in Philippi with her.

It would have been worth it, no matter what it cost, if it had kept him here.

With a sigh Rachel got to her feet. "I will go down and tell Euodia you still cannot come."

Lydia didn't reply. She knew that after dinner Euodia would come up to see her. She hated her visits more than anyone else's. Partly it was the desperate brilliance of Euodia's hope—a hope Lydia found exhausting and deceptive. But mostly it was her own guilt.

If she had not barred their way so many years ago, her son and Euodia might have married long since. Epaphroditus might never have wandered from the path of Jesus. Happily joined to the woman he loved, he might have been well settled here in Philippi with a young family of his own. At least she might have had a grandchild to carry on his name and his memory.

"Lord, why didn't You answer my prayers? When Jesus walked among us here on earth, He had power over every kind of disease and illness. Now that He sits at Your right hand, Father, does He have less power? Can You not protect Your people?"

Heaven did not answer. Nor did any human voice break the silence. The evening meal must be long finished, but Rachel had not returned nor had Euodia come to see her.

Lydia struggled to sit upright. Two hours ago she had desired nothing more than to be left alone, but now the emptiness of the room oppressed her, and she realized that she actually wanted to see Euodia, no matter how much a problem the girl's presence was.

She waited till Ariane appeared before bedtime to help her get ready for the night. As the woman changed the bedclothes and poured a fresh cup of water to place by the bedside Lydia silently watched. "Is there anything else you need, mistress?"

"Yes. Will you ask Euodia to see me before she goes to sleep?"

"She is working in the shop, mistress. I will ask her to come, but it may be a little while before she can get here."

"It doesn't matter. I won't be asleep." If Euodia was working late, there must still be customers, orders, dyes being prepared, and fabrics being dyed. Once she had managed every detail of this business. Now she felt remote, distant, unconcerned. What was the point of her business if she had no son to pass it on to? And her son, she remembered now, had never even wanted to be a dye merchant. If she had known how few years he had to serve the Lord, she would never have forced him to spend so many of those years selling purple dye.

A few minutes later Euodia slipped into the room and spoke quietly to Ariane as the other woman left. Lydia had not returned to the bed, but still waited on the bench across from it. Euodia came and sat at the other end of the bench, and for a moment neither of them spoke.

Lydia looked at the woman who had been her slave girl, the woman her son had loved. She still thought of Euodia as a young girl but she could see that time had left its mark. Euodia looked older, now, than Epaphroditus. A thread of silver had even woven itself through her dark hair and faint lines edged her mouth and eyes. Or were those not the signs of years but of days—these past days since they had heard about Epaphroditus? Lydia was sure she herself had aged 10 years in the past 10 days, and she knew Euodia was suffering too.

"I was a fool," she heard herself saying aloud.

Euodia didn't ask what she meant, or how she had been a fool. "You have always made the decisions you thought were right. We are only human. Sometimes we do not see God's will clearly." She paused, and the next words came slowly, as if they cost her dearly. "I, too, have made foolish decisions that I thought at the time were God's will."

"And now we have both lost someone we loved dearly," Lydia said.

"You should be comforted to know that he died in the faith of Jesus. You will see him again. And before he died, he had a part in carrying the gospel to the world—that was his great dream." For a moment Euodia's eyes looked almost hungry.

"It is your dream, too. You should have been with him."

They were both quiet, then, for a long time, the silence broken only by faint voices that drifted up from the street outside and a dog barking somewhere. Finally Euodia spoke. "He asked me to marry him and go with him. I said no."

"It's strange to say it after all these years, but I wish you had said yes. Perhaps if you had been with him, you would have cared for him better than he cared for himself. And it would have given him such happiness." She studied the face of the younger woman, her severe but lovely face lit only by flickering lamplight. "I think it might have given you happiness, too."

"We are not here to worry about our own happiness, but about how best to serve God. Epaphroditus would not have wanted us to mourn like this, but to keep doing the Lord's work."

"You have done better than I. You have kept busy."

"You are his mother," Euodia pointed out. "And in a way, I think it helps me to keep busy. There is so much happening in the church—and so many people have come to share our grief.

Even some of the—of the others, have sent their regards. Epaphroditus was well loved by everyone. Rufus came today to visit. It was kind of him, given that their household has had its own sorrow to bear."

"What sorrow?" Lydia realized that she had been so completely cut off by grief that she had no idea what was happening in the church, in Philippi, in the world. Surely she should have known that hers was not the only loss in the world.

"Clement's daughter, Julia—she died in childbirth."

"No! Not Julia! How terrible." Lydia had not seen much of the girl since her marriage, now that the two congregations no longer worshipped together. But she remembered the younger Julia well from the days when the family had lived here in the house, and she had enjoyed watching her grow up into a confident and assured young woman.

"I must go see Syntyche," Lydia said after a moment. "Poor woman. She and Julia were so close, she must be devastated."

"You're going to go see her?"

"Yes, of course. Why would I not?"

"You haven't left this room for two weeks."

"My own grief kept me here. Now someone else's grief will take me out."

"What of *my* grief?"

The words were so harsh, so raw with pain that Lydia glanced around to see if another person had entered the room. She had known Euodia 10 years and always thought of her as someone with a controlled passion, like a fire carefully banked and tended in the grate. Except for the moments when her anger flared, Euodia kept herself in check, never allowing others to see whatever pain she felt. Now her eyes were wide and wet with tears. Lydia slid next to her on the bench and put an arm around her, and she felt Euodia shudder with the effort of gathering her breath and holding back sobs. *It's all right to cry*, Lydia wanted to say to her, but she knew that for Euodia, it was far from all right.

"Your grief is part of mine," she said simply. "We are family, you and I. But we also owe something to the greater family, our brothers and sisters in Jesus. We have had our differences with Syntyche, but she has lost a child just as I have. I am going to visit her tomorrow morning, and I wish you would come with me."

Stiffening, Euodia edged away. "I am sure you are doing what you believe is right, sister Lydia. But for me—no. Syntyche has made it clear I will never be welcome in her home, even with a word of sympathy and kindness."

"You may not find her as harsh as you think, not after what she has been through."

"Perhaps. But even if she welcomed me, I—I would not think it right to call on her. To treat her as a sister suggests that we are united as believers, and you know that is a lie. I won't pretend a fellowship that isn't there."

"Is it pretending, Euodia, or just treating others the way we want to be treated—as Jesus told His followers to do?"

The younger woman was quiet for a long time. When Lydia looked up at her again it was as if she had seen an actor before going on stage, then watched him put on his mask. The naked grief and pain momentarily revealed on Euodia's face had once again vanished completely behind her composure and calm. "I have thought about those words of Jesus," she said. "But truly, it doesn't take so much imagination. We are ourselves grieving now. Has Syntyche come here to offer her sympathies? No. Would I wish her to? No. I would feel we were playing a part, being false with each other. So I will do what I would wish her to do for me—stay away, and pray that the Holy Spirit comforts her and convicts her."

Lydia knew better than to urge Euodia further. She, too, would pray—pray that somehow her heart would soften, and that the rift between the two women would be healed.

Rachel went with her the next day to the house church of Clement and Syntyche, leaving Euodia behind to work with Ariane and Tacitus. As they walked, Lydia thought wearily about what to do with the business. She wanted to talk to Rachel about it, but discussing it would mean saying aloud, " . . . now that Epaphroditus is dead." She couldn't quite use those words—not just yet. But if he were . . . not coming home, then she had no son to inherit her life's work. Plenty of merchants would be interested in buying it, and the money could go for the Lord's work. *That will be the only legacy Lydia the dye merchant leaves behind*, she thought.

When she reached the spacious villa that had once been Flavia's, one of the church members who lived there greeted her with two clasped hands and a kiss. "Sister Lydia, how sorry we all were to hear about brother Epaphroditus. We are all praying for you."

"Thank you. I came to visit with sister Syntyche."

The woman invited Lydia and Rachel in to sit down while she went to get Syntyche. They waited alone in the pleasant atrium, listening to the hum and murmur of voices as people worked around the household.

"I admire the way they care for each other here," Rachel said. "As we have done in your house, but on a larger scale, with so many families living in the same villa. I think perhaps this is what the Lord Jesus intended the church to be like."

"Yet these same Christians will not invite us here to eat the Lord's Supper," Lydia reminded her softly. "They have unity, but only within their small corner of the Body of Christ."

It was unfortunate that Syntyche chose that moment to enter the room. Though she could not have heard the words, she perhaps caught the tone. Or maybe it was the sight of Lydia and Rachel whispering together like conspirators that put her on the defensive. She walked toward them with her shoulders back and head up, her solid form beneath her flowing robes reminding one of a ship under full sail.

"Lydia. What brings you here?" Her tone was barely civil.

"Respect, Syntyche." Lydia let the word fall into a little well of silence, then said, "Whatever the differences between our churches, we are sisters in Christ, and we are both mothers who have lost a child. I heard only yesterday about Julia's death. I came to tell you how sorry I am and to offer you my prayers."

Syntyche relaxed just a fraction, enough to take a seat and offer them something to drink. She looked awkward and uneasy. "We were sorry, too, to hear about your son. The same day Urbanus brought the sad news, I was called to Julia's bedside to help with the birthing, so I had no—opportunity to visit you. We hoped that you might have better news—that perhaps he had recovered after all."

Rachel opened her mouth to speak, but Lydia shook her head quickly. The fragile grasp on sanity she still held depended on accepting that Epaphroditus was dead. To allow hope and then let it be shattered would be too cruel. Syntyche turned to Rachel. "And you, of course, are still grieving for your husband. What a lot of sorrow we have borne in a short time."

"Yet we do not mourn like the pagans do," Rachel said. "We have the hope of the resurrection. Some days the knowledge that I will see Simeon again is all that keeps me alive."

"Yes, we are supposed to believe in the resurrection," Syntyche said heavily. Lydia saw the same thing in the woman's face that she had noticed in Euodia's—grief had aged her, sketching new lines on her brow and cheeks. "But it seems so hard to have Julia taken from us. She was so young, ready to begin life with her new family."

"I know," Lydia agreed. "It's easy to talk of resurrection and new life—until you lose a loved one. Then, when you need faith most, it seems so much harder to hold onto."

As she said it she also realized that Rachel had not struggled like this—her faith seemed stronger, almost unshakeable. Perhaps it was because Simeon was older and had lived a full life, unlike Epaphroditus and Julia who had died in the prime of their youth. Syntyche's eyes met Lydia's with perfect understanding. They had walked the same paths, these past dark weeks.

They did not fall into each other's arms or weep on each other's shoulders. But they did talk a little longer, and before

Lydia and Rachel left, it was Syntyche who suggested they pray together. Their prayers were slow and hesitant, as if searching for the right words, speaking and praying only about their personal grief, not about the troubles of the church, but in that prayer Lydia felt the presence of the Spirit of Jesus and a tentative movement toward reconciliation.

She tried another step at the door, as she turned to go. "Euodia also sends her sympathy and remembers you in her prayers."

Syntyche's face grew still and hard, just as Euodia's had when Lydia had mentioned Syntyche's name.

"You did a kind thing by coming to me, Lydia—you were both kinder and braver than I. Don't spoil it now by trying to make peace between me and your slave girl." Then Syntyche stepped back and swung the heavy door shut, leaving Lydia staring at its polished surface.

She turned to see Syntyche's husband Clement coming up the street toward the villa. He must have noted Lydia's surprised expression, for he said, "We're honored to have you visit our home, sister Lydia. What troubles you?"

Lydia sought for words but found none. It was Rachel who answered. "We have just visited with your wife. The visit was pleasant but when we parted—there was some strain between Syntyche and Lydia."

Clement looked weary. "Please forgive my wife. You know she has always been a woman of strong opinions, but she is grieving now, as you yourselves are, and she does not think before she speaks. She is—this is a very difficult time for her. For us all. Even I find it hard to offer her any help. It was kind of you to come."

"You have my prayers," Lydia said, and bid him farewell.

When she returned home she did not mention the incident to Euodia. She wanted to add no more fuel to the fires of dissension. What could be gained by telling Euodia that the woman had closed the door in her face?

To Lydia's surprise, life resumed something like a normal pattern. Although she had thought that the news about Epaphroditus would destroy her, it merely crippled her. Gradually she was able to return to her normal routine, to supervise the shop and household and even the church. The joy and purpose had gone out of doing those things, but they still had to be done and Lydia discovered that she could still manage them. She hired two more artisans, a young Christian couple, to work in the shop where help was badly needed. Business picked up. Even church life continued as it had done before. They still had poor and hungry believers to feed and care for, still new converts wanting to learn the gospel, still petty quarrels and disagreements to straighten out. The larger rift, between her congregation and the one led by Clement and Syntyche, showed no signs of healing, nor did she have any further contact with them.

As Lydia went through the daily routines she noticed with a shock of pain that other people had accepted Epaphroditus's death and moved on. Only Euodia, she thought, still felt the grief as fresh and sharp as she herself did. But they did not speak of him even between themselves. Lydia walked around with a pain the size of a fist beneath her breastbone and thought she would have to learn to live with it until she, too, died.

Every night she knelt alone in her room at prayer—the only time in the day she could cry freely, the only time she could let down the façade of being well. She begged the Lord to help her believe more truly in the resurrection, to look forward to that day instead of thinking about the empty years that would pass before she could be united with her son. And she prayed that she would think more of the eternal things, of Jesus' coming kingdom, and less about the present world. It was so unimportant, really, that her life's work in this world had been for nothing, that she had no son to carry on after her, no grandchildren to play with. Epaphroditus's death revealed to her that she had been, as the Lord Jesus had said, laying up her treasure here on earth rather than in heaven.

Her final prayer each night was simple: "Lord God, please walk with me through this dark valley. Be by my side." It was the only prayer that ever seemed to be answered, for though her sorrow never lessened, she never felt as if she was bearing it all alone.

The cool, wet months of winter passed and spring came finally, dazzling Lydia's tired eyes with brilliant golden sunshine. But she felt as if she was still locked in winter as the land around her came to life—she wasn't ready for blossoms and warmer days and new life.

One day in early summer she sat on the bench outside her shop, listening to the noises of the busy street all around. She kept her own hands busy embroidering a border on a piece of cloth as she talked to the wife of Caius Memmius who came over from her shop to show off a length of fine linen. "Rachel told me of a dye you had that could color the linen a very faint purple—the color of lavender," the woman said. "I thought perhaps if we dyed a few lengths to show customers we could both benefit if it became popular."

"It's a risk, though," Lydia observed. "Both the fabric and the dye are so expensive. If customers don't like the color we will have lost a good deal. Maybe we should—"

"Lydia! Who is that coming down the street?" The other woman's voice was suddenly sharp, almost shrill, as she pointed up the busy street. Many people strolled or hurried between the shops of the weavers and dyers, but Lydia saw the stranger at once. A tall young man dressed in the robes of a traveler, weighed down by a heavy pack, walking with long confident strides so that people on either side parted to let him pass.

Her hand went to her chest as her heart pounded like an animal beating against the bars of its cage. She got to her feet, stumbled, and her neighbor had to offer a hand to help her upright.

He was close enough then that she could see his face, see it truly was no dream, but reality. Epaphroditus ran the last few steps, holding out his arms, folding her in his embrace.

"Mother. Mother. I'm so sorry, sorry Urbanus brought you such terrible news. I didn't realize until I reached Philippi and

people began stopping in the streets to marvel that I was alive—
I didn't realize he told you I was dying."

Lydia threw back her tear wet face to look into the eyes of her
son. "He told us you were likely already dead by the time he
came. I've lived all winter thinking you were gone—we all
mourned you . . . " Then she moved back a step, trying to behave once again as a proper Philippian matron. She had made a
fool of them both in the public street—but her dead son had
come back to her alive, and he didn't seem to care that she had
cried and embraced him and behaved so unseemly. Epaphroditus
was alive. Nothing else mattered.

People were now rushing out, not just from the shops and
homes around them but from their own house, to greet
Epaphroditus. Ariane and Tacitus, the new artisans, then Rachel.
Epaphroditus enfolded Rachel in a hug almost as big as the one
he had given his mother and looked over her head as if expecting to see Simeon there.

Then Euodia came, last of all, out of the house and stood in the
doorway, close enough to see Epaphroditus but not, at first, to be
seen by him. He kept glancing back toward the house though, over
the heads of the people all around him, and smiled when he finally
saw Euodia. Although she returned his smile, hers was only a small
curving of the lips. She, at least, was restrained and proper.

Epaphroditus laid down his bag and said to Lydia, "I bring
messages from the believers in Rome, but most important, a long
letter from Paul. He addressed it to you, but of course it's for all
the believers."

"We'll gather everyone as soon as we can, and you can read
it," she said as the family and a small crowd of neighbors followed him into the shop. "Our scribes can copy it as you read,
and we'll send copies to the other congregations at once—"

"No." His voice was firm. "Paul had one request, and it is my
wish too. We both desire that this letter be read to *all* the believers in Philippi at the same time. Tomorrow is the Sabbath.
Can we ask everyone to meet at the place of prayer by the river?

The scribes can bring their writing instruments and papyrus and parchment there and copy as I read, but all our people must be together to hear this letter."

Lydia opened her mouth to protest, then shut it again. Epaphroditus spoke with an air of command. Something had happened on the long journey to Rome and back—and perhaps to the doorstep of death and back—that had added an assurance and confidence he had not had before. She would not think of disobeying or questioning his words anymore than she would have done with Paul himself. It had been two years or more since the various factions of believers in Philippi had gathered to worship together, but if it was Paul's wish and Epaphroditus's that they should be together to hear the apostle's letter, then she would summon them.

She remembered the words Luke had taught her long ago, the joyful ending to one of the Lord Jesus' most loved stories, and now she said aloud to the crowd in her workroom, "Come, let us rejoice and celebrate! This son of mine was lost, and is found—he was dead, and now he is alive again!"

CHAPTER 27
SYNTYCHE

"It's a mistake. We shouldn't go. We manage all right as long as we keep apart from them. Going will only cause trouble." Syntyche knew her own chatter was a way of covering her nervousness but that didn't make it any easier to stop. She walked next to Clement as their little group—about 20 believers who lived in Flavia's villa—made their way through the city gate on the road toward the river.

They were not alone. The road was always busy, but at this

early hour on a Sabbath morning most of those going toward the river were Christians. Some were friends from their own church or Nikolai's, but others greeted them with silence and a wary glance.

"Syntyche," her husband said, "the apostle Paul is alive and being released from prison, probably on his way here to see us soon. Our brother Epaphroditus—hush, he is our brother—is alive, when everyone had given him up for dead. We have a letter from Paul himself, and both he and Epaphroditus have this one request: that we come together as one family to hear the letter. It is little enough to ask."

She sighed, and Clement slipped her arm through his. At his touch she stiffened a little and almost pulled away. It had been so natural, once, for them to walk arm in arm or hand in hand, even after many years of marriage. But the long winter had been a difficult time for them both. Grief for Julia, instead of bringing them closer, had made them strangers to each other. Syntyche knew that her husband was trying to cross the distance between them, to reach out to her, but her heart felt frozen. When he tried to talk with her, she had nothing but silence to offer. In bed at night, when he held out his arms, she turned away. The distance hurt her as much as she knew it must him, but it was as if all her emotions had died when Julia had.

Now she let her hand remain tucked in the crook of his arm as they walked. The sun was warm on her face, and for the first time in a long time she felt her spirits lift just a little. On a day like this, it was easier to believe in the resurrection, to believe that someday she would hold in her arms her daughter and the grandson that she'd never known. It was almost possible to believe once more in a God who cared what happened to His people.

She had been distant, too, from God. Of course she was angry at Him for allowing her daughter to die. Then, when she saw how patiently others bore their sorrows, she was furious at herself for having so little faith. Had she served Jesus so long only to find that in her great crisis her faith had rested on sand? Why could she not comfort herself with the hope of resurrection as others did? Perhaps, she thought during those dark nights of winter, she had never been much of a Christ follower after all. Too headstrong, too quick to quarrel and make trouble, too shallow and stubborn to really trust the One she called Lord and Savior.

Yet now, seeing the green trees edging the riverbank around her and feeling the warmth of summer against her skin, she knew God was still there and still loved her. She thought of Him much as she did Clement—as someone who loved her despite the barriers she put up, despite how difficult she persisted in being. The first smile in months tugged at the corner of her mouth. "I am a great trial to you sometimes, aren't I?" she said aloud, not sure whether she was speaking to Clement or to Jesus.

Her husband laughed. She hadn't heard him do that for so long. "What makes you say that?"

"For 20 years you have been putting up with my moods. It can't be easy."

He squeezed the hand that rested on his arm. "I love you, Syntyche. You're my wife. What more do I need to say?"

A sizable crowd had already gathered on the riverbank by the time they arrived. Syntyche noticed, as she took a seat on the grass alongside the others from her household, that the believers were seated in two camps according to their alliances. A few people wandered back and forth between the two groups, or stood chatting on the grassy space in the middle, but the dividing line was clear.

Four scribes sat at makeshift tables with parchment or papyrus, pens, and inkpots, close to the spot at the front of the group where Epaphroditus would stand to read the letter. They would transcribe as he read, so that when he finished there would be four new copies of Paul's letter. Although addressed to the believers at Philippi, they would distribute it to other churches too, just as the believers here at Philippi had read his letters to Corinth and Galatia. Though Paul wrote about people and problems specific to each church, every one of his letters also contained teachings that any believer could learn from.

More people gathered around them. A couple hundred Christians had assembled on the riverside now, a large crowd to listen to a letter being read, but Syntyche remembered that Epaphroditus's voice was strong and clear and no doubt would carry well in the still morning air. As he rose to speak, she saw that he looked thinner and older than he had when he went away. He was a few years older than her own son Lucius, who sat nearby with his bride to be. When Lydia's son had left for Rome he had still something of the boy about his face, just as there was about Lucius. Now his face and body were those of a man—young, but tough and serious.

He spoke for a few minutes about his experiences in Rome, about his illness and recovery, and about the believers there. Mostly he talked of Paul, soon to be released from his imprisonment and hoping to see the people of Philippi again. "But I will not keep you long, brothers and sisters, telling these tales, for it is not my words you have come to hear, but Paul's."

Clearing his throat, he unrolled the scroll and began to read. "Paul and Timothy, servants of Christ Jesus, to all the saints in Christ Jesus who are in Philippi, with the overseers and deacons. Grace to you and peace from God our father and the Lord Jesus Christ. I thank my God every time I remember you, constantly praying with joy in every one of my prayers for all of you, because of your sharing in the gospel from the first day until now. I am confident of this, that the one who began a good work among you will bring it to completion by the day of Jesus Christ."

The words rolled out and although the voice was

Epaphroditus's, Syntyche instantly knew the words as Paul's. They sank into her heart and for the first time in a long time—perhaps since Julia died, but possibly even longer—she felt truly at peace. She knew the truth of what Paul was saying. It was not she herself, but Jesus, who had begun this good work in her. He was faithful, and He would finish it so that she *would* be ready whenever that day of Jesus came—ready to meet Julia again, ready to meet her Lord.

Epaphroditus read on. Paul wrote about his imprisonment, how he rejoiced that despite his loss of freedom it offered one more opportunity to proclaim the gospel. He mentioned others who preached the story of Christ from false motives, but said only that he was glad that the message was being heard, no matter what the motives. Syntyche wondered what he would say if he knew about the division here in the Philippi church. Then she realized that he probably already did. Lydia's son would have had plenty of time to tell him.

That was clear a moment later, when Epaphroditus read: "Make my joy complete: be of the same mind, having the same love, being in full accord and of one mind. Do nothing from selfish ambition or conceit . . . "

Syntyche felt the blood rush to her cheeks: it was as if Paul were here before her, leaning toward her a little and fixing her with his bright gaze as he had so often done in the past, telling her that she should be of one mind with Euodia and all the others. *No, that can't be what he means,* she thought. *That division didn't come about because of selfishness or conceit—not on my part, anyway.*

"Let each of you look not to your own interests, but to the interests of others." Epaphroditus then paused. When he read the next lines he did so in the tune that fitted the words they all knew so well.

"Let this mind be in you
That was also in Christ Jesus . . . "

Instantly Syntyche remembered the first time she had heard

Paul sing that, how he had taught them the words of the hymn about Jesus' humility that believers all over Asia were singing. How many times through the years since then had she sung it? How often had she stopped to think about humility, about what it would really mean to lower herself the way that Jesus had done when He came to live among humanity?

Other voices joined Epaphroditus in the familiar and loved words, singing as if they were accompanying Paul himself.

" . . . so that at the name of Jesus
Every knee should bend
In heaven and on earth and under the earth,
And every tongue should confess
That Jesus Christ is Lord,
To the glory of God the Father."

The singing died away. As the voices fell, Epaphroditus continued. "Therefore, my beloved, just as you have always obeyed me, not only in my presence, but much more now in my absence, work out your own salvation with fear and trembling; for it is God who is at work in you, enabling you both to will and to work for his good pleasure. Do all things without murmuring and arguing . . . "

The words were as sharp and pointed as if the apostle had been here these past two years, watching everything that went on. He had some stern words for the Judaizers, those who insisted on circumcising Gentiles. Syntyche glanced, as many of those around her did, over at the other group, where Judah, Benjamin and Joshua sat close to Euodia, Lydia, and Rachel. She could see the shock on their faces at the words. But Paul rolled quickly on from there to talk about his own past, reminding everyone that he was a faithful Jew, perfect according to the law of Moses, but his hope was not in those things, but in what Jesus had done for him.

But if that direct hit at the Judaizers was a shock, worse was to come. Syntyche knew, from hearing Paul's other letters read in the past, that at the close of the letter he usually named individuals, sent personal messages to and from particular people. But nothing prepared her for the words that came out of Epaphroditus's mouth a few moments later.

"Therefore, my brothers and sisters, whom I love and long for, my joy and crown, stand firm in the Lord. I urge Euodia and I urge Syntyche—"

It was obvious from the surprise in Epaphroditus's voice that he had not read the letter before, perhaps wanting to wait to hear it in company with the other believers. Now he cleared his throat and started the sentence again, glancing briefly at each person as he read their names.

"I urge Euodia and I urge Syntyche to be of the same mind in the Lord. Yes, and I ask you also, my loyal yokefellow—" here he turned to look at his mother Lydia, to whom the letter had been officially addressed, "help these women, for they have struggled beside me in the work of the gospel, together with Clement and the rest of my coworkers, whose names are in the book of life.

"Rejoice in the Lord always; again I will say, Rejoice!"

Epaphroditus went on through the closing words of the epistle, but Syntyche's mind had locked on to, as she knew most of the other listeners would be, that brief but unsparing admonition. The praise would have warmed her heart in any other context—Paul had written of her as a coworker who had fought by his side in the great battle for the gospel—but the rebuke stung. He had pleaded with both of them—her and Euodia—to make peace. No mention of who was right or wrong, no suggestion as to how to resolve the dispute. Not even an order from the great apostle, but rather a heartfelt plea. She could almost see tears in Paul's eyes, hear a quiver in his voice as he begged them to make peace.

Tears sprang to her own eyes as Epaphroditus read the final words. She felt Clement's hand close around hers. Suddenly she didn't want the service to end, for everyone would surely stare at her and at Euodia, curious to see how they would respond to Paul's public rebuke. Yet she didn't for a moment feel that it was wrong, that he ought not to have written it, or that he should have addressed her and Euodia privately. It was not a private problem. She looked again at the two groups of people on the grass, at the bright green strip dividing them, and thought of Paul's words again: "Make my joy complete by being of the same mind, having the same love."

The reading ended and the people sang a few more songs. The leaders dismissed the people present who were not baptized members, and as they began to make their way back toward the city gate the deacons and deaconesses from the four house churches rose to bring bread and wine around to share.

Now Syntyche thought of another of Paul's teachings: it was a sin to eat the Lord's meal with strife or dissension in the heart. Jesus, too, had said that if you came to worship with bitterness in your heart against a brother, it was better to leave your offering at the altar and go make peace.

Before the deaconess could approach with the basket of bread that she would be responsible for, Syntyche got to her feet. She caught Clement's quick questioning look and whispered, "If I don't do it now, here, with everyone watching, I don't know if I ever will."

As she crossed the strip of grass she held her head high, even though her breath came fast and her heart raced. The murmur of conversation from those around her dropped into the background. Clement rose too, not to follow her but to join Epaphroditus, Lydia, and the other overseers who would pray over the bread and wine and lead the worshippers in the sacred meal.

Syntyche walked past everyone to where Euodia stood filling cups to pass among the seated groups of worshippers. She took a cup and held it out silently. As Euodia poured, their eyes met.

The older woman raised the cup. "I cannot drink this until we do as Paul asked us, and make peace. Unless we can drink this cup together as sisters, it means nothing."

Euodia passed the jug to Rachel without a word and looked at Syntyche over the brimming cup of wine. For a moment Syntyche feared that she had risked shame for nothing, that Euodia would reject her gesture as she herself had closed the door to peace so many times.

As the silence grew, Syntyche could read nothing from Euodia's cool expression, her dark serious eyes. Finally, Synyche cleared her throat.

"I ask your forgiveness, Euodia," she spoke again, putting whatever faith she had into the words. "We have honest disagreements, it is true, but I have not dealt with those as a sister in Christ should. I have been cold, harsh, and critical. I've said things about you that weren't true and were cruel. Will you forgive me?"

CHAPTER 28
EUODIA

She stood in front of Syntyche, summer sun pouring down on them both. The grass around them was crowded with people, but for that moment it seemed that they were alone.

In the 24 hours since Epaphroditus's return, Euodia had thought of nothing but him. He had not sought her out to speak to her alone, and she would not do so unless he did. But the memory of his marriage proposal, and the searing grief that she had felt when she thought he was dead, had filled every corner of her mind. God had brought him back to her—but for what purpose? Were they meant to be together after all?

Although she had lain awake all night thinking and praying, she had found no clear answer. This morning, listening as Epaphroditus read the letter, she had been jolted from her own reverie by Paul's stern words. She had other business, she realized, business that must be settled before anything else about her future could be.

These past few years she had agonized much about what God's will was for her, what future He was calling her toward, and in all that time she had blinded herself to what He was summoning her to do here and now. Lydia had tried to tell her, but she had wrapped herself in the cloak of her own self-righteousness. If she shed that, she would be standing alone and cold, but she would take a step in the direction God wanted her to go.

Reaching out, she put her hand around Syntyche's on the cup. The other woman's fingers were warm. *The same blood that flows through her veins, flows in mine,* Euodia thought. *We are sisters in Jesus, no matter how we disagree, no matter how much I have denied it.*

"You are braver than I," she said finally. "What you have just said, I should have said long ago. It grieves me to think that the story of our quarrels played on Paul's mind while he was in chains. I do forgive you. And I ask your forgiveness too, for all that I have done and said."

They stood there a moment looking at each other. Neither was the sort of woman to step forward and take the other in her arms, but Syntyche finally smiled a slow smile and brought the cup to her lips. She took a single sip, then handed it to Euodia, who drank also.

From the front of the assembly Epaphroditus spoke: "This is the blood of our Lord Jesus Christ, which was shed for us. Let us all drink of it."

"We have much to talk about, sister," Syntyche said, "and some of it will not be easy. But I am determined that we will begin to mend this quarrel. Will you come, along with Epaphroditus and Lydia and Rachel, to our house to share our Sabbath meal today?"

Euodia nodded. "I am honored by your invitation."

It was that easy, she reflected as she passed out baskets of bread for the other worshippers. That easy, and that hard, for real divisions lay between them and there was much to be worked out before all the Christians in Philippi could truly worship as one family. But at least they were talking. If they could talk and eat and pray and perhaps, someday, even laugh together, then the rest of the road might not be too hard.

Syntyche went to Lydia and Rachel then, and when the service by the riverside concluded they all walked together back through the city to the house that they all still called Flavia's villa, in honor of the woman who had given so much to the church she loved.

As the women returned together Clement and Epaphroditus strode ahead, the latter telling more stories of the things he had seen and heard in Rome, of how the Christians there lived under daily fear of the capricious emperor Nero. "The small persecutions we have suffered here in Philippi seem so little by comparison to the fear they live with," Lydia said as a little of the men's conversation drifted back to them.

"Euodia has suffered more than a little," Syntyche said. Remembering how sharply Syntyche had criticized her when she was in jail, Euodia shot a grateful look at the other woman. She could not quite manage a smile, but she did her best.

Many believers had gathered for the meal. For the most part the men and women kept to their separate circles as they ate and visited afterward. It was late afternoon before Epaphroditus came to find Euodia alone on a bench in the gardens.

"You did bravely today," he said, sitting down next to her.

"Not me. Syntyche was the brave one. I just followed her lead."

"If she hadn't done it, perhaps you would have. Paul is never afraid to rebuke people if he feels they need it, but not everyone responds so graciously."

"I've known for a long time that I was doing wrong by holding onto this quarrel—that we both were," Euodia admitted. "Your mother told me, you tried to tell me. And the Spirit told me, in my heart. But to give up the quarrel would mean—undoing part of who I was. Humbling myself—just as Paul said. Like Jesus did."

"So you have walked a little further along the path of Jesus. I traveled that road, too, while I was in Rome. Urbanus was too hasty in announcing my death, but he told no lies—I truly was close to death."

The thought of him, sick and dying faraway, had burned itself into her mind for so long that it took an effort to remember that he was alive and well beside her now. "Were you frightened? Did you feel you were ready?"

"I was afraid. I stayed in the same house where Paul was being held, and he came to sit at my bedside. He told me that he had faced death many times, and that it was only a step bringing us closer to being with Jesus. I tried to see it that way, but I couldn't help thinking of my mother—and of you."

"When I thought you were dead—it was hard for me to accept."

Epaphroditus laughed. "You are such a strange mixture, my Euodia. So fiery and passionate about what you believe, yet so careful and reserved about your own emotions. Tell me what you really thought when you heard I was dead."

She closed her eyes and gathered her thoughts. He was right—she could speak with great fervor about the Lord, but she seldom spoke about Euodia, keeping her feelings locked close inside. Tears were very close to the edge, ready to spill over. She had never trusted herself, her heart, her feelings to anyone but Jesus. Certainly not to any other human being.

"When I heard you were dead, I was glad you had died in the Lord," she said at last. "If you had died while you were still wandering from Him—I could not have borne that. But even thinking that you were safe in Jesus—still, I was so miserable I wished I could die too." She remembered her silent nights of stormy weeping, the pain she could offer only to God, never share with anyone else. And she remembered getting up each morning and putting on a face of calm serenity for Lydia and Rachel. "I laid awake nights and struggled with the Lord, praying that He would save you and bring you back." Opening her eyes, she looked at him, saw his beloved face, his eyes on hers. His face in the sunshine was so bright that it dazzled her.

"He answered your prayer."

"Long before He did, He gave me peace," Euodia said. "In the darkest part of winter I finally, somehow, came to believe that whatever happened, whether you were alive or dead, whether we were together or parted, it was all part of His plan. Then I felt a little more peace. But I never stopped hoping you would come home, and—" Then she hesitated. What she wanted to say was far too bold. But Epaphroditus had never made a secret of his feelings about her, and now it was clear that he truly wanted to know what she felt. She had almost lost him twice—once when he had left the Way of Jesus, and once when he had nearly died. Twice God had brought him back to her, still loving her, still wanting to marry her. *I hope I have enough sense to know when You are giving me a gift, Lord,* she prayed silently. *Only let me be worthy of it.*

"I hoped you would come home," she finished, "and ask me again the question you asked before."

He took her hand. "I prayed, too, Euodia on the way here. I

thought perhaps you were right and I was wrong—that the Lord had called us each to serve Him separately, that we could do His will better if we both remained single and committed only to Him. But I remembered that in the darkest hour of winter—when even I believed I would die—that it was not just His love, but yours that kept me going. The thought of you, praying for me back home—sometimes I would just picture your face and it gave me the strength to take another breath. I decided then that a love so strong and deep had to be His gift, and that if He spared my life I would come back and try to convince you once again that we were meant to walk this road together."

Her tears came now, hard and fast, untangling the tight knot in her throat that seemed to have been there forever. She couldn't imagine being a wife, perhaps even a mother. Nor did she know what the future might hold, whether they would go away again to carry the gospel to other places, or whether they would live out all their lives here in Philippi, selling purple dye and leading the church. No, she had not the slightest idea what the future might hold—except that she was a free woman, she was a follower of Jesus, and she was no longer alone. Her fingers tightened around his hand. "Ask me," she said. "Ask me again."

EPILOGUE
LYDIA

Five Years Later

The house was still dark when Lydia rose from her bed and went downstairs. She heard soft sounds from the other rooms—snoring, coughing, someone turning over in bed. Pulling a woolen wrap around her shoulders, she went down the stairs.

The shop was empty and silent, samples neatly stacked on the shelves for customers who would come later in the day. From the street outside the first gray light of dawn seeped through the shuttered windows onto the tiled floor.

At this early hour the street of dyers and weavers was quiet, the other shopkeepers' doors and windows still shuttered. Not even the beggars on the corner had taken up their posts. A dog howled in the distance and two roosters crowed as if competing with each other. Philippi was slowly waking.

Turning away from the outside world, Lydia returned inside. Not even Ariane, always the first to rise, was in the kitchen yet. Lydia went into her courtyard. The air was fresh and cool against her skin.

The courtyard, too, was empty and silent, though in her mind it was crowded with the faces and voices of memory. Sabbath after Sabbath for nearly 15 years this courtyard had been filled with her fellow believers, praying and singing together. Paul had preached to them here, most recently after his release from prison in Rome five years ago. He was imprisoned there again now, and Lydia did not know if she would ever see him again in this life. She thought of the other visiting missionaries who had passed through the city during the years and spoken about Jesus in this courtyard. Luke, of course, and Timothy and Silas. John Mark and Barnabas, Priscilla and Aquila, and so many others.

This past Sabbath it had been her own dear ones, Epaphroditus and Euodia, returned from a long missionary journey, who had risen to share the Lord's Word with the believers. Their travels had taken them as far as Antioch, where they had met Luke and brought back a treasure more precious than gold. The physician had finally written the book he had planned so long ago—his great collection of the words and deeds of Jesus. Epaphroditus and Euodia had brought back a copy of Luke's scroll and read it aloud to the members of Lydia's church. It had now gone to Clement and Syntyche, whose scribes would make a copy before passing it on to the other Philippian church groups.

"The church in Lydia's house," Lydia whispered aloud as she

looked around the empty courtyard. An apt name for so long—but that would soon change. This morning it was not the voices of preachers and teachers that echoed most in her memory, but the faces and voices of those gathered to worship and pray together. Paul called the believers in Christ a body—Jesus' body—one creature with many parts. Others called the church a family, and that was how Lydia thought of her fellow Christians. A family—close and comfortable, but also prone to quarrels and misunderstandings. They disagreed and hurt each other and then, just as a family did, banded together to protect each other from the world outside, which became more hostile every year. Euodia's and Syntyche's bitter quarrel was many years past now, but there were always fresh disputes and difficulties to settle. Sometimes Lydia wondered if they would ever reach that unity that Jesus had spoken of.

Yet for all the troubles and conflict there was still something precious here, a Spirit that moved through this courtyard when it was full and made it an extension of her own beloved household—people she cherished despite their flaws . . . and her own.

The sun was rising, not yet visible above the walls but sending golden shafts of light onto the upper stories of the surrounding buildings, warming the air a little. Lydia crossed the empty courtyard and went into the dye works at the back. Here, too, everything was still, the vats covered, skeins of wool and linen folded on shelves or hanging on racks. Soon this place would be busy again, mixing the dyes and dyeing the fabrics that had supported her and her family all her life.

That would end later today—not the business, of course, but her ownership of it. Her neighbor Caius Memmius had made several offers through the years, but in the end she had decided to sell to a fellow Christian. Her old friend Demos would run the dye works well and would use the proceeds, as she had done, to support the Lord's work. The house, too, would remain a center for worship, but it would no longer be her home. Demos was moving his family in. Ariane and Tacitus would remain to work for him. Lydia had rented a modest apartment, suitable for two elderly widows, for herself and Rachel. Euodia and Epaphroditus would stay with them for awhile, but Lydia knew her son and daughter-in-law would soon take to the road again.

At Demos's request Lydia had agreed to remain an overseer along with him for one more year. But this house and its church would now be his, while the members of Lydia's household moved on to new destinies.

It had taken her a long time to accept that Epaphroditus did not want either her business or her house. He had continued to work dutifully by her side after his return from Rome, but his relief when she spoke of selling the business was obvious. He and Euodia were free now to do the work they loved. And Lydia had learned, finally, that leaving a family business behind for her heirs mattered so much less than leaving them a heritage of faith.

Uncovering one of the vats, she looked inside, thinking of the purple dye upon which her family's fortune had been built. She imagined the tiny sea snails dying on a far-off Phoenician beach, their shells crushed and their bodies collected in basins to decompose. The resulting dye traveled across the seas to dye works like hers, where it was mixed with a mordant to fix the color before the fabric was plunged into it. The color became more brilliant and true as it seeped and aged into that rich purple cloth so coveted by the wealthy. The process was long, hard, and costly, yet the result was vivid and lovely.

The life of faith, she thought, was like that. She knew what her own faith had been through, and how strong it had become with the years.

Turning, she walked back through the courtyard, now awash with morning sunlight. There was much to do today, as Demos would arrive to take over the business and she and her family would begin the process of moving out of the house. From the kitchen came the smell of bread baking and she smiled. Ariane was awake and busy as usual. Soon the others would arouse and gather for the morning meal. She would lead them in prayer, thanking God for His blessings, asking for strength to do their daily tasks. And she would remind them, on this last day together in the house, that every ending was only a new beginning. But perhaps she wouldn't need to. They all understood.

AUTHOR'S AFTERWORD

Where did the idea for this book come from?

Although the book is named for Lydia, the two characters who first seized my attention were Euodia and Syntyche. I've always liked Philippians, the best of Paul's epistles, because of its warm, personal tone, and in reading it I really felt Paul was writing to people he knew and loved well. Then, near the end, we get this sudden admonition to two women, who are obviously influential in the community, to make up a quarrel. No hint of what the quarrel is about or how they should solve the problem, just a heartfelt plea from the apostle to heal their rift.

Naturally, my storyteller's mind was intrigued. Who were Euodia and Syntyche, what were they quarrelling about, and how had the story of the Philippian church unfolded in such a way that two contentious women could cause such division? From there, I began piecing together clues about Philippi from Acts 16 and the Epistle to the Philippians.

What is the Biblical basis for this story?

The New Testament tells us about the Philippian church in two places: Luke gives an account of Paul's first visit there in Acts 16, and then—some years later, according to biblical scholars— Paul himself writes a letter to Philippi, mentioning several church members by name.

The Acts account is full of exciting incidents. Paul brings the gospel to a group meeting on a Sabbath morning near the river. His first convert is an influential woman named Lydia, a seller of purple dye, who invites the apostles to stay at her home. Paul and Silas get thrown in prison for casting demons out of a slave girl, and when an earthquake shakes the prison, the missionaries end up going home with the jailer and baptizing him and his whole family before they leave town.

The letter to the Philippian church, probably written about 13 years later while Paul was in prison in Rome, mentions none of these events. It does, however, name several people: Euodia and Syntyche, whose quarrel Paul begs them to make up; Epaphroditus, who brought gifts to Paul in Rome from the Philippians and almost died while there; Clement, whom Paul recognizes as one of his fellow workers in the gospel.

I had to use my imagination to connect the unnamed individuals in Acts 16 with the names in the Philippian epistle, as well as in imagining what events might have happened in that church in the years after Paul's first missionary visit.

One problem troubled me: Paul never mentions Lydia, his first Macedonian convert, in the letter to the Philippians. Of course, he might simply have chosen not to address her by name, but Paul routinely sent personal greetings to many people in his letters, and the Acts 16 account suggests that Lydia's role in the church, and her connection with Paul, would have been important enough to deserve a mention. This left me with the possibility that Lydia had died in the intervening years—but for the purposes of my story, I wanted her to live!

In Philippians 4, in the midst of his plea to Euodia and Syntyche, Paul addresses a plea for help to someone whom he calls *syzygus*. This might be a person's name, but is usually translated as "yokefellow"—an unnamed person who would recognize himself or herself as Paul's yokefellow or coworker. I imagined that, just possibly, Paul's first friend and convert in Philippi might also be his "loyal yokefellow," the one with whom he pleaded for help in healing the divisions in the congregation. Some Bible commentators over the years have suggested Lydia might have been the "yokefellow" Paul referred to, though others reject the suggestion because the grammar of the passage may fit better with a male "yokefellow." As always, when scholars disagree, I claim the storyteller's privilege of choosing the interpretation that fits best with my story!

Why a story about the early church?

The last two biblical narratives I wrote were about Esther and Deborah, heroines of the Old Testament. Entering the Greco-Roman world of the first century meant plunging into an entirely different culture. But researching the early church, imagining what life might have been like in one of those first Christian communities, is some of the most interesting work I've ever done. We are so familiar, today, with the message of Jesus that it's hard to imagine how it might have been to try to live out that message in a world where Jesus' teachings and ideas were entirely new.

A Bible verse that guided me in imagining this world comes not from Paul's letter to the Philippians but to another of those early churches, the church in Galatia. We are all familiar with the words of Galatians 3:28: "There is neither Jew nor Greek, slave nor free, male nor female, for you are all one in Christ Jesus." In a society such as ours, that presumes everyone is created equal, these words don't have the shock value they must have had in Paul's world, in which social divisions between Jews and Gentiles, slaves and their masters, men and women were so rigid and deeply entrenched. What was it like to live in a community that was trying to transcend those boundaries and figure out what it really meant to be "all one in Christ Jesus"? Obviously it didn't happen without conflict. We sometimes have an idealized image of the early church as a perfect place where everyone worshipped together in harmony, but Paul's letters make it clear that divisions and disagreements existed from the very beginning—the rift between Euodia and Syntyche in the Philippian church being just one of many.

Although that world and that time are so far removed from us, so different from ours, there are lessons we can learn from the church at Philippi and the other early Christians. They were as prone to disagreements–both doctrinal and personal–as we are. Furthermore, they were human beings striving their best to know God's will and follow it, just like us. And they were people for whom the message of the gospel was completely fresh, new, and even shocking. With 2,000 years of Christian history behind us, we don't have the luxury of hearing the story of Jesus for the first time. But we are called to keep the flame of our "first love" for Him alive. Perhaps putting ourselves in the sandals of the people who first heard of Him will help us to keep that story, and that relationship, always fresh and new.

For more of the author's background to this story and these characters, you can visit http://www.lydiaofphilippi.com.

QUESTIONS FOR DISCUSSION

If you use this book in a book club or discussion group, you might like to consider some of the following questions. Your understanding of the story will be enhanced if you read Acts 16: 11–40 and the entire letter to the Philippians, along with this book.

1. What do you think first drew Lydia to the message of Jesus? Why was she ready to be the first convert in Philippi?

2. What motivated Paul and Silas to sing in jail? Do you think they expected a miraculous delivery? If so, why didn't they run away after the earthquake (as Peter did when an angel led him out of prison in Acts 12)?

3. Did you empathize with Euodia's situation before the spirits were cast out of her? How would her conversion experience be different from those of the other characters portrayed in this story?

4. How did you feel about Syntyche's struggle to give up her worship of Isis? Why do you think such a change might have been difficult for a woman like her? How was Syntyche's experience of worshipping pagan gods different than Clement's experience?

5. Discuss how the believers in this story cared for and supported one another as a community. What can we learn from the early church that we can apply to our church communities today?

6. What did you think of the romance between Euodia and Epaphroditus? Was it believable? Were you hoping they would marry? Why or why not?

7. What are Epaphroditus's motives for turning away from Christianity? What is it that draws him back?

8. What are the roots of the division between Euodia and Syntyche? Is one woman more to blame than the other? What might either of them have done at any point in the story to prevent their differences from becoming so severe?

9. How is the apostle Paul portrayed in this story? Is it similar to the way you picture him when you read the New Testament? If your image of Paul is different, discuss the differences.

10. Many scholars believe Philippians 2:5-11 to be an early Christian hymn. I have used it several times in this book. Why do you think these words might have been especially meaningful to early believers such as those at Philippi?